Who Invented America's Gasoline Automobile?

WHO INVENTED AMERICA'S GASOLINE AUTOMOBILE?

Carol Jean Lambert

Great-granddaughter of
John W. Lambert
Designer, Builder, Driver
America's First Gasoline Automobile
1891
Ohio City, Ohio

Merrimack Media, Cambridge, Massachusetts

Carol Jean Lambert
Who Invented America's Gasoline Automobile?

Copyright @ Carol Jean Lambert, Clinton, MA

caroljeanlambertbooks.com

ISBN: 978-1-939166-29-6 (print)
ISBN: 978-1-939166-30-2 (ebook)

Library of Congress Control Number: 2013954138

Research bibliography available upon request.

Merrimack Media, Cambridge, MA

*This book is dedicated to my Dad
and to all members of John's legacy*

*Cover Image is from a picture in an Art Association
of Randolph County 1984 calendar of a 1978 mural in
the Randolph County Courthouse by Roy Barnes, artist,
Winchester, Indiana.*

Contents

Family Tree

Mike & Betsy
from Lost Mountain,
Pennsylvania 1820's

| William & wife | Michael & wife | Joseph & wife | **George & Christiana** m. 1855 | Betsy & husb. | Mary & husb. | Barbara & husb. | Margaret & husb. |

1. Anna Elizabeth (Libby)

2. George Albert (Al)

3. John William (JW)
b. 1860

4. Savina Ellen

5. Emma Melissa

6. Christian Harry

7. Mary Ida (Mollie)

8. Benjamin Franklin

9. Samuel Webster

10. Levi Calvin (Babe)

| Libby & Dan | Al & Eva | **John & Minnie** m. 1885 | Emma & N. Glunt | Mollie (more) & H. Longnecker |

1. Ethel Mae
b. 1886

2. Alvin Ray
b. 1888

Preface

John Lambert never told. Even though he designed, built and operated America's first working gasoline automobile, he never stepped forward to champion this primary deed. In his day, trains took people from one railroad station to another, and then they rode a horse to get home. Some ambitious folks built contraptions for travel propelled by a variety of unlikely means: sails, rubber bands, steam and electricity. John, a former farm boy, dreamed of a self-propelled vehicle using gasoline for fuel because it was cheap, plentiful and locally available. The son of a successful carriage manufacturer, he built a buggy explicitly to carry the gasoline engine he crafted for his purpose. To the amazement of his neighbors and the consternation of his wife, John rode the startling vehicle on the dirt streets of Van Wert County, Ohio as early as January 1891. High on his custom leather seat, riding under a surried top, he maneuvered his three-wheeled machine first with levers at his feet, and then also with a tiller stick at his hand. But he never insisted on recognition for his invention. How could the inventor of America's gasoline-powered car not raise his voice to claim his accomplishment? What kind of man lets that go?

John eventually became a successful car manufacturer and achieved recognition for many contributions to the automobile industry. He lived into his ninety-third year but in most of those years he did not address the topic of priority. In private conversations toward the end of his life he cited two reasons to explain why he never came forward. Foremost in his mind was the financial failure of that first car. When John first rode in his prototype in 1891, he advertised widely but attracted not one buyer. It had been too early in the game and in his mind he linked the invention to its lack of production. He proceeded to manufacture and sell the compact gasoline engine as a stationary model and found commercial success, as he did in later years with the automobile. The second reason includes the story of Elwood Haynes, John's friend in Indiana. In the later 1890's Elwood produced a gasoline-powered car of his own design and wanted to advertise it as "America's First". When asked, John promised he would not contradict him. As John told it, these two factors were reason enough not to toot his own horn.

At the time the promise was made it would have been impossible to foresee the explosive importance the automobile would make in our national life or the universal interest there is in its historical impact. Over the years John may have visualized some of the changes automobiles would create, but he did not seek to glorify himself as being the starting point of what would be a colossal industry. His silence has left students to wonder who invented the car. Michiganders may say they know but Henry Ford did not invent the automobile; he mass-produced it. In fact the automobile was invented by a man who, when the success of Henry Ford's organizational idea took over the automotive industry, turned his attention to motorized tractors and invented the interlocking continuous wheel pad, a technology that helped create the field tank, a major contributor to Allied victory in WWI. The passion of John's expansive mind was in considering the workings of the things in front of him. His interest began as a boy on his father's farm where he repaired the many tools. His first patent, for a farm tool, came at age sixteen. Over the course of his career he collected over 600 patents. The inventor tinkered into old age, long passed losing his sight and his hearing. I saw a drawing he did without sight in his late eighties. It was a design for an automatic pancake flipper.

It is only in knowing the scope of the man that the reader can glean the more complicated reasons John did not tell, even over the years as he watched others make the claim. A complete answer includes his family background and the country's stage of development. Indeed he was living in a time that saw an explosion of mechanical and industrial progress hatched by ingenuity, plentiful resources and the freedom to try. This story of John's automobile is the history of American transportation, commerce and the Industrial Revolution.

The backbone of my story is based on a hand-written family tree, a copy of which Dad mailed me back in the 1970's. I kept it in a slim folder marked "Lambert history" along with a reprint of an article on the Lambert car in the prestigious *Antique Automobile* (October-November 1960, Volume 24 No. 5), an essay by John's son Ray on his father's invention and a copy of a letter written by "Aunt Lib" (John's older sister) about their childhood before the Civil War on an Ohio farm. The Lambert family tree shows John's family and his parent's family, including all of John's cousins starting in the 1820's with the Lamberts of Lost Mountain, PA. I was quickly enchanted with those early Lamberts whose numbers flourished and the life I imagined in a remote Appalachian community. Through the transition from Lost Mountain to Ohio I envisioned a story to set the stage for John's accomplishment. At a time when Americans transported themselves and their goods laboriously, slowly, and with great manual effort, John's uncles walked off their mountain to the farmlands of Ohio. By the time John got interested in building a self-propelled mechanical carriage a generation later, railroad locomotives, fired by coal, blazed past the old human-power pace and were ushering in paved roads and widespread travel lust in preparation for the automobile.

There are several irresistible stories not included in the text of my book. In 1913, years into John's in-the-clover automotive career, a fellow contacted him with a request for financial backing. This entrepreneur had the idea to mass-produce automobiles for the common man. Having a touch of social elitism, John must have scoffed at the idea that the car could be cheap enough for the mainstream; he thought of the automobile as a luxury item as indeed his products were. Contented in his own circumstances, as I imagine him, John had nothing to gain by abandoning his position and joining Henry Ford's company. Successful, popular and established in Anderson, he had considerable time to pursue his first passion of spending time in his work shed devising methods and machines. Besides, Dad guessed, the fifty-three-year-old knew his wife would be against moving to Detroit. The bottom line, as Dad imagined it, was John preferred to be his own boss. He told Mr. Ford no, but eventually offered to send his nineteen-year-old son Ray to the meeting of potential investors with the intention of sponsoring Ray's involvement if he deemed it worthy to pursue. As well, I found in my research, he referred Mr. Ford to a friend in Detroit, a Mr. Cousins who became an original investor and a board member of the Ford Motor Company. Dad told me Ray traveled to Dearborn, Michigan and attended the meeting Ford set up in a restaurant, as was the custom back then. The potential investors who gathered in the various red-leather high back booths included the Dodge Brothers and Ransom Olds. Dad tells the story of Ray's return report to his father that included Ray's assessment that "Ford had no charm." He was not interested in joining his team. The son of the day's famous car maker did not want to throw in with another man's dream and so chose to remain under the Lambert roof. In spite of Ford's fabulous fame and monetary success, I doubt either Lambert, father or son, ever regretted his decision.

I told my teenage son this story out in our driveway as he washed his 1996 Ford Mustang, a beautiful dark satin green vehicle with 225 horsepower in its 4.6-liter V-8 engine, a beloved car he had bought himself. He stopped wiping the seventeen-inch alloy wheels, the white wooly mitts on both hands dripping suds and water, to look at me. Gesturing slightly to the car, he gasped, "You mean this could have been a Lambert Mustang!?"

As John approached his seventieth year in 1929, the national economy was in crisis. Local banks were failing, so John walked down the street to his bank intending to withdraw his holdings. The owner, a neighbor and a man John looked upon as a friend, pleaded to John that the bank was solid. In the name of friendship he asked John not to withdraw his considerable money, because it may set off a panic among other Anderson depositors. John walked home empty-handed. The very next day the bank closed and John lost his wealth. How did he react to this betrayal and reversal of fortune? "He didn't care," his daughter told a reporter after her father's death. His interests were centered in his work shed. Family lore cites the lost sum as over one million dollars.

When Warren G. Harding was President, the President's father married my great grandmother's sister Dora. Thus for a while John was brother-in-law to a member of the President's family. Dora was much younger than the senior Mr. Harding; they divorced after four years.

As I worked on this project, I encountered several outlandish coincidences. For example, I discovered that the address for John's business representatives in downtown Boston was the very place where my sister worked for a number of years. She had had no idea. Of all the old buildings in Boston, she worked in the very one out of which Lambert cars were sold almost eighty years prior. How could this happen? Maybe all families have these connections that pass through the generations. Could ancestor shadowing have reached so far as to affect my story? Upon locating Lost Mountain, I realized I had been to this remote place thirty years before. After I found my Writers' Group, I was amazed to discover that some members had known Dad's sister. I see these unlikely connections that characterize my writing experience as referential to the nature of John's invention. I suspect John himself was charmed by what he was able to build. The marvels of chance that decorate my project elicit amazement which is the way I imagine the cute little noise machine inspired those who witnessed it as it peppered along the roads of rural Ohio.

Whether John would tell you or not, he designed and built the first gas-propelled automobile in America. The story of this mechanical genius would stand on its own but because of his primary accomplishment the story centers on the charm of the attractive little runabout. Proud of this gem in the Lambert family's past, I wanted to bring forth the characters so that you, my reader, can experience for yourself where John came from and what life might have been like for him. He was the first American to ride in a gasoline-motorized car; there have been many who follow.

1

1843: The Beginning

The gravedigger's boot slipped off the shovel so the edge of the blade knocked his shin and left a line on bare skin that widened with red. After another thrust he let go of his shovel long enough to draw his arm across his face. The moisture his body was producing was indistinguishable from the wet in the air. It had been raining all morning, all through last night, and most of yesterday. Maybe time stood still and this picture of the land is how it will stay forever. Maybe time will go on, the rain will never stop, and the land will disappear under widening creeks and lakes. Most assuredly, life as it was is gone; Death was leaving its mark. The future is obscured beyond the dark sky and drenching sheets of rain.

The grave was filling in on itself as the water running over the ground carried mud off the higher end and swamped the lower. Joseph grunted as his digging partner yelled at him through the precipitation, "Should be a diversion to guard the site," he formed the words through the dark morning air. The light from inside the little church next to the graveyard offered a contrast; it was nearly noon, yet dark as late evening.

"What say?" Joseph looked at his older brother and waited as thunder exploded and the dominating rumble moved around the mountain. Michael created a winged-shaped barrier of rocks on a spot of land above the hole. Joseph eyed Michael working above him and kept on in the grave site. "Now, how'd you think of that? That makes it a lot easier." The water now moved around their work, leaving only the actually falling rain to pester their progress. As Michael finished inside the hole, his chest and shoulders disappeared. The extracted earth completely covered a companion grave settled many years ago. The new grave was wide; the coffin was the biggest their brother William had ever crafted. "What's the point in putting her in so big a box?" Joseph seemed to be posing the question rhetorically. Michael threw a last shovelfull up over his left shoulder and answered him like a town crier, as though such a fact could be understood by reciting an explanation: "It was her own idea. She wrote down a whole set of instructions for the funeral, a list of songs we're to sing, which pies to bake." This was sufficient information for Joseph's need to know. As though someone had jabbed a tickle-spot, his teeth flashed white through the dark air. His smile brightened their whole endeavor. "Seems to me she's been taking care of business for so long she don't know when to quit."

Joseph pulled his older brother out of the hole to ground level. Once up he said, "We're going to miss her but not like some folks. Lots of them are going to feel like lost sheep, but we'll be alright."

"That's what Ma says too."

The optimistic older brother took purposeful steps toward the building. "Where are those tarps?" he asked to the corner of the yard. Near the door of the church he bent down and picked up two large-sized oil cloths. "We'll need eight rocks the size of your head, Joseph." He shook out the larger of the two coverings over the newly dug grave, and like clockwork Joseph supplied rocks to weigh down the corners as Michael scooted around to put them in place. They danced the steps again with the second oil cloth to cover the pile of loose dirt. Their job accomplished, they passed out of the dreary day and into the bustling activity of the tiny chapel. They were immediately set upon by animated children and concerned women who wrapped them in blankets and led them to the fireplace. Others stepped back as the brothers extended their hands to catch the dry warmth from the flames and coal-red logs. One of their aunts, Star, was huddled in a corner of the hearth, also wrapped in a blanket although it was warm inside, too warm to be dry and covered in a blanket. She was staring into the room with a strange expression of befuddlement and rapture. Those small eyes seemed to hold up her broad brow. Her hair was staging a revolution under her cap, and many an escapee was flooding her forehead and neck. The other women had returned to arranging dishes on the tables they had assembled. The benches were already in place in the front half of the room where the altar and pulpit stood.

Back at their home, the youngest brother was in charge of bringing the four young sisters to the burial. George was seventeen under William, Michael and Joseph, but he was older than all four of his sisters. He was a practical joker who rarely had an audience for his cleverness outside of the girls. For some reason Grandma's death had inspired him. While the girls were finishing up in the loft, he had laid out a rag doll as a corpse on the kitchen table downstairs and had lit candles on all four of its corners as well as around the large room. He let the curtains fall shut at the two big windows, more for effect than to block light, as the day was dark as it was. One at a time his sisters stepped down the ladder, turned to face the room, discovered the scene he had set, screamed, covered her face and melted into terrified giggles. Each was greeted by his silent signal, finger to his lips, to stop her from giving away his efforts to his next descending victim.

Finally all four girls were downstairs, the doll was rescued and the flames carefully blown out. His sisters dutifully told him how naughty his prank was and how ashamed he should be. All the while they smiled with affection. In varying degrees each was grateful to be distracted. The house had been so sullen the last two days, since Grandma had dropped dead while counting bags of flour: oat, rye, corn and wheat at the mill. It is not that the young people did not love their Grandmother; they did. And they respected her as they had been taught. But they were just five of thirty-seven grandchildren on the mountain and Grandma had never gotten their names straight.

The horse and wagon waited in the rain for the four females to climb in. George also ascended his seat and checked around him one more time; he was comfortable in this role. Many times it was he who drove the sturdy mountain pony whose forebears were bred by the Delaware Indians. He gave a snap to the reins and they were off.

George's oldest brother William was in an out building down the road from Grandma's house where he was putting the fin-ishing touches on the coffin. Timber was the main product of this remote country community, and William felt the pulse of the planks like it was in his own hands. He lingered as curls of blond wood floated to the floor. He was more comfortable here than he was with people, and a large group has surely gathered. Some were at the chapel, preparing for the funeral service; some were at Grandma's house, where the body was, waiting for the minister to arrive. The body was surrounded by burning candles on the big table in the parlor and around the room at every available surface to cover the smell on this humid July day. Her face and hands, the only visible flesh, were covered with muslin material to hold down the odor. Other family members were making their way to the chapel or stopping by the house, in wagons and carts, on mules and on foot, plodding through the rain and mud, laden with food, children and questions about their future, now that the backbone of their community was dead.

The door to the out building opened, and William heard his mother let herself in. Betsy was the youngest of Grandma's ten children. There were ten until Elias succumbed to diphtheria many years ago, so, nine healthy offspring, if you count Star as healthy. Her body has always been strong but she is dim-witted. That's why the next oldest constantly prattles around her. Star had gotten her name from her father who rigidly enforced rules against teasing. He said she was his Morning Star there to reassure him each day of life's purity. There had been other deaths on the mountain but the one today would have the biggest impact since Grandpa's death in 1795. Being just a toddler when that tragedy struck Betsy did not remember much about that funeral. During her growing up years she heard a few stories about her father that emphasized his tremendous accomplishment of founding their home. Grandma told a host of stories about his being a war hero but the children realized he could not have been in every battle she mentioned. They figured her stories were more truthful as history lessons. Still, Uncle John, who remembered his father, said the war veteran told stories when they were out together cutting trees, of chasing the British and surviving through the winter with little to eat or to wear.

The main story to survive Grandpa's death and funeral, aside from the horrible loss of his presence, was John's romance with the daughter of the minister who came to officiate at the burial. The two fifteen-year-olds fell in love stealing looks over the coffin. Two years later they got married in a ceremony also officiated by her father. Grandma's response was to say, "Lose one, gain one." The old traveling minister is gone but his daughter organizes prayer meetings on Sundays when the new minister does not make the trip down the perilous dirt road but attends to other of the scattered sheep in his flock, or unless the ice or fog make it too dangerous to travel the steep inner roads of the community. This family of cousins, nieces and nephews, uncles and aunts and brothers and sisters has gathered each Sunday for dozens of years. Jesus is a member among them. He is talked about daily, consulted with problems, called on to shame wayward behavior and looked to for comfort when times are tough. Today's funeral would be officiated by the Reverend Jeremiah Lischy, a man greatly loved and followed, with books published and politicians for friends. He had known the old Ben Franklin and met with President James Madison. He was flawlessly righteous in his habits, and his preaching inspired even the most hardhearted. The softhearted cleric cried as he greeted the loved ones on Lost Mountain and spoke laudatory words about their now departed Tower of Strength.

Others arrived at the woodwork shed to carry the coffin to the house, collect the body and begin the procession to the chapel. As per Grandma's instructions, her old pug dog had been exhumed and its bones, in a thick burlap bag, were placed in the coffin beside her. So close in the small public room, the men sat on their side while the women held small children on the other. All waited for the designated beginning hymn. The Reverend Lischy sang out the first notes. Their voices joined together, raising a reverberation that sounded like boulders rocking on the mountainside. Vibrations went rolling through the valley to join ancient echoes of tom-toms and the legacy of rituals enacted over millennium on this mountain. Together in the little church house, facing the large simple cross William had made as a teenager replacing the two sticks Grandpa had tied together last century, and with Grandma's coffin in their midst, her descendants took turns offering a memory as they bade her farewell. The Reverend led them in sharing a thought or a wish; even the small children were invited to speak. They exonerated the woman who married her childhood sweetheart and settled on the western slopes of the Allegheny Mountains.

The rain had started up again by the time the service was over and the congregation moved outside. The coffin was slowly lowered into the grave for Grandma to rest next to the grave of her husband. Betsy knew this event was a line of demarcation. As the coffin disappeared under the dirt, the inevitable end had come. Her mother was dead and gone. She knew change would not happen overnight but she was sure their secure, secluded world had to break open. The young ones had to spread out, beyond Lost

Mountain, perhaps even beyond Pennsylvania. Although one or two people lingered behind, most returned to the chapel to eat cottage cheese, dark bread and strudel. Betsy had seen that the last of her family was entering the building when she turned to give a look to the raw spot where her mother now lay buried. Under the mound of dirt lay a force of nature. Grandma had extended herself over the lives of so many she was a family tree all by herself. Betsy glanced at her feet and right there as though beckoning was a newly-opened clover of not three but four green leaves of good luck, there for her reassurance. She bent to pick it and standing, she smiled, "Thank you, Mother."

After the funeral in the Lamberts' one-room home, Betsy sat, too tired to pick up the lace which usually occupied her hands, but ready to reflect on the day's implications for her family. She was in for a surprise, as well. Through the years Mike had taken the boys, one at a time, to Philadelphia. Not too long ago the second oldest son Michael had made the trip with his father. They followed their lumber by canal across mountains and farmland to the lumberyard at the edge of the city. From there the two men proceeded to the furniture store owned by Mike's brother in the same neighborhood Germantown as the chairshop made famous by their Prussian-born father. In his short visit, young Michael had met an office girl and made plans to wed. They would go West to Ohio, but not alone. Her cousin, a redhead, only fifteen, laid a claim on Joseph, sight unseen, for the chance to live in Ohio. Having heard good reports of her charms and her health, Joseph was willing. They had communicated by letter and sealed their intentions. The brothers thought tonight might be a good time to announce their plans. Michael studied his mother then spoke for both himself and his brother, "We will help with the harvest, then head to Philadelphia to become married men. Early in the spring, we'll be back with our wives. We plan to travel the National Road to Ohio." Betsy was delighted.

This was one of those rare occasions Mike brought down the bottle he kept on a shelf over the dishes. "I think a drink of this brandy is in order. What would Grandma say, 'Lose one, gain one'? I think that applies to us." He raised his glass, "To a woman who was unique in her time, although she didn't know it. To a mother, a grandmother and a leader who will be greatly missed but never forgotten!" They all took a sip. "And to the future of this family, those present and those gathered in their own homes across this mountain and this commonwealth." He paused, raised his glass again, and again they each took a sip. "And to our two boys, Michael and Joseph, who are preparing to set out on life's adventure." His smile was deep.

When the muted light from the overcast sky faded, the younger girls prepared for bed by taking trips to the water pump and outhouse, changing into nightgowns, brushing out hair and winding strands on each other's head with rags for curls in the morning. They settled down to games of Cat's Cradle before climbing up to the loft to go to sleep. Not too much later, the rest of the family was also securely tucked in their beds for their customary ten hours of rest. The rain prowled the mountain through the hemlocks and maples, and the lightening and thunder rolled in. The sky released a huge thunderstorm that took over the mountain, as though Grandma were tantruming all night in protest for giving up her life.

As planned, after the harvest the prospective bridegrooms traveled the long dusty roads to Philadelphia. In early Spring on their way to Ohio, the young newlyweds made the long detour back to Lost Mountain. Their visit was short. With stifled tears and well-wishing, the rest of the family saw them set out again. Deep in the wagon were rifles, knives, dishes, shovels, round iron pipes for their stoves and a large heavy plow nestled in between bags of seed, wheat, corn and rye, wedding gifts of the mountainside community. There were packets of seeds for the young brides, vegetables, flowers and herbs. All this was covered with quilts, blankets and clothes and on top a rocking chair. Finally a cutting of mountain laurel was tucked in a safe corner of the wagon to be the first planting in the ground of Ohio. With their talkative wives walking beside them, Michael and Joseph led their mule teams as they traveled the Conemaugh Path to pick up the National Road to Ohio.

Indian raids were a thing of the past and Ohio was blossoming. The first few years brought the middle boys and their wives widening prosperity. At the same time, life back on Lost Mountain continued much as it had been before. One afternoon Mike and George were working alone with two sturdy Durham oxen on their mountainside field. After two years of corn, they were plowing in fertilizer for the coming two years of alfalfa, in plan with crop rotation. The September air was nippy and the older man was eager to finish their labor and head back to the homestead. Across the steep mountainside, the patches of fields repeated into a quilt of yellow, gold and brown earth, as cousins and uncles, likewise good shepherds of the land, tended their acres. In all, fewer fields were worked than last year. The Lamberts were not the only couple saying good-bye to their children. As Betsy had predicted, Grandma's death marked big changes to their community life. Mike and his youngest son finished the last of their field-work and led the oxen back to the barn where they unhitched and cleaned the plow. The young son had filled out physically as well as mentally as he learned the skills of a farmer. He was happy in his tasks and sang out hymns as he worked. Mike was an excellent teacher, for he remembered the process by which he had learned when he gave up the furniture business and took up life on the western slope of the Alleghenies. Father and son lingered together for hours discussing the details of what had to be done. The seventeen-year-old who had helped bury his grandmother and who had waved good-bye to two beloved brothers, had changed and matured with the seasons. Three winters now had come and gone, and George was looking forward to his twentieth birthday which coincided with Easter this year.

For Easter the Lambert family had gathered at the chapel by the graveyard with the now older uncles, aunts, cousins and children. After the service, William and his wife Lizzie, who was pregnant again, and their toddler twins joined the Lamberts for dinner of golden corn mush, fried pork and onions. After the carpenter and his family headed back to their own homestead, the seven remaining family members sat quietly around the table by the large window. As the center of attention, George received small gifts from each of his sisters, a sash for his waist, a scarf for his neck, new mittens made of wool, one each from the two younger sisters. Mike and Betsy offered to arrange for George to go to school in Philadelphia and to work in some capacity in the furniture business. It would take time for the necessary letters but with the proper response expected, after the harvest, away he must go. The young people found the plan as natural as night following day.

In late summer tragedy found the young William Lamberts. While William was down at the woodworking shop, his wife was outside in the garden of their homestead. Both twins were sleeping inside the small house with the thick log walls. Lizzie had deliberately secured the latch to prevent them, in the unlikely event they awoke, from wandering to the wide stone well which was so close to the front door. She was picking vegetables for dinner and clearing weeds from the zinnia patch when she heard the whoosh of the flames and saw the tendrils of smoke curling to the clouds. The basket of vegetables fell to the ground as she ran to the house. The flames had moved quickly. She managed to get the door open and tried to walk into the heat but instead in her shock found herself aflame on the front yard. She rolled on the ground to regain control of herself. Quickly, she hitched up the horse to run for help; in terror and guilt, she reached William back at the shop. Her clothes were charred and burned, her face smeared with soot, her hair practically gone, her fingers black, bleeding and raw. She shook as he held her and they both fell to the ground.

The community again gathered to say the funeral service but with no little bones to bury, no coffin, just one little headstone for two perished toddlers, a sister and brother.

With the loss of their house and all their possessions, the young William Lamberts moved back in with his parents. They all worried about Lizzie, away from her own mother, now childless and pregnant, and in the weeks that followed, so distraught and self-blaming, claiming she deserved to be dead, except for the thought of the little one on the way. For the sake of the unborn she re-assembled her life. Her hair grew back and the bandages came off. William benefited from the therapy of working with wood. But the shadow of grief nonetheless hovered. After one supper late in the fall, when the family as usual lingered at the table to talk, Betsy, her voice full of intent, announced her solution: "Go to Ohio. Once the baby is here, there is nothing to stop you. You can stay with Michael or Joseph."

William and Lizzie made plans for their new start. George waited to hear from his relatives in regards to his move to Philadelphia but no letters arrived before the winter isolation of the mountain. The silence came as a reprieve for it allowed the family time together to buffer the trauma of the fire. It also allowed George to be close for the birth of William's son. And if that were not enough reason, the rains came hard in October and flooded much of the county, which made travel a misery and loosened the ripening pumpkins that floated away from their fields.

The spare time winter brings was spent preparing for the oldest son's move to Ohio. Betsy and Mike involved themselves in the details of the preparations which were complicated by the uncertainty of Lizzie's confinement. Even assuming all would go well there were the special needs of a new baby to consider. As the time approached for the birth, a midwife moved into the loft on the girls' side thereby making herself available morning, noon and night. She was a cousin they had known all their lives. Betsy would not allow anyone to mention The Worst, should mother or child not survive the birth. Lizzie herself showed a brave attitude which made it easier for the rest of them. Everyone tried extra hard to be cheerful and helpful, in order not to upset Lizzie, and to keep the place even more sparkling clean than their usual scrubbed tidiness inside and out. The baby must have known of their efforts; he was so polite in his convenient arrival, requiring only a morning of labor, appearing a healthy pink with a loud yelp of announcement, then gurgling contentment to seven adoring women and sleeping through the later return and viewing by the men. Awestruck, George was not shy about asking to hold the big baby boy he called *lambie-pie.* He marveled at the perfect little fingers with their miniature nails complete with half-moons that the baby wrapped around his newly grown-up finger, and at the variety of sounds that came out of the perfect little budding mouth, along with dribbles and bubbles and other less savory stuff. On that occasion little Harry won a trip back to his mother's lap. Still, George had never seen a more adorable creature than his little nephew William Harrison Lambert, named for his father and before him, the war hero President. William Harrison had spent much of his life securing Ohio from the Indians: Wyandot, Shawnee, Miami and Iroquois with names like Blue Jacket, White Pigeon, Little Turtle, Leatherlips and Logan, from Xenia to Piqua, Fort Defiance and Fort Recovery and from Greene Ville to Fort Wayne. A Lambert was present at the signing of the Greene Ville Treaty in 1795 and had secured a package of land near Springfield in Clark County that the two Lambert brothers now farm. Cleared of its ancient, giant trees only a generation ago, the land in Clark County was rich and generous, enough for two successful farming brothers with ample opportunity laying in wait.

Harry's aunties spent the winter vying to change his little clothes and prance him around the farmyard when the weather permitted. They brought him out to the backyard when Betsy baked in the large clay oven beyond the kitchen door. Harry helped each one of them forget the horror of the fire and the two tragic deaths. As the winter wore on, the promise of new life he represented was as sweet as the sound of his contentment, recipient he was of much adoring attention. He filled their gray winter lives with delicate beauty. As the winds blew and snow covered one side of the house, the family gathered on a Sunday too treacherous to go to the chapel. Betsy read aloud from the Bible before they ate their sausage, biscuits and gravy. Mike was the only one who could speak of the coming separation and expressed for all of them the mixed feelings about the plans. "We'll be sad to see you leave us but you are doing the right thing. You'll find your success in Ohio." His leadership eased the awkwardness of everyone's emotions. "You'll have your own home and your own shop before a year's out. That's my prediction," he told his oldest son. "And while you're at it, why don't you three brothers put your thick heads together and develop a vehicle your Ma and I can use to come see you? I'll have a hard time talking her on to a train." George heard that and laughed with the rest of them. Betsy was notorious for her reluctance to venture beyond her mountain home. "It's not healthy to ride in so close a space with strangers," Betsy defended herself, referring to the newly developing, revolutionary speedy railroad systems. "Don't you worry, William. We'll make good use of that mail coach, just as we have with your brothers."

In order for mail with the outside world to resume, the long single road around half of the mountain needed to dry and be repaired after the rush and added destruction of the muddy spring surge. Communication opened with the first snow drop blossom and with it, the letter from Philadelphia arrived. George would be welcomed to a point and Mike decided George should postpone his move as his Philadelphia brother requested. Betsy sighed in relief, for she needed a break between good-byes. Agreeable though George was to set out on his own in the City of Brotherly Love, he was content in the familiar environment of the fresh mountain air. Spending a lot of time with his sisters, George was reluctant to leave them and the plans they had been concocting.

Soon after the letter arrived regarding George came the much anticipated time for William's departure. As soon as the road off of the mountain had dried solid enough to take the wagon's weight and not slide with soft mud down the side of the ravine, William packed up his young family for their journey and a new lifetime, new bedding, new clothes, along with the sole salvaged item of the fire, a cast iron pot from their hearth. William stowed a lathe, his hammers and saws, and other tools of his trade. As soon as the first wild jonquil appeared, they were gone. George and the two older of his sisters traveled the two days to Johnstown alongside William and Lizzie and baby Harry. The carpenter and his young family then continued on alone toward the National Road. Other unmarried cousins from the mountainside community made the trip to Johnstown as well for the Spring Festival Fair. Before the young people got home, both Lambert girls considered themselves engaged. The oldest of George's younger sisters married the boy she met at the Fair in a ceremony at the chapel late in the fall of 1849 and the following year had a little girl. The next sister, Mary, married her beau Jake from that Fair as well. The two of them moved to Minnesota where land was cheap and he had relatives settled already. Shortly after George left for Philadelphia in '51, the third sister Barbara married and moved to Iowa, with her husband and new brother-in-law who was blind and who played the mandolin and dulcimer. He gaily serenaded them all the way to their new western home. Margaret, the youngest, married and settled closer to Pittsburgh.

Mike, recognizing the change of seasons in his own life, farmed fewer acres and spent more time with his bees. He was less eager to travel now although unlike his wife he liked the clickety-clack of the iron horse. He had gone back and forth to Philadelphia at least every third year and so had adjusted to the new transportation. He brought back tales of his adventures for he loved to talk, and he thoughtfully brought back books from the city shops for his studious wife. He told the story of one ride across Pennsylvania farmlands in a railroad car whose wheels hugged rails now re-enforced with a steel band layered on top of the parallel wooden tracks. All riders knew the infrequent danger posed by those strips of steel. A strip could break at any time, and a "snake-head" would suddenly pierce the wood floor of the traveling train. Mike was riding a car that was hit when the layer of steel broke under the train's thundering wheels. A growing, hot strip of steel suddenly waved wildly inside the cabin. By God's miracle, no one was killed but the train had to stop and terrified passengers convinced to re-board.

Perhaps George's imagination was stimulated by his father's tales or by his own anticipation of leaving the mountain. One night, as he was sleeping in his corner of the loft and the crisp air through the opening of his window moved over him, he dreamed of an unknown place. George dreamed he was standing in an expansive flat yard and could see distances 360° around himself. He felt small against the land and unprotected like a target. When he looked down where he was standing, he saw a large group of children playing like a litter of kittens. He knew there were ten. One face came into focus, the round and sweet visage of a little girl and another one, a boy, moved away from the rest. Then the dream changed and George was riding a large buggy that had no horse, over the same terrain from the earlier part of the dream. He again felt vulnerable to the very air that moved over his face and abandoned by whatever horse should have been there. He knew he owned several horses but their familial companionship was a conspicuous absence. The vehicle moved forward with nothing in front of it. Nonetheless he was riding, sitting in the seat of a three-wheeled wagon-like contraption that was guided by levers at his feet, with no apparent means of propulsion, except that did not puzzle him in the dream. He dreamed the smell, not unlike horse manure, but sweet. He dreamed the feel, a vibration like the end of thunder, but constant and pleasant. He dreamed the sound, loud and encompassing. The male child who had stood apart earlier in the dream was there as an adult. He was waving his arms with excitement as George passed in the phantom machine. The look he saw covering the animated face left George believing the vehicle belonged to this young man. His amazement in the dream coincided with sparks of energy that began to course his body urging the young worker away form his sleep and into the day. He lay thinking of chores that needed to be done, then got out of bed.

As he moved around pulling on his clothes, his circulating blood cleaned the twitches out of his muscular limbs, and he climbed down the ladder into the main room of the darkened, silent house. The dream stayed with him as he sat in the cow barn, performing the ritual to relieve each cow and replenish the family's milk supply. Still bleary, George brought back the events he could remember and made a strong mental note to hold on to the images in his mind. *What a ride!* He felt rested and intrigued. *Where in heaven's name was the horse?*

In 1851 twenty-five-year old George made his move off the mountain. With no thoughts of Ohio or joining the crowd heading for California to prospect for gold, he rode the mule- and pony-powered railroad to Philadelphia. He located some rooms for himself on the third floor of a widow's house and with his uncle's letter of introduction, secured a part-time job in a printer's office. Mike and Betsy helped George pick out a course of study for the law and enrolled him at the University of Pennsylvania. His home away from home was Library Hall.

On Saturdays, George fell into the habit of walking the city and eating his noonday meal at an open farmer's market where he had tried to catch the attention of a certain brown-haired girl. One Saturday it happened inadvertently. He stood in the crowd admiring some carnations and dahlias, their fiery colors and trance-inducing blooms, when she came up beside him to reach for a blossom near his fingertips. She had been speaking to the older black woman who was with her. Without a moment to connive George deadpanned, "That's my flower," as she lifted a bright orange dahlia from the bucket.

Startled, she looked at him and her face turned red from her neck to her cheeks. He felt the heat of her embarrassment and showed her a deep and sunny smile, "I'm just kidding. Forgive me. Please, let me get it for you. I insist."

So he bought her flowers before he learned her name and they walked toward a bench to sit down. Her companion insisted on leaving them, explaining she would take their packages home. He asked Christianna about herself. "I live a few blocks from here in the Musselman estate. Annie is one of the cooks and I help her." George accepted the pieces of information she gave him and did not question that a serving girl be educated along with the Musselman children. "I've been on my own forever," Christianna explained with a shy smile. "My mother left me with the Musselmans because she was re-marrying and her new husband didn't want to risk taking a young baby to Ohio." George thought of little Harry, now settled in Ohio with a new younger sister. "I don't hear from her. I never did, but the Musselmans have been so kind and generous. I have no complaints." Christianna had a face full of kindness. He was falling in love. They were drawn to each other from this start.

After two years of study, George was restless to proceed beyond a printer's assistant. He had no passion to practice law or to develop as a journalist, but he had to do something. He was concerned with establishing himself, becoming a landowner, gaining security, the vote, and the right in his own mind to raise a family. His boss saw his dilemma and offered him the job of covering a concert featuring a new style piano. On the designated evening, with notebook and pencil, he and Christianna arrived at the concert early to assure seats close to the front. As the lights were lowered, the spotlight was directed to the large wooden box on the stage. The audience "ahh-ed" as it was a piece of art all by itself. The instrument was much grander than any piano they had ever seen, even more so when it's wide lid was propped up with a long stick. George jotted down the adjectives that came to his mind and that passed through Christianna's whispering lips. Afterward, Christianna commented that the Steinway piano was as far as could be from the tinkle tinkle tin pan tones of the harpsichord in the Musselman parlor. She felt she saw angels filling the air space and George, too, had felt God embrace first his shoulders and then opened wide His arms to include Christianna and the pianist. Who knew a live performance could weave such magic! George tried to write his experience but it was beyond words.

Christianna showed George her favorite site in Philadelphia. She had first visited Ben Franklin's grave many years before with the Musselman tutor and the Musselman children. The tutor's admiration for the American icon was infectious; she had told the children he was one of a few characters who played the role of father to this country. In her childlike ears Christianna heard she could assume Ben Franklin as her father-figure. She did not think of herself as an orphan but neither did she have her father or mother in her life. A part of her ached to know them and to have them know her. Here was an illustrious man whom the tutor said was her father. She began to think of him that way, until she was old enough to understand the biology and dates involved. Now she brought George and shared her vulnerability over her situation. He said few words in response to the emotionally charged story, but showed such compassion on his face she knew her feelings were safe with him. In response, he told her of his deep feelings for her and was rewarded with her vows of mutual love. They made their pledge to marry.

Christianna went to tell her employer of her plans. Old Mr. Musselman sat at his leather-covered desk straightening papers; he hardly moved a facial muscle as he looked up at her entrance. He had heard of the man who sat in his kitchen paying court to the young serving girl, yet frowned at her news and advised her in no uncertain terms against it. When George heard this, he was furious. Confronting the wealthy old man, George explained in as diplomatic terms as he could muster their decision was final. Sorry as he was to be taking her away from a place that she loved and was loved in return, she would indeed be leaving.

"Not so fast, young Lambert, if that is your name. I have already sent a letter to this so-called town of yours out in the wilderness – Lost Mountain, indeed!" George and Christianna confidently waited it out. The messenger returned promptly with reassurances from George's parents who had only recently read George's letter. Once the plans were in motion, the old Philadelphia couple were inexplicably generous to the departing young people. George had told his parents that he would be returning to Lost Mountain to present his intended. From there he would take his bride to Ohio to join his brothers. Both Mike and Betsy had immediately responded to George to express their pleasure at this turn of events. They also took the liberty of writing his three brothers in Ohio to announce his news and instruct them how they were to make George and Christianna welcome. "George," his mother wrote to her baby boy, "we expect you and your bride to winter with us. We want to get to know this girl who has captured your heart."

The wedding was sweet after being postponed long enough for Christianna and Betsy to stitch a dress out of the delicate silk brocade, the color of fresh cream, which had been given to the bride by the Musselmans. Mike hired a photographer, an invention newly available. The family sat still the six seconds in front of the box camera balanced on a three-legged contraption, and held their faces so the likeness would not blur, and then marveled at the outcome on the tintypes they held in their hands. Their time on the mountain passed quickly.

As soon as the newly-weds set out for Ohio, Christianna confided to her groom she could say with confidence she would make him a father in the fall. He was so excited he announced it to fellow travelers on the train, who smiled, pumped his hand and nodded their heads knowingly. He wired his parents from the Pittsburgh station. George had run through the crowd of passengers waiting with luggage for arriving parties; he wove around children and old people to reach the telegraph desk and return before the train, with his seat and his bride, rumbled out of the station so near to the Ohio state line. The soon-to-be mother asked him to not mention her condition to the Ohio fold until she could see what they would encounter in their new home. George stoically agreed and respected her direction. He was used to following female cues; he had been the guardian of four younger sisters and the youngest son of a strong-willed mother in a community run by his grandmother.

George and Christianna arrived in Ohio by stepping off the train in Springfield Station on an overcast March day. William and Lizzie were there to greet them with nine-year-old Harry and his sister seven-year-old Katy, all dressed in very fine clothes. The excited children performed their welcoming speeches ably with curtsies and bows. Some singular energy inside George leapt out to his hands and feet when he saw the dark Ohio earth. He could smell it as soon as he stepped off the train. Here was a land that begged to be plowed and planted. He was eager to put his plans for his crops into action, to get out into the sun, to sweat and work until sweet exhaustion at his own farm. He and his father had debated and detailed those plans over the winter and struggled at times over who was the master of methods, Mike with his experience or George with his education. Eventually they combined perspectives and came up with schedules for crop rotations and cash-producing endeavors to create prosperity for the not-so-young man who was eager to start and care for an expanding family. The two reunited brothers stepped off the elevated platform of the station onto a wooden sidewalk which stretched over a sea of thick mud. William waved at the black earth. "Welcome to Ohio in the springtime!"

William and Lizzie had written to George at the time of the wedding and graciously offered to house them on their arrival. George was astounded at the generosity of the quarters he and Christianna enjoyed in William's house. William had constructed a new wing to his spacious home in preparation for George's stay. In his mind's eye, George had pictured a small bed curtained off in a large room, much like the accommodations William and Lizzie had shared with the family after the fire. This was something else all together. George looked forward to seeing his two older brothers Michael and Joseph who had arrived in Ohio about a decade ago. Christianna had looked forward to meeting all of George's brothers but derived the most pleasure from the anticipation of meeting the two female Philadelphia natives, for she assumed a bond already cast from their mutual roots in the city of Brotherly

Love. It did not take long after their arrival for the other brothers to gather. Michael and Joseph appeared at William's home with their families, each in a riding carriage led by two beautiful horses. Their faces were all smiles and their brightly colored clothes were freshly pressed. Each female wore what looked like a new bonnet that encircled her head. These families were growing and prospering. Life looked grand in Ohio.

No brother or sister-in-law mentioned the tragic fire on Lost Mountain. George wondered if they ever had discussed it among themselves. The silence seemed to persist to protect Lizzie, who kept her own counsel and maintained her habit of spending long hours by herself. George whispered his feelings to Christianna in regards to the subject that seemed to drift silently around the oldest brother's household. No traces of the little lost lives decorated the rooms which were various and comfortable as William, true to his father's predictions, had found immediate prosperity in the madly expanding Miami Valley. He had a construction company with ten hired men, and his workers were building on several sites. And he owned a large facility that housed numerous workstations that alternated in producing barrels, horse troughs and wagon parts.

"Ohio," Christianna said, "was a place to put the past behind you."

Lizzie arranged for the new style of floor covering, a Bigelow carpet, to be put down over the raw wood floor in the new room offered to her husband's brother. She ordered curtains for the windows that went all the way to the floor. A beautiful wooden chest William crafted and gave to the newlyweds was on display as a centerpiece in the room, surrounded by simple furniture, a rocker, a washstand, a mirror and small bed. The view out the windows was filled with trees and flowers on a gradual incline to a fence covered with pussy willows, beyond which were cornfields, rows and rows of small, baby corn plants, each asserting its green fingerly leaves up out of the wide, level expanse of dark earth.

In spite of the lovely accommodations, George wanted to be out on his own. Before his money slipped away, he needed to make his move. With William's advice and contacts, he and Christianna soon moved into a small farm southwest of Springfield. The owner had been called suddenly to his mother's bedside in Virginia. He left the fields cleared and standing ready to be planted. George had bought the livestock outright, two mules, four cows and a bull, chickens, a rooster, three pigs and numerous barn cats. The Virginian had taken his dog and his horse when he left Ohio. George and William had signed the deed before they traveled the dirt county road to see it, so were relieved to find it as described. They alighted from William's coach and went up the front walk. While William was opening the door, George glanced down and spotted a four-leaf clover in a patch by the steps. "By Golly, now can you believe that," he said as he bent to pick it. William stopped to see what was amazing his brother. The only other time either had seen this phenomenon was the four-leaf clover their mother had found after Grandma's funeral which was pressed and framed over the family table on Lost Mountain. Without gazing toward him, William said to his brother, "It is a good omen. This place will bring you happiness, little brother. Once you have it pressed and dried, I'll make a frame."

During their stay with the William Lamberts, George got to know the young man he had held as a baby and called "lambie-pie." Nine-year-old Harry likewise took an interest in his uncle and the two males walked all over Springfield. Harry proudly pointed out his father's holdings and projects.

Just before the move to the new farm, the four brothers and their families gathered at the oldest brother's large home for an outdoor meal of fried chicken and gravy, cooked by Lizzie's maid, with potatoes that Lizzie mashed with cream, garlic and butter, set next to a large earthenware bowl of succotash, lima beans, corn, carrots and butter. The other families brought pickles and bread, apple pies and custard cake and freshly brewed beer. After dinner the croquet set was pushed into the freshly mowed lawn, and the adults played teams against each other while tolerating the children who were attracted to the colorful balls and the idea of smacking them across the yard with little clubs. As the evening drew dark, the croquet was put away and the lightening bugs came out. The children ran around in an effort to catch them. The older boys had jars into which the captured bugs were collected, but easily escaped, because so many little faces wanted to lift the wooden lids and peer into the contents. Joseph gathered the children together and had them gaze at the sky. He pointed out the Big Dipper and taught them to find the North Star. George joined the group of mostly little people and asked the children if they ever heard of their Great Aunt Star who had been named after a star that appeared in the early morning. Katy said no, but it was a pretty name. George told the children of the woman who was special and kind and who had a friend and protector in her older sister. Joseph said that was the way all siblings were supposed to be with each other.

The smallest children were asking for bed as the large extended family re-grouped inside. In the midst of this contentment, standing in front of a marble fireplace, looking tall and lean in his waist coat and vest, William produced a bottle of brandy to pour into clear glass goblets. "To George and Christianna, welcome and congratulations on your new home." William sounded like their father. He lifted his glass and smiled at his newly arrived brother. George rose to his feet. The flush of excitement and alcohol colored his cheeks. Christianna looked at the hands in her lap; she knew what he was about to say as they had planned this moment together. The others waited for him to continue.

"My brothers," his voice was low, "join me in toasting my beautiful wife who is soon to make me a father!" The other three men, plus Harry, leapt to their feet with "Ha-zahs". The warmth of the moment filled the room.

William arranged with some of his workers to come around on moving day to transport George's things to the new farm. The transfer took place on a bright spring day with a deep blue sky.

Overgrown lilac bushes encircled most of the little farmhouse's front face. The roof beam had a slight sag, but the white washed walls were stout. The deep front porch had a two-seater swing tied to a cross beam. Christianna was charmed to call it home. Her pregnancy seemed to emphasize her robust health rather than threaten it. It made her happy to unpack their things, and she hummed as she heated her irons to straighten out the curtains before she hung them. With water easy to get from the pump just outside the kitchen door, she washed every inch of the place. George took right to the fields.

Although they were a good distance from Springfield, they were far from alone. One of William's best business clients was a horse farmer located only a few miles south in Harmony Township near where George and Christianna were now farming. They were soon to make each other's acquaintance. The two middle Lambert brothers had talked with William to arrange with this client to present, on their behalf, two beautiful young riding horses to George and Christianna, as wedding presents and as assurances they would visit their brothers who lived in a different township called Mad River. Before too many days went by, George and Christianna rode their powerful mules three or four miles to the Furst farm. It was more like a plantation. They came up a ridge to see the house under a canopy of several large trees which George immediately recognized: a large horse chestnut out by the road, maple, oak and poplars up by the house and a large elm towering over the rest from the back yard. He said to Christianna, "The Fursts have a beautiful place. It looks like the one I can see in my mind for us." He touched her elbow as they walked up the broad steps to the porch in front of the house. There were large white pillars to the roof of the overhang which provided a space of shade and kept the house cool. At the top step George looked around him. As far as he could see were fields of young plants dotted with orchards in the distance which made an overall pattern out front of low fields and cool patches of trees flanked by wildflowers. Toward the sides and rear of the home were horse pastures. Christianna knocked on the door, and George stepped up behind her to be greeted by a Negro woman in a gray muslin dress with a long white apron smock. She smiled kindly and waited for the strangers to speak. George spoke while removing the hat he had worn on the ride, "Good day. We are the George Lamberts, brought here by invitation of my brothers, who made arrangements with Mr. Furst."

The servant bowed slightly and leaving the door open for light, stepped back into the house with a sweeping gesture of her arm. She disappeared into the back of the house while the young couple stood alone in the large hallway. They looked at each other as loud steps sounded in the hall. They heard the voice before its owner appeared. "You must be the young people from out East. Welcome to Ohio! Welcome to Clark County!" She was round with strength to her frame, topped with silver-speckled brown hair. Hurrying up to them the middle-aged woman held out both hands to grab at first Christianna and then George. After greeting George, her hands went back to Christianna, "Oh, my dear, how wonderful! I am a mid-wife, you know. I want you to call on me." Christianna flashed red with embarrassment at such a blatant reference but kept her voice steady, "Why, thank you. I will." *How did the woman know about the coming baby?*

Mrs. Furst took them out through the back and down a short gravel path beyond a flower garden and over to a huge red barn. Beyond the barn began several lines of white rail fencing around clusters of horses.

"Levi!" She yelled out; George and Christianna noticed a tall slender man about his father's age coming around the far corner. He took his time as he walked while his wife spoke alternately to him and to their visitors. After introductions and pleasantries were made, he walked George down to the stalls at the far end of the barn. Christianna could see their silhouettes and the two women watched as Mr. Furst pulled first one horse then another out of the stall. George bent to rub his hands down each leg and up over their backs and necks. He pulled pieces of carrots out of his pockets to place between eager lips. Each man took a bridle and guided the horses toward the women.

"My, what beautiful horses," Christianna tried to sound knowledgeable. The horses were tied to a post closer to the house, and the group took seats in the shade on stone benches. A tray of lemonade had been left on a stone table between two of the granite settees. George expressed his pleasure in the animals. "We used a much smaller breed where I come from." Levi continued talk of breeding and special grasses while Savina, his wife, went out in the dirt and dug up plantlets to give to Christianna, nasturtiums, poppies, and other varieties of flowers and herbs. After a very pleasant visit which included celery soup and biscuits, George hitched a mule behind each horse, helped his wife up to her new perch, joined her on his and with much hand-waving and promises to visit, left their new friends and neighbors.

As the summer passed Christianna welcomed the changes in her body, for she had always longed for her own family. George sang as he did his work, and the plants in the fields grew strong and tall. His new plow sliced the sticky black earth like magic so that the fields rolled out as fast as he could dispense the seeds. He planted all his wheat, corn, rye and three bags of soy Michael had given him. The sun lingered in the summer sky, baking the fields and throwing strength to the young plants. The air was hot and humid. The rain seemed to know when it was time for a drink, and watered the young plants on a regular schedule. George learned from his brothers about local mills and machine shops to take advantage of the constant flow of new devices to save effort and maximize profit. His farmer brothers Michael and Joseph had become machinists and blacksmiths and members of the Grange.

Christianna heard in her mind the soothing tones of Annie's voice who had taught her about a woman's body and the gift of childbearing, an uncommon attitude in her generation. Because she was well acquainted with what to expect, she knew when her labor came she would need someone strong enough to save her should something go wrong. She knew who that person was and made her plans to visit Mrs. Furst. Once there, she received the shock of her life.

"I wasn't sure if telling you now was the right thing to do, with the baby coming, but then I figured, with the baby coming I had to tell you," Mrs. Furst explained with a shrug and a touch to Christianna's arm. "When I first saw you, I knew in my heart but my mind wouldn't accept it. I had Levi ask William where in Pennsylvania you were from, and when he came back and said Philadelphia, well, it was falling into place. You look so much like I did when I was your age." Christianna was not so quick to believe what she was being told. But Mrs. Furst could name the Musselmans and knew Christianna's birth date and finally convinced her that it was true. She could not wait to tell George: Mrs. Furst was her mother!

"And you have a half brother. He is in Kentucky with Levi's family, but he'll be back. He inherited a love of horses from them." She smiled big and never sat still. She brought framed photographs from various locations in the big parlor to show Christianna and talked of how Levi had promised her he would help George get established. "He might want to consider horses," her mother suggested. Christianna stayed much longer than she had planned. She needed to recover from her shock, which of course would really take much longer. She wanted to stay and feel the connection which could not be put into words with this woman, her mother. Savina was not one to sit wordlessly and sentimentally sigh into her daughter's eyes, but she was jovial to beat the band and rubbed Christianna's arm so much Christianna finally flung her arms wide and offered to be hugged, and then struggled not to smother in the enthusiastic embrace. When it was absolutely time to go, no more stalls or doddling, Savina insisted she take home a container of her famous molasses baked beans and brown bread with a slice of her sweetbutter. The Negro servant who packed the food was a different woman from the servant who opened the door several weeks back. Christianna surprised herself by saying so.

"Oh, my dear, we don't want to tell all our secrets right away but since you are from Philadelphia perhaps you will agree about the abomination of slavery." Christianna nodded seriously. "These girls that you see are with me only a short while. I figure the best disguise is right out in the open. They are on their way to Canada." Upon hearing this, Christianna felt more awed by this force of a woman. And here was another bond between them.

As Christianna rode back to the familiar rhythms of her life with George, she marveled at the revelations of the day. Her mother had always been in the back of her mind. A day did not go by in the last twenty years in which her thoughts did not drift to her mother. With coming to Ohio, she had privately wondered if she could learn about her and had planned maybe in a few years to find a way to make some inquiries. She had anticipated the welcome of George's brothers and their families and has been so happy to make them her family. Now she had kin of her own! She had never had that, in all those comfortable years with the Musselmans. She eagerly awaited seeing George and his reaction to her startling news.

"What?!" he said initially. "No, how could it be?!"

It took convincing him as well. Eventually, even he could not deny the truth after hearing all Savina could recite about the Musselmans and Christianna's early life. George suggested they kneel in thanksgiving, which indeed they did with tears in their eyes and streaming down her cheeks, grateful to God for His mysterious ways. They asked as well for guidance for the embarkment of this adventure of a mother, a new brother and in-laws, on top of all the other new adventures they were having. In the excitement, no one had thought to ask about Christianna's father, and when she did ask her mother, Savina replied, "That's better left unsaid. Let us be satisfied to have found each other, for indeed it is a miracle."

As high summer waned, Christianna and George made another trip to the large horse farm to visit Christianna's new found family. Levi Junior was back from Kentucky. George was impressed by the horses the Furst men relished showing off, but he felt guarded about jumping in with their financial endeavors. He stuck to the plans he and his father had laid out. He did, however, pick up on the idea of animal husbandry and learned from his step-father-in-law the methods of raising animals for profit.

Savina recruited George and Christianna to help in her subversive activities with runaway slaves. She seemed unconscious of the dangerous waters she swam in, and her lack of intimidation probably was her best protection. Many visitors came to her farm to speak to her husband or her son, any of whom might report her and she had in-laws in Kentucky who owned slaves! She, in fact, boasted of helping one of her father-in-law's field hands travel to freedom. The Fursts of Kentucky never suspected their daughter-in-law whom they saw as flighty, unkempt and unschooled which made her laugh all the harder. Truth be told, Levi enjoyed the dramatic subversions as well. George engaged Levi in constructing a hidden cellar beneath a floorboard in one of the horse barns, to provide some protection should Savina's luck wear out. The family on Lost Mountain had built similar precautions for alongside the limber trade, they had been part of a network to help runaway slaves that Mike had set up from Philadelphia before he married Betsy.

Over the summer Christianna had worked in her own home with a young women sent over by Savina. Her "brother" helped George in the fields. George had built a secret room behind the barn, half under his woodpile and half underground, should bounty hunters come snooping around. A man recently had been tarred and feathered by some pro-slavery folks up from Cedarville after they broke open his large covered wagon to reveal eight terrified wayfarers lying hidden under a false bottom.

The leaves in the trees had turned bright yellow, gold and scarlet and fallen to the ground, brown and crispy, and still George and Christianna waited for their first baby to arrive. At last the labor began. On that day in early November, on her way to the spring house they had built a few weeks back in the lull of the summer, a pain seized Christianna's abdomen which stopped her in mid-step. She reflexively called out as she struggled to endure until the grip of the contraction released, then she turned right around and returned to the house. She wanted to be inside. After some time, another attack controlled her body. She had to square herself to face what was coming; her body, which was so used to continuous moderate activity, had become a clenched fist. Both Annie and her mother Savina had said it would hurt but nothing prepared her for this complete occupation of her body. The awkward young black woman, who was spinning in the corner, opened her eyes wider as Christianna struggled, but never wavered the rhythm of the wheel as she turned flax into thread.

Savina had made a habit over the summer of traveling the two long dirt roads between fields and pastures to the Lambert farm and more frequently as the days grew shorter and the sun's shadows longer. She had come every day for the past five days. As Christianna looked out the window up the west road, sure enough, the bouncing bonnet of her mother could be seen at the head of a tunneling cloud of dust. The air had a mild chill wind and the sky held not a cloud. With the leaves stripped from the trees, Christianna had a clear view of her mother traveling the final half mile to the house. Never had the sight of Savina felt so good, and Christianna's body dropped a lot of its anxiety in response to the arriving figure, just in time for another total invasion of penetrating pain. The older woman entered the house between contractions but diagnosed the situation immediately, "I told Levi I won't be home tonight because you're having a baby." Savina Furst filled up any room she was in, and this small house seemed to bulge with her expansive energy. She placed several baskets on the table as she smiled at her daughter. "So they only just started?" she asked, again demonstrating her uncanny ability to know things outright that others needed to be told.

Savina put more logs on the fire and worked the pump just outside the back door. She lay out utensils and spread fresh sheets over the bed in the backroom, all the while talking to Christianna who said nothing, encouraging her to walk, move about, with soft tones like Levi would use with his horses. When the next contraction came, Christianna, although gripped and blanched, had an easier time meeting its demands. After waving a few words to the young woman spinning, Savina went out to tell George of the happenings. The night of bringing a baby into the world was in motion. By dawn, Christianna was sleeping deeply with her arms around her healthy newborn girl, likewise sleeping.

Although George had hoped his oldest child would be a boy like all three of his brothers', as soon as he saw Anna Elizabeth he forgave her. He was content she was healthy and immensely relieved Christianna got through the ordeal safely and that the precious little thing had waited until all the crops were in and the fields bedded for the winter. The bounty from his efforts of the last few months would provide for expanding crops next season with plenty for themselves and to sell. He shipped a bag of his soy beans in a box by train to his father on Lost Mountain, along with word of Anna Elizabeth's arrival, named for Christianna and his mother Betsy.

George and Christianna had no idea that something so small could create so much work. Little Libby Baby did not like to sleep at night and was fretful to have her mother out of her sight, so George and Christianna had to steel themselves to her protests. They told each other her screaming and crying were good for her lungs. With those powerful lungs they bundled her up to face the winter's cold, for they made a habit of visiting their families on Sundays unless it was snowing. One Sunday, as they approached the dual farms of the long established brothers, a lone rider came out to meet them while he carefully balanced a blanketed bundle in his lap. It was Michael. "You might want to turn back. My wife is terrible sick and we don't want you or the baby to catch it."

George and Christianna hardly knew what to say. Michael turned back the corner of the bundle he held close by the pommel of his horse, and two little fists emerged. "Oh, my!" Christianna exclaimed, as Michael continued, "So far it's passed Jake by.

Would you take him with you? We're so busy and with so much sickness, we thought asking you was his best hope."

Christianna touched George's arm, and he turned to see her nodding her head. Then he said to his distraught brother, "Of course, Michael. Golly, what else can we do? I'm so sorry to hear of the conditions here. Does William know?"

"William knows," Michael said, not masking his disgust.

His brother continued, "I know Libby won't mind sharing with her cousin. We'll take good care of little Jake, Michael. Rest your mind about that. I am happy to take him for as long as you need us." Christianna had already taken the child out of the blanket and after whispering soft words cold nose to little nose, turned to wrap him next to the quiet, for once, baby Libby.

Christianna handed over the pies and bread she had baked, and Michael nestled them in a pile in front of him where his son had been. Waving a wan smile, he turned his horse and returned to his home. When Savina heard from Christianna about The Fever attacking the sister-in-law, she took it upon herself to make the long ride to Mad River Township to look in on the patient. What she had to report after her return was not good news. Both of Christianna's sisters-in-law were ill with scarlet fever, as were three of the children and Joseph as well. She had left remedies and detailed instructions and scoffed about the doctor from Springfield William had sent.

The children were not so sick as the adults; Joseph and his wife were sickest of all. Michael somehow remained healthy and was working his best to tend to the patients in his brother's house. He was grateful the sickness had waited until the demands of the farms had slackened for the winter. His wife, although weak, refused to lie down. By sheer will she rallied in order to tend her cousin. The happy red-head, who had walked most of the way from Philadelphia to Springfield including a long detour in and out of Lost Mountain with a man she had met a day before their wedding, was now near death. The pain was searing her throat and burning deep in her chest. Large dark areas shadowed her eyes. Alice wrung out a rag in a bowl of cool water by the bed, fragranced by the eucalyptus, lavender and peppermint they used in the soap they had made together and sold each year at the County Fair. She was already mourning the now silent woman. The end came peacefully, but not before Joseph, who had rallied to embrace his young children, suddenly got worse and died. Scarlet fever claimed them both. Michael's wife regained most of her health but no longer could she run up the hill from her garden, and she needed to rest through the evening. The children recovered as though the sickness had never inhabited their sturdy young frames.

William made coffins for his brother and sister-in-law, and they were buried side by side on a corner of the farm that Joseph and Michael had worked together. They were so young to be taken and would be so sorely missed. Inexplicably, Lizzie was absent at the funeral service but sent her two children each dressed in brand new black velvet and white lace. The survivors Michael and Alice were desolate. George and Christianna quietly held their hands through the service. There was a child or two in every lap. William eulogized his brother and sister-in-law and closed his remarks by again welcoming George, his bride and new daughter. Quoting their grandmother of Lost Mountain, he tried to smile: "There is a motto that for generations has sustained our family in the face of tragedy and loss: lose one; gain one."

Although grateful to his brother for the words, this was not the welcome George would have preferred. Stunned and sad, he huddled with Michael and William to discuss the fates of Joseph's two children. Baby Jake was returned to his family, and Christianna was given the newly orphaned children at least temporarily, which relieved Michael and his wife who were busy with two rambunctious little boys and baby Jake. By Christmas they were expecting their fourth.

2

JW is Born

First impressions of the prospering relatives had changed. There were private problems in William's house which were becoming more public. Drinking was Lizzie's big secret, a secret so she blindly thought, and William kept up the charade. But the stories of her tirades were well known in Springfield. Christmas Eve she got her horse out, hitched it to a two-wheeler wagon and drove like the devil for twenty miles in the dark and cold. William had to go find her. She had cuts on her hands and large bruises blossoming up and down her left side with swelling around her eyes, but she would recover.

When the unsuspecting relatives, George, Michael and the others, arrived in Springfield Christmas day they saw that something was strangely amiss. The servants were laying out food as usual but threw harrowing looks to the visitors. William looked haggard but welcomed his brothers by helping them off with their coats and directing them into the parlor where the tree was sparkling and a present for each child was waiting to be unwrapped. Christianna asked after her sister-in-law. William made light of her absence by saying she was feeling a bit under the weather. But Harry volunteered that his mother looked beat up, whereupon the farming brothers turned to William in alarm. Unwilling to be implicated as a wife beater, William told the story of the mad late night ride and explained when she took to drinking she lost all her reason. William strained to allow the underpinnings of his life to show, and Christianna suspected the situation must be grave. Other incidents took on a clearer understanding once the problem with alcohol was defined, like why Lizzie was a no-show at Joseph's burial service.

William was at his wit's end and drew comfort from the company of his brothers. Harry seemed to sense his father's emotional exhaustion and took over some of the authority by giving needed instructions to the servants. Little Katy sat motionless in the parlor and later at the table, except to bring the silver fork to her mouth to eat the baked lamb and gravy. The chocolate custard dessert inspired some spirit from the sad little girl. William announced he would that very day sign The Pledge and would rid his household of all alcohol including beer. George and Joseph raised their eyebrows at this, as Christianna spoke up in support of her brother-in-law's extreme measure, "Under the circumstances, I am sure we all will go along with your wishes." The Temperance Union's Pledge was one part of a large campaign to rid society of the evil of alcohol.

On the following Saturday, George and Christianna bundled up Libby for the cold ride to celebrate the holiday with the Fursts. Joseph's two children, Lewis and Frances, were spending this time with Michael, his three boys and his newly pregnant, hallow-eyed wife. Upon their arrival Savina, always unpredictable, declared a new moniker for Christianna. She announced henceforth she would call her "Anna". "Anna of Ohio, after all," she beamed. Telling George she expected him to do the same, she brought them to the large parlor brimming with cut greens. The centerpiece was a large, freshly hewed spruce tree. The fragrance of pine embraced them like a massage and perked up their spirits; the stress of the Springfield situation poured off their bodies and evaporated at their feet. Here they joined the two Levis whose heads were bent over a map on the desk but tilted up in unison to greet their guests. There was no shortage of alcoholic beverages here, and the laughter was deep all around. Libby, in an eyelet lace bonnet and red velvet dress, stayed awake the entire visit. She spent her time on one adult lap and then another. Even the men welcomed a stay by the round-faced infant who laughed along with her larger relatives.

George and Anna were reassured of Ohio's promise with this generous celebration in Harmony Township. George squared his shoulders as he considered the future and faced how much depended on his own doing. The deaths impressed him that life can be short and this family gathering nourished him. Young Levi was a college scholar as his father had been, with great plans for the future. Both his parents beamed in his presence. Levi and Savina were delighted to learn of George's past collegiate successes as well. Levi showed no resentment at sharing his throne with Anna and her family; he had been relieved to discover there was a half sister to dilute the combined attention of his parents. Growing up he always looked forward to spending time in Kentucky with his father's people, for there were a lot of them. Plus nothing about his mother surprised him.

George decided to sell the Virginia man's farm where Libby was born and, after destroying the hidden room used to house runaway slaves, move his family into the home vacated by the death of his brother. The move enabled Joseph's children to have their old beds back and be together with their accustomed companions. George and Michael threw in as partners. First they bought a thrashing machine run by horsepower, which significantly increased the amount of wheat they could manage. They planned to produce a large amount of straw and hay which would come in handy to care for the large numbers of livestock they invested in and brought to the dual farm: hogs, mules and colts, sheep, cattle and cows. Every day through the winter that didn't have snow in the air, they were out chopping down chestnut trees to make fences and construct a large barn. The work was a balm for the two brothers who were grieving for their losses, concerned about the ominous political signs in the air and excited about the anticipated prosperity coming in the future. Springfield was a good market for their produce. William had arranged with one of his railroad executive friends for space on the bay at the station to ship what they could to Columbus and Dayton. Access to the railroads with their bellowing smoke stacks and loud steam engines gave the brothers an advantage over their neighbors.

By mid-summer Anna knew she was having another baby, hopefully a boy this time. She told George the news the same night she cried over missing her mother. The new location, though close to Michael and a promising financial opportunity, was quite far from her newly-found mother. Her condition enhanced her longing for Savina, but she adjusted to the distance through Savina's extended visits. The outgoing woman enjoyed the noisy new railroad travel, for there was little that could intimidate her. Around the homestead, Anna kept her news to herself and watched her sister-in-law grow large with her fourth. In the midst of the harvest season came their sought after daughter, but the weary mother weakened and seemed simply to drift away in the days following the delivery. Michael was stoic. Distracted with the tasks of the farm, he confided to George that he had known he would lose her. They laid her to rest next to her cousin on the edge of the field, surrounded by a white link fence. Anna made sure forget-me-nots and Queen Anne's lace encircled the space. Under the weeping willow to the left she planted lily of the valley given by Savina so her sisters, whom she had been able to know only briefly, could hear their angel bells.

The brothers reaped a fine harvest, as though God and the earth were rewarding them for the steadfastness they showed through the losses they had been hit with so soon after George's arrival in Ohio. The crop sales to Springfield, Dayton and Columbus had put coins in their pockets, smiles on their faces and money in the bank. By candlelight at the desk that William had recently presented him, George drew up his plans for his expanding empire. In spite of his tragedies, he felt on the upswing. He loved being a businessman farmer, relished the opportunities he saw out there begging to be taken and thought only his own physical limitations stopped him from conquering the world! So he hired helpers for the fields and a farmhand to live in. He nurtured his relationships with the blacksmith and men at the machine shops in Springfield, who worked on engines to run the machines to take over pieces of his labor, sowing, reaping, sheathing and sheering. The boys there had a planter they fashioned themselves and were studying a McCormick's reaper manufactured in Chicago. James Leffel's success with his waterpower machine and his double turbine engines fascinated the men. They took turns visiting his foundry shop, to buy a knife or a sickle, and then regrouped to discuss what they had seen. It was big excitement when Leffel and his sometimes partner, sometimes competitor set up their machines to race. They drew a big crowd and, no matter who won, gained a lot of publicity for their businesses. Like his brother, William also loved the noise of the machines and talking about the promise of steam power. He could recite the numeral specifications of an engine and took interest in the one Lizzie's brother in Greenville was trying to adapt to practical, laborsaving devices. Michael, mourning, had no attention for the new inventions.

Christmas was again celebrated at the William Lamberts. Lizzie looked trim but still had a distant look in her eye. Her children vied to take turns helping cute chubby Libby, dressed with ribbons and lace, walk on wide little legs around the room while holding on to fingers held for her service in front of her ever-expanding path. Anna had not seen Lizzie all last winter, until mid-August and she was present at the burial in the fall. She made it clear she did not want to talk about her absence. But she told Anna about Daniel Hume from England who had spent a week in Springfield and an evening with her. He had held her hands over the table in the parlor and called upon spirits to enter the room. Lizzie claimed he rose out of his chair and hovered, trembling in her hands. Anna did not know how to respond. She could tell this was an important event to Lizzie but had no context to understand its meaning. As much as Anna tried to forge a friendship with her older, more stylish sister-in-law, she could not find an opening that worked. It was a bit awkward between the women but their feeling did not dominate the scene; the brothers set the mood. No one spoke aloud of last year except in financial terms, for the three brothers were making, each in his own standard, more money than ever before. No one mentioned The Pledge William had signed last Christmas, but the men enjoyed brandy and cigars in the parlor after the meal where talk turned to politics. They talked about the race for governor, William's chronic lament about the price of wood, and the over-the-top railroad bosses. They chewed over politicians. Giving each other the right of indignant expression, they laughed at their pretenses. The lightheartedness eventually turned serious, for the temper of the country did concern them. Michael turned moody while the two other brothers went over what they knew of the bloody attack at Harper's Ferry. They enthusiastically called themselves Republicans to be part of the new political party that was so clearly anti-slavery. Debate focused on the Kansas-Nebraska Act that in effect opened up slavery to new states. It was frustrating because the Missouri Compromise had stipulated no expansion of the institution, leaving it to die of attrition. This was a step backwards. A lawyer from over in Illinois whom William had consulted about the railroads and who was running for the United States Senate, best articulated the issue as they themselves understood it: eager to maintain peace and preserve the union, but seeing the threat of division rooted in slavery. Slavery was an evil, amoral wrong and a reality neither of the brothers could stomach. Their mother had taught them well on this political issue. Although raised by an informed and vocal mother about political affairs, William did not look to his wife to discuss political parties, legislation or candidates; he looked to other men to go over the chess-like maneuvering of political game playing. This oversight was re-enforced by female disenfranchisement; women did not vote. With their power to vote, the brothers would become Republican regulars and talked about ways to promote their party.

Michael who was making a big decision, interrupted his brothers' political banter to open a discussion on his private considerations. He wanted to take his four motherless children and Joseph's two orphans to Lost Mountain. He hoped he would have time to get the children out of harm's way before the inevitable Coming Conflict. Talk of war was increasing in parlors across the nation. Those crazy politicians from the southern states were not coming to their senses about the sinfulness of slavery. As William had said, the pro-slavery crowd was frantic to expand their lifestyle into the new western states. They needed to be taught a lesson. The killings in Kansas amounted to a civil war; no one was stopping it. Michael felt he could not fight a war and raise six children as well. He would take them to the protected isolation of the steep mountainside and rely on the haven presided over by their mother and father. It was their sister Betsy who suggested the move, imploring her brother to escape to their birthplace in a letter included in the Christmas correspondence, written directly to him, "This is your home. Mother and father could use your help and the company of the children. It would brighten our world and you could stay just as long as the conflict lasts, which should only be a short while, as right has might and the slavery question must be answered once and for all."

The brothers focused on Michael's troubles and put together a plan. Their unspoken assumption of mutual concern for each other's welfare and unhesitating attention to solve each other's problems came as naturally as one season after another. After another year's cycle of harvest and profits, Michael could comfortably make his move, and George would be set as well. Michael proposed George buy him out before he packed up the six children and left for Lost Mountain. But George, knowing Anna wanted to be closer to her mother and wanting his own green pastures, opted out and decided to look for land in the county north of Springfield. William stepped forward with the solution. Successful in his manufacturing and with his many landholdings, he was a bank unto himself. The economic panic of the previous year passed him by, so that he offered to finance George's new farm. Michael would then sell the dual farm, pocket the profits and take the children to the mountain with immediate financial security for them all.

Through the cold winter months, the six cousins, plus fat and sassy Libby, played together around Aunt Anna, who acted as step-mother. The space was cramped, for the children were used to long runs in the green expanse of summer. Savina was staying with her daughter because the ride to her home was a good distance and the baby was soon due. With her usual companions, the railroads were fast becoming too dangerous even for Savina. She was with a woman from Georgia, a lone traveler on the highway to Canada but willing to linger during this cold season to help in the delivery. As Anna's time approached, Savina's engaging authority chastened the children to be helpful and cooperative. The grown men were harder to manage and Savina had to be more direct with them. On this particular day she bade them, "Ride over to Springfield and take any three of the children. Fetch me the things on this list, but do not come back without more blankets." She smiled and shooed them out of her way, including George out of his own home. Savina orchestrated them all, along with the cooking and tending to Anna who felt she was giving birth in the middle of a road show. But she had never known privacy at any point in her life, so having the others did not hinder the progress of her laboring. She cherished each little voice as she knew in a few short months they would board the train for Pennsylvania. The new baby George Albert, called Al, arrived on a crisp morning early in February when the snow was glistening around the steps to the front door and around the redbrick farmhouse. Never had Savina seen a father beam so much over a baby; he was so pleased to welcome a son. From behind his line of vision she had looked at her exhausted daughter and spun her finger in a circle over her ear to indicate goodnaturedly she thought he had gone crazy. She allowed him his excesses; she had a few of her own.

A boy, ah, the real thing, George said to himself and held the little fellow up to the window light to examine his face, his hands and all the details of his little body. *And a right royal brand he is, too.* He had the look of that other little boy he had held and called "lambie-pie" and who now, so grown, begged to spend time helping on the farm. Harry often spent weekends with George and Anna and called their farm his "country escape". George smiled thinking of Harry. They had become quite the companions and took obvious pleasure in each other's company. George studied the little wizened face of his newborn son, highlighted in the filtered sunlight. Truth be told, in spite of how he razzed Anna about a dozen more children, with this little boy, he felt his family was complete.

Michael, the widower, shouldered on through that winter and as the time approached to leave, Savina organized his things and lent him household help for the packing. The children scrubbed clothes and spread them to dry and later gathered the garments in their little arms, and then folded them in stipulated piles. They volunteered to leave behind most of their toys "for Wibby and Aah" and were praised for their generosity. Household items were sorted, and those few that made the grade were packed into the trunks with William's signature carvings of oak leaves decorating the front and the sides. There were sentimental items that Michael shunned. Savina stepped in to discard them, most sadly the rag doll from an earlier childhood, carried over the expanse of Pennsylvania. Michael had cried into his hands as he stood on his doorstep and looked for the last time at the the flourishing plant of mountain laurel brought from the old home so long ago. Soon he would see a glorious abundance of the evergreen shrub.

With the terror of the Coming Conflict on every adult mind, the Ohio Lamberts gathered on the platform at the Springfield railroad station and waved good-bye to Michael, the survivor who relied on his natural optimism, as he settled into seats with his six little charges. The older ones were minding the younger, their faces pressed up against the glass, as they left for their adventure and new life in Pennsylvania.

So much attention was diverted into all the details of Michael's leaving that the start of Anna's third pregnancy received little recognition. Anna could tell her hard-working husband was less than thrilled about this new arrival. She assumed it was because the first two were still so small. She tried to cheer him by asserting that by logic of timing their new arrival should be another boy. *Ah, well,* George had thought to himself, with a healthy wife he had to expect this, and he tried to find a positive attitude toward this third arrival. *I guess having a brood is a Lambert tradition. Too bad it couldn't be put off until all the bank notes are paid off.*

With Michael and the children gone to Lost Mountain, George closed the deal on a large farm near Mechanicsburg and moved all the livestock and machinery that Michael had generously surrendered to him along with the bank notes to be paid to William. He and Anna took the time leading up to their third Ohio Christmas to pack. Michael had left behind a good many items, including lots of fragrant and colorful soap. While George finished his dealings at the dual farms, he and Anna prepared their new home, red brick like where they were leaving but with three additional upstairs bedrooms. He dug a cellar under the kitchen and they placed a rug over the trap door. Mechanicsburg was a popular stop on the Underground Railroad. Their involvement was a bond they had shared since their first conversation back in Philadelphia. It grounded them in the Christian values they most wanted to live. Church services had never been a regular part of their adult lives, but prayer and good works, remembering and emulating Jesus were always top priorities. They moved for a third time and settled into their home. The dried, pressed, framed four leaf clover from the Virginia man's farmhouse served as a reminder of their many blessings and took them back to a moment that seemed like a long time ago.

George quickly became engaged in his business by learning the quirks of his farm, making business connections, dealing animals and their hides, selling grain and produce throughout central Ohio to the Indiana border. His was the only thrasher in the township; he rented it out to other farmers which brought in additional revenue. Harry would often come with George to the neighboring farms to set up the process. Horsepower ran the multi-spoked machine. George would hook up the wheel and the blades, and young Harry would encourage the two horses, after they were bridled to the bits on the wheel.

Anna had no idea what the capitol investment had been when they moved here, but George had no complaints about his wife's economy. She made home-making look easy by organizing her new environment in no time. Even under the burden of pregnancy she accomplished more tasks than most women could think of in a day. The donut jar was always full and she had fresh baked cakes, breads and fruit pies to offer him along side his dinners which were simple, but delicious and hearty. She regularly presented him with a dish he had never tasted before. "Oh, Annie's old recipe," she would smile and toss off his compliments for she had made the dish not from a recipe, but straight from her heart, or, "I thought you might enjoy the tomatoes in that broth," or, "It's the same thing as last Thursday, but with rosemary and thyme instead of onion." He was happy when he was eating and enjoyed the friendly atmosphere of their table. Her company, raised as he was with an abundance of female companionship, nourished him. Anna had the entire house decorated with many of her own handiwork. Little spaces were transformed into spotlights of beauty. Her needlework was some of the most intricate and difficult embroidery in all of Ohio, George was sure. He envisioned her in a mansion on a hill, with trees lining the sloping path to the door, the front of the house filled with tall windows and lace curtains, and in one window, her form beckoning, and of course, his farm unfolding behind.

This Christmas the William Lamberts were over in Greenville with Lizzie's brother. Left to their own devices, George and Anna expected to be lonely with visiting only Savina and Levi, but were not, and had a quiet time in their new home with their two young children. Anna was agile despite her large size and made Christmas goose with all the trimmings for her husband. She cooked things separately to saturate their home with the savory smells of the culinary delights and to pace herself, for at this stage of the pregnancy her breath was short. Little Libby was old enough to pass an opinion on every event that unfolded, but Al was just old enough to revel in the adulation that his cuteness and his gender earned him. He was hearty and passed right by the influenza Libby suffered after Christmas with sniffles, sneezes and fever, scaring her mother but recovering after only a week. It was the week they read in the newspaper about the mill factory that collapsed in Massachusetts, killing so many innocent young people. The news affected Anna; she was afraid it was an omen to the structure of her family and could not get it out of her mind. But those ominous thoughts evaporated along with the sickness, and George chuckled over the superstitions that came along with pregnancy. Al had left babyhood quickly; he took his first steps before his first birthday as his father crowed with pride. He was now talking in sentences and pointing to objects to his left and his right, chatting nonsense syllables interspersed with real words. He assumed he was Master, as Libby assumed she was Queen. George and Anna got many a good laugh over the antics of their two little children.

Savina was delighted to have the family in Union Township. This part of Champaign County was closer than the dual farm near New Carlisle in Clark County, so the two-hour ride to Mechanicsburg seemed like an instant compared to the inaccessibility of the other. She marveled at Anna's fertility as proved by this third pregnancy and openly teased George which left the younger couple embarrassed and lost for words. Anna wore her expected bundle with a self-conscious gait, which tickled her outspoken mother and prompted even more jokes. Perhaps Savina was trying to disperse the sense she picked up that this pregnancy was not received with the joy that met the others producing Libby and Al.

In spite of her proximity and her attitude, Savina was not with them when Anna's labor began, as her husband had out-of-state guests who commanded her presence through the weekend. The young mother was left to put her fallback plan into action. Her neighbor and new friend Mrs. Longnecker had given her the name of a local midwife who was on hand for the blessed event. For several days leading up to the birth, the weather had warmed which brought a steady drip from the snow on the roof and slushy puddles in the paths around the yard. Then the wind picked up and breathed new life into winter, freezing the puddles and bringing a blizzard on Friday. On Sunday morning, little John William rode into this life assisted by a stranger of a midwife. His father ignored him as he was busy digging paths through the high snow, and his mother, having made the delivery, got up and made dinner for herself, her family and the farmhands. Libby was three when this extra baby was born, and Al had difficulty contending with the new arrival so close to his second birthday. He was not at all sure what kind of a present this was. John William was a quiet thing and, from the start, watched all that went on around him. He tolerated the pokes and jabs of his two older siblings who vacillated between ignoring and tormenting him. George accepted his presence and with a long look at the infant, told his wife this new one was the spare to the heir. Anna, always patient, allowed the others their ambivalence. She loved her precious little newcomer and stroked his chin whenever she passed his cradle. She relished the smell of a newborn and thought this round-faced one adorable in his hand-me-down clothes. At night she rocked him with a rhythm in her foot as she worked with her needles by candlelight. She was making a garden picture and crafted her own stitches to illustrate different blossoms. She included a butterfly and stitched its wings so that they left the canvas.

As winter turned to spring, George had much to absorb his attention. He dashed from developing one end of his enterprise to the other. The two little toddlers entertained each other and colluded in their denial of the new baby's presence. They helped with chores, churning butter, stirring batter, bringing in firewood, but they balked at fetching nappies or shushing the baby. Anna had to use a curt voice to impress upon her defiant little ones she meant Business. JW remained unaware of the rebellion his presence inspired. His mother was also preparing for the biggest event since her wedding. It was a rare occasion that put hoop skirts on Anna, but just such an occasion occurred in the political arena. As the weather warmed, the political climate heated up with the anticipation of the Republican Convention gathering in May in the great city of Chicago. William was a member of the Ohio delegation, and George was involved up to his nose as well. Savina took in the toddlers so that the two Lambert couples could participate child-free in their civic duty. They packed their bags, boarded the Big Four train to Anderson, Indiana, and then switched to the C.C.C. and St. Louis line to bounce and rattle up to the big city convention.

In the last few years William had thrown his political loyalties in with the lanky lawyer from Illinois. He had been among those who had brought young Abe Lincoln to Ohio to help in the campaign when William Dennison was running for governor. The Illinois native had proved himself to be witty, ready and popular. So, William had gone over to Illinois when he in turn ran for the Senate from that state, to offer his experience in organizing, finding the right settings and overseeing the construction of the debate platforms. For six weeks, Abraham Lincoln and Stephen Douglas had met and matched their wits on the issues of the day, but predominately the issue of slavery. The debates were wildly successful and caught plenty of national coverage. William was proud to promote Abe's ambition and at the Chicago convention helped the Ohio delegation swing its votes to his candidate, which paved the way for Lincoln's run to the White House. Throughout the week in the Windy City there were functions and balls for the conventioneers. Anna had seen the kind of entertaining she encountered in Chicago in the Musselman home when she was growing up in Philadelphia. There were large groups of women dressed to the nines and men full of self-importance wheeling and dealing. The time went all too quickly; the trip was a whirlwind and then they were back on the farm.

Savina had had a ball with the three young children while the parents were away. The returning mother soon discovered the attitude of the two older toward the youngest was mysteriously transformed. Not wanting to look a gift horse in the mouth, Anna welcomed the changes Savina had orchestrated without question and was glad to have her three children in unison. The two older ones now interspersed their squabbles of who gets to pull the toy wooden dog or who gets to knock down the tower Papa made out of blocks with generous acts of sharing with their curious, patient baby brother.

Toward the end of the summer George made a trip to Springfield, which was not unusual, but his demeanor upon his return was. He was agitated and jumpy, then sullen and cross. He left for his fields after supper, not lingering to enjoy the chatter of his children, but went out the door like a shot. Anna left Libby in charge in the kitchen and followed her husband to discover what was bothering him. "George, wait for me," she called after her husband who was planting his feet heavily with each step down the path. He might not have heard her for he missed not a beat, and she had to pick up her skirts and run after him. "George!" She sounded too shrill, but she was out of breath. She let her trailing him be her question.

"Ah, Anna. I have bad news and I can't find the words to say it." Anna's stomach turned over and she put her arm around her husband's waist. She slowly lifted her head to his face.

"Oh, good God in Heaven, Anna. I am sorry. It's not all that bad," he was struggling to stay in emotional control; he put his arm across her back and they walked into the fields.

"I can hear the corn growing," she smiled, trying to relax them both and looked at him with a warmth in her eye.

"This air is the best I ever inhaled," he said, settling into her company.

"Yes, the smell of the corn is divine." They walked a few more steps in silence. "I saw William this morning," he said as he strolled. She hardly breathed in anticipation of what he would say. "He's taking Lizzie to Harrisburg to see a doctor." Anna exhaled an "oh," while he fought for more words. Anna dared to be relieved, for this news was easier than the report of an injury or death. "He's selling his holdings, his manufacturing complex, the house, everything."

"Oh," she said more vocally. Now Anna was concerned, as he revealed the catastrophic nature of his news. "He's leaving Springfield and going back to Pennsylvania permanently." He looked at her, willing himself to not cry and thereby getting her to express his emotions. She began weeping. He put his arms around her as she sobbed into his shoulder, for William and for all the other losses. "Poor Lizzie," George continued. "He is taking her up to Lake Erie for a vacation right away on the Fannie Dugan. He said she's always wanted a steamboat ride and this is one fancy outfit. They'll travel through Port Huron all the way up to Mackinac Island. As soon as they get back, they're leaving. There's a doctor who claims to have cured some of these poor besotted victims of alcohol. William's grasping at straws but this flimsy chance is all he has left. The Christmas Eve incident with the horse and the wagon has been repeated more than once. It's tearing him apart." George stopped speaking. Saying it out loud hollowed him out. He watched her wipe her face with her apron and saw her beauty. He pulled her close and she enveloped her arms around him in turn. They stood in a hug in the shadow of the corn which was higher than his shoulders. The smell of the bounty encircled and refreshed them. "We're not alone," she said huskily. "We have Savina and Levi. Don't worry, George. You'll see them again. They may even come back after Lizzie is better and the war is over."

"That's not all," George let go of her. "Harry isn't speaking to either of them. He's a character all right. I offered to let him stay with us."

"That's wonderful, George. You didn't think I would object, did you? Of course Harry can live with us. Katy too."

"Katy wants to stay with her mother. I'm sure she's worried sick. I think it's been a trial for all of them. William said Lizzie alternates between the pretense of making the move to return to a higher civilization East of the Alleghenies – even though she was born on a mountain farm same as us – and raging over William's insistence she is sick. She accused him of greed, corrupt business deals and even dallying in town with women of ill repute."

"Oh, no!"

"Of course he hasn't done any of those things. It pains him to hear it. She's out of her mind, Anna. I just hope they get the help they need. William heard of this doctor from two different people. He's such a proud man and he has accomplished so much . . . . ." George's voice trailed off.

Anna picked up, "I think she never got over losing those twins. Maybe going back will help her let them go."

George looked at his wife for a moment, "I'm a lucky man to be with the likes of you." In spite of the August heat, the dirt and the bugs, they made love in the cornfields while Libby, absorbed, played patty-cake with Al, which entertained the baby in the house.

By Christmas William, Lizzie and Katy were gone. In the red-brick farmhouse outside Mechanicsburg in Union Township of Champaign County, fifteen-year-old Harry, Al and JW were ensconced upstairs in one bedroom, Queen Libby was solo in the other and across the hall were her mother and father. Abe Lincoln was in the White House and South Carolina was out of the

Union, quickly followed by six additional states then four more. In April at Fort Sumner, the guns began firing and the effort to restore the union began. War fever gripped the nation and Anna was pregnant again.

In the summer, President Lincoln's call for volunteer soldiers from Ohio was met with an overwhelming enlistment of young men as much from the farms across the state as from the big cities, Marietta, Cincinnati, Cleveland and Springfield. Tens of thousands more were turned away. The Lamberts hoped Betsy was right, that a quick stern spanking would settle the attitude of the South once and for all. But it was not to be. George geared up for the added wartime demand for produce and knew he was well positioned to sell a large number of hides, for soldiers needed shoes, coats and boots. They stopped eating lamb that summer, as he needed all sheep for wool-making duty.

In late September Anna gave birth to a daughter, a placid little thing whom nonetheless Anna named after her mother. Little Savina Ellen grew more slowly than her three lively older siblings, and by Christmas they knew something serious was wrong with her. She did not have the healthy fire which shone in the eyes of the others and had no interest in crawling around on the floor. Libby or Al could entertain her endlessly with something as simple as a button on a string. Little JW, left to his own devices as he often was, got in to everything. Out of the range of his mother's gaze, he took apart whatever he got his hands on and then carefully examined the parts of the thing he had disassembled. His slight little sister monopolized his parents' attention; their concern for her health burned through the winter. Savina came often between snowfalls to visit and help, but the little girl failed to grow like the others. None of Savina's concoctions could reach her.

Struck with pangs of guilt, George remembered his Aunt Star and saw the same look on his daughter. But, unlike Star who lived a full life, little Savina surrendered to God's call. They laid her to rest with much weeping. As the flowers of spring colored their landscape, the loss of their precious infant and fond treasure drained Anna's heart to think little Savina was beyond her mother's love. At two, JW was too little to understand, but responded to the ocean of sadness pouring from each of his older family members with a quiet demeanor, as though in respect for their grief. Harry took it upon himself to shepherd the independent tyke through the daze of the death rites which allowed the fond, loving mother and father to indulge in their grief for the innocent life now called to bounteous heaven. With trembling lips and hearts, George and Anna gave her back over to God. Mimicking their parents, Libby comforted four-year-old Al while crying and petting him; at the same time, he, like his father, held back his tears. Of all the losses the adults had braved since coming to Ohio, this hurt the most. And anything would they give to have her back among them for just one day or one tiny hour. This time Anna planted only bleeding heart near the little grave; but Savina, the grandmother, came unannounced and unbeckoned and planted a wide expanse of lilies of the valley for the spirit of her namesake. She swore she heard the child's cooing to the ring of their bells.

Their sorrow was echoed in the White House, as their political mentor and his wife lost their son Willie just five weeks prior, their third child to die. Anna sent a message to Mary Todd as from one grieving mother to another and cherished the hand written note she received in return.

Harry's sturdy body had grown into manhood, and he worked hard in the fields alongside his Uncle George, the tenant man named Given and the other men George hired as seasonal workers. But inside the home, Harry spent his time with the children. He lay sprawled for hours on the floor with Al and JW, even Libby, sometimes playing marbles or checkers or with the expanded collection of wooden blocks William had made. For most of the year when the weather was good, he accompanied the young boys on their chores, silently supervising, directing and protecting like a shepherd his little Lamberts through their routines. Their biggest job was milking the Bessies, along with feeding the long line of cows, the colts, mules and workhorses. Given took care of the cattle and the sheep. It was he who did the lambing in the spring by bunking with the ewes in their pen. Libby's job was to skim the twenty to thirty crocks of milk the boys got each day and pack them up in the cellar. She would then wash the crocks and the boys would hang the big wet containers on a fence, all before breakfast.

One morning Harry was milking a cow next to JW who sat on his stool, his body largely in baby proportions, and still he was agilely wrapping his little boy fingers around the udder of his cow and pulling with efficient authority. To his left one of the big barn cats, this one grey and white, made an appearance with some small prey in his mouth. Feathers followed the big Tom as he brought the flailing bird to a corner of the barn in clear view of both Harry and JW. As they continued their pulling, they watched as the cat bat the injured bird up against the wooden wall and into the corner. When the doomed sparrow tried to flutter away, a big paw reached out like lightening and cut him down. The noises the cat made were eerie and the bird cried out as well. Tiny JW was fascinated and mortified watching the deadly play. Harry found it entertaining and laughed with nerve at the sight. Later that evening Harry knew his little nephew was ruminating about life and death issues. Inspired, he told JW he had a new game to teach him, "I'm the cat, you're the birdie." He stooped and put his hands to his feet, then turned his body and stretched himself flat on his back on the floor. "You flutter around me and I'll try to catch you. And if I do, I get to tickle you until you say "'Uncle.'" His provocative smile could be seen under the waving and reaching he was doing on the floor.

"I won't say 'Uncle'," JW puffed out his three-year-old chest, "And you won't catch me." He ran to Harry's feet and made a quick step in to bat at his boots. Harry surprised JW by quickly bending at the waist and grabbed the little fellow who shrieked before he could back away. Harry held him trapped between his legs, both laughing, and gave him a dose of tickling, then turned to Al who joined in the play. Al took a swat at the strong teenager's head. Quick as a wink Harry swung his arm around and just missed Al who jumped in retreat with a shout of glee. At that JW wiggled free, and Harry pretended outrage at losing his prisoner. "Come here! I'm gonna get you," he used a deep voice and tried to sound forceful. As the game continued, Harry grabbed each of the boys and then tickled like crazy as his pretended threats joined in the cadence of their laughter. Each in turn yelled "Uncle". Before any one lost his supper, for the older cousin knew just when to stop, Harry got up and mussed the sweaty hair on each of their heads. They pulled on his arms, "More, Harry, more." Harry gave each an affectionate squeeze in the ribs, eliciting more laughter but Harry was firm about the game being over. He said, "'Uncle,' you two; I'm crying 'Uncle.'" The game was a rollicking success as the children mimicked the deadly antics they witnessed on the farm, transforming the morning's serious battle into laughter and joy.

Less than a year after the precious little sister was laid in the earth surrounded by the circle of her loving family singing her spirit to heaven, Anna gave birth to a new daughter Emma Melissa. It helped Anna during the sad anniversary of last year's springtime good-bye to see a new baby in the cradle, to hold another dear, dependent child to her breast, although no one would replace Savina Ellen. Even with a new baby in the cradle, Anna produced her usual fare for her family and workers plus extra every week for her bake club. A group of women had organized to collect bread to send to the boys fighting the war. At the Champaign County Fair, Anna set up a booth with Mrs. Longnecker and collected old clothing and money to buy supplies for the front. There was discouraging news about the progress of Lincoln's campaign but George and Anna refused to believe that the northern troops would not eventually be victorious. Anna believed every citizen needed to pitch in. She put her needlework aside and spent her evenings tearing up old sheets and petticoats, and then rolling the strips into bandages. All the children, except Emma, helped with the task. She sent basketsful along with George and his farm contributions when he made his trips into Springfield. The produce, supplies and bandages traveled by train and otherwise made their way to the boys in hospitals, in route and at the front. Their conditions and suffering were unimaginable to the farm family in beautiful Ohio. George read the Bible and led his young family in prayers every night. They lined up in front of the fireplace, down on their knees in supplication, and asked God to help the Union soldiers. And they thanked God for their safety and blessings.

That safety was threatened this summer of 1863. A crazy Rebel had a large band of blue-clad cavalry soldiers marauding too close to home. He marched up through Kentucky and into Indiana and penetrated Ohio north of Cincinnati. George did what he could to take precautions for his farm and his family, even though the escapade was a hundred miles away. The children knew about the secret cellar under the kitchen floor. George drilled them to open the hatch and silently lower themselves into their hiding place; each knew his or her position. Libby's job as oldest was to close the wooden cover so that the rug disguised it as best she could. George knew his bold daughter could do this even if pressured by eminent threat. She was fearless like her grandmother and his grandmother had been. Of course, if the parents were present, as likely at least Anna would be, they would lead the children, but they could not always be present. George buried his pewter, a sugar bowl, pitcher and scrolled little tray, and other precious items in the backyard.

George and Anna were horrified to read about this General Morgan and how he escaped again and again. The youthful Harry was incensed. The state militia was giving good chase with their squirrel guns brought out from the back of old closets, but reports were conflicting. Eventually the Rebel was captured and taken to the Ohio penitentiary. By then, when George went to retrieve the precious pewter, he found he had lost track of where he had buried their valuables. When he took his shovel to the place where he was sure he had interred it, he turned up only dirt. He dug in several more places before he finally gave up. What a joke on himself! He apologized to Anna, but Anna only laughed. She was grateful this was their only loss.

The terror of Morgan's raid added to the general discouragement the news of the battles brought them. Over at the horse farm, Levi hung a big map in his study so they could follow the progress of the various regiments with what information they could gather. Anna tried to keep the children distracted during the war conversation at her mother's house. Savina joined in with the men, George, Levi and Harry, and offered many a good suggestion for what the Generals may be thinking and the different possibilities for the way the war could go. George filled Anna in later, once little ears were safely in bed. George sought her thinking. Unlike his absent older brother, he had been raised more in the company of his articulate sisters and he knew the value of a female voice.

Then the news came of the victory at Gettysburg and hope grew in their hearts and minds. It was hard to imagine a three-day battle. Little Libby openly lamented the carnage, the casualties and the wounded. Anna announced they would focus on the courage and be grateful for the heroism of their men. She took the jump rope out to the yard; she and Harry turned while the younger ones ran through the loop. Soon all were making up rhymes of victory and odes to valor and peace. They ran double dutch, each calling out a word in their turn and made up rapid rhyme games requiring quick thinking, until the children and Anna had exhausted their nervous energy.

Throughout the summer there was no word from Lost Mountain, but George was not worried about that community for it was protected by geography and the spirit of his blood. Miraculously three months after he wrote it, they had received a letter from William who, in Harrisburg, lives so close to the battlefields. He described events in his dispassionate way, thereby letting the

Ohio Lamberts know of their safety. His sisters' letters from Pittsburgh, Iowa and Minnesota continued in their sporadic pattern.

In September, Anna and George celebrated their eighth anniversary. Anna had had five children in their eight years of marriage and at twenty-six, she felt fit and strong. But she was not prepared for the shock that Harry's sudden announcement placed on the family: "I signed up for muster. I'm joining the Thirteenth Regiment of the Ohio Volunteer Infantry. They're accepting recruits and I signed up yesterday. I report next Saturday morning."

More Ohio boys had been called up, and for one of those calls, Harry had left them. George understood his nephew's decision, had secured him a breech-loading rifle and helped him organize his supplies, a canteen, a knife and sleeping roll. It all happened so quickly. Anna had cheese, hard tack and biscuits for him to place in his blankets. George had gone with him to the GAR Post #98 muster early one foggy morning. There they met up with other farm boys of the county ready to join Abe Lincoln's army. George had come home with a heart both heavy and proud and wrote to Harry's father and mother in Harrisburg. William had written that Lizzie was doing better, but the war was hard on all women. George hoped Harry's enlistment would not set her back.

After Harry left, George agreed the children could pick a dog for a pet from the Longnecker's litter, to help ease the void left by their affable cousin who now fought for the Union. The family made the mile and a half trip to their neighbor's farm, each walking the distance singing, running and waiting, and helping to carry the baskets of favors Mama had made to offer for the dog. The Longneckers had trouble keeping their working dogs away from their house dog, so every year she gave birth to a large litter of puppies of unpredictable talents. The Lamberts had been offered a puppy in the past but had resisted until now. The Longneckers got rid of the others somehow.

The Longnecker clan came out to greet the Lamberts as they came into sight. The children ran ahead with their too numerous dogs under their heels, followed by Mr. and Mrs. Longnecker arm-in-arm down the incline of their wide drive and out onto the dirty road. The children met up and mingled a good quarter of an hour before the adults reached each other. They zigged and zagged in the ever-decreasing space between their parents who walked toward each other like soldiers advancing in battle. "Howdy, neighbor!" George yelled out. The children pierced their excited chattering with an occasional squeal of joy or cry of protest. Back at the homestead cluttered with decaying junk scattered throughout the yard, the Lamberts were welcomed with barbequed meat and dark sweet baked beans, along side fresh cooked vegetables marinated in Mrs. Longnecker's famous garlic vinegar. Anna had brought brown bread and early corn from their fields along with jars of jellies and marmalades to put in the Longnecker pantry. No matter how hard Mrs. Longnecker worked, her husband's inconsistent efforts undermined their family's prosperity. Anna knew special sweet treats were beyond their routine and that her jars would be welcome. Their friends were jovial and talkative, quick with a joke and clever with words and so were good company. George enjoyed learning about Mr. Longnecker's numerous projects, few of them ever completed, and joined in the sampling of his homemade beers.

The sun was high when they arrived, and although Mr. Longnecker was already teetering, he brought out his placid old mule and managed to give each child a ride. He led the patient beast around the gravel courtyard or did the animal lead him? The Longnecker children matched the ages of the Lamberts, so each had a companion to run and play games with. Libby and the oldest Longnecker girl, both clutching short batons, were good at batting their thick, wooden hoops up and down the slope of the yard. Mr. Longnecker had put pieces of Osage orange around the yard to discourage the insects. Al and Harvey Longnecker took off down to the brook which passed through their cow pasture in clear sight of the adults, there to build dams and bridges out of stones and leaves and to find a beetle or two to detain, in the name of General Grant, in miniature barracks they built with sticks and mud. The child for JW was a girl who preferred the clothes of a boy. So attired, she engaged her fellow young friend in exploring the tools in the barn. JW was an eager participant and came home with stories detailing the Longnecker collection of levers and pulleys, wedges and wheels. If his Longnecker companion preferred to be a boy, it never crossed his mind as peculiar.

As the afternoon wore on, it became time to make the selection of which little dog would come home with them. The children were excited by the cute farmshepherd puppies and wanted to take them all home, but their parents would have none of that. "You must select one," their father told them decisively. He put three twigs in his hand. He gathered his three little voters, held the twigs up, each stick looking the same in his hand and explained, "There is one short stick and two long ones. Each of you will draw. The child who draws the short stick gets to pick the puppy we bring home. But before we do, I want each of you to vow to love the dog who is chosen. I don't want to hear a word of complaint from any of you. When a Lambert gives his word, the case is closed. Are all agreed?"

The children agreed and sticks were drawn. Before the family returned to their farmhouse, each child had bonded to the newly selected four-footed friend. The puppy named Rex, with long ears and soft coat, was a companion to them all but it was Mama who made sure he had food and kept his water dish filled.

Late in the fall, the men and older children went out in the fields, for all threw in to gather the ripened grain. The smallest ones, toddlers included, carried water in leather containers to the sun-baked workers, each in a wide-brimmed straw hat as light as a feather. George reaped a healthy profit from the sale of his grain and large numbers of his stock, for he sold their hides to be made into harnesses, satchels and boots, as well as for their meat. *The war is not all bad,* he spoke to himself as he sat at his desk, going over the ledgers and calculating his assets. The debt on the farm was totally paid off. He had been able to provide large numbers of raw materials to the war efforts of President Lincoln, as had farmers all over the North. Still, the Union suffered weariness as the end was nowhere in sight. Then Lincoln did what he was so good at: he delivered a speech with the right words in the right place. Savina had traveled to the Lambert farm on her dappled horse, unannounced, and brought a copy of the *Gazette*. She was inspired by what she had read and wanted to be the first to share the news with her children.

"His heart is as big as the ocean!" Savina said as she handed George the newspaper, folded neatly so that the text of the speech delivered over the battlefield at Gettysburg could easily be read. It was not very long. "He has the vision and the know-how. God Bless him," she beamed. "It's as powerful as the Inaugural Address." George took the paper. The words of the speech had a similar effect on him. Instead of handing the paper to Anna so she could read it for herself, he gathered his children along with his wife and read aloud to them the words which were inspiring a nation,

Four score and seven years ago, our fathers brought forth a new nation conceived in liberty and dedicated to the proposition that all men are created equal.

Libby had tears in her eyes; Anna had to use the corner of her apron to soak up escaping pearls of national pride. JW sat cross-legged like an Indian on the floor with the dog's head in his lap and listened, reflectively caressing the silky ears. The cadence of the spoken word hypnotized the young boy, and he seemed to take in the meaning.

We here highly resolve that these dead shall not have died in vain, that this nation, under God, should have a new birth of freedom – and that government of the people, by the people, for the people shall not perish from the earth.

When the father finished reading, it was JW who first spoke to the awed audience of family members, "Papa, do you suppose our Harry was among the soldiers who heard President Lincoln say this speech?" George looked at his son, struck thoughtful to hear such a serious question come from so small a frame. JW was a strong boy growing normally, but he was not yet four. George was glad JW had not forgotten Harry. They had never heard from the young soldier, but if reports were to be believed, his regiment was in Virginia guarding troops and raiding railroads. George worried about Harry, left by his mother and father in stages at too young an age. Anna had verbalized George's worst fear when she had told her husband one night she hoped soldiering would not set him adrift. He needed to know he had a family who loved him; adrift it would be harder to survive. George truly loved the boy, as did Anna.

George answered, "No, son, your cousin Harry is most likely down in Virginia keeping those Rebels from using their trains. Wherever he is, he's doing a man's job and we're mighty proud of him, aren't we?" JW nodded; Al and Libby assented as well.

Mama continued reacting to what they had just heard, "What beautiful words! How wonderful that in the worst of dark times such an enlightening vision comes to brighten our day. Yes, God Bless our Abraham Lincoln." Savina was proud to be the bearer of such a heartening development, but then again, she always seemed to have her finger on the pulse of political developments. All over the North families were gathering to share the news of the speech that re-galvanized a nation. Standing, Papa extended his arms, took hold of JW's and Savina's hand and nodded around the room for them all to join the circle. This was a posture Savina had taught them. "I want to offer a prayer." He waited until each of them held hands and bowed their heads. "Lord, look down on all our fighting men and let them know the comfort of Your Presence. Stay close to our Harry, protect and guide him, and make sure he knows he does have a family that is focused in their love of him. God, bless our leaders and thank you for sending us Abraham Lincoln. Help us to be a worthy nation. In Jesus' name we ask this. And thank you for your continuing generosity to this family here gathered." They all said "Amen" and then there was silence. Even Savina was quiet. At last Mama let go her hands, reached up to George's face with them both, broke open her face with warm sunlight, then kissed him openly on the mouth. She was quick about it, but it was so rare a sight, each child carried the warm memory throughout their entire lives. After she did it, they all laughed and started talking at once. JW was proud; he had asked an important question and mentioned the name of his absent friend and older playmate. He had missed him in silence, and now that was broken. Harry's name had not been said aloud since he joined up for the War.

One early morning while Anna and Libby were setting up the two-day kitchen project of peeling and slicing their peaches, with the best of the bunch being preserved should Harry return for it was his favorite, George took his two young sons across two counties to Greenville. He had received an invitation from Lizzie's brother who was now married and settled in Darke County. George was eager to inspect his current mechanical project involving a steam-powered, mobile cannon or gun. Papa told his boys it was innovative men like Mr. House who will win the war. There was an unsettled feeling in the air from the long national struggle, and George was restless staying put in the house. The long ride for the father and two young boys was a time to talk and relax. George told them of his admiration for the old German precision, set free in America, meaning Ohio. He said Ohio was the place to create social progress, like an engine driving the country. JW knew it was true of the farmers who fed the warring troops for he had heard his father say so. And although Al and Papa, who did the most talking, spoke in hyperbole and exaggeration, it was true that they lived in an age of leaping advancements. George told his sons he expected them to be more successful than he, as he was more than his father, for that was the natural order of things. Throughout the winter between snowstorms, the Lambert men made additional and more extended trips over to Darke County. Both boys were interested in the talk of war and guns and the display of machines and tools going on in Greenville and followed the older men around, absorbed, for hours. They visited the sawmill and lumberyards, explored the grain elevator and stopped by the various machine shops and hardware stores displaying the latest innovations in farming equipment, plows, reapers and harvesters. One of their usual stops was the blacksmith's shop where George struck up a friendship with the box-built older man who ran the forge. The more George learned about the man with the engaging English accent and biceps the size of Texas, the more he wanted to know. His interest soon won them an invitation to the man's farm just over the border in Indiana.

John Koerner lived with his Virginia-born wife on their large farm where they had raised their children. Mr. Koerner was particularly fond of talking about the daughter who married the itinerant preacher, now a bishop and editor in Dayton, for he held to the strict Brethren ways dictated by his adopted religion. He was very proud to have his daughter married and raising a family with an esteemed man of his faith. George and his boys were more interested in the goings-on around the farm and patiently out-waited the talk of religion. Koerner had learned the carriage-making trade when he arrived in this country from his Saxony home. He flourished in the trade even after his move to Virginia to marry his shy, quiet wife, and he brought it with him to Indiana when they left her family to strike out on their own. He was a hard worker. Along side his farming he augmented his vehicle repair business piece by piece until he now produced almost every part of a carriage in various buildings spread around his expansive farm: the wheels, the body, canopy tops, the step or sideboard, and the cushioned seats, as well as the poles and shafts. He had a tannery, a harness-making shop and his own forge. In all there were fourteen buildings which had gone up over the years.

George and his boys enjoyed sitting with this mountain of a man in any shop they found him, and he talked a blue streak to such eager and clever listeners. With all parts of buggies and carriages now being produced, last year he completed another large shed to assemble the parts into a whole and had put his vehicles on the market. He sent out a mailing to dealers as far away as

Pittsburgh and with his signature and his reputation, orders were already coming back in response. The Lambert men took this all in. Each of the three made mental notes to himself, JW for the innovative process by which Mr. Koerner visualized the operation of mechanisms and tinkered and forged that vision into a buggy; Al, with an eye for a plump reward, for the sales techniques with both a personal touch and personable tone; and Papa for the manufacturing homestead of various enterprises – repairing, smithing, compiling – now joined into a united effort. The restlessness that drove Anna's males to wander was burned into learning, for all three Lamberts gained an education from the hard-working men of Greenville, especially the ham-handed Saxony blacksmith.

By Springtime Anna was pregnant again. Her morning sickness hobbled her energy until noontime. She depended on Libby to watch one-year-old Emma who had discovered her legs and delighted in the revelations her added range unmasked. Seven-year-old Libby took over much of the kitchen operation and provided meals for the score of hungry laborers who helped to prepare and plant George's far stretching fields, as well as for the family and the tenant man Given. She also fed Rex.

Good-natured Emma was wild on her wobbly legs. Her falls stimulated some funny bone in her cute body and her little belly-laughing brightened the home as much as the hearth, lamps and candles. Her doe eyes shone with love lights for any family member but especially JW. She was very attached to her next older brother and instinctively went to him when Libby or more likely Al teased him with words or with more physical shoves. He, in turn, always had his hand out to pull her to her feet or to sit in his lap. Mama and Papa, but more openly Mama, still mourned baby Savina Ellen, but Emma did not know she was living for two and modestly responded to the void of death with a loving attitude toward all, unless she was overly tired. Then she just cried. She never complained about a wet nappie and never demanded a toy that another child already had. The benefit of her goodness was not lost on Anna. As she came out of the early stages of this latest pregnancy and her sickness lifted, she was able to take over the ritual of Emma's feeding and thus re-established her relationship with her littlest girl. In the process she freed Libby up to take on other responsibilities, just as George was occupying the time of Al and JW by teaching them the details of his farming and working with them from sunrise to sunset.

3

Farm Boy Childhood

The boys followed the brook by jumping from rock to bank and occasionally dropping a foot into the cold water. Al was ahead, leaving JW to worry about Libby whom they had left standing at the rail gate, warning them not to leave the edge of the yard. "I'm making pancakes for supper," their eight-year-old sister hollered out. "Come back in good time."

The little brother's legs were short but his determination made up for what his physical development lacked. He pushed himself to a faster clip, to tell Al what Libby had said. Breathless, JW caught up to his brother and nodded faithfully. "Libby says be home in good time," JW recited the message.

"We'll be home in good time," Al was a bit curt. Ever since little Savina Ellen was buried, Libby was even more determined to rule the boys and run the kitchen. Al felt bad about losing his little sister, but he did not like being bossed. "Let's pretend we're Indian braves, walking through the forest. I'm the oldest brave and I'm in charge. You follow me." Al headed down the path made by the stream and picked up his pace as JW fell in behind. Al whispered back over his shoulder, "We have to be silent as we go. It's good practice." For what, JW did not want to imagine. The real war raged not too far away. The two boys came upon a bend in the stream where Al stopped, and together they approached the widening waterway. Large rocks were scattered about. JW stopped by one which was waist-high and held on as he looked across the small deep pool of moving water. Al had his piece of wood he called his ship and stood at the edge of the water. "Our Viking vessel is at our command! Stand aside, mate, and I'll set her out to sail!" He was rocking the little wooden craft over the surface of the water.

"Then put her in the current, Al. The current will add go," JW told his brother matter-of-factly. Al snickered under his breath and shook his head. Then he moved a few steps to his left. With a smooth sweep of his arm he sent the five-inch piece of wood skimming across the tiny pond and it was propelled by the current as well. The boys lost themselves in their game of marauding pirates and valiant seamen but were jolted out of their revelry by the squawk of a blue jay. Having no sense of time but strong consciences, they pulled themselves away from the sailing ships of yesteryear and headed back toward the house with Al leading the way.

Libby stood on a box near the griddle on the stove and flipped pancakes. Soon the three children were eating pancakes smothered in butter and maple syrup. Under her quilted blankets in her wooden cradle on the floor, baby Emma slept through it all. This child's arrival had re-lit the spark in Anna's eyes. Emma's spirit showed an intent on living which reassured her parents. Losing baby Savina Ellen had touched them all deeply. George believed little Savina's death had been God's reminder to cherish his children, and so he did. Over the past year, he had noticed for the first time that little JW was a rather unique young fellow.

For Christmas George had bought Anna a music box imported from Switzerland. The wood was inlaid and when it was opened a little figure of a ballerina popped up and began to twirl with the sounds of the music. The song it played was the reason he bought it. It was one of the pieces he and Anna had heard played on the beautiful boxy piano at the magical performance in Philadelphia. When she first opened the box to hear the music, she recognized the tune. Anna made a place of honor for it in the parlor on the long walnut table. Before the new year arrived, JW had taken that expensive gift, crawled off with it out of sight, worked off the cover to the roller and gears, snapped out the roller, taken apart the gears and then was putting it all back together when his crime was discovered. George had flashed anger at the sight of his second son sitting amidst pieces of the delicate instrument, "You better get that back together just the way you found it." JW was calm in the wake of his father's tone and continued working his little fingers on the box in his lap, each time picking up just the right piece to work back into place. He had a hairpin he used as a tool. Soon the box was back together and working. George was amazed. Respect for this serious, quiet child dawned in his heart.

"How did he do that?" he later asked Anna.

"He's a smart little tyke and he likes to tinker with all kinds of things. He repaired my breadbox when the cover was stuck, and he studies the pull toy dog more than he drags it around. He must have inherited William's creative talent because he didn't get it from you or from me," she teased her enterprising husband. Belying her comment was the needlework in her lap.

Soon after the music box was safely restored to the darkly polished table in the parlor, Anna gave birth to another boy. She gave no special attention to its gender, but George was jubilant and told her she was giving him his own private army. Anna named the child Christian Harry, to soften the paternal militaristic endowment and to call cousin Harry to mind.

Family conversations at dinner were the classroom for Lambert children, and the young Lamberts were benefiting from the purposeful stories their parents told at each meal. A formal education was put on hold as the nearest schoolhouse stood empty. All hands, large and work worn as well as chubby and small, toiled to support the Union efforts, shucking corn, pulling weeds, wrapping cheese, as well as forging steel, tilling fields and running railroads.

What a relief April brought to the family and across the land when Lee surrendered to General Grant. General Grant allowed the Southern leader to keep his sword, and George worried the surrender was a sham but that fear was forgotten when it was overlaid by a much worse scenario. Horrible news came. This time George got the word on his own while in Springfield. The boys were talking about it when he dropped by the carriage livery. President Lincoln was dead, shot through the head by a crazy man while he sat beside his poor fragile wife in a theater near the White House. George leaned against an anvil and wiped at his eyes along with the other men. The boy from the telegraph office had run into the shop not ten minutes before and told them the news. Then he left to spread the sad word to others. Outside along the wooden sidewalk women held their children into their wide skirts, and men joined in their shocked response as the news spread down the street. The Furst farm was closer than home so George rode straight there. The family had been so happy when last they gathered just days ago, for they had been celebrating the surrender at Appomattox and the inevitable end of the dreary, old war.

How much can the nation take? George mourned to himself, holding the reins and focusing on the space between his horse's ears. He was calm when he reached the Furst farm. Savina's daffodils were golden in the afternoon sun. He detached Bonnie from the wagon and walked up the peeling white stairs to the entrance and into the spacious front hall. There had been no rotating runaway servant to open the door in several years now. The Emancipation Proclamation had done that. He heard Savina in the back of the house, clanging around in the kitchen.

"I don't have a gentle way to tell you this, Mama Savina, but I can tell you it's serious enough you may want to collect Levi so I can tell you together." George spoke softly and Savina listened to every word.

"That's mighty thoughtful of you, George, but you can tell me right out. Then we'll both go to Levi, if need be." Savina was concerned something had happened to Anna or one of the children.

"President Lincoln," George choked. His voice caught in his throat and he gave half a sob, then he got out the words, "has been shot. He's dead." Her eyes filled with tears. They stood together among the counters for workspace and utensils, many dangling in the air around the large room dominated by the cast iron stove.

"Let's go to Levi," she said. They walked passed her garden of herbs and flowers, passed the shaded area with the stone seats and table where so many pleasant sociable hours had been spent even through the years of the Conflict, down by the large red horse barn when they saw him over by the smithing building. He was hammering a horseshoe along side his hired man. Levi, too, read the seriousness in the air and stopped what he was doing. When he received the news, he put his arm around Savina's shoulder. The three of them walked up to the house while the work man spread the news to the hands.

George went home and told Anna. They prayed with their family and the laborers whom they had called in from the fields. Dirt-covered worker and small child alike took time to say something aloud to the fallen President, mostly "I'm sorry" or "thank you" and "good-bye." It was the same group George organized to travel south through Xenia to Wilmington to watch together in silence as the train which carried the body passed by, from Washington, DC back home to Illinois to bury a President. JW was still as the train went by and missed nothing of its majesty or mechanics. "What was that other kind of car?" he asked, referring to the new Barney and Smith Pullman coach.

One of the first things to happen after President Lincoln was shot was Lewis and Frances came to live with the family. Lewis and Frances were Lambert cousins like Harry. When their parents died of scarlet fever, Uncle Michael adopted them and raised them with his own children in Pennsylvania. George said they were born in Ohio, so rightly were "Buckeyes" but Frances bristled at that and insisted they were Pennsylvanians.

As soon as they moved in, all the children except the littlest two started going to school. The schoolhouse was about a mile away in the corner of the township; it took less than half an hour to walk along or ride the mule whose name was Jack. George built a shed near the schoolhouse so Jack had a place to stay in case it rained or even worse. Their father said it was important to plan for worst contingencies. It did not hail often but when it did, any thing outside could get hurt. Lewis and Frances were older than the Lambert children, and Frances was a handful. She stayed only a season before Uncle Michael rode the train back from Pennsylvania to collect her. During the week of his stay, he spent his entire time with George. He and his four children and now Frances were moving to Harrisburg, joining the oldest brother William and Lizzie and Harry's sister Katy. They were all leaving Lost Mountain. Grandma and Grandpa Lambert were moving to Philadelphia with Aunt Betsy and her family, but first they would travel to Ohio for a visit.

Lewis stayed in Ohio with George and the family. Young Libby and Al colluded he was mighty stuck on himself but they were just jealous because he was older. George and Anna were delighted to have him, not only because he was family but also because they missed Harry. They expected Harry to return to them any day and were eager for the confirmation he was at least alive. Soldiers were coming home now, but there was no word from Harry. Lewis was eager to work on the farm. After spending the war years on the confines of Lost Mountain, he was awed by the expanse George controlled by himself. The newcomer cousin kept largely to himself, reading books, magazines and newspapers. When he had finished what he brought with him from Grandma Betsy's extensive collection, he read through the volumes Anna and George had accumulated. He made himself known in Springfield as he scoured the libraries of George's friends for new reading material. He had never had formal schooling, so joined Al, Libby and JW in the one room schoolhouse. He listened quietly but he was in a grade by himself. Anna thought Lewis might know more than the teacher who was a young woman living with her father and five younger brothers and sisters, those five included in the classroom.

Before going to school, the children tended their morning chores, milking, feeding, shifting, washing and storing. Libby cooked breakfast and on Sundays, their Mama and Papa stayed in bed until breakfast was ready for the table. After Mary Ida, called Mollie, was born, came the new baby named after the man who stood in Mama's mind as her father, even though he was not even alive when Mama was born. Little Benjamin Franklin came just before All Saints' Day and was now about six months old. Twelve-year-old Libby spent most of her time in the house minding the baby, Mollie and Christian. Emma, six, was Libby's helper. George and the men including Lewis, Al and JW, were usually in the far fields distributing wheat seeds or tending to another task. When Anna had a good hour she could safely steal for herself, she gathered her yarn and needles and headed to the path beyond the springhouse to an abandoned grave she had turned into a garden. She sloshed through the mud in early spring and crunched over the frost in late fall. The only weather which kept her back was thick ice on the ground, fog and snowfalls. George asked her one time why she went out there and bothered with abandoned bones. She said that is exactly why. Grandma Furst claimed to know the story of the unmarked grave. She said the grave was that of an old Indian woman who had stayed behind after Fallen Timbers. She had lived alone in a log cabin. When settlers came and bought the land she was on, they just left her alone. Eventually they sheltered her by making sure she was warm and fed. One time they checked and she was laying in her bed, dead.

The other part of the story was about the Longneckers. Grandma Furst said that old Wyondot in the grave was Olive Longnecker's grandmother. Grandma Furst knew a lot of old stories about Ohio. She never talked about who her first husband was, or whether she was married to him at all, or why she did not raise Anna. She liked to say, "West was where people don't ask questions." Although the pioneer never talked about her early life in Pennsylvania, she loved to talk about her life in Ohio. She told how when Levi was a teenager, he joined his father in selling horses. The best way to show them off was to race them, so they organized colorful racing events. Half the county, including plenty of horse buyers, came from as far away as Hamilton County. After the War, young Levi moved the horse business to Kentucky because the land was naturally plentiful in grass horses loved. Now, his father Levi was not well. He walked with a cane and slurred his words.

The first Christmas after the end of the War, George made a bench for Anna which he carried down the path and put near the grave site. She used it as often as she could. Anna said the grave was a symbol of all people who had got lost and their people never saw them again. That applied in this case to cousin Harry. The family hadn't heard from him since he went to fight in the War. His father and mother and sister in Harrisburg had not heard of him either. Anna said because we did not know where Harry was, she needed to go out there to think about him and all the mothers who lost their boys. She thought about people from her past as she sat and wondered about life's complexities. She missed her baby Savina Ellen. She felt this time of reflection was somehow part of her responsibility in her role as the homemaker.

One day in the spring of '69, four years after the last of the Confederate troops had surrendered, Harry came walking up to the house, all by himself, in clothes which were dirty and put together funny. He appeared totally different, skinny and wearing a hard look on his face. His hair was pulled back reminiscent of earlier patriots. He spent most of his time with George although

Anna made huge peach pies for each of the eight days of his stay. Harry smiled at her in return, a sweet expression obviously foreign to his current face.

The morning he left he took nine-year-old JW for a walk who told him about school and the machine shops in Springfield and Greenville and the tools Mrs. Longnecker gave him when Mr. Longnecker died. JW had never talked so much and Harry listened to every word. Then he collected the items and food Anna and George gave him along with a horse, and packed up the old wagon George forced him to take. George was sentimental in his insistence that Harry take the gifts, "You gave me a lot of your time in the fields, Harry. And we all are grateful for the job you did for the country. You always have a home with us, Harry."

After he left, George told Anna that Harry had told him horrific stories about what he had seen and done in the army. After the Surrender the soldiers wanted desperately to go home. Harry was headed for Ohio because he intended to return to George and Anna. In the part of the country down where Harry was, the quickest way was to get a ticket on a steamboat. For each ticket sold the boat owner got a commission, so the boats were crowded and slow. Harry's ship was overflowing with thin, dirty men in rags of blue. In Memphis, when the *Sultana* as the boat was named, stopped to refuel, Harry lost her from drinking too much in a pub on the harbor side. He slept through the whistles and threw off the boys from his adopted regiment who tried to rouse him. While he was awakening twelve hours later the news of the explosion reached his ears. The overworked steam engine blew timber, steel and men into the sky and the river. From there for years, Harry wandered through Georgia, Tennessee and Virginia. He recently stopped to see his mother, sister and father up in Harrisburg and now planned to head West. Anna was grateful he had all his limbs and in general talked sense, unlike so many of the poor boys who came home. George had tried to convince him to stay here but Harry was skittish and would not sit still. When

Grandma Furst heard George's report, she upset Anna by saying, "I believe that War will claim him yet."

When Harry left he said he was headed for Iowa and his Aunt Mary who lived there with her Somerset County husband, his blind musician brother and their several children. But over the next several years, Mary wrote to her brother George in Ohio and reported each time they never had a visit from Harry.

JW spent much of his time in the implement shed where saws, knives, gauges and files hung up and down the large walls. In earlier days, he would ask his father if anything needed polishing or sharpening and he willingly did that. George noticed how dexterous his son was at handling the instruments, many of which had an awkward distribution of weight and sharp edges. The young farm boy sat all by himself and went over the tools and the machines. George encouraged his ideas, but did not spend much time with his inventive son. George was a businessman and Al was the one who showed an interest in the books. When George traveled for business, he took Al; when he went to look at machines and equipment, JW came along as well. Meetings with men smoking cigars while they discuss banknotes, credit plans and railroad rates was not JW's idea of a good time. Al, on the other hand, emulated the men and piped up in the conversations. George complimented Al on these efforts for they were a mutual admiration society.

One trip to Greenville proved to be different. As they turned off the well-rutted main road, George looked at his handsome boys conspiratorially, "Want to see the home I have always dreamed of owning and now intend to buy??!!" His voice got louder and his eyes bigger with each turn of a phrase. The boys could hardly refuse. George turned the light carriage pulled by a pair of identical glistening horses to a road by the creek, then went through short woods to an opening. Up a gentle incline was a large two-and-a-half-story house, with porches and windows and a long sloping roof, each side of which covered a space as large as the home in Union Township. Al whooped and JW asked if

Papa intended on moving the family away from the farm between Urbana and Mechanicsburg.

"Not completely, JW. Given has been with me for years and I'm putting him in charge back home. I'm not going to sell, so the farm will always be ours. But yes, the entire family will move here to Hill Grove. As for Lewis, he can decide for himself to stay or come with us. What do you think?"

"May I bring my tools?" JW asked, for he had conditions to negotiate before he agreed to big changes.

Al ignored the question, too excited not to interrupt, "This is grand, father! We shall be so happy here. How much acreage?"

"Fifteen hundred. It is not just the size of the place, Al. The railroad station in Greenville is closer than our trip to Springfield and that will save money. It goes right through this property, so I think I can create a station just for us. We'll ship our vegetables, grain and livestock to Anderson, Indianapolis and Chicago, as well as keeping Cincinnati and Dayton." The family already brought their hides to a tannery north of Greenville. The move felt like part of a natural progression to Al. He liked being in on the secret.

"Mama doesn't know?" He had to be sure.

"None of them at home, except Given. You boys are the first to know."

"I'm willing to give the new place a try," JW wanted to reassure his father. His father slapped the nine-year-old's back, "Sure you are, JW, sure you are."

Their father continued talking to them both, "This afternoon I sign the papers and then it is mine. I want you men to help me plant maples up that path to the front before your mother comes over. I want the trees already in there when she sees it for the first time."

Back at home JW had no trouble concealing the big secret. Al, on the other hand, had to say to Libby something about "and you don't even know" which put her on the trail. She started asking a lot of questions, so George took her outside and told her the tale while asking her to respect his surprise for his wife. Libby returned to the house satisfied, re-established on her throne.

George made the plans to take Anna to Hill Grove the following week, just the two of them, but little Ben had been sick and she would not leave him. So the three of them made the ride through Urbana and Piqua over Miami County to Greenville bouncing along in their best light carriage. Anna knew there was a surprise, and she was sure she had guessed what her husband was planning. She expected a new carriage. Over the years of success in Ohio, they had added a number of luxuries to their lives – a tall grandfather clock in their little front hall, a set of hand-painted china from Italy, and they now regularly bought leather shoes for themselves and their eight children. Anna resisted standardized clothes but hired a dressmaker who brought her sewing machine with its foot pedal to the house twice a year to replace items worn out and supply new needs not covered by her hand-me-down system. She was proud of her husband. Although she did not need so many nice things, now the War was over, she enjoyed the comfort of having them. She thought her suspicions were confirmed when George continued driving through the town of Greenville and beyond. She thought he was taking her to the Koerner farm on the Indiana border, for they made beautiful vehicles. So he took her by surprise when he turned off on the shady little path, followed the creek for a few hundred yards then stopped in front of an opening which revealed a surprising depth climbing up from the road. From where Anna sat her eyes followed the driveway up a gentle grade between two rows of young trees. At the end of the dozen new trees, she could see a large brick house which rose to a grand two-and-one-half stories. Protruding from the center of the house was a wide angular tower, each façade of which was broken by tall windows. This house had size but the interconnecting designs of the façade along with the lace-like quality of the large windows, made it seem unified and cozy. The house stood by itself. No trees canopied its sides, but instead two large sycamores stood freely with cathedral grandeur on either side and stretched their limbs unhindered into a symmetrical balance. The land continued a gentle slope behind the house to the right. The creek must twist its way to the left, for the land was lower there. Cleared fields showed themselves bathed in sunlight beyond immediate view. Anna could see colorful songbirds passing over the driveway, laying claim to new nests in the young trees not far from where she sat. She could not imagine why George was so giddy to display this scene before her eyes.

"Do you like it?" he asked inexplicably.

"Why, yes, George, it is a lovely homestead," she said patiently.

"Anna, it's yours!" He was so proud. For years he had held the vision of her in just this house only he had never really seen it, a place which she could fill with her needlework and their children. "I bought it last week. I wanted it to be my surprise to you. Remember the first time we went to Levi's farm to collect the horses my brothers had given us, and I told you how their house approximated a picture in my mind? This is it, Anna!" He was squeezing her hand when little Benjamin awoke and asked to be let out of the stilled carriage. These small things distracted her from the moment. She loosened the child from his blankets, wiped his nose of the remnants of the cold he had suffered and moved her skirts so he could crawl down to the ground.

"But George, I don't want to move. We're so happy where we are. I don't want to leave Savina to care for Levi all by herself." She did not mean to sound ungrateful, but she was happily planted on the sprawling farm which currently housed her children and whose ground held the child who departed to God's care.

"I know it's a big change, sweetheart. The children will love it here and I plan to build a second home over there to the right so that eventually Savina can bring Levi here. We're not far from Greenville, so the children will have the best education around. The library has 10,000 volumes," he exaggerated. His face was so open and filled with delight she couldn't resist him and so let go of all her objections.

"Oh, all right, George, if it makes you so happy. Come on, show me my kitchen." She was teasing him to cover her anxiety. She trusted his instincts, but also did not share his ability to jump forward without looking back.

He unlocked the massive front door and two-year-old Benjamin ran through the cavernous hallway and parlor, his footsteps ringing in all the corners of the house. Anna swept in and could not restrain her outcry, "Why, George, it is marvelous! Look at the light in these rooms!" She looked up and stared at the metal embossed ceilings then surveyed the angular hallway. "What a great spot for the Grandfather clock." She went from the parlor to the dining room and moved her sensitive fingers over the mahogany carvings of the wainscot covering the lower half of the walls. "Oh, my!" she let loose as George tried to hurry her along. In the kitchen was a built-in icebox and a water pump right outside the door in a mudroom with sinks and shelves for storage. In the main kitchen, windows with ironwork lattice surrounded the work area.

George leaned an elbow on the counter and smiled with amusement at his wife. "Now I won't have any more burned dinners, Mrs. Lambert. With this space to work in I want all my meals on time and in excellent condition," he deadpanned.

"Oh, George," she did not look at him, but was examining the built-in cupboards with glass doors, "when did I ever serve you burned food?"

"OK, never, but I am putting my foot down and hiring a girl to help in the kitchen. You have proved your ability to make a pie crust; let someone else take over the details."

Now he had her attention. "You mean it, don't you? All of it." She went to embrace him.

"Of course I do. Nothing makes me happier than providing for my family. I bless the day I bought you those flowers in Independence Square. Let's plant dahlias all over the backyard in celebra-

tion. Come look out the back. The land is as grand as the house."
She followed him to the window, and he led her to the back door.

"Benjamin! Benjamin Franklin, come here!" She collected the
adventurous toddler and together they went to explore the outside.

Moving was arduous, for Anna insisted on overseeing every
detail herself. The hardest part of leaving the old home was telling
her mother. But, Savina was won over to the new plans and even
acknowledged how impressed she was by George's successes,
"and all with carrots and pigs," she snorted, meaning he made
his fortune with produce and livestock, not horses. Levi, her husband, who had made a fortune with horses followed in kind by his
son now in Kentucky, had drifted farther away from this world.
Soon after his stroke, she had hired a couple to live in to help
in his recovery. She would hold on at the horse farm for a while
longer, she pledged, but eventually she knew they would give up
their home and retire to George's side yard. Anna understood her
mother's reluctance to change and although she hated to leave
her mother back in Clark County, the new distance was not so
much a burden as to break their bond of affection. Like in the
old days when the young George Lamberts moved so frequently,
Anna capably established the family in the new home and in no
time had the household running. A year later, in the spring of
1871, she was pregnant again. "Well, we now know these children
are not the result of the well water around Springfield," George
teased his wife.

The agricultural entrepreneur had changed in his new environment and was less interested in farming and more interested
in the larger profits to be got in manufacturing. Each time he
walked his fields he found himself at the edge looking out at new
lands rather than focusing on the soil, the health of his plants,
the size of his harvest, the price of grain, the means of transport.
He had conquered those problems. He wanted new challenges.
With the War over, the fruit of possibility was lush. The national
economy was expanding at an unstoppable pace. He hired more

workers, including a clerk to keep the books for the farms so he and his oldest son could put together a plan for a plant in or near Greenville. Foregoing whenever he could the routine repetition of farm chores, JW, now eleven, maintained his focus on machinery. He was a whiz with the tools and could coax almost any machine back into working order.

Exciting as the new endeavors were, George did not completely let go of the farm near Mechanicsburg in Champaign County. The first year after moving his family to Hill Grove, he made several trips back to check on things and to install the systems with Given and Lewis which enabled them to finish taking over his roles, buying, planting, harvesting, selling, fertilizing. George put young Lewis in charge of the overall operation, including the business of renting out the thresher to farmers who had come to rely on using the machine. The young men thought they had inherited the opportunity of a lifetime. George's interest was in meeting expenses and paying the taxes. For any unusual problem he was available, but they understood his aim was for them to accomplish as much as they could on their own. The herds were sold off after George took his best breeders to Darke County, so the only animals left were workers.

While the boys in Union Township went through their paces, George's plan was to set up the new farm using the latest technology and to invest in machinery of which much was developed in this post-War boon. One of the most innovative projects was installing a big steam engine unlike anything in any of the counties nearby. If George was enthusiastic over accomplishing this change, JW was ecstatic. He was attracted to the power of the machine and enticed by the manufacture of "go", as he referred to it. George had studied the literature and talked to Lizzie's brother in Greenville, as well as his friends in the machine and hardware shops. He had arrived at a decision about the size and model of engine for the needs he anticipated. To purchase the model he would take the two boys to Cleveland. For the few days between planning and leaving, JW was so excited he could hardly sleep.

Once en route, the bouncy rumble of the train ride echoed the itch in his feet. JW was alone with his excitement, as his father was preoccupied with working out the details for the new business site in Greenville. In the seats across from where the younger son stretched out, he and Al had their noses in notebooks spread across their laps. They had settled on the idea of manufacturing wooden buggy and carriage parts, so that involved lumber. George knew a lot about wood, more than he did about leather, steel or the new material called rubber. Al suggested they talk to Levi about getting wood from down South. It could come up the Mississippi River, which was more practical than going back to Lost Mountain, the forests around which were suffering from strip mining for iron ore. JW heard their voices, but his mind was wandering all over the engine he imagined upon its wheeled trolley which will sit in the barn now being built to house the new machine. Then his ears caught the drift of their speculating over power for the plant in Greenville and possibly buying two of the engines instead of just the one. "Maybe we can talk the fellow into a deal for two of the same," Al suggested. He loved his own ideas.

"Let's see how the power works out at the farm before we make any more plans," George encouraged Al to voice his plentiful ideas and patiently listened to details of even the most far flung notions, confident he alone made the decisions. For this idea, he put the brakes on his capitalistic thirteen-year-old son.

"Energy for the work at the farm should transfer to manufacturing, Papa." JW opened his eyes. "You could even take the farm engine up to Greenville to try out different functions at the plant. You may want several smaller motors for things in different areas of the factory, rather than a central unit like at the farm. The farm will use the energy in a serial manner – one task after another, over a year's time. The factory will have constant smaller needs." JW emerged from his other worldly posture to say these words. His father and brother had not realized he had been following their conversation. Al was a bit miffed at hearing the comment, but George saw the wisdom of the eleven-year-old's observation.

"Yes, JW, I see what you mean. We'll wait on our factory needs until we understand what they are."

Once along the harborside, the boys reverted to younger days. They ran up and down the waterfront where large ships were docked to refuel and repack goods and passengers. Their father sent them off on their own, within limits, while he alone met with the representative from the Case Engine Company. He made his money-deal privately from his economically curious oldest son. There was no sense in letting on any specifics about the depth of the family fortune. He was content this purchase would catapult him over his competitors. Although he was taking a big risk with this new product from an outfit in Wisconsin, its design and construction promised to deliver the energy he needed for many operations and should pay for itself easily in the next few years. When George re-emerged to collect his sons, he found them standing on the edge of the water, throwing stones at the seagulls and waving greetings to the men working on the decks of the nearest ship. The boys were enthralled by the size of the vessels and the bustle of the area. George's purchase would be packed and shipped by railroad car down the Chicago-Indianapolis Line and weighed almost 5,000 pounds, including the engine, boiler, feed-pump, a trolley and wheels.

On the way home, Al was full of questions about what goods the ships carried and where they went as well as about the competition between the ships and the railroad lines. George explained the determination of destination and went into detail about rate rebates and the status to be enjoyed of being a favored customer of one line or another. He had more trouble answering the questions from his younger son. JW wanted to know what fueled the various transports and asked about the principals of thermodynamics which the newly purchased machine used. He also asked why steam was so popular when it had killed so many of Harry's friends.

The large steam engine George set up in his new building was off limits to his tinkering third born. Under no circumstances was JW to touch anything on the expensive equipment George now depended upon as a vital support to the farm enterprise. Its use was scheduled, as JW predicted, according to the time of year. It was dragged through fields at harvest time to drive the blades which cut the grain and the binder which collected the sheaths and pulled them into bundles. As they witnessed the work, George was amazed and nearly as excited as his son JW, but for different reasons. JW was tantalized by the clever machines with their mechanized operations run by the steam engine. His father remembered the pride of hand binding the sheaves, binding one before the last hit the ground, the deft twist and tuck of the binders' knot, the flailing fun he had as a boy. He was bedazzled that the long processes of old were accomplished in what seemed like the wink of an eye. The corn was harvested twice as fast as before, for the new engine ran a combine which picked the ears from the stalk, removed the husks, shelled the corn then collected the clean kernels in a bucket. A conveyor belt carried away the straw. The forage harvester hooked up to the steam engine right in the field, cut the stalks into pieces and blew them into a wagon which took them to a silo for fermentation.

JW had an idea for using the steam engine to help with milking the thirty-some cows. He worked out his idea by drawing it on paper, then showed it to his father. George pointed at the paper and asked about specific points along the line and thereby helped the young inventor to work out details before he began constructing his machine. George helped rig up the small conveyor belt which carried pails of freshly extracted milk to the yard where it was strained and poured into crocks by hand, then returned the pails to the cow barn. This process saved hauling and some washing when the big steam engine was not needed for bigger uses, but pails fell off the line and loss of milk became significant. Although this idea did not bring a revolution in the milk cow chores, JW established himself, at least within the confines of his family, as a lad with a useful imagination. More than that, he pleased himself, for he had taken an idea for making something better and brought that mental picture into material reality.

4

Post War Boom Becomes the Industrial Revolution

JW took special care to comb his hair back just so. He made the part razor straight by directing each side to flow back from his face and used goose grease to keep it in place. He was a handsome eleven-year-old trying to look older. Last year he had accompanied Libby and Al to their first Darke County Fair dance, but the evening had ended all too quickly when he fell asleep early near the pie table. Now he was older and more mature. He grinned into the mirror, straightened his collar and headed down the stairs. He walked into the parlor where his sister and brother were waiting. Eight-year-old Emma was holding Benjamin, still the youngest, while four-year-old Mollie combed her sister's hair in front of the fire. On the floor Christian was building with wooden blocks.

"We'll miss the Virginia Reel if you don't shake a leg," Libby was crabby because she was nervous. Not quite fifteen, she frowned and grabbed her hat. Putting it on her head, she flashed a smile to her two brothers, "Well, you're supposed to tell me how lovely I look."

"You look oh, so beautiful, Jenny Lind." Al submitted dutifully and winked at his brother. "And doesn't our brother cut a fine cloth? I don't know if I want you along, JW; you'll turn the ladies' eyes away from me." Mollie held the comb aloft while she giggled.

JW was ready; "I think I'm going to ask Eva Parent for a dance just to show you how it's done." He walked up close to his older brother's face, his eyes twinkling. "You were acting like a peacock after Sunday Services last week. There was nothing she could do but pay you attention." JW puffed up his chest and strutted in front of his tall, dark-haired brother. Al's face crinkled with amusement as he raised his fist up near JW's face. The boys broke into simultaneous grins as JW shook him off and ran his palms over his temples to smooth his shining hair. Al, his young face rosy with hormones and the fire's glow, pulled his jacket down and flattened the material to his form.

Anna peered into the room with a ladle in her hand. Her body bulged with the latest stork offering. "The three of you will look out for each other," she chimed right in. Holding her left hand under the dripping utensil, she approached her three oldest children. She could not move fast these days, but as always her hearing was impeccable. "JW, you'll find your own dance partner." She could not tie her apron so the strings hung down by her sides.

Turning to his older sister with a smile, JW placed his thumb next to his abdomen and offered her his elbow with an exaggerated bend at the waist. Libby curled her fingers under his arm and turned to do the same with Al's similarly offered arm. The three of them faced their mother, as their father came into the room to stand beside her. Christian got up from his fantasy play on the floor and stood beside Mollie in order to hear what Papa had to say. He reached for three-year-old Benjamin who was holding up his arms to be picked up. Emma brushed her skirts after the large toddler vacated her lap. "Well, well, look at this. My favorite farm hands sure clean up nice. I'm guessing there is some special event planned for this evening." Papa's voice had a tease.

"There is, Pa, and you know it," Libby wanted more of her father's reassurances.

George patted Libby's back and whispered, "You'll be the prettiest girl there." She broke into a pleased grin. After hearing their father's instructions on Lambert manners, they left the parlor for the outside shadows of the late afternoon where the wagon was ready with the nag restless to get going.

The sun still offered some light as the three excited siblings arrived at the new Grange Hall in Greenville. The sounds of fiddle playing made Libby give JW a little shove to hurry out of the wagon. He hopped down and turned to help his older sister, but she was down and running to greet her girl friends who seemed to materialize out of nowhere. Al moved the wagon over to the field away from the crowd. JW wandered over to the barbecue-pits by himself. The meat was sizzling and dripping juices. A boy from school recognized him.

"John Lambert! How goes it, neighbor?" Russell Smith pumped his hand. They fell into a conversation patterned after their elders about the harvest at their respective family farms. Russell looked at the meat being taken off the grill and placed on large platters. Other young people were crowding up to the red-checked tablecloth as the platters were set down between stacks of clean plates and napkins rolled around utensils. The boys looked at each other. "Want to get some of that?"

The long, wooden tables had crocks of baked beans at each center. Bread and pitchers of lemonade spotted the ends of the narrow tables. Someone had collected wildflowers and set out bouquets in glass jars. Russell and JW made their way over to the platters of meat and helped themselves to steaming pieces of pork, beef and lamb. In sync they headed toward the far end of the hungry crowd. Most of the lively conversation was carried on by the older teenagers who seemed to have no notice of their peripheral younger siblings. JW caught a glimpse of Al as he shook a pork rib off a big fork and on to Eva Parent's plate. It seemed like a long way from eating next to Russell to where his brother stood. Other young boys were taking seats next to Russell. JW rose to shake their hands. To have the leisure to sit and eat with peers was a luxury these farm boys rarely enjoyed. If they were not with their families, their heads were bent into a reader at the schoolhouse with Miss Hawk's voice cajoling them and waving her pointer stick. JW and his friends made several trips to the barbecue pits, then switched to the inside pie tables. As the meal wore on, their conversation was sparse but their smiles eased over the spaces. They filled their glasses and buttered their bread and ate ear after ear of fresh-picked sweet corn. As the musicians played for the dancing crowd inside, outside Russell, JW and their friends gathered in the dirt across the yard in front of the big barn to play marbles almost by feel it was so dark. Around nine o'clock the music slowed. A few couples drifted out to the shadows around the other side of the building. Libby's voice rang out in the yard from the lighted doorway, "JW! JW!"

"We're all out here, Lib," JW yelled back.

"Oh! We're getting ready to leave." JW was tired, and once they got going on the dark road, the ride back was quiet. Al let Mercy pick her own pace. Libby alternated between yawns and giggles, but did not talk. Al asked her once what was so funny and she made a dreamy hum but did not answer. Al kept hold of the reins and did not ask again. The sky was filled with a thousand million stars. The black of the land stretched deep around the horse and wagon, and the vastness of the heavens spread even beyond that. JW's mind seemed to leave the wagon and sail up into the velvety darkness, swaying around one star then another. He knew the names of some stars and had studied a book on the rotation of their configurations. The multilayered meanings of the heavens was like a playground to him and gazing at the sky was relaxing. He was thinking about God and imagining Jesus sashaying around the stars in similar fashion to his own mental escapades. It was a comforting sense of companionship lulled by the rhythm of Mercy's feet on the dirt and stones of the road. The light from the house grew brighter and sharper through the trees, until the big windows were straight-lined boxes. Mercy had picked up her pace; no doubt she was imagining her own bed at the end of the trip. Al let his sister and younger brother off near the front door and went to put the horse away by himself. Entering the house after Libby, JW felt like he was in a dream. The evening had been out of his usual routine and yet was securely encompassed by ordinary expectations. It was good to be home, to enter the warmth of the full house with his mother and father sitting together in the parlor, the fire out but the kerosene lamps blaring. JW blinked in the bright light and reached to rub Rex's silky ears. His mother asked, "Well, you are all three home safe?"

"Yes, Mama. Al will be in as soon as he brushes down Mercy."

Upstairs, JW splashed cold water from the bowl on the washstand over his face. As he slipped into bed, he looked out to the vast dark sky, twinkling with a thousand million little lights, and that feeling of quiet calm took over his body. He could hear Christian, or was it Benjamin?, breathing through an open mouth. Al was whispering with Papa in the hallway. Before he even got in the room, JW was asleep.

As winter settled in, news came from the Urbana farm Lewis was engaged to the school principal who had taught the older children in one room back in their Union Township days. George joked now there was no doubt, Lewis was in a class by himself. The family traveled back to Champaign County and made a good showing for the young man whose own parents had died in his youth and whose only sister was at that time lost with a man she had married who was thirty years her senior. In the first years of their marriage, Lewis and his wife started a theater group, to the shock of their Methodist neighbors and to the delight of everyone else. They hosted readings in their parlor and eventually, they traveled with three others to give shows in small towns throughout Ohio. Though distracted, Lewis continued his farming. George was content to allow the levels of production to settle to a lower, more modest and therefore more reliable income for these times. After the War the price of wool dropped considerably.

Lewis and his bride reciprocated with the George Lamberts by traveling to Hill Grove to celebrate Christmas. They brought Savina and poor Levi to join the family gathering. The large house was festive but Grandma Furst could not sit back and allow her daughter to reign in her own home. She asserted herself by ordering her grandchildren to her bidding, thereby doubling the decorations in the front of the house and the menus from the kitchen in the rear. Anna, with her husband's affection and being large with child, tolerated her mother's assertiveness. She understood this was her mother's first Christmas away from the rambling house on the horse farm. George had cleared half the apple orchard, laid stone for a foundation, purchased lumber and was waiting for warm weather to construct Savina and Levi's new house. Savina knew the move was coming. At Lewis's wedding, when it had taken four grandchildren to escort her and Levi into the small chapel, she had said to her daughter, "Old age isn't for sissies." Savina who started her life in the civilized East and came to Ohio when the land was still new, and who fought slavery right out in the open, was certainly no sissy.

On Christmas morning the family bundled themselves in wool coats and mittens, leggings and hats and tucked themselves under blankets to ride in the large family carriage with seats facing each other, a smaller child on each adult lap which added warmth, and traveled to St. Paul's Presbyterian Church in Greenville. A large prospering family, the Lamberts took up two pews. The only other family to do so was the Parents, so it seemed natural to stop and greet them after the service. Eva's grandfather was co-founder of Darke County. She looked beautiful standing between her two sisters in her green velvet coat with the braided black piping. She kept a steady gaze at Al while her tall, soft-spoken father talked to George. Mr. Parent ran the big grain elevator in town. Anna wished Eva a Merry Christmas and introduced her to Savina, on the other side of whom stood Libby. This friendly holiday scenario was unfolding while JW was leading Levi, along with the youngsters, Lewis and his wife, to their vehicle, for it took some time to get Levi to step up the suspended cast-iron buckboard of the large carriage and into a comfortable position. With his hands directing the old man, JW stole glances back at the scene in front of the large stone church. Libby was watching as her parents exchanged pleasantries with Eva's parents. Her eyes had a distinct green tint as she silently witnessed her younger brother's romantic aspirations receive a boost in this most dreamy of seasons. All this attention and encouragement to Al in his pursuit of Eva seemed unreasonable for, after all, she was the oldest. At the county fair dance last month, Libby had met the boy she believed would make her a bride. She had her plans. She didn't understand her parents were in no hurry for matchmaking and considered Al's infatuation to be a youthful effort in a long game. She felt taken for granted around her parents' home and reasoned she could work as hard for her own household. Her intended was the son of a manufacturer in the same type business Papa was building in Union City. What a coup it will be when this cozy little group discovers her intentions! She will not be the silent one by Savina's side then; she will be the center of attention, the queen of her world, with no more farm chores or tending the children. She will live in town in a grand home and have store-bought clothes. Oh, well, the others would have to wait and see.

The amiable conversation between the two families broke up with warm wishes hanging in the air like the white of their breath. Earlier that morning, Anna and Savina had put a large turkey shot by George in the deep oven, so when the family returned after church the house was filled with its intoxicating smell. The stockings and presents were quickly unwrapped. The children were content to be occupied with their new toys: box blocks from Grandma Lambert decorated with Bible verses, pictures of garden swings and nursery rhymes, also a scooter, a rooster bank, wooden boats and a stereoscope with pictures of Niagara Falls and Civil War battles. JW disappeared, for along with the card which announced a subscription to *Scientific American* in his name, were copies of half a dozen back issues. He was devouring them as fast as his eyes could read.

George was with Al and Lewis in the library which was just like the parlor on the other side of the front hall. Levi sat silently with them while George detailed his business adventures. He grew fidgety when he was not expanding his dreams. He had bid on property in nearby Union City which was more affordable than land in Greenville and still well connected to the railroad lines. He had ordered wood from Tennessee, paint from Akron and lathes from Harrisburg where William flourished anew as a builder and master craftsman. His wife Lizzie was deeply involved in Veteran's affairs with her much overweight daughter Katy. Al told the older men of his interest in fire prevention after a spectacular blaze burned nearly all of Chicago earlier in the year. It was his idea the catastrophe would stimulate a large demand for fire fighting apparatus in small towns across the nation. He had written to fire protection organizations in Philadelphia and New York to study construction of their equipment. He wanted his father to manufacture pieces for these specialized items to add to the Lambert inventory. The father and son sparkled with enthusiasm. Lewis was a good audience for he admired the dramatic flare with which they presented their vision.

By springtime the new home for Savina and Levi was nearly complete. When it was done George wanted to travel to Tennessee to inspect the timberland he had acquired through Anna's half brother Levi and which would supply his manufacturing plant. He asked Anna how she felt about gathering all the children and taking them for a full family adventure. Anna was at first hesitant to venture into the South. "You don't suppose some Confederate veteran will object to our presence and seek revenge on one of our children, do you?" It was not like Anna to give in to her fears, but George offered reassurance.

"You've got three males to protect you and your pups, my darling." George knew he would let no ruffian anywhere bring harm to any member of his family, especially a newborn baby and its mother. Anna had given birth in January, and the four-month-old child was outfitted for traveling. "It's our patriotic duty to present ourselves to these Southerners, Anna. Let them see we are not horned devils, but people just like them. It will be our sacrifice for the reunion effort." He was half teasing her, half re-assuring himself. George had read many former slaves were now starving. Wanting his business venture to be part of a new national unity, he decided to find Negro workers in Tennessee to cut and haul the timber. He would make the business arrangements with his lumberjacks man-to-man; color would not stand in the way. Truth be told, George believed the most dangerous stop on a trip South would be Cincinnati where foreigners from Eastern Europe, unaccustomed to American ways, with their gruff language and dark looks, were stirring up trouble with labor rallies and strikes. George carefully routed his family through Indianapolis and Louisville to avoid trouble in the quagmire of Cincinnati. In spite of trepidations, he made the travel arrangements and accommodations; he insisted to his wife he anticipated no problem. Soon Anna looked forward to seeing a different part of the country. It occurred to her their absence would give her independent mother privacy as she made herself comfortable in her new home. When she told Savina of their plans to be gone at the same time the moving would take place, Savina gave a checked response thereby confirming Anna's hunch she preferred to be on her own.

The children were dressed in stylish new clothes including spring coats. Their new cloth valises were packed, one for each child, and together they would ride the Jeffersonville line past Louisville and into the foothills of the Smokey Mountains to the small town of Gallatin north of Nashville. This was similar to the terrain George had grown up in, if farther south. He was amazed at the power of his nostalgic feelings as the train passed from rolling countryside to higher hills. He relaxed as the train covered ground and the topography became more varied. The constantly changing views outside the windows provided amusement to the children. The passing farms and small towns were the topic of questions and speculating, for what must life be like for the people who lived there? At some spots, small groups of local inhabitants, sometimes white sometimes black, all poor, gathered by the tracks with their scrawny loyal mongrels to wave to the trainload of passengers as the loud, smelly engine sped by, most of them dressed in rags and thin as rails, their mouths spotted toothless, their feet bare. The well-dressed Lambert children waved back to these figures as the train sped by. They saw pig farms and covered bridges and beautiful blooming lavender wisteria. They counted sheep and cattle and debated the names of the breeds. Constantly outside the window was the punctuation of the poles which held the telegraph wire. The wire ran close to the top of the train, drooping between poles, seemingly close enough to touch, if not interrupted by glass. It swooped and looped and accompanied them their entire trip.

As the hours fled by, the children became acclimated to the bounce of the moving car and grew more adventuresome. For the midday meal the family, each smaller child led by a larger one, filed between the rows of seats, opened the heavy doors at the end to pass between cars, jumped with squeals drowned by the roar of the steel wheels on steel rails screeching over the loud grinding connecting gears and passed through the next set of doors into the smoking car where big leather chairs and deep carpet worked with the smoke in the air to capture all sound. Silent, single old men stared at each child and held their faces stonelike. The Lamberts passed through to the next passenger car, thus making their way to the special dining car. They sat down on red velvet-lined benches, five on a side including the baby, and ordered their lunches. The land outside the window kept moving, kept moving, kept moving.

Not far from the setting of their unusual mealtime were mail cars packed with packages and bags of letters, and muddy stock cars filled with hogs and cattle. Each animal was packed in one next to the other like captured Africans used to be assembled in ships traveling to American markets. And there were freight cars loaded with Northern produce and farm implements manufactured in Northern factories, McCormick and Deere. Up front in the engine car two grimy, sweaty men alternated with each other heaving shovelsful of coal into the fire to keep the big steam engine burning which kept the train rolling. They passed by some of the small depots, the train slowing only for the switchman to wave his lantern "Good-bye and Good Day" as the train went rolling through. At other stations they stopped and alighted which stretched the travel time but added to the variety of sights the children observed. At each stop the stationmaster, dressed in a white shirt, suspenders and a visor over his eyes, was the telegraph operator as well. Waving his directions with his hand and holding a clipboard over his arm, he signaled the train out of the station with a whistle. The steam engine would roar and lurch the train into motion. After each stop the children were more familiar with the routine. They imitated the stationmaster, pretended to blow the whistle, braced themselves for the initiating jolt, and in general, had a rollicking good time. After each stop the conductor would pass through their car to check tickets. This sober man in uniform inspired straight backs and silent behavior as he paused to inspect the bundle of papers George wordlessly handed to him.

They pulled into the small town of Gallatin in late afternoon while many of the younger children were napping. The station had recently been rebuilt. It, along with many stations throughout the South, had been destroyed during the War as the Union forces battled to choke off supplies to Rebel lines. George knew Harry had been stationed at several different spots along Southern railroad lines. But during his brief visit that one time George had not questioned him on specifics of his service so he could only guess if this were a spot controlled by the Ohio boys in blue. These thoughts had little time to detain George. The train would resume its itinerary in a few moments, and the family needed to gather their belongings and deboard. George had arranged for their stay at a mountain log cabin which advertised a long front porch made for sitting and watching sunsets. He walked over to the livery stable and hired the driver with the largest vehicle to take them to their retreat. Their cabin was one large room dominated by an expansive fireplace. Once there, Al and JW quickly built up a fire. Soon the sweet scent of the pinewood filled their air. George described a similar room where he and his seven brothers and sisters grew up, the family table they gathered around and the ladder to the sleeping loft where the space was divided between girls and boys. He told his children the inspiring story of his Grandmother who had been left a widow with ten children in the wilderness and had built a community which prospered for two generations. They heard about the determination and ingenuity which went into the making of life in primitive times and they marveled to hear of no schools, few books, no steam power or railroads, of a place so isolated it took more than half a day to ride on the only road out to the nearest neighbor and of the cooperation among family members which helped them all survive.

George took his two older boys into Gallatin to meet with the agent who sold him the timberland. While they were in town, George proposed they stop by the local carriage dealer and strike up a conversation. He was glad he did, for George found a welcoming Southern businessman whose partner was a Northern transplant. They contracted for future purchases of his wagon and carriage parts. Thus the vacation paid for itself. The next day the three men joined the agent to inspect their newly purchased forests which stood in an isolated part of the county. The trees, including birch for foot boards and oak for the wheel spokes, would supply all the Ohio entrepreneur needed, if managed right, for years to come.

The ride back North was more challenging to Anna and George. The entire family was tired. Anna had purchased maple sugar candy which she offered in pieces throughout the day as a reward for the competitions George set up. The first child to count fifty Marino sheep won a piece of the candy, or thirty black and white cows or one hundred telephone poles. They arrived back in Hill Grove on a cool spring night. Savina had ordered a fire in each fireplace, so their Northern house was warm and welcoming for their return.

Anna had been wise to allow her mother this time to claim her new home. Being there to welcome her daughter and family was a familiar dynamic but as dominate as Savina felt, she was a shadow of her former self. In the implement barn, JW put together a wheelchair for transporting Levi across the short yard each day for dinner with the rest of the family. The old horse dealer had lost all his speech and never got out of the rig except to sleep, but he followed conversation with his eyes and seemed to understand what he heard.

The property George had secured for his business in Union City housed a two-story brick factory building, but George's vision was larger than that. When they returned from Tennessee, George and Al spent a lot of time pouring over ideas for the factory. He named his company the Union City Carriage Manufacturing Company. George wanted eventually to manufacture whole buggies and so stretched his plans to accommodate the manufacturing of wheels, poles, shafts, axles and all wooden parts of the body. Eventually he would upholster the seats at this site as well. Koerner was doing it, so why could not he? But unlike Koerner, whose production was spotted all over his expansive property, George believed his plans were better for he was consolidating the process to one centralized location. The necessary starting tools would be delivered by the end of the summer, so he needed more space. He ordered bricks and hired a construction crew.

Al had turned himself into a fire fighting apparatus expert. He and his father mapped out the floor plan for producing the various parts which went into these special vehicles, except the pumps which they would special order and install themselves. The two men devised an overall organization of the factory space, first to produce the wooden pieces for carriages, buggies and fire pumpers and then to include the other pieces of the complete product. They determined they would hire ten workers and start their payroll when the first wave of tools were in place. They interviewed former railroad workers, sons of farmers, a veteran, and transient men looking to put down roots. These workers would supplement the few old friends from the machine shops in Greenville who were already promised jobs and eagerly throwing in with the efforts of the enterprising farmers.

While George and Al were busy empire building, JW kept the farm chores up to date by overseeing the permanent workers and his young brother Christian Harry, as well as the laborers who helped by the season. He spent his time repairing tools and keeping the vast army of equipment in running condition. Still, the twelve-year-old found time to dally; he divided his stolen time between reading a book or magazine and toying in his tool shop. The light was good in the hayloft above the big cow barn and the place was out of the way enough to avoid interruptions, but still central enough for him to hear if his help were called for. Lately he had been reading about steam engines for transportation, inspired by the big locomotive which pulled the train he had ridden. A train line ran the edge of their property, following the line of the creek. Each time one passed JW lifted his head or ran out of a shed to catch a glimpse of its steel power, the pressured billowing smoke and the screeching thundering noise.

George was expanding the Hill Grove farm to accommodate his overall vision. He was re-building his livestock herds by focusing on prime cattle for leather. In this way he would eventually supply his own needs for upholstering the seats of his buggies and carriages. It would take a few seasons, but step-by-step, he would build up his production until he indeed was manufacturing whole vehicles.

JW liked to show his father the innovations he was working on in the tool shop. He was building his own little steam engine by trying to come up with a smaller version of the large apparatus which drove so much of the farm work. Each smaller model sacrificed power and, so rendered, became virtually useless except as a toy. George was at a loss for suggestions. JW wanted to separate strength and size, but in order to build up enough compression to drive the pistons, he needed a large boiler. The puzzle obsessed him. How he longed to dissemble the large engine his father had purchased, but with respect for his father's property, to his credit, he never did. Although the mysterious conundrum did not reveal its secrets to the curious adolescent, JW was entertained for hours. Not only did he spend time tinkering on the impossible engine, but he also turned his attention to more practical and successful designs. He rigged up a wide, stage-like platform under the farm's spacious storage silo. In the silo he collected grain which the large mechanical harvester had separated in the fields. From the silo, built next to the railroad tracks, the grain was released directly into the boxcar as the train waited to pass along the Lambert property. Thus he built a system to funnel the grain from the fields on to the trains headed for the markets. He modeled his system on what he saw at Mr. Parent's granary in Greenville and others in Urbana and Mechanicsburg.

At the end of the day, while the supper dishes were being washed, JW often got on the floor of the great angular hallway to be the "cat" for a game of "Cat and Birdies" with the three younger children, for Mollie doggedly joined in. It gave them a release; the screams and giggling exhausted them and rendered them useless for protesting wash-ups and bed. JW loved grabbing and tickling the squirming children and enjoyed his own laughter and feigned predatory nature. On a deeper level, these games linked him to his absent cousin who had become in his mind a reason for always doing his best. Harry was a war hero; no one could debate that. He was also a personal hero to JW. Occasionally someone, usually George, wondered out loud what ever happened to Harry. Anna said he was lost and sadly acknowledged he was likely dead, for no one had heard from him since he showed up one day at their old home and stayed for an eight day visit. He could have become a railroad man and made it all the way to California, or married a farmer's daughter and inherited a plot of land for himself, or joined the circus or some other traveling show. JW did not like to think of him as dead and occupying some anonymous plot in the ground like the grave Mama had turned into a garden back in Champaign County. Memories of Harry came easy to JW; he remembered the older boy taking his hand at a country burial and squeezing it with meaning as a small wooden coffin was lowered into the ground and covered with dirt. He remembered Harry looking into his eyes on their last walk together as JW, uncharacteristically, bubbled over with words to tell stories and ideas, his mouth barely keeping up with the mental images he was trying to share. There had been admiration and interest in Harry's eyes as he listened to the gangly young boy. Just before he left to fight in the War, Harry had made up the game of Cat and Birdies. Now it was so much a part of Lambert family life young Benjamin thought it dated back to the Indians.

Round-cheeked baby Sam had been born in January, just before JW turned twelve. For sitting in the parlor in the evening, George had purchased a mammy bench, a couch with one seat being a place like a cradle which held the baby, so Anna could enjoy quiet time to work with her needles by rocking the bench to keep the baby content. Emma was the perfect age to play at being a mother and made up games and amused the young one with "mousy creep" by walking her fingers all over his cute little body or "buzzy bee" by waving her pointer finger around his face and poking him gently, thus evoking smiles. When he was able, he gave her that delicious baby laughter. Libby ignored the baby and in an outburst accused her mother of throwing her life away for her children. Anna had patiently explained that feeding and caring for her children were very fulfilling to her. She wondered at Libby's attitude because Anna, remembering such loneliness in her own childhood, experienced the world of her household as marvelously diverse and constantly challenging. She knew her influence had an important effect on each of her developing children. She was serious in her intent to direct that influence to the highest good her God could reveal to her. She read her personal Bible daily as George read to them all after supper from the large family Bible which had pictures of Jesus holding little children, as well as of Him with his mother. This purpose filled her with happiness and a questioning will to discover how next to respond and handle the problems which came up through the course of the day. Poor Libby, her mother worried, seemed like a loose cannon. She wrote out a favorite verse about motherhood and left it on Libby's pillow. She spoke to her husband about their restless oldest daughter, "Perhaps after the Bible readings we should re-institute the practice of each child thanking God for specific blessings, George, because she does not seem to appreciate what she has here." It did not cross the minds of George and Anna that the kindling romance of their oldest daughter would blow into a blaze. But when it was discovered, with practical response a wedding was planned for the early fall. Libby married Dan Cook a month before her sixteenth birthday. Anna was angry but blamed the Waverly novels with their stories of brave knights and ladies fair which the girl had been reading. Yet she rallied to give her daughter a beautiful wedding. Libby swelled with pregnancy shortly after the ceremony. To this day George believes the child was delivered a month "early" due to the mother's tender age. It helped that he liked the young man. At the wedding he said, "It's a Lambert tradition to look at situations this way: I'm not losing a daughter; I'm gaining a son."

He paid particular attention to Libby's new in-laws, for Colonel Cook had been manufacturing carriage parts since his return to Ohio after serving in the Grand Army of the Republic. The Pioneer Pole and Shaft Company was a substantial business in central Ohio, and the Colonel was quite open to expansion, or "conquering new territory" as he liked to put it. Before the wedding ceremony was completed and certainly before the mutual grandchild, a boy, thank God, appeared, the Lambert men of Union City were thinking up ways to do business with the firm in Piqua, Ohio. Young Dan was a salesman and began traveling to Cleveland, Chicago and St. Louis to keep the two plants busy with orders for parts for various vehicles. George's timberland in Tennessee was a wise investment for both companies. Miss Libby, now Mrs. Cook, in spite of herself, had made a success by bringing these two families together.

All members of the family had to adjust to Libby's exit by marriage from the Hill Grove farm, but it changed nine-year-old Emma's life most dramatically. She took over more responsibility for morning chores and work in the kitchen to prepare meals along with Mama and Mama's cook. If Emma were to tell it, she would express her relief at the change, for Libby was a handful, always guarding her rights and monitoring the rewards she saw doled out by her parents. The premature marriage of Queen Libby only enhanced Emma's attachment to JW. She had never been part of or even understood the fierce competition between Al and Libby which left JW out, but it had kept him available to her. In addition he was able to appreciate her devotion, while Al teased her for the same trait. She saw in JW's quiet moods a calm strength and wished to pay homage to the ideals she envisioned in him. Whether he was worthy, his other brothers and sisters would debate. To Emma, he was high on a pedestal. She saw to it he received at least his share of food; she hid his mistakes and smiled at his remarks at dinner. Unlike Al the show-off, JW was interested in things the others had no way of understanding. She knew he was special and considered herself lucky to have such an older brother. On the train ride to Tennessee she positioned herself next to him and hushed the younger ones so as not to interrupt his reading. She did the same on the return trip.

As Emma admired JW, JW smiled kindly on his little sister as well. It helps they shared the same coloring, the same shaped face, mouth, nose and brow. They looked more alike than any other two of the children. Both were strong and always healthy. Emma's favoritism did not go unappreciated by her older brother. He, in turn, would lend a hand in her labors whenever he was about, if she had something to carry or lift, like a child or a crock of milk. Although they rarely spoke at length to each other, they each were able to enjoy the mutual goodwill.

The Christmas after Libby was married, Grandma and Grandpa Lambert came from Philadelphia for a three-week visit. It was a big deal because Grandma Betsy did not like riding in trains. She admitted this trip was not so bad as the one they took shortly after the War. Ever one to emphasize the importance of the written word, Betsy was writing her memoirs to preserve the story of life on Lost Mountain. Emma took her sentiments to heart and began a journal of her own life in Hill Grove. She would quiet herself in a corner of the kitchen or upstairs in the bedroom she shared with her little sister and write down her thoughts.

Savina brought Levi over to the parlor in his wheelchair for an hour or so in the morning and sometimes again in the afternoon. George had hired a maid's helper for the kitchen so Anna could spend her time with the family. But even with out-of-state company the Fursts took their meals in their own home, the little house in the side yard by the old apple orchard. Levi had not said a word in over a year. The Saturday after Christmas, Anna hosted a festive holiday Open House for neighbors, the Denlingers, the Glunts, the Bickels, the Snells, the Kenards, the Everetts and the Stockdales and friends from church, the Fishers, the Greens and the Parents, but no Eva who was staying with chums at the Golden Lamb Inn near Lebanon north of Cincinnati. Grandma Betsy's hair was still brown. She combed it back from her face and caught it in a bentwood barrette, an object which fascinated

Christian Harry. She wore garnet earrings on the day of the Open House which livened the lights in her brown eyes. When she walked, she held on to Mike who at ninety was still strong and lean. Libby, who a few short weeks ago was as integral to the family farmhouse as anyone, now visited from her new home in town, with her husband. The sixteen-year-old wife could still hide the pregnancy so it was not generally known. On the occasions they were together, the East Coast relatives had a good chance to look over this young man. Even though Libby's smiling, well-dressed husband talked mostly to George, Betsy took a good look and announced she liked Dan Cook. On the other hand, as soon as she could, Savina cornered Anna in the kitchen to say her peace about the changes in the Lambert family. She spoke pointedly, "Libby has made her bed, now she must lie in it." Anna understood her mother's good intentions and knew her mother knew the whole story that Libby was going to have a baby, even though they had never talked about it. She shot her mother a look. In her mind she went back to the first time she met this woman, eighteen years ago. She had been a young bride, recently immigrated to Ohio and newly pregnant like her own daughter is now. Savina had known it then without being told. Who could overestimate this woman? Anna sighed to herself. In acquiescence she said, "I know, Mother; I know."

5

1876

The surge of voices nearly lifted Anna out of her seat among the thousands of attendees at the Opening Ceremony of the International Exhibition of Arts, Manufacturing and Products of Soil and Mine in the City of Philadelphia, 1876. For the second time in her life – both here in her hometown – she felt surrounded by invisible, oversized angels. Today the sound of their feathery wings was absorbed by the joined vocal efforts of the one thousand choral members standing on the wooden rafters, dressed alike in shining long robes. The combined orchestras of strings, drums, trumpets and bugles gave lift to the resounding sentiment of the hymn. There were church bells and factory whistles sounding across the city on this bright, clear May afternoon and ringing in steely determination. The audience rose to its feet as one. The giant red, white and blue Union flag was hoisted to the sky while the yelling crowd swelled their roar and threw hundreds of hats in the air. Old Glory continued its billowing above the crowd like it was dispensing a blessing. The one hundred-gun salute shook their bones, the seats and the ground. Earlier the words of John Greenleaf Whittier's *Centennial Hymn* brought tears to all eyes.

Now Anna's two-year-old baby was crying; eight-year-old Benjamin, whistling with his fingers in his mouth had saliva running down to his wrist; four-year-old Sam clung to Mama's knees and was invisible in the copious material of her skirt. Emma thrust a handkerchief into her mother's hand; Anna had not felt the tears streaming down her face. This visit was an emotional time for reasons beyond the Centennial Exposition. It had occurred to her as she prepared for this trip she was returning to the place where she had grown up but she had put it out of her mind. In this city lived the family who had fostered her including an old black woman who had looked after her like a mother. Once in Ohio, Anna had written only to Annie, but her old friend did not read or write and never replied. Once the Rebellion began so many years ago Anna had stopped trying.

"God Bless America!" She was yelling with the crowd. Those close around her, many of them relatives, were yelling as well. "God Bless America!" She encouraged her children to join in.

President Ulysses S. Grant kept the chant echoing through the crowd so it bounced off the walls of the newly erected Machinery Hall and traveled over to the Agricultural Building and the Art Gallery. This grand opening of the long-planned Exposition on the one hundredth anniversary of the Declaration of Independence was intended to be an affirmation of national unity. It had opened with President and Mrs. Grant graciously taking the podium as the combined military bands played *Hail to the Chief.* All members of Congress, the Supreme Court and the Cabinet, along with the crowd of 150,000 spectators, were standing to greet them. The Declaration of Independence was read by Richard Henry Lee from the original manuscript. The nightmare of the War Between the States was now passing into memory; the rivalry was over. "God Bless the United States of America!" Grant pounded the podium. He waited for the echoes to die out and for those on the far reaches of the crowd to complete their cheers. Then the President and former General of the Union Forces raised his voice to an extraordinary level and repeated his most-quoted phrase. He emphasized each syllable so no soul present would miss his meaning, "Let – us – have – peace!"

There were two hundred fifty individual pavilions covering two acres of Fairmount Park to celebrate the achievements which exemplified America around the world. Individual American initiative had produced tools and machines which created a new world. The progress of the last dozen years announced America as an industrial world power. Emphasis at the Fair was on technology and America's many engineering marvels. In defiance of the devastating economic downturn of the last three years, America was united and moving forward. And so it was declared and affirmed on this Centennial anniversary of America's birth. Anna's hands were red and beginning to swell from the clapping she had done. She wiped Levi Calvin's nose. He was the family's tenth and last baby. When he was first born, George had referred to him only as "baby" and so he became "Babe". Musicians of all stripes were belting out Richard Wagner's marching song, *The Centennial March* for the second time this day. The crowd was beginning to disperse, streaming to the various buildings of the Exhibition, many following President Grant and the group of dignitaries to Machinery Hall where they would start the immense Corliss steam engine. Anna heard the 1400 horse-powered machine start up, and from where she stood outside the building, the crowd "ahh-ed" and then cheered as the electric lights fueled by the loud engine blazed before their eyes. Thomas Edison seemed to have his influence everywhere.

The Pennsylvania cousins were gathering their things. George was talking with Al and JW, each pointing to buildings and pathways and referring to the programs in their hands. Emma and Mollie were gathering their four brothers, each of the six well versed in these symbiotic roles. Libby and her small family bade them all farewell, as they would make their own way around the exhibits. Anna looked about their seats to collect any belongings they may have forgotten. The shots of the large cannons still reverberated in her chest. Libby, Dan and their son had traveled with the large Lambert family on the overnight train across Ohio and Pennsylvania in a fancy new Pullman car on the Penn Central Railroad. They checked into a grand hotel that had a cavernous lobby filled with the haze of cigar smoke, a two-story fountain, sweeping palms, Persian rugs and furniture gilded with cherubs and roses. This hotel was in close proximity to Grandpa Lambert, now ninety-four. He had decided to "retire to Ohio" after the recent death of his wife Betsy and would return with the family to Hill Grove. Although saddened by his mother's death, it struck George as ironic his father would be joining them so soon after the death of old silent Levi, who had been like a grandfather to the Hill Grove children. "Lose one; gain one," he whispered with a private smile to his wife.

The children were chomping at the bit to see the sights. The young ones wanted to see petrified wood, meteorites, marble and crystal, the big animals, elk, walrus, all kinds of bears and the birds and the unusual display of fresh fish frozen in ice and viewed through the transparent sides of a special refrigerator. They pointed to the giant torch seen above the crowd and were promised a trip to the metal hand of the magnanimous French gift, the Statue of Liberty, which was being assembled behind schedule in Paris. The children later stood under the knuckle and looked up at the base of the balcony encircling the flaming torch thirty feet above them. Visitors had climbed interior stairs and were now waving handkerchiefs from the viewing platform of the torch to their loved ones on the ground below. "The real statue must be huge, Mama," Emma's eyes grew enormous with aston-ishment.

This was the first time George and Anna had been in Philadel-phia since they were married twenty-one years ago, but any romantic sentiments were overshadowed by many factors: the immediate demands of traveling with their ten children, includ-ing a son-in-law and three year-old grandson; the emotional reunion with George's two living brothers and their families; missing Harry; the sadness of visiting Grandma Betsy's grave; the excitement of the Exhibition, with its speeches and chorus, sights and crowds and their specific personal interests in the inventions, for the Lambert men of Hill Grove were a curious, tinkering lot who now held patented inventions of their own, one of which was featured here at the Exposition.

Sixteen-year-old JW had two projects for which his father had sought legal protection in binding patents. The first was a combined hay rake and loader and the other was a clever, little corn-planter. Some farmers swore the one-handed machine, which miraculously dispensed the preferred number of seeds with each thrust in the ground, was revolutionizing corn growing. George anticipated a market for both of the useful, innovative machines and dedicated factory space to their production. Within a short time they were selling quite nicely in central Ohio and Indiana. With the patent protection secured for the rake, he could safely go ahead and offer them to a wider market. To add to the Lambert travel excitement, notification the corn-planter was granted a patent arrived the day before they left on the train.

The Ohioans certainly felt they were part of the show here in Philadelphia. The Lambert hay-loader was on display in the Agricultural Building which is where they would go first to view their contribution to America's great advances. That patent had been granted in January. Al and his father were prepared to sign up sales representatives for they believed their machine could rake and load hay better than any other machine on the market. Once it was shown in this expansive venue, they expected swift sales and were already producing dozens of machines each week back in the plant in Union City. Al had designed a pamphlet, gotten it printed and had arranged for a stack to stand beside the display. The men led the family across the grounds to Agricultural Hall to check on the interest they confidently knew they would attract in this vast sea of people.

JW had fooled around with ideas for the two-wheeled hay-loader for a couple of months before he came up with the clever adaptation to the farm's hay-rake. His machine, made largely of wood, stood up the stalks of hay after it cut them with sharp spring-wire teeth. Hinged wooden arms compressed the stalks together into a compact bundle at the same time the moving belt guided and lifted the batch up to where it was released into a horse-drawn wagon. He had carefully sketched two views of his machine with a pencil and paper and numbered each of the parts. When he showed the plans to his father, George immediately recognized the implications of the clever, simple additions and new combinations JW had devised. Together he and his father had fashioned the first prototype in the spacious tool shop on the farm near the railroad tracks. Their new hay rake and loader was fueled by its own propulsion. As the carrier frame was pulled through the field hooked to a horse-drawn wagon, gears and pulleys kept the teeth, arms and belt in motion. The cutting apparatus was retractable from the ground for easy transport from place to place. Combining the cutting, gathering and lifting saved many man-hours of work. Last fall, George hired a lawyer and filled out the application for the patent while JW concentrated on perfecting the one-handed corn-planter. By spring, JW was satisfied he had found what he was looking for. As their Philadelphia plans were coming together, the lawyer sent off the second Lambert application. It took only six weeks to be confirmed.

George had made the decision for his family as to which part of the six-month long Exposition they would attend. He had written away for tickets for the Opening on a lark eighteen months before it happened. He contacted Alfred Goshorn, whom he had met several times back in Urbana and who now was vice-president of the committee planning the entire event. George was delighted to receive the thirty or so tickets admitting them and their cousins from Urbana, Philadelphia and Harrisburg to the seating section not too far back from the front of the staged platform with the main podium. By deciding to attend the Opening Celebrations they would miss later events, for the entire summer and fall had a full schedule. There had been a lot to choose from, contests pitting various farm machines, the special Ohio celebration and parade, the big military parade on the Fourth of July, but George did not regret how things had worked out. He was proud to put his children in the presence of the President of the United States and the entire national government. Critical as George could be of individual political leaders, he was grateful for their service, for while they were tending to national decisions he was free to earn as much money as he could, in a way that most interested him. It had not occurred to George to ask his wife if she wanted to look up any members of the old household with whom she had lived as a child in Philadelphia, and she did not mention it to him.

As the long line of family members walked by a string of food booths, George offered to buy ribbon candy for them all. Soon a score or more of Lamberts lapping colorful strips of curly candy entered Agricultural Hall and went straight toward their own Ohio machine. George joked it should have a pedestal and spotlight, but it looked impressive enough. They spent the afternoon looking at reapers, mowers, other rakes, at plows, drills, wagons, pumps, lifts, hammers and other seeders. The Pennsylvania Lamberts moved on but even the small Ohio children took an interest in the farm equipment and wandered from object to object, absorbed in seeing the special display of land-working objects.

The George Lamberts, the Dan Cooks and Grandpa Mike when he was not asleep, talked on the train ride home about what they had seen and done in Philadelphia. They looked over the small gifts they had collected as souvenirs and retold the highlights of the Exposition. The children listened as their parents discussed their concern for their relatives, especially Lizzie. George gathered his six younger children close to him, as the older ones also listened and told the story of the fire on Lost Mountain and the tragic deaths of their tiny two cousins.

"That's a horrible story," empathetic Emma resounded.

"Yes, dear, it is. It started a chain of events which nearly killed Aunt Lizzie so it was especially good to see her looking well," Mama said. "She may be a bit over-involved with veterans' affairs, but she did not touch a drop of alcohol." Lizzie had been her same aloof self but had become talkative when the subject of politics came up. She had no patience for hearing the stories of corruption in the Republican Old Guard Grant administration. She was adamant about veterans' rights and she directed the men in her family to "vote the way they shot" even though none were former soldiers; her missing son Harry was the only family member who had taken part. Anyway, the Lambert men had been Republicans from the beginning of the Rebellion and were now Stalwarts of Abe Lincoln's party.

George explained to his children, "Aunt Lizzie fell in with an old friend who bit her back something fierce. Alcohol. She fell pretty hard into her cups." The children were silent. They had read about the evils of alcohol in their McGuffey readers and seen traces of the problem with a neighboring family back in Urbana. "So, we're glad for her and for her family her problems seem to be in the past. Life isn't easy and it doesn't always go the way you want it. The important thing is to keep trying, pull yourself back if need be, and keep trying." George patted Mollie and she smiled up at him from under his arm. George spoke of the street urchins whom his children saw on the streets of Philadelphia, the likes of which did not exist in their rural setting, for the penniless could at least grow their own food on the vast stretches of rich farmland. These were children who had to beg for food to survive. On more than one occasion the well-dressed Lamberts found a small, dirty hand tugging at a sleeve and gazed into a mud-covered face with pleading, sad eyes on a frail little body dressed only in rags. George had pulled his children away from the beggars, and Anna discreetly slipped a coin into each grubby hand. Their father turned these poor creatures into an object lesson and posed a challenging question: "The Good Lord rewards those who help themselves. If you never want to end up a beggar, you must work hard to take care of yourself. If something were to happen, and you were left to support yourself now, what would you do?"

"Farm!" "Be a seamstress." The naive, well-cared for children answered with courage.

Soon after returning to Hill Grove, the family's canine companion took himself down the creek and did not return. In order to locate the missing dog, George assigned territory for each family member to scour. In this systematized way, they would find their beloved elderly pet. JW headed out the front door and down the driveway under a canopy of leaves. As his eyes scanned the edges of the yard, he thought he caught a glimpse of movement through the lilac bushes down toward the creek, so he headed in that direction. As he approached he saw no repetition of the promising effect; it must have been light between the flickering foliage. He looked down toward his feet. He was standing in a green sea of clover, some grown to the size of a big buckeye. And yes, he saw an exception to the rule of three, reached down, and picked a four-leaf specimen. He continued scanning the curved faces of the clovers, looking for the exception to the triangular configuration of the pleasantly rounded little leaves. He had discovered a patch and picked fourteen four-leafed clovers all together. JW temporarily forgot his anxiety about Rex being lost, but he heard sounds from the backyard indicating the mystery was solved and the news was not good. He ran through the house to put his clovers in a cup of water before running out the back door to where his family had gathered. George told him the news Rex's body had been discovered under a protruding rock. Grandma Furst explained to the children this is what animals do when they know they are going to die. The heady experience with the clovers softened Rex's death for JW. George said he was not sure he could compare dogs to clovers, but if he did, then he could apply that old family motto to Rex's death and JW's find: lose one; gain one.

The Lamberts planned to join their neighbors and folks from all of Darke County in Greenville for the gala Centennial Fourth of July celebration. On the way, George cautioned his children, "No one is to show any smugness over the celebration here. It may not be as grand as what we experienced in Philadelphia, but we are all to have fun and not show off. Do you hear me?" Strong and little voices responded, "Yes, Papa."

But Papa was wrong, for the Town of Greenville had transformed itself for the occasion. The granite courthouse was decorated with red, white and blue banners and a large wooden stage had been erected over its steps. After parading down the main street now called Lincoln Highway, bands played on the platform and speeches were made throughout the day. The music was followed by a reading of the Declaration of Independence and the Constitution, including the Bill of Rights, by Miss Hawk in her school teacher voice, accompanied by an alternating cannon salute. "Boom!" the sound came from one side; then, "Boom!" it came from the other. People were dressed in their finest and were in such festive moods the Lamberts had no time to compare their experience in Philadelphia to the delights they found in Greenville.

Throughout the warm summer months, a favorite outside game of the four younger brothers was Cowboys and Indians. Whooping and yelling they rode sticks for horses, shot arrows from makeshift bows and brandished tomahawks made from flat rocks tied to old wooden handles JW found for them in the implement shed. Their yelling was at times high-pitched and ghostlike like the Rebels of the late war. They ran around the feed room shed and hog pens and rattled the hogs and the pigs. Anna smiled from the window thinking Rex was lucky not to be subject to their harassment. There were real Indian wars going on in the broad open spaces of the West. This summer there was a huge tragedy on the Little Big Horn River which JW read about and told his younger brothers. Lieutenant Colonel George Custer was from Ohio and he died that summer, along with two-hundred twenty-five of his men, killed by Indians who had lived on the land. By the end of the summer the Lambert boys' fantasy play focused on the lawmen and outlaws out West. JW used his tin snips to cut out stars from the bottom circle of leftover tin cans, and the youngsters pinned these to their jackets to designate themselves authentic deputies of Wyatt Earp or Bat Masterson. For a week they were entranced in a Texas fantasy and insisted to others in the family that they be addressed as Rangers. "Ranger, have you brushed your teeth?" George went along with their wishes.

George was home early one afternoon for a change. He and Anna stood in the kitchen doorway and watched their five youngest children play in the yard. George was struck by a sense of inexplicable familiarity with their movements. They never actually hurt one another as they jumped over and rolled on top of each other while giggling and shouting in their soft, immature voices or hid at barn corners laying in wait to pounce in play attack. "They look like big kittens the way they move around each other," Anna said and her words added to the irrational mood of knowingness. He felt he was in another dimension. The sun was low in the late afternoon sky and had gone behind a cloud. Even the yard took on a strange aura, like it was the setting of an experience he had had from a long time ago. JW entered the yard and greeted his parents as they gazed out from the kitchen door into the yard. George was half remembering a dream he had had a long time ago of a ride and the excited face of JW beaming pride in ownership of something new and promising. George knew his son well enough not to underestimate his cleverness, so he did not scoff at himself for surmising JW would make another significant contribution to the family enterprise, bigger than the corn planter whose run could not last forever. Already there were rumors of new planting machines. Anna noticed the dusk as it stole around the yard while George enjoyed his reverie. She called out into the yard, "Calling all Rangers. Giddy on up to the house. It's time for supper now." George willed himself to put his thoughts somewhere else, and the feelings submerged into the dark waters of his deeper mind.

While the boys were out in the yard, the girls were more likely to spend their sparse free time thumbing through the Montgomery Ward catalog and making lists of things to buy, tools for the kitchen, petticoats and stockings or muffs to keep their hands warm. Often they curled up near Anna while she read *Mary Had a Little Lamb* and other poems by Henry Wadsworth Longfellow. When the entire family joined in, they set up memory contests in which each child chose a passage then stood to perform their lines in front of the others.

Early on a September day George asked JW to accompany him on a trip to Greenville. He had business in town, which was not unusual, but it was rare to make his rounds without Al. Al was in Chicago to collect a shipment of water pumps bound for Union City where they will be installed on fire wagons. JW did not often have the exclusive company of his father, so he leaped at the chance for the notable time of one-on-one conversation. George lit a cigar as JW skitched to the horse and maneuvered the carriage down the slight incline of the canopied driveway. Dressed in clean work clothes over expensive boots and sporting a perfectly manicured haircut, beard and mustache all tempered with white, JW's fifty-year-old father was in a talkative mood. Before they turned off the path by the creek, he was talking about the role of technology in the late War for the Union. "New technology is always the ruler of the future. You read about the gun turret on the *Moniter*." He turned to his son who nodded. "The more you study history, the more examples you collect, from the catapult to the submarine." It did not occur to JW his father's choice of topic was deliberate to encourage his son's inventive habits. To JW this sounded like an observation of the obvious order of things. JW simultaneously listened to his father and mused about the large, spidery-looking steel apparatus he had seen which had been used recently to clear this main road of small tree stumps. Two giant prongs pulled by mules, with additional pulling power provided by a steam boiler engine, had grabbed each protruding wooden neck and extracted the tentacles of its roots from right out of the ground. "Technology won the war for the North," George continued. "It was our ability to build machines – guns, boats, whatever – that enabled us to overcome their forces. They were fighting for a way of life that was over, and we were moving toward the future. The impulse of progress was on our side. The triumph of technology continues with the railroads. Pretty soon we'll have quick means to ship our products all over the country. The sky's the limit. You build a better machine and you're going to sell better than the next guy. Did I tell you I want to open up another wing on the factory? I asked Al to size up the price of bricks over in Chicago so I can get construction started this winter. I've put some boys on it already."

As JW listened, he noticed nature's show on either side of the road, the silvery, shimmering leaves of the ash trees as the wind of the carriage passed, the dashing lines of color from a male cardinal streaking through the branches, the smell of the dirt and dung coming up from the street on this hot day. He knew a lot about the business in Union City, how his father adopted methods he gathered from established businessmen and combined them with ideas he learned from his brothers, to put together a plan for production which was bringing the family undeniable wealth, not on the scale of the Vanderbilts or Rockefellers, but in their county a respectable level. "I'm going to buy more land in Tennessee. We'll need wood for years to come. My boys told me about a package of poplar acres I think I'll grab." JW enjoyed the confidence his father had in him and knew his father recognized his contributions. His suggestions have been integrated into George's farm practices ever since JW was big enough to think them up. Incorporating his son's contributions came naturally to George, who had experienced the same encouraging attitude from his father on Lost Mountain. Grandpa Mike said, *Every one lends a hand; everyone makes a contribution.* Grandma Betsy used to say, *We each need to express the talents God gave us or else it is a sin.*

His father asked, "Were you old enough to remember the horse races back in Clark County?" JW recalled the multitude of beautiful sleek, shining horses whose necks and tails were decorated with colorful ribbons, and the large jovial crowds in which the ladies carried parasols even though it was sunny on the large farm his grandmother's husband ran, but he let his father tell the story anyway. "Levi would invite all his neighbors and friends, then throw in a politician or two and invite the general public. He always drew a big crowd. They dressed up and showed off for each other just the way the animals did. He would race his most attractive horses. What a show! Young Levi is doing the same thing now in Kentucky. He built a permanent race track and holds regular competitions. I hear he's got customers waiting years for an animal. That's the kind of business to run." JW was silent. The best conversations with his father were when he did not interrupt. George continued, "So, I'm thinking of setting up a corn planting competition. We put out the challenge we can plant a row of corn in less time than anybody else and offer $10.00 to anyone who can beat us. We'll get Davis over in Chicago to write it up in the papers. That's the kind of thing the nationals pick up. Every paper in the country will carry the story. And then," he looked over at his son with a charming grin, "we make a lot of money selling our corn planter." JW smiled back. He would like to see a corn planting competition.

After a while, George used his cigar to point over a field of soy beans. "I bought that tract of land on the other side of Snell's place and put your name on it." Sixteen-year-old JW was taken by surprise and shot his father a look. "Now, don't go jumping to conclusions." George continued, "I did the same thing for your brother and sister Lib. Land is a good investment in any case, but in the worst case, I want you taken care of. I wanted Lib to have something of her own to hold up to Cook if she needs to, and you boys will be expecting to get out on your own eventually. If needs be, I know I can count on you to take care of Emma and the younger ones. We can stop by on the way back if you like." JW felt awkward. As obvious as his father's prosperity was, he was not used to generous gestures.

"Thank you," he managed to say and to put on a smile. His father added, "Now, don't think I'm trying to get rid of you. It's an investment. Your mother would be very upset if you moved out.

You don't have to jump the gun like your older sister." JW stole a glance at his father for he had heard the farm hands who told the tales of Libby's secret meetings with her now husband and so he understood what had never been acknowledged in the family. This comment, JW saw from his father's face, did not mean what it sounded like; his father remained in denial.

Both men rode along in silence. The opening in the conversation to speak of JW's personal future made JW feel self-conscious while Papa got thoughtful. Eventually, George stepped into the silence, "Someday you'll fall in love, John William. Take a look at your mother when you do. If your girl measures up to your mother, then marry her. Your mother is a fine woman and a wonderful wife. Looks like she's done alright as a mother too." He smiled at his son and put the cigar out on the bottom of his boot, then tucked the remaining butt into his pocket. The two Lambert men took a leisurely pace to travel the ten miles to Greenville. The way was familiar like family; trees along the way were like neighbors, their rustling like gossip over the fence. On occasion they glimpsed a human neighbor from their perch on the carriage seat and waved a friendly hello. As they rolled past the Redmond place, their shaggy mongrel shepherd dog bounded out to greet them and ran along side for a quarter of a mile or so. They passed a wagon overburdened with bales of hay and they saw Judge Kains hurrying by riding a fine English bay. George regarded his second son; he knew still waters ran deep. The boy had demonstrated time and again his powers of observation and his clever, practical ideas about what he saw. He was a hard worker, able to manage his younger siblings and the hired men who now did all of the field farming. Although he spent the majority of his working time with Al, George was proud of this handsome, reticent, ruddy-faced youth.

"I have a bit of a surprise for you," George said invitingly. "I know you love engines and I heard about one heck of an unusual contraption last time I was up this way. We'll have time today to take a look."

This inspired JW, so he spoke up. "What's so special about it?" His curiosity was paramount now. He would be interested in *any* engine.

George knew he had caught the cat, so he milked the situation. He could not resist teasing this serious boy. "There's no boiler," was all he said.

JW's face flushed with energy. George waited him out. Reddened now, JW asked his father and thereby doubled the number of words he had spoken in the first eight miles of their journey. "No boiler?" George nodded nonchalantly as he cleaned one fingernail with another. "How big is it?" JW was getting down right conversational.

"Not nearly so big as our steam engine." George replied and chortled to himself. JW resisted the urge to ask more questions, but Papa could tell his mind was sailing around. Finally George gave up his withholding and offered all he knew. "One of the boys in the lumberyard was telling me last week about seeing an engine with no boiler up near Versailles. It's powered by gasoline. The fellow at the tannery uses it to run the fans in the drying rooms. I thought you'd be interested, so I asked him to take us up there." The conversation trailed off as driver and rider were distracted by the quickly concentrating landmarks as they approached Greenville. After George had completed his business and abbreviated social calls, the father and son headed north of town to Parent Lumber where Jim Brown strolled out to greet them. Jim informed them of the fire the night before, at the very tannery in which George had expressed an interest. With a shrug he said, "We'll go anyway."

Once at the tannery they viewed the devastation of the fire. It was a common liability which hung over every citizen and businessman. The Lambert men offered their condolences to the tanner and asked if they could poke around. The ashes were still warm so the tanner offered old metal railroad shovels, and the three men set upon the task of digging out the intact but ruined engine which they had located without too much trouble. Once they got to it, they wrapped a thick chain around it and pulled it out of the ashes, then dowsed it down to clean and cool it. George handed his son a clanking burlap bag then pulled out his half-smoked cigar and walked off with the tanner. The tanner invited JW to do what he would to the engine.

What a moment! Engines fascinated this young man with sensitive fingers, and truth be told, they occupied his mind a lot of the time. The manufacture of "go" held infinite puzzles. He often lay in bed at night trying to calculate the result of different combinations of functions, the effect of altering this step or a substitution of that, and thinking up an entirely new construction for one of the steps. Here before him was the real thing, not a steam or battery device which he had seen before. JW studied the machine from all angles before he dissembled it. With each deconstruction the secrets of the foreign-made engine were revealed. It was a slide valve coal gasoline engine and had been made in France. JW had read about these gasoline engines in *Scientific American* and guessed it was an authentic Otto design. The four cycle principal caught JW's attention. If only he had seen it run! As he was tinkering, the tanner came over to chat. His tongue had a foreign accent JW assumed to be French due to the proximity of Versailles, Ohio where the language is still common. And it would fit with the results of his investigation which showed the engine to be manufactured by a French company. The tanner proved willing to talk, so the young man asked questions about its operation. It had created a large amount of power, yet the whole thing was so much smaller than a steam engine of similar strength. JW asked if the engine had set the fire which destroyed the extensive building. The tanner said he could not be sure, but he suspected a spark from the fires which warmed the vats of water where the hides soaked ignited straw on the ground nearby. JW was relieved his little mechanical friend would not be held responsible for the blaze of the night before. George walked over to the yard full of engine pieces. The sun was low in the sky, so with handshakes all around, the two Lambert men resumed their positions on George's two-wheeled luxury carriage. JW turned it around and they cantered toward Hill Grove.

6

The Young Inventor Comes of Age

Savina looked through her lace curtains to watch fifteen-year-old Emma cross the yard. Like clockwork the young teenager brought a pot or a platter each day in the late afternoon, accompanied by her Grandfather Mike who each day carried a small basket of bread and sweets. And every day Grandma Furst set two places on the kitchen table by the window overlooking the old apple orchard. Today she had made lemonade. Each day Emma only stayed long enough to hear a short story either of Clark County or Lost Mountain before she headed back to the kitchen of the main house. Later she would summarize the story in her journal. The old folks took one meal a day together, away from the buzz of the children in the big house next door. "You're not shutting us out," the strong-minded Savina had in fact brightened at Anna's suggestion food could be sent over to the small neighboring house once a day. "It's a fine solution to the situation at hand. I will stay in my own home for supper. It wears me out to eat with you all." Grandpa Mike had volunteered immediately to join his fellow senior for a quiet meal at the end of the day. In the two years he had been on the farm, the ninety-six-year-old had acclimated to Ohio with ease. His self-appointed job was to tend the bees and before long the hives were flourishing, producing honey which was sweet and clear. Every day the retired farmer spent hours singing and talking to his swarming friends. He had fastened a hammock between two trees like the Indians did. He could fall asleep in a minute at any time. He was likely to nap at Savina's table but Grandma Furst did not take offense. She was happy to sit quietly finishing her meal and enjoy the view out the window.

On one such slow trip through the yard with her grandfather, Emma's eye caught a flicker of flames through the open half door of the tool shed which stood beyond the orchard. She practically threw the large platter of meatcakes and vegetables on the ground before she yelled at the top of her lungs, "FIRE!" Grandpa Mike's gaze followed her wild gesturing where he saw a beautiful sky around the usual sight of the red and white shed. Emma was back at the house and pointing instructions to Mollie through the open back door to alert their mother. Men were emerging from the far barns in response to her original cry. Mike could see the men in their overalls and work shirts point to the shed as Emma was running toward them, herself pointing to the shed. One man ran the other way to ring the bell by the fields to bring all hands to the fore while some pulled the fire pumper out of the livery and ran the hose to the well. Still others were firing up the steam-engine pump. The flames heating the boiler took their own time to bring steam and while the engine lulled, men formed a bucket brigade around Emma. JW was the first man in from the fields and ran straight for the wooden building brimming with smoke. Before anyone would stop him, and Emma tried, he disappeared behind the walls where flames could be seen through the cracks in the wallboards. He re-emerged within seconds, dragging out the kerosene barrel. A nearby man recognized what he was doing and leaped to help in the dangerous task of pulling the highly explosive fuel away from the fast growing fire. Streams of water were beginning to reach the flames through the door JW had left open. Smoke rose in opening rolls above their heads and stained the blue sky.

In minutes the flames were extinguished yet the shed continued to receive a soaking. Outside, JW was covered with black soot. Tears were streaming down Emma's face as she held fast to his arm, to hold him back and to hold herself in physical connection for her own sake as well. She spoke without hysteria as the flow from her eyes came of their own accord. She used her apron to wipe at JW's face, but he had no use for that. He ignored her calm tones and shouted directions to the men still controlling the fight against the smoldering fire. He broke away from her and re-entered the shed while a couple of men accompanying him pulled the hose inside with them. The smoke was still thick, although spaces of clear air showed through. Emma now stood with Mike and Savina. "Your brother reacted quickly," Mike observed. For his part, he had picked up the platter of meatcakes and taken it in to Savina's kitchen along with his basket of baked goods. "We would have seen a real show if that barrel had ignited."

Emma shuddered. She would not say out loud, "*and if it had blown up my brother would be dead now,*" but with crossed brows she looked from Savina to Mike. Both deeply lined faces were relaxed and they spoke proudly of JW. "Not a major catastrophe," Mike was saying. "Looks like it's all under control now."

Later that night, scrubbed and drained now of adrenaline, JW did not feel well. After hardly touching his supper he asked his mother to be excused from the table and he went up to bed. Again, Emma crossed her brows in concern for JW's welfare while others were oblivious to what to her was obvious. Although not present for the near tragedy, George praised the superb performance of Al's fire pumper apparatus manufactured two miles down the road at the Union City Carriage Manufacturing Company. Al and George were full of self-congratulations and the rest understood that although serious, the fire had caused little actual damage. Anna had murmured repeated reassurances to the children, but the entire family knew the seriousness of any fire. Emma's role of discovering the fire and sounding the alarm, her poise in the emergency, and efficiency in collecting help, were all lost to her father.

The next day JW felt too tired to get out of bed. He had a deep cough which he stifled by holding his breath. Emma knew this was a result of his daring acts during the fire. She kept silent as no one else mentioned the connection, except Grandfather Mike who said to her, "Being a hero is not always so smart." Emma did not want to point out anything which could get JW in trouble, so she kept her thoughts to herself. She checked in on him throughout the day and found him sleeping most of the time. His recovery was slow, and he stayed in bed, asleep.

There was little time to wonder about JW's condition, as shortly before the small fire, Al and Eva Parent had, at long last, confided their plans to be married. Her parents began orchestrating a lavish garden party at their home in late April to announce the engagement. This was a very good reason to showcase Al as the hero of averted catastrophes and unfortunately, to suspect that JW's recovery was impeded by jealousy or a fear of loss of some kind. Because JW showed no visible bruises or scars, his mother suspected he was malingering. So, she had a talk with him about his duty to put mind over matter. She told him not to make a show of the coughing and to resolve to be productive and contributing and not take advantage of other members of the family. JW, who had never been a conniver, was speechless and had no strength to summon his own defense. She interpreted his passivity as a dismissal of her good intentions. The poor mother was reluctant to imagine another child in mortal danger. Losing little Savina Ellen played on her mind and that allowed the misunderstanding with her second-born son.

After Anna's talk with him, JW rallied to get out of bed every day, dress and put on the appearance of going to work. He forced a robust demeanor around his family but fell into bed each night deeply exhausted. He stole sleep in the hayloft during the day where he was used to stealing time to read. The farmhands covered for him, for in fact they knew he was not himself. Many had witnessed his impulsive dive into the smoky shed and had stories of other occasions where smoke had done severe damage to someone's health. Their conventional observations told them if he survived the first hour, he would get better in time. He did not burn his lungs, only damaged them with the particles of debris in the smoke. Christian and Benjamin, now full-fledged field hands, were easily diverted from the family subplot, so they did not betray JW's schedule. The expanding plans for Al and Eva's party was the main subject of most conversations in the house. A seamstress had moved in and was working full time making two new party outfits for each family member, one for the large formal party in the afternoon and another for after the party when later that evening just the families would dine.

Emma was worried sick about her brother and ran her thoughts in circles over her dilemma: should she approach her mother about medical care for JW and risk causing a worse and unnecessary situation, or do nothing but go along with the assumption he was on the mend and all would be alright. Finally, she told her two grandparents about JW's charade, his deep cough and lack of energy. Savina rose to the challenge. She made poultices and teas to give to JW and wrote out a list of instructions including number one, her insistence he eat more green vegetables. Emma was the courier. He received them silently but she could see he used them.

The day of the engagement party was sunny and unusually hot for April in Ohio. The Parent garden was manicured so no blade of grass stuck out by itself. Eva looked lovely in a pale yellow organdy dress with blue, pink and yellow embroidered flowers dotting the skirt; the bodice was ribboned with soft satin strands of the same three colors. She wore tiny flowers in her shiny brown hair. She looked so grown-up but then again she was twenty-three. Al turned twenty just last month. He was a proud young man, indeed a peacock, strutting and posturing himself at her side. Although Al would deny it, Mr. Parent had hired an investigator to dig up dirt on this newly successful family who had lived in Darke County not yet a decade. Eva's father apparently had received a good report, for here was the happy couple now, enjoying the punch and chatting to two of Eva's college friends. For most of the soiree the handsome young couple had stood side by side with their parents and received each one of their guests.

JW stayed in the background. He got dizzy when he stood for any length of time, but his behavior drew no attention, for it was his older brother's day. He was happy for Al, tired of being tired, and willing to be optimistic both about the upcoming marriage and the state of his health. But the day after the party he suffered a relapse. His condition could no longer be kept from his parents and Emma sought her mother with alarm and determination. Anna was immediately concerned and summoned a doctor from Greenville who placed JW on his medications. Grandma Furst harrumphed to Emma about it but Emma was relieved with what she had done in turning the responsibility of his care over to their mother. JW, however, did not respond to the treatment. When the Greenville doctor had called it a possible condition of consumption, George remembered how his mother used to cough and wondered if it were an inherited condition. Now that both parents were alarmed, a series of doctors were called in. The last was a peculiar fellow with a full white beard and a threadbare jacket which at one time had been top quality. He was Dr. Kelley from Dallas, a small town north of Greenville. George was at first adamant no Irish Catholic doctor tend his son, but Anna peshawed that and then learned Dr. Kelley's name was French Protestant, his family one of the original settlers of Versailles.

Dr. Kelley was an unusual man with thick unruly hair and intelligent eyes. He entered the well-ordered Lambert household, spent some time with JW and then sat in the parlor with Mama, as willing to report about evacuations of Indian artifacts as about his patient upstairs. "Do you have any Elderberry wine, Mrs. Lambert?" Anna replied in the affirmative and rang the little bell to summon the girl in the kitchen. "No, no, you misunderstand. I want a glass set beside JW's washbowl each morning, for he is to gargle with it." Dr. Kelley's methods were old-fashioned and reminded Anna of Savina's suggestions. She preferred modern science but recognized his seemingly social visits brought a noticeable change in her son. JW found the man interesting and unlike anyone he had ever met. He was not an industrialist or a manufacturer, not essentially a businessman. He had been a farmer, but loved the science of it more than the profit. He read copies of JW's beloved *Scientific American* and brought a stack of medical journals and other science magazines for JW to look over at his leisure. This gave the two men, doctor and patient, more subjects to cover when they talked. JW told him about the fire and the smoke. It was Dr. Kelley's theory his lungs had been damaged. He set up a regimen not unlike Savina's. Dr. Kelley's philosophy of human health was based on four fundamentals: enough sleep, enough exercise, cleanliness and good food. And on top of those essentials: productivity and happiness. JW was to walk in the fresh air every morning and afternoon, in order to revive his lungs and invigorate his circulation, and to have strict rest in between. He could resume other activities slowly. There were mixtures to swallow every night, one made from willow bark which unknown to the doctor Savina had administered, another of marshmallow commonly grown in the swamps near his home and grape seed oil, an old French remedy his own mother had used. The patient was to sleep with the window open. Dr. Kelley handed the cook a list of foods he wanted included in JW's meals which was easy to do as the farm family ate a plentiful variety of fresh food anyway. He wanted dandelions and garlic put in his salads and soups. Onions were to be added to everything, along side a special dish of onions cooked in milk to accompany each of his meals.

Anna and the children grew used to Dr. Kelley's presence around the house for he arrived twice weekly to check on his patient. Savina listened to Emma's accounts of what was transpiring in the big house with fascination and approval. Nowhere else had Savina heard of a physician who so openly promoted and used remedies patterned after the practices of the Indians like she did. He carried dried plants and seeds in his dark leather medical bag. When six-year-old Sam fell and received a big cut on his head, Dr. Kelley tied the gash shut with the boy's own hair. When JW complained of muscle ache which accompanied his increased activity, Dr. Kelley advised him to hold himself in the cold water of the nearby stream to relieve the pain.

The date set for Al and Eva's wedding was March 16, 1879, four days before Emma's sixteenth birthday. As the day approached, Al was nervous and touchy. It had been about a year since the fire, or since the more commonly sited milestone, the engagement party. JW could now draw a deep breath without a sharp pain. Dr. Kelley's visits dropped back to infrequent, and by Al and Eva's wedding day, JW stood by his brother the picture of health.

At the last minute, Anna thought of inviting Dr. Kelley to the festivities. When she spoke to him, Dr. Kelley showed amazement and declined, for attending had not crossed his mind. Indian treasure hunting was a different matter. He always carried artifacts around in his pockets and pulled one out now to show Anna. He launched into an explanation about the different sizes designed to kill what type of animal. Anna quickly excused herself to see to some wedding detail. The Indian arrowhead he held in his palm was one of hundreds in his collection he had gathered as he walked the furrows of his fields. As the plow turned the earth, it uncovered old treasures. He collected each specimen in a gunnysack strapped over his back and had done it for years. Undaunted by Anna, he climbed the stairs to show JW the sculpted stone. To him he told about its artistry and the hunting methods of the tribesmen who used it. On other occasions he had brought oddly shaped stone tools to his patient he said were for grinding and cutting. Once he showed JW what he called human bones which were carved with designs. They looked like old cow bones to JW but the young man was fascinated by most of the Indian tales Dr. Kelley told. Talk of Indians in long ago Ohio was a pleasant diversion for JW from the endless talk of the wedding and of the return to his farm duties, the same springtime duties he had performed year after year since the factory was built. He was tanned from the early spring sunshine and had regained the weight he had lost. With his face filled out he looked as handsome as his jittery brother.

Uncle William, Aunt Lizzie and Katy had arrived from Harrisburg by riding the Pennsy Rail Road through Pittsburgh where they picked up Margaret. At Wheeling they changed to the Ohio Central which took them right to Urbana. They joined Uncle Michael, his four older sons and his young wife and new daughter who had spent the week prior to the festivities on George's old farm near Mechanicsburg now run by cousin Lewis. They all traveled together on the Ohio Central straight through to Hill Grove and the Darke County home of their relatives. Betsy from Philadelphia had come earlier with her husband and daughter; she had been missing her father and wanted extra time with him. Margaret arrived with all her possessions for she intended to stay. Her husband had died in a mill accident last year, and she was now joining her brother's household to start life over in Ohio. Anna was happy to welcome her sister-in-law. Emma noticed the let up in her workload, for her Aunt Margaret knew how to join in to help. The other two sisters from the Lost Mountain Lambert family did not make the trip from their homes in Iowa and Minnesota where they lived with their own families, but they sent gifts and best wishes to the young people. Anna's half-brother Levi brought his family up from Kentucky and stayed in the little house with his mother.

Not one of the relatives had heard from Harry for years; in fact he was hardly mentioned at all. So much had happened since the last time they saw him, and life was so different now, it was hard to imagine his being a part of the gathering. Harry was in limbo, not remembered along with the dead and not joining in as among the living. It was hard to know what to say about Harry.

The Lambert party of the night before The Big Event had been lovely. Eva's mother was gracious in her compliments to Anna. The wedding itself took place at St. Paul's Presbyterian Church in Greenville. The sanctuary was decorated with white ribbons and bouquets of lilies, roses and greens which had been shipped up from Georgia by train. An archway of white roses had been erected at the foot of the nave. It had been Eva's idea; she thought it would be romantic to pass through the fragrance of the flowers as a symbol of entering her new life as Mrs. George Albert Lambert. Eva floated down the aisle on the arm of her aristocratic father. She spoke the words of her vows loudly and clearly to pledge herself to her husband. When Al spoke in turn, he used his Lambert luster to full effect. The newly wed couple endured the party at her parents' home with patience and grace, even though they were eager to leave on their wedding trip to California, which was a gift from the parents of the groom. JW, newly restored to health, unwisely drank too deeply from the champagne punch bowl and ended the day with his head spinning. Emma, along with Mollie and Eva's two sisters, enjoyed his untypically comical behavior for they had sampled the libations as well. Even the little boys, Sam and Babe, had a good time playing with other children and stealing chocolate-covered strawberries from a silver tray in the hallway of the Parent's sprawling home.

With Al out of the house and with the late departure of the wedding guests who stayed for nearly a month now gone, George announced his intentions to change his farm production. Christian Harry, now fourteen, would work with JW throughout the summer in order to take over as supervisor of the agricultural efforts, which would be scaled back to produce only materials for the factory and food for the family. George was leaving the grain and produce business. Market prices had not rebounded and profits were slim. After the fall harvest JW, his father proclaimed, would go to work in Union City to learn the ropes of the factory. Al now carried the title of Business and Sales Manager and was having a large home built in Union City. Union City was a small town but three railroad lines, the Bellefontaine, the Central Ohio and the Dayton and Union, converged there making it ideal as a source of manufactured products. JW accepted his father's orchestrations of family member activity without much question. He relished a change. His first thoughts were to have private conversations with the more experienced of the hired farm men to ease their transition and engage their cooperation in accepting the teenager as their boss. A number of them would be moving over with JW to work in the factory. Returning to work after these conversations, JW came upon Emma in the cow barn. It was curious for the milking was done, and she was usually at work in the kitchen. As he came closer, he saw she was crying.

"I'm sorry to disturb you," he turned to leave her to her private feeling. She was sitting on a three-legged milking stool by the door of the largest stall.

"No, don't go." She wiped at her eyes and stood up. Then she sat right back down as a wave of tears overtook her. She covered her face to hide her involuntary emotion.

Her brother stood in silence and waited her out. At last she peered up at him from behind the apron she was holding to her face and he asked, "What's the matter?"

"I'm just being selfish. It's only self-pity." She kept the apron near.

JW put down the rakes he was carrying and knelt on one knee by his brown-haired sister. Again he repeated, "What's the matter?"

Now when she peered out of her apron, his face was right in front of hers. She lowered the material after wiping at her wet face and smiled, like the sun breaking through dark rain clouds. "I feel better now. I just need a cry now and then." JW crossed his brows, the same design of brow she had herself and looked in her eyes. "OK," she stood to break his show of concern and he followed her up. He repeated in a more matter-of-fact tone, "What's the matter?" like he wanted an explanation of a broken utensil. She told him. "Mama and Papa never acknowledged my sixteenth birthday. I've been sixteen for four months and neither one ever even said Happy Birthday." She had such sadness on her face. He put his arm around her shoulder and showed her his own face full of empathy. He had left a present of a pen and some ink on her bed the night of her birthday, which was four nights after Al's wedding. JW had not noticed the oversight by their parents, although looking back it did seem peculiar no mention had been made at the time. He knew other girls who had been given big parties to mark their sixteenth birthday, but of course Libby was married before hers. The wedding celebrations seemed to leave no room for other family events, and at the time JW had been occupied with his own recovery, Dr. Kelley's visits and tales of old Indian tribes. He was sorry now he had not done something more. "It's not you," she read his mind. "And I know the wedding was important. I'm just feeling sorry for myself. I've got to get back to the kitchen." She patted his arm and crossed in front of him to head back to her baking, for it was a Tuesday when the week's worth of bread, donuts, pies and cakes were baked, usually Emma's favorite day.

The next day Anna put a candle on one of the cakes and the family celebrated Emma's birthday at the noontime dinner table. Along with the five younger children, Aunt Margaret, Grandpa Mike and Grandma Furst were there to add their love, for each of them had a special relationship with the nearly broken-hearted, sometimes invisible Emma. Although there were no presents, George gave a speech praising his daughter's soft beauty and her sensitive, delicate ways. Anna declared her the master maker of cookies and donuts along with her other culinary and needlework skills. Neither one mentioned the fire which had become just another page in the history of the busy family farm. But it was still vivid in Emma's memory, especially those first few flames she had seen before she called, "Fire!" JW raised his glass of cider to his sister and predicted her writing would bring her fame and fortune like Emily Dickinson to which Emma blushed and shook her head. JW had done some behind-the-scenes work on behalf of his sister by urging his busy mother to "do the right thing" for her second, no third, born daughter. Emma knew JW had prompted the party, but each time she intended to acknowledge it to him she grew so emotional she knew if she spoke she would break into tears, so she never said anything at all.

The following fall, JW started the three mile daily commute to Union City and was put to work assembling wheels for the higher end carriages. Immediately he saw ways to improve the design of the spokes, and his father allowed him to institute the changes. The curious young man could not face a machine without surmising a way to make it run better. George decided to rotate JW's job every few months thereby showing him all the facets of the busy factory and also troll for his ideas and improvements. JW could not have asked for a better arrangement. Al got a little stand-offish after JW discovered a major design flaw in their construction of the fire wagon, but in general the older established brother encouraged his younger sibling. He knew the rewards the Lambert enterprise had accumulated was based in no small part on JW's constructive ideas. JW fit in with the crowd at the factory; the men could tell JW about their jobs and the troubles which came up. A number of his former farm hands rallied together each day around the lunch wagon. JW recognized a few machinists from the shops in Greenville alongside classmates, neighbors and new acquaintances. They were a spirited group of men captivated by the Lambert luster and united in the common cause of producing Lambert goods. The new young worker, not officially a supervisor, was still the boss' son. His skills and his genuine, easy-going nature authorized his powerful status. He was not so interested in the sales and management of the company, but he understood the upper level goings on. He had been raised with it as part of his blood. JW's biggest adjustment to his new position was being inside for so much of the day. He missed the fresh air, the sunshine and the quiet of the fields which was lost in the brick factory building in spite of the huge windows. As he got to know each workstation, he did find adjustments to suggest at each for the over-all method of production as well as to the mechanics itself.

In the fall of 1880 an incident occurred which, when he learned about it, stabbed the young man emotionally the way the smoke from the shed fire seared his lungs. His younger sister Mollie was assaulted by a vagabond wanderer. The stranger had approached the Hill Grove farm like others occasionally in the past and spoke to Christian Harry about day work. The young supervisor took him on to pick tomatoes. But the rag-clad man left the fertile field on the second morning and doubled back toward the house. He sidled past the hog pens and feed room, then sneaked behind the barns toward the large redbrick home where the day before he had seen a young woman alone in the yard. Without detection he hid for hours in the hen house until fourteen-year-old Mollie entered to collect eggs. He held a knife to her throat as he covered her mouth with his other hand. The air coming out from between his clenched, grimy teeth was putrid. He had a large open sore under his beard on his pasty white skin. Gruffly he told her he would kill every member of the household, should she scream. Then he raped her. When he was done, he told her he would come back to kill her mother if she ever told anybody what he had done. He fled and left her sobbing among the squawking birds who seemed to know they had witnessed a terrible thing. Mollie willed herself back to a presence of mind by praying to Jesus to help her cope. Fearful of the threats and wishing fervently the incident had never happened, she re-entered the house. She told Aunt Margaret she was not well which Margaret and Emma accepted easily, as Mollie did not look right and one of the cooks had yesterday gone down with the throws. So Mollie went to her bedroom; in private she scrubbed at her scratched and defiled young body with renewed panic. She shook so much she had to concentrate to get the cloth in her hand to reach her skin, but cleaning herself was her overriding mission. When Emma looked in on her sister sometime later that morning to ask could she bring her some hot bean and bacon soup, the poor young girl was buried under the covers and feigned sleep until Emma softly closed the door again.

The now long-gone desperado had not counted on Emma's sensitive perceptions. After the large mid-day meal, as she stood at the sink with her hands in the dishwater, her skin unaccountably crawled. Her mind kept going up to her sister. She tried to throw off the creepy feelings as a reaction to any member of the healthy Lamberts being sick. Rarely did any of them have more than a sniffle. *I'm still jittery over JW's running into that shed*, she told herself, but did not succeed in assuaging her uncomfortable mind. With the last pan washed and dried, she again headed up to peek in on her sister. This time she found her in a deep sleep of exhaustion, so she left her, and told herself, *See, all is well.* Emma replaced the chamber pot, for the girl had been sick.

The following day Mollie rejoined the others. Emma and her three next younger siblings rode the old farm wagon to the Union City schoolhouse. On the way, field supervisor Christian Harry mentioned a mysterious vagabond who seemed desperate for work, yet had disappeared without finishing his assignment or collecting his money. Christian, the reins in his hands, was talking down about dirt bag transients who had not the self-control to make a success of themselves. Mollie was rigid under her clothes and held her own arms so tightly under her shawl she added new bruises to the brightly colored but healing and hidden marks on her arms. Emma had her eye on Mollie, but told herself the girl was upset about their brother's arrogant attitude toward one of God's unfortunate creatures.

The shameful secret came out that night while the girls were alone in their large bedroom. Mollie told Emma only on the condition Mama never find out because she believed to her core the tramp would torture and kill her. Emma could tell Mollie needed to set the terms of the story of her violation and so went along. Both girls knew instinctively this was something Papa should never hear of. Together they kept the secret, and alone Emma helped Mollie heal. There were tears every night and dreams which interrupted their sleep, for the fears were profound: what if he came back? How could Mollie ever have a boy friend or get married? What if she were pregnant?

The weeks passed and an awful reality began to seep into their consciousness. "No," Emma fought the idea and rubbed her sister's arm. "You're just late because you're scared. It will come. Let's try to forget about it and you'll see. Your friend will visit." They kept up with their chores and read poetry to each other. They sat with Margaret in the evenings for she was teaching them to make lace. But the telltale flow of blood never came. Emma tried always to be by Mollie's side and never let her be alone. Her protectiveness inadvertently helped Mollie to cover up the crime committed against her. Emma was the one to gather eggs, for she wanted to save Mollie the painful confrontation of returning to the scene of her molestation. By her sister's rape, the hen house had become a horror chamber. Emma felt badly for the noble little hens and spoke to them reassuringly and thereby helped herself bear the time in their coop. The two girls had delightedly broke dozens of those first eggs, because, they said to each other, how could those eggs not be rotten, after what the hens had witnessed? Mollie wondered the same of the pregnancy she knew in her heart was alive in her still largely child-shaped body. It was the younger Mollie who put her foot down to the older Emma, "Yes, I am. I know I am. Oh, Emma, what's to become of me?"

Emma knew of only one possible source of help, Savina. Grandpa Mike had died and Emma took all meals to her ancient grandmother who spent all her time in the little house on the side of the old apple orchard across the yard from the big family home. Although she was frail, she knew the goings on in the family and welcomed Emma who lingered as long as she could when she delivered the hot, nutritious food. This day Emma sat down at the kitchen table by the window, and the old pioneer woman knew she was about to hear a trouble which was burdening her open-faced young granddaughter.

"Grandma, when you were trying to get Levi," Emma started. She was determined to speak openly for she knew her grandmother's famous forthrightness.

"Yes, dear?" Savina hoped the young women was not in trouble herself. Emma's butterflies nearly stole her voice.

"You know, I mean, I know you found a way to get Levi, even though you had lost three babies before him." Emma knew because the story had often been told.

"That's right, dear. When I was young, I had an old Indian friend. She taught me many tricks of the trade. Now, how can I help you?" Savina was almost positive Emma was not pregnant. Pregnant women put out a glow which appeared to Savina's eyes, and there was no such glow around Emma. "What do you need, Emma? I promise I will try to help."

Emma and her sister were so close it was impossible to know where one ended and the other began, so this ordeal naturally was traumatic for Emma as well. "Mollie..." Emma ventured into her subject, then stopped to cry a little. Grandma Furst handed her a napkin. Those who knew Emma knew tears were a part of who she was. "Mollie," she tried again and then blurted out, "Oh, Grandma, Mollie is pregnant!" Savina reached out her blue-veined hand to Emma's glistening face. "But that's not the worst part," the young girl said. Savina knew she was about to hear horrible news. "That dirty, filthy scourge of a man, not a man, a monster, a horrible monster," Emma was distracted by her feelings for the perpetrator so Savina gently directed her back to the facts which needed to be said. "Tell me, child. What happened to our

Mollie?" The seventeen-year-old met the clear eyes of her grand-mother.

"She was raped." Emma hated hearing the word come out of her mouth. She told as much of the story as she knew. Savina murmured, "I'm so sorry, honey. You bring Mollie to me. I'll speak to her. This is not something that can't be handled. Of course I can help. There is no reason your sister has to suffer alone one minute longer. We'll help her together. Now get down that tin over the icebox and you go fetch Mollie. We'll do this right away." Before Emma left, she set two pots on Savina's stove for hot water, one to clean the instruments Savina had in the tin and one to brew a mixture of yarrow tea. Emma felt she was in a dream as she crossed the lawn to the kitchen door but had enough wits to feel relieved at Mollie's good luck. She knew her grandmother was different, but she had no idea she would receive the totally helpful response she had gotten. She reminded herself her activ-ities must remain Top Secret. She squared her shoulders before re-entering the large sunny kitchen. Once she located Mollie, she whispered into her sister's ear, a common sight to those who lived and worked around the two girls. Mollie's knees buckled but she held to the counter and did not fall. With a quick wink, Emma said out loud, "Will you help me with Savina, then?" and Mollie said, "Oh, OK, then, I'll come." And the two girls headed through the cold November air to their grandmother's kitchen.

Savina's skills as a midwife had never left her. She calmed the girls and gave Mollie the medicinal tea. Her hands deftly per-formed the procedure which quite literally may have saved the life of the desperate young girl. Grandma Furst insisted Mollie stay with her that night. She told Emma to excuse Mollie to the others by saying Savina needs her. Thus Mollie was successfully relieved of the physical legacy of the nightmare she had endured in the hen house, and no one questioned the goings-on except Anna who asked after her mother and accepted Emma's assurances Grandma Furst was fine. Emma valiantly held the Big Secret to herself. She was awed by the afternoon's events as well as the terror which lingered from the threats of the knife-wielding rapist. Mollie's recovery coincided with the rest of the family's happy anticipation of Christmas, and somehow the holiday with its special emphasis on birth and new life was both sad and encouraging to the all-too-wise young women. Throughout the winter, the two sisters kept up a lively relationship with their grandmother. Savina talked often to both girls at her kitchen table about men and life, self-determination, relationships, faith and perspective while they sipped Chamomile tea. Each time before they left, she had them all hold hands and say The Lord's Prayer together. The three females deepened their relationships with Jesus whom they each found to be compassionate, all knowing and forgiving. His very real Presence gave the young girls hope life could be good even after so great a personal tragedy. Grandma Furst said that is what His death was all about.

When the next fall rolled around and the smells in the air were the same as the time the rape had occurred, both girls grew afraid the monster man would return. After discussing it with Mollie, Emma decided to consult their older brother JW. She would have to tell him at least part of their secret, but trusted he would have ideas about what to do and be able to help in their protection. She stopped by the tool shed the next Saturday afternoon where he customarily spent time fixing the problems with the farming instruments which could not be solved by Christian Harry. Her words to him about the undisclosed deeds in the hen house hurt him deeply. He felt helpless spending so much of his time far away from the farm in Union City. She could see he was upset and so quickly added their emotionally hearty grandmother knew as well and was helping Mollie so that she could eventually face the reality of married life. That embarrassed them both, so JW, convinced his sisters were being cared for in that regard, let that part drop. Emma was asking him for protection. That was the problem for him to solve. Using a voice from deep in his chest, he reassured her he would see to it no further harm would come to her or to Mollie.

But what could he do? Emma had been earnest about keeping the incident discreet so JW agreed to help and still avoid talking about it to his father or older brother. He devised a plan which would maintain his pledge. He spoke to Christian Harry at the farm in Hill Grove and told him a story about a strange fellow who had showed up at the factory, worked a few days and then took off. When he left, he may have stolen some goods. Before he brought the situation to Papa's attention, he would make the half-lie to his sixteen-year-old brother to try to discover who this fellow was. *Had there been a straggler looking for work in the past year?* Christian Harry remembered there had been one fellow last fall who had struck him as odd. He had looked enough like he needed money but had worked fewer days than they contracted then had run off without collecting his pay. The profile fit the description Emma had given. JW told his younger brother to watch out for this man, to tell the other hands to be on the lookout for him also and to report it immediately should he come around. And if he did show up, JW's tone was serious, Christian Harry was not to leave the man out of his sight for he could be dangerous. He was to send for JW first thing. The young supervisor, who relished excitement, promised to do as his older brother and mentor was instructing him. At the factory JW let it be known there had been a bit of a fracas on the farm caused by a vagabond who may come to the Lambert facility in Union City. This disorderly bum was in need of money and likely looking for work. JW described the fellow's appearance according to his brother and what Emma repeated his sister Mollie as having said. He let his co-workers know they were to fetch him should ever the man show up. The workers understood JW was serious.

Still JW was not satisfied he had done enough to spread his net to capture his sister's assailant. He racked his brain and thought of Elwood Haynes, who stopped by the office on occasion to visit with his father and brother. JW had recently spoken with the traveling high school teacher about being away at college in Massachusetts. He was an interesting, articulate man and told tales of his travels and the unusual people he met on his assignments. The next time Elwood came for a visit, JW approached him as he was soothing his horse in the courtyard of the factory buildings. "Hello, Elwood," JW greeted the man who was three years his senior and told him about the dangerous outsider. He asked Elwood if, in his travels, he had run across a man of that description. Elwood said, "I reckon I haven't, but I'll keep my eyes and ears open for you and let you know what I find out."

Later that very week Elwood came riding up to the array of connecting brick buildings. Instead of heading to the President's Office, he asked around for JW and found him watching over a man's shoulder as he used a wrench to tighten bolts. The former farmboy looked up and saw Elwood, "Elwood! Are you looking for me?"

"I sure am." He reached out to shake JW's hand and walked with him over to the side of the cavernous, noisy room, under one of the large bright windows. "I've got something important to report." JW knew he must have news about the man who had harmed his sister. "I thought you would want to hear right away. I didn't come across a live fellow, but I found a stiff who fits your description. Fellow must have been camping out for some time by himself on a little piece of abandoned property just below Bluff Point. Buried him right there, after the sheriff had a look at him. He had the scar under his beard like you were looking for. Same size, same coloring. Must be your guy." JW looked at the ground. This was grim business. Elwood asked, "What did the dearly deceased do?"

JW did not want to lie, but he could not betray his sisters. So he stuck with his original story, "I thought he might have been a thief, but it doesn't matter now. I am mighty grateful for your help, Elwood."

"Well, good. I gather this is not a matter you ever discussed with your Papa, so mum is the word. Maybe you'll show me that new fire pumper your brother was talking about." JW led him through the large room, to an adjacent equally large room and happily chatted about spoke-lengths and spacing to the interested ears of the dapper gentleman who nonetheless rode a horse on the dusty roads of the back country for a living.

As soon as he could, JW relayed the news to Emma. She ran to tell Mollie who said she was only sorry she could not kill him herself. But now the two girls, in fact all four family members who had known of the crime, could let the matter recede from terrifying their daily lives. This Christmas season seemed to sparkle like none in the past, for Mollie and Emma directed their relief into making cookies and cakes, spiced drinks and delicious meats. They concocted a tiny village made of gingerbread, icing and candies and little objects which seemed to jump out at them to be used as clever ornaments for the fantasy scenario.

Before the winter was out, JW took a Sunday afternoon to travel to Dallas to visit his former doctor and friend Dr. Kelley. The invitation had been sent months before, but JW had been busy as usual with his family-related occupations. He had been in no hurry to respond to the unique request which would take him away from the drama of the last few months and the mechanical world he tinkered in. Now Mollie's culprit had his toes turned up to the daisies, the tiller was repaired, Christian Harry was visiting friends and nothing stood in his way. He took the light family carriage with its buttoned-leather seat for the fifteen-mile drive to the house. He had considerable time to imagine in what kind of place this eccentric man would be living – maybe he still walked on dirt floors, maybe his wife only spoke French. The area north of Greenville was settled by those who left France disgusted with the failure of Bonaparte to institute democracy. Versailles was a busy town filled with a mixture of recent and old arrivals.

It never crossed JW's mind the Indian history aficionado had four beautiful daughters, but he found out that afternoon. The four girls had seen JW at the County Dances and had early on agreed John Lambert would make a likely boyfriend for Minnie. Of the four, young Minnie spoke her claim as her two older sisters conveniently had their eyes on other young men. They saw their father's commission to attend the Lambert boy in his illness as a sign the relationship was fated to be. They consolidated their mission and conspired to make it happen. They got their mother to offer the invitation, and they bundled up their father with instructions, and then sent him to the Lambert farm to deliver the note. If the girls had known their father had turned down an invitation to the big Parent/Lambert wedding, they would have been beside themselves. It had never occurred to him to tell and what they did not know did not hurt them, but they watched with fascination the newspaper coverage and grasped every bit of information they could gather from their girl friends. When Anna looked at the Kelley invitation, back in Hill Grove, she told JW she assumed it was a gesture of good will and concern for the problem successfully treated by the good doctor.

As the handsome, six-foot-three, twenty-one-year-old unsuspecting son of possibly the most successful entrepreneur in the county entered the trim, richly decorated foyer, Dr. Kelley greeted him while standing next to his wife. She was a tall, sober woman with gaunt cheeks who matter-of-factly welcomed him. Without expression she gestured for him to sit in their parlor, a dark room with large dark furniture dotted with lace doilies and ornate pillows. Much to JW's chagrin, Dr. Kelley disappeared and left his former patient alone with his wife and daughters. Mrs. Kelley made the introductions to her four trim girls and pointed JW to the dark gold velvet davenport where a daughter sat adjusting the silver tray on the coffee table. Once JW's eyes grew accustomed to the dim lighting, he caught the mischievous smiles smirking below the surface of the polite expressions of the four petite young women and thought to himself, *My, don't they enjoy each other.* His couch mate took the lead in conversing with him. She had been introduced as Mary Francis, but she purposely touched JW's hand when she said, "I want you to call me Minnie." The touch of Minnie's fingers was momentary, but the sensation it caused was unlike anything JW had ever experienced. It shot up his arm and possessed him briefly on all counts. He did not dare open his mouth, for his body was reacting enough already. "And I will call you John." Her smile was determined, her attitude familiar. She had been working on her trousseau since she was a young girl and often day-dreamed of her wedding. The isolated farm boy drew on his years of training in Lambert manners. "Why, thank you. It is a pleasure to meet all of you." The use of the word pleasure had been a mistake, so he just shut his mouth and the blood blazed on his cheeks. He tried to cover his nervousness in this unfamiliar environment and willed his hand not to move to his neck for that old collar-adjusting gesture. He had arrived at the Dallas farmhouse expecting a tour of arrowheads accompanied by a lecture on Iroquois natives, but now he found himself in a cloud of perfume. This scene had been discussed and orchestrated; the girls' movements were synchronized as though rehearsed. One of Minnie's sisters offered a tray of fruit tarts and delicate chocolate cookies. Sweet smelling tea was steeping in its pot on the table at their knees. Eighteen-year-old Minnie reached out her little hands to pour from the ornate big bellied teapot. She offered her regret over his recent illness as she handed him a bright yellow china cup with a band of gold on the delicately scalloped top, the saucer and the handle and looked right in his eyes. She won a smile before he looked around the room. The girls chatted and carried the conversation themselves. Mrs. Kelley was the only one silent and not smiling; her gray face was a stone façade including deep gauges under her eyes and cheekbones which made her look much older than her actual years. She seemed to recede into the large armchair she sat in while her daughters' animation absorbed all the attention. After what seemed like an eternity, Dr. Kelley reappeared and JW was treated to his tour of the artifacts, rescued at last from the feminine web of artistry beautifully drawn to sting the young man.

On the long, quiet road home, to the sound of the horse's clippity-clop, JW was haunted by the feel of Minnie's hand. Her touch had intended to lay claim, and he had indeed been infected. Had she known, she would have been well pleased. The view he had of her eyes dropped from his memory, but the picture of her hands encasing her yellow teacup enveloped his mind. He had never felt anything like this; the infinitely interesting sensation buoyed him above the soft leather seat, so he floated over the road. At his leave-taking, he had stood in front of their home and had promised he would return soon, as all four girls had insisted. As he rode along he could think of no reason not to honor his promise. By the time he reached Hill Grove he was very relaxed. His mind had turned to the puzzle of improving a certain boring tool. A mile or so ago it had occurred to him that the shape of the handle may hold the key to unlocking the dilemma of the tool. After putting the carriage away and delivering the horse to the stable, he rushed to the tool shed to test his hypothesis.

7

Life in Enterprise, now called Ohio City

Anna held her mother's shriveled hand and heaved a sigh. The tiny figure of the old woman lay quiet under the wrinkled mess of bed sheets. How her bed got so upset was a mystery to the orderly Anna for she did not understand that while Savina's body was exhausted, her mind was rushing to accomplish an inventory. It moved over the whole scope of her life, letting go of it piece by piece. Anna fretted.

This morning in the quiet shell of her body, Savina felt close to the bright shining Jesus she knew so surely was waiting on the other side. She knew her husband Levi was close too; she could sense his amusement, as always, at her psychic audacity, for he had long appreciated her unorthodox ways. Last night she had revisited a scene unfit for human eyes. It was 1837. She and Levi were on the last few days of their long walk, alongside all of their belongings in a wide-plank wagon pulled by one mule from Philadelphia to Ohio. They walked on a deeply shadowy, secondary road off the National Highway, both carrying long guns, through the thick, giant hardwood trees. They saw a lightening off to the left which indicated a clearing, so they made the long side trip expecting to find settlers like themselves who would offer shelter, company and warm food. They found rotting bodies mutilated and defiled. Though weary, she and Levi buried as much as they could, all the while saying prayers and singing hymns. Anna had known then, in her heart, the harsh realities of life in the wilds of Ohio. The spirit of the unknown woman whose body she buried appeared last night and let Savina see she was whole and peaceful. The revelation brought Savina healing. She now knew the prayers she had sent through the years had reached the two nameless victims. Invisible to Anna, Savina's imaginative mind was completing some list before her old body gave out. Out of love and consideration for Anna, Savina willed herself to turn away from the density of the difficult times and move to a gentle place. She took herself for a walk in her mind's eye and experienced through her memory the crunch of brown crispy leaves under her heavy leather shoes and the sharp smell of rotting apples which were scattered under the autumnal carpet. She looked up at a deep blue sky. Her body was too weak for her to acknowledge her daughter.

Anna straightened the bed covers, leaving barely a rumple under which the slight body lay. The routines of homemaking now were done by others; Anna directed the large household and farm while her husband and older sons were running the manufacturing business. Her youngest child was near ten. She herself was a grandmother twice over for Libby had a son and Al had a daughter. Savina was her mother but not her mother. The woman who raised her had had a black face and it was that woman whom Anna carried into her own mothering. As Anna had cared for her young children, it was Annie's old instructions which spoke in her mind and guided her actions. She ran her household using the organizational systems Annie had run in the prosperous Philadelphia home in which she grew up. Savina had been a good grandmother to her children and Anna loved the old woman even though she purposely held a part of herself away, a legacy of the original abandonment. Now that her mother was going to be gone, Anna began to think of all she would never know. Anna looked at the wrinkled hand she was holding and wished her mother had been willing to tell her the truth about her background. She had intended to ask her here at the end: *Who is my father?* But Savina left without answering. She was buried in the small family graveyard between her husband Levi and the old dog Rex. Instead of being recognized as a force of nature, her life passed like the era; the time of land loving and survival slipped away, overtaken by the time of mechanical progress and large-scale profit. Emma, now a young woman, knew best how her grandmother would be missed. Savina had served as an anchor to the family in more ways than one.

After his mother-in-law's death, George wired a railroad friend in Urbana who arranged for the rental of an entire Pullman car so he and his wife could travel in comfort on a pleasure trip back to Philadelphia. Their current itinerary included time with George's family. They had no plans to look up any of the prominent family members in whose home Anna had worked as a girl. George remembered the old patriarch, certainly dead now, who had caused such a ruckus over Anna's leaving. He had tried to impede them, had even sent a courier to Lost Mountain in an attempt to discredit him. It still got him angry to think of the audacity of the old man to assume any right to complain about her freedom to go anywhere she chose.

Once in Philadelphia, Anna expressed her desire to look up Annie, the black woman who had fostered her. The fashionable farm couple from the heart of the nation approached the Musselman house with the intention of calling at the back door, which they did. The uniformed individual who answered their knock politely gave them an address for the now elderly housekeeper. George read the driver the address and spoke to him at some length before the carriage started moving again. George patted Anna's gloved hand and repeated what the driver had told him, "It's not in the best part of town. He'll only wait for us for an hour, for he says it is imperative we all be out of the neighborhood before dusk." She looked out at the dilapidated buildings and groups of ragged children gathered on the street. The carriage stopped and they walked to the front doorway. A barefoot young girl in a short cotton shift let them in and led them to an unlit upstairs bedroom.

"Annie, is that you?" Anna called out. The old woman was not in her bed, but sat in a dark corner of the room tapping her foot tied in rags to move the old rocker back and forth.

There was silence in the shadows of the corner, then an explosion of sound, "Oh, Lawd Jesus, come here, chil' – let me touch you." Anna knelt at her feet, so the blind woman could reach her. The old black fingers capped Anna's head, then her fingertips gently traced the contours of the younger woman's face. The old cook chuckled to remember George and claimed she saw Christianna's future with him the first day they met. She said she was not surprised he had made such a success of himself. Anna told the story of her life in Ohio, but left out Savina and the deaths and all the war years. She talked of her children and the recipes she continued to use which had begun in the kitchen with Annie. "Ten children, my God Lawd Almighty. You are a hearty girl, eh?" She giggled and chatted and repeated her sentences in delight. At length, for the cab would not linger, Anna asked the question which was of late ever in her throat, "Annie, did you know who my father was?"

"Well, my goodness, everyone knew that. You didn't know, chil'? that your daddy was the old man's son, the tailor who lived in New York City? Sho', honey, sho' 'nough, you were a granddaughter same as the children at the big table." She added, musing, "You were a happy little thing; you never missed them. Umhum. And I sho' loved having you with me."

Anna could not help but smile as her stomach turned to liquid. "No," she agreed with her foster mother. "No, I never missed them. You were all the mother I ever needed." The sentiment emboldened Anna to ask, "Have you heard of him?" Anna braced herself, for a walking, talking father was hard to imagine.

"Oh, Baby, he went with the chicken pox right after the War. Tore the old man up and he died soon after. Um hum. I stayed on with the young missus for a while, but she put me up. I asked and she put me up."

George put his hand on his wife's shoulder as they stepped out of the tenement building to their waiting vehicle. She gave a little shrug before she stepped up to her seat, "No wonder Savina never spoke of them. It must have been horrible for her. Well, now I know." George remained silent and his wife continued, "I'm not angry. They were good to me in their way."

That night in the hotel room George offered his suggestion, "Let them see you. Let's go back to the house and show them how successful you are, all without them." But Anna laughed, "Oh, George, there's no one to show. I only care about Annie. I want her to come back with us. Can we ask her? Do you think she will?"

Annie did not consider their offer for a minute. "I'm not leaving my home here, darlin, but you're kind to think of your ol' Annie."

"We could fetch you at any time; just send word. You'll hear from me now." Before leaving, she put paper money into the thick old hands. George now understood what irritated the old man those many years ago when he had tried to block his unnamed granddaughter from moving away. That old man was his own children's great grandfather.

The weather had been fair in Ohio. JW stood in the sun on the wooden elevator platform by the railroad tracks with his bright red rag. In a few minutes the train would come by and JW intended to flag it down for a ride to Union City. He hitched a ride every morning around 6:45 and jumped off on his return twelve hours later. Last Sunday he had flagged a ride on two trains to get to Dallas to visit Minnie and her sisters, his third or fourth visit in a year. Dr. Kelley showed him different Indian things each visit. In his own mind, JW thought that was why he was there, but the lure was more than the Indian legends.

While his father was out of town, twenty-three-year-old JW had sat in his place in the second floor office of the baked brick building near the Indiana border. George's second son was behind the expansive mahogany desk when Elwood Haynes came in. Expecting the father, Elwood was surprised to see JW. "JW, you ol' hornswoggler, good to see you in your proper place. I knew it was time for your father to retire. He's getting old." The smartly dressed worker grinned at his own playful banter. JW smiled back. Elwood kept talking, "Say, I wonder if I don't have some information you might be interested in."

"What's it about, Elwood?" The two men made themselves comfortable. JW offered his friend a cigar from his father's humidor and then picked one out for himself by digging to the bottom of the box. The two men clipped off the ends and lit their long dark smokes. Blue haze filled the air. JW leaned back, pushed the window open wider and put his feet up on the desk.

Elwood loosened his lapel and gazed at his cigar. He laughed out loud and then looked up. "Well, I ran into a fellow who claims to be kin to you. Where'd you Lamberts come from before you moved to Darke County?"

"I grew up on a farm in Champaign County."

"Urbana?"

"Near there."

"Well, that's the place this fellow was headed. Had a ponytail to his waist. Was traveling all by himself." The hair stood up on JW's neck. Something rang familiar in what Elwood was describing. "You people send any boys to the War for the Union? He looked like an old veteran."

"Yep. Yep, we did. My cousin Harry."

"Harry?"

"Yep, Harry. Joined the Thirteenth Regiment. Infantry. He survived but went wandering and we haven't seen him in years." JW was looking intently at his friend. *Could Harry be alive?*

"I think I talked to your cousin, JW. This guy said his name was Harry Lambert." In general, Elwood had a way of playing things up, so he relished the drama of the news. And he only knew the half of it, for he could not have known how special Harry had been to JW. *Was Harry back from the dead?* A visit from his older cousin was like a miracle. Putting out his cigar, JW was nearly standing as he said, "Where was he? What was he doing? Is he coming this way?"

"I saw him over by Anderson in a little restaurant by the Pennsylvania Depot. Said he was riding the Central line to Greenville on his way to Urbana. Then I told him about you Lamberts in Hill Grove. He may be there already."

JW hopped the early afternoon train back to Hill Grove. When he jumped off the train, he could sense something was abuzz in the big farmhouse. Sure enough, there at the kitchen table was Emma and Margaret along with various smaller children, sitting with a thin, etched, weary man who looked up at JW with eyes which nonetheless showed spark at seeing the full-grown boy who had been his charge in earlier times. He was eating a bowl of oatmeal and drinking a beer. When JW came into the room, long-haired Harry struggled to stand and extended his hand to greet his now grown cousin man-to-man. The teeth left in his mouth were brown and fuzzy but his smile was sincere. Late in the afternoon the two of them made their way to the implement barn for some privacy and found the old connection was still intact. Relaxing amongst the tools, Harry told about his adventures and hardships, how he had settled in St. Louis, married and made a living as a mason. Then a year ago, his wife and children were stricken with typhoid and all three died within two weeks. Harry started to rebuild his life in the gateway town, but one day it occurred to him a mason could work in Ohio as easily as in St. Louis. Maybe he could go back. He did not even know if George and Anna were still alive. All of a sudden it became important to find out. After a year of bereavement, he saw reason to hope and his life took shape again. More than a dozen years had passed since he had last seen any of his family. He sold all his things for the trip back to Ohio. Harry told JW these things but did not speak of the War or the years afterwards which got him to St. Louis.

Pointing out some of his work amongst the tools, JW bragged about the two Lambert patents and described the commercial success of the corn planter. Harry knew of the concept, how with a push and a pull the job was done, but he had no idea his cousin had built the machine. Harry learned his Uncle George had become a manufacturing entrepreneur and built a factory which produced farm implements, farm wagons, fire pumpers and carriage parts, all sold far and wide. The marketing included St. Louis, but Harry said he never saw the Lambert label. "I didn't know to look," he smiled apologetically. He had a scar running down his cheek, but besides that his earlier good looks were still discernible under the tough exterior. He walked with a limp and relied on a cane but denied he had any pain. "Just a reminder of an earlier time," he smiled mysteriously.

Animated, JW pointed to long pieces of wood laying on a bench and talked about the process of bending the wood to sculpt it into a comfortable harness for attaching horses to a carriage. Of late, JW had become fixated on improving the process of adjusting the wood in order to bend it at just the right angle to accommodate the stresses and movement of the vehicle and the animals. His work included finding a clever way to attach the hardware. Harry watched the enthusiastic young man in silence, then spoke, "Don't let me put a damper on your project, JW, but shouldn't you be thinking about getting out on your own? Sounds to me like your father and brother are getting rich off this operation. Why don't you start an enterprise of your own?" With his mother's history of alcoholism and indifference, Harry was a bit suspicious and naturally independent.

The more complacent JW said, "Oh, I'm happy. I like working with the tools. I'm more interested in inventing things than in building an empire."

"But that's just it. You invent, they get rich. Get out on your own and when you invent, you get rich." Harry was grinning ear to ear. JW was listening now. Thinking that improving poles and shafts suited the needs of the company more than it served his young cousin, the older Harry continued, "Maybe you don't want to invent a process to bend wood, maybe you want to do something else." JW's first thought was of the engine which ran with coal gas which he and his father had dug out of the ashes of the tanner's burned building.

"There are a lot of things I'd like to do, but at least around here I can work with the process. If I went out on my own, I'd starve to death."

"Get out of town! You're telling me you'd starve? What kind of sissy are you? You would not. I left here when I was a lot younger than you are, saw things worse than you ever will, God willing. I found a way. You could too. If you wanted to. If you really wanted to." Harry drove his point home.

When the two men returned to the house, Harry agreed to accept Emma's invitation to stay on at Hill Grove at least until George and Anna returned, although he was inclined to avoid even second-hand closeness to his elderly parents. As scheduled, in a few days George and Anna stepped off the Ohio Central train to discover their surprise visitor. But before they did, JW had become convinced of the need, nurtured by Harry, to move out of Hill Grove in order to establish himself as an independent man. This news came as a shock to George and Anna. With the new discoveries about the father who had denied and ignored her, Anna was looking forward to feathering her nest in Hill Grove. The timing could not have been worse for hearing of JW's assertion of independence. Misunderstanding his need for self-reliance, she felt betrayed he was moving out just at the time she needed her family most. He, in turn, was hurt at her lack of encouragement. His father's response was a neutral silence.

The family gathered for a big, formal dinner to honor the returned veteran which included not only Anna, George, Margaret, Harry and JW, but also Libby, Dan and ten-year-old Charlie and Al, Eva and their toddler Maggie, as well as the near-grown six younger sisters and brothers including Emma and Mollie, Christopher and the three younger boys, Benjamin Franklin, Samuel Webster and Levi Calvin. They gathered for a meal prepared and served by the family's three full-time serving cooks. Harry was the center of attention. George reminisced about the old family gatherings at the rough wood table in the one room home on the side of Lost Mountain. He told the joyful story of Harry's birth, but left out the story of the fire which had happened a few months prior to his arrival, and which had destroyed the home and nearly the lives of Harry's mother and father. George did not realize Harry had never been told about his little brother and sister who died tragically in the fire on Lost Mountain, although most assuredly he had heard the story of his welcomed birth many times and how, with their infant Harry, the two mountain-bred parents, leading a wagon with tools of his carpenter trade, walked to Ohio and prosperity. Throughout the meal, no allusion was made of JW's intentions to move out on his own until George made a toast to the prodigal relative who had decided to live in the Urbana farmhouse with Lewis and his family and find work as a mason. Holding his glass aloft, George told his family with a sad smile, "Lose one; gain one."

After dinner with the family, Harry told JW his parents' lack of support was the least of the obstacles the world might throw at him, so he better toughen up and get used to it. JW continued to think out his plans as Harry moved on to the old family farm near Mechanicsburg in Champaign County where JW was born, on a piece of property his own father had helped George buy, land he himself had once farmed. JW continued his work at the factory where his father approached him about an opportunity he heard of in the northern part of the state. He had heard through the grapevine a grain elevator in rural Van Wert County was for sale. George offered to float his second son a loan so JW could buy the operation which stood at the conjunction of not two but three railroad lines. Following railroad lines had brought George success, for he recognized early that sufficient means of transportation was essential to any man's financial well being, as well as necessary to a community's economic growth and prosperity. Every one needed to eat, so a granary had built-in protection from the ravaging economic whims of the wider economy. As a youth, JW had himself built a grain elevator on the Hill Grove farm. With this experience and the opportunity in Van Wert, George saw two necessary factors come together for a unique opportunity. At first JW was stand-offish because he thought he should make his move on his own, but he accepted Papa's generous proposal when he recalled one of Harry's directives: *Develop the means to invest. Make yourself enough money so that you can afford to play with tools and ideas.* George said the business was a sure bet, so JW agreed and planned to relocate as soon as the sale went through in order to be there before the fall harvest was ready for market. His new granary business took off before he actually moved.

With the help of his father and his four younger brothers, JW took all his personal belongings to the second floor of a widow's house in the very small town of Enterprise, Van Wert County, Ohio, about fifty miles from Hill Grove as the crow flies. The round, pleasant woman had moved her bedroom into her own parlor and for a few dollars more was willing to provide meals. She placed steaming vegetables, warm bread and juicy pork chops on her table for the six Lambert men; the youngest Levi Calvin was ten. To him the move was an awesome adventure. George was enthusiastic about JW's prospects in this little town. As they sat at the widow's table, he told the story of his moving off Lost Mountain at roughly JW's same age into a second floor apartment of a widow's house in Philadelphia.

Although George understood the importance of JW's decision to be out on his own, JW's mother was still nursing her wounds of abandonment. She believed she was losing her next oldest son. To her, fifty miles could have been an entire continent. George went so far as to say to JW her disapproval was not his fault, but more a combination of things including Libby's marriage which was now going through trouble. George left out the ambivalence of trying to keep up with the Parents, a sport largely played only in Anna's mind. But he talked at length about the recently learned truth of her father's identity. He hoped his sensitive second son would find compassion for the woman who discovered her father's identity when she was nearly fifty years old. JW could follow the tone of his father's explanation, but he had no context to understand the significance of this recent discovery in his mother's life. In all the years to come, as now, neither parent would ever refer to the man who had been Anna's father as "grandfather" to the children. It was as though his paternity would not reach past the denied daughter.

At his age, JW was sure enough of himself to see his mother's mistake in not accepting his decision. He was not inclined to resentment or to assigning negative motives, so with a patient-style bore her disapproval. Emma was the one JW felt badly about leaving. A sadness shadowed her eyes since hearing of JW's intentions, although she never tried to talk him out of his decision. She gave him a special present before he left, his only sibling to think of such a gesture. He would use and treasure the fountain pen forever. A Lambert neighbor, Newtie Glunt who, although he had recently lost his wife in childbirth, was vying for Emma's attention. Ever one to be sympathetic, Emma had been kind to the older man when she and Mama spoke to him after Sunday Services. Both mother and daughter were surprised he had come calling soon after. The appropriate mourning period had hardly begun. Emma denied he was courting, but that soon died as a defense for the widower spoke to George only six weeks after burying his wife and baby. George put off the man in concern for his daughter and told him to ask again after a time. Although the man was an adequately successful farmer and businessman, George had heard he could let loose a temper which was not good for a wife; so he had several reasons to be protective of his gentle daughter.

Emma forgot the proposal and her parents made their trip to Philadelphia. Then, Harry came back, JW began his move to Enterprise and when Mama and Papa returned, Emma told her father she would accept Newton Glunt. She wanted his dear surviving child to have a mother whether a proper mourning period had elapsed or not. The child needed her and so for that matter did Mr. Glunt. By the fall of 1884, just weeks after JW moved to Enterprise, twenty-one-year-old Emma became engaged to the serious, out-spoken older man. JW returned to Hill Grove for the engagement party late in October and brought Dr. Kelley's second youngest daughter as his guest. JW had visited the strongly feminine household in early October. While sipping tea in the parlor, he casually related to the family the news of his business venture and his recent move north to Van Wert County. This seemed of special significance to the sisters for much whispering took place immediately after JW made his report. Upon questioning their male visitor, the sisters discovered the news of Emma's engagement, and before he left, without intending to, JW, or John as she called him, had invited Minnie to accompany him to his parents' party for his beloved sister. Minnie was thrilled to be included in the affair, and JW's family noticed her feeling.

When JW made his final move out of his father's household, George and Anna presented him with a shiny new carriage and a beautiful fifteen-hand horse from Ira's Kentucky stock. George wanted his son to have the accoutrements of his new position in the small, farming town. When JW arrived at the widow's house, indeed his new home address, he hesitated deciding to ring or just walk in and happened to see a lone pink clover blossom by the fossil-ridden stepping-stone at his feet. Upon closer examination, a little white-laced green four-leaf clover caught his eye. He broke out in goose bumps. Without saying a word he picked it, laid it in his wallet and rang the bell. The granary was under his leadership now and he had made the acquaintance of several of the bigger, more entrepreneurial farmers. By coincidence, at least two Enterprise residents had connections to Darke County, so descriptions of JW were not short as word spread of his arrival.

One of his first goals in his new community was to host a large social at the granary site. The first floor of the granary was a large open space, with broad sliding doors which connected the room to a fan-shaped yard. During the work week the yard held trucks and wagons as farmers arrived with their grain to be sold in Columbus, Chicago, Indianapolis, and as JW soon discovered, Toledo and Detroit. The dirt had been pounded hard to make a fine dance floor. JW wanted to create a splash in the area to attract the attention of his potential customers. He wanted everyone to know the granary at Enterprise was operating again, and its new owner meant to do business. He wanted the people to see a dynamic, good-natured man who was ready to turn grain into gold. It never occurred to him he could fail. He entered Enterprise with a vigor which matched the town's name. There was a strut to his step as he gathered in men to do his bidding. His enthusiasm was infectious to the four men who accepted jobs, along side their curiosity about the simple novelty of the new owner. All the neighbors were talking. But John did not think about that. He enjoyed the kind favors of the landlady while behind his back she was telling her friends details of his personal doings. There was no shortage of interest in the subject for which she was the front row commentator. Through chains of friendships the word spread the newcomer came with good credentials, or so said their friends and relatives in Darke County. He was obviously rich, smart and good-looking, a very interesting addition to the local pool of eligible bachelors.

The fete was a huge success. Mrs. Schmidt, his landlady, had spread the word cash prizes were being offered for the Best Pie and that, along with newspaper advertisements, brought in a lot of baked goods. The four new employees barbequed chicken and pork ribs on a makeshift grill. Cider was passed out from ladles which were dipped into deep barrels. The new businessman's promotional effort was a big success as he shook hands with a long list of far-flung farmers. Besides meeting the new neighbor, they had enjoyed the excuse to bring their wives and children to town.

News of the social reached the Kelley household in Dallas after the fact and had a devastating effect. Although JW had been in her presence only a half dozen times in the eighteen months since they met, Minnie was inconsolable not to have been invited and paraded as JW's companion. She was on the verge of panic, for she could just imagine the mothers and daughters of Van Wert County would know the marriageable prize which had fallen into their midst. Nothing had been said between them, but she assumed after his sister's engagement party of last month she and JW had an understanding, a thought he obviously had not had. She and her sisters agreed circumstances had to change, for it was too painful to contemplate a repeat of this disaster. They put their heads together to set up a scene so Minnie could make her move. Whether JW admitted it to himself or not, he had shown memorable interest to the delicate, articulate daughter of the retired doctor who had cured his bout of lung disease. JW still ate a lot of onions, the only direct legacy of his yearlong sickness. Dr. Kelley did not give it a second thought when his daughters directed him to travel to Enterprise up the Toledo-Cincinnati line to call on the young Lambert boy. They convinced him he should visit the granary and drop in on the new young owner. The good doctor was inclined to go, for he had long considered investigating some rock formations in the area.

Minnie penned a note and folded in a pressed flower before sealing the pretty pink envelope which she sprayed with perfume. Then she announced to her father she would accompany him as far as the stop passed Celina, the one before Enterprise. Oblivious to her motives, Dr. Kelley told his twenty-three-year-old daughter to suit herself, which she did by dressing in her best coordinated outfit, complete with plumage in her cocoa-brown hat, which matched her gloves, shoes and the bag which hung from her wrist on a dark brown velvet cord, the same cord which outlined the shaped bodice of her dress. She waited stoically in the Mercer depot as her father traveled on to Enterprise where he stepped off the train directly into JW's presence. The young entrepreneur was surprised but delighted to see his old friend. Elwood Haynes had been up to visit last week; so as with him, JW welcomed the bearded doctor with pleasure. He showed the man around and then they settled into his office on the corner of the building. There was no cigar smoking with Dr. Kelley. After forty-five minutes a waft of fragrance served to remind the good doctor of the letter he had to give to JW. It was an awkward thing for JW, being handed a pink envelope saturated with perfume from the man who was father to the sender. JW held it in his hand for a moment and then laid it on the desk. Both men paused, watching the other, for the letter was calling for more attention. Dr. Kelley pointed to it, and with a sober face he said, "You better open that." He was used to things of a delicate nature being taken care of by others. JW was also used to things of a delicate nature being taken care of by others. The men were in uncharted territory. JW picked up the envelope, ignored its color and smell, and opened it with a sleek devise which he returned to the top drawer of his desk. He opened the folded paper to read the words and a delicate, colorful sprig fell to the floor. Neither man picked it up. JW read these words:

"Mr. Lambert, I am waiting in the Mercer Depot and I urgently need to speak to you. Please send my father on an errand. (He wishes to visit certain rocks in your area.) Please understand you must do this and I will be forever grateful. Sincerely, Mary F. Kelley."

Baffled, JW handed the opened epistle to Minnie's father. Upon reading his daughter's words, he said, "We better do as she says," for he was relieved to have direction on how to proceed. JW lent the older man his new two-wheeled carriage and a driver. He told his helper not to let the doctor wander too deep into the woods, to keep an eye on him and the carriage, and to direct him back before it got too late. Then JW hopped a train to Mercer. He knew in his heart what was happening. He was meeting his destiny. He sat back and thought of the lively little Minnie, with her intelligent eyes and tiny waist. He thought he would ask her to step onto the train so they could ride one stop to Celina where they could walk along the Grand Lake in the afternoon sun. He sat back and smiled to himself at the thought. When he stepped off the train, she was nowhere in sight. He found her inside the little box of a station where the stationmaster was sweeping the floor. He raised his eyebrows in playful warning when JW stuck his head in and rolled his gaze to Minnie sitting on a bench in a beam of sunshine looking so demure and pretty. JW's heart began to gallop like a horse. He rushed to her side but she purposely turned to him slowly still sitting, cast him sheep eyes, and then broke open her smile. He took her hands and lightly lifted as she stood. They were silent, smiling at each other when the stationmaster, not eight feet from them, tipped his visor and left the small room. Alone, the young couple took notice they still held each other's hands. Minnie moved her gloved fingers ever so slightly deeper into his larger bare hands, and he moved his thumbs to cover the backs of her hands. From his height he could look at both her gloved hands and her down-turned face which she brought back up to smile into his eyes, a gesture which brushed the feather of her hat against his cheek. They both spoke at the same time, "I'm so glad you came." "How nice to see you."

Then they laughed and he made his suggestion. They made a dash for the train, which waited because JW had tipped the engineer, and rode to Celina. The day was brisk, for it was late in the fall. In spite of the temperature the large lake attracted a good many people. The long thin feather in her hat rippled with the breeze. Minnie was hoping to be engaged by Christmas and married in the spring. As they walked the boardwalk, she smiled up at her intended and wondered how to make her dreams come true. Well, she did not come this far to let the afternoon pass without his verbal proposal. As they stepped up to a dock to view the few boats on the expansive water, she pulled her skirt up just enough to display layers of lace from her petticoats, and then moved her foot through the foam of the lace to give him a glimpse of her ankle. He caught the bait. She could see his eyes enlarge, so she grabbed at his wrist as though in need of support as she finished her step up to the viewing platform. He extended his other arm and she glided into his gentle near-embrace. "Why, John, it is marvelous being close to you by the water. But, goodness, the air is cold." She frowned but achieved the desired effect for her gentleman friend reflectively pulled her a little closer. She held there a minute, then stepped back. He was hers and she knew it. There was no need to make more of a scene. Lightly, teasingly, she spoke to her besotted companion, "You know, John Lambert, you should not display me like this without speaking to me of your intentions."

John was truly dumbfounded. His heart, hardly quieted from his first glimpse of her, now pounded in his throat. Tongue-tied and delighted, he could find no words but he managed to smile. She looked so small and precious standing beside him. She smelled divine; even in the breeze off the water her perfume reached his nose. The ripples on the lake glistened from the golden sun low in the November sky. He held her in his view against the water, ready to hear her prompt. He could still see the image of her little leather shoe with its row of tiny buttons nestled in the white eyelet. "Well, John," Minnie smiled warmly although her tone took on the hint of a reprimand, "Now you need to ask me the question I traveled all this way to answer." She looked in his handsome face with patience and determination. Underneath she was giddy.

"Will you marry me?" he said without thinking, as though he said, "The sky is blue."

She said, "Of course I will." She offered her cheek which he bent down to meet for a quick connection before returning his head to his usual height, a good foot above hers. He felt carried by a celestial wind. Having touched her skin, John's lips were sending streams of current all over his body. She was an exciting phenomenon and her company fascinated him. This told him they should marry.

"I will speak to your father when I see him this afternoon," John announced as he suddenly thought of the gentleman still in Enterprise with his hired help. "You must come back to Enterprise for I don't want you traveling alone." They walked across the muddy, wide rutty road to the Red Rooster Inn for tea to warm themselves and to pass time until the train was due to come through again. John was happy and unusually chatty. He told her about the physical building of the granary, the success of his "get-to-know-me" event, and she understood the social event had been a business move in his mind, not a snub to her. She listened with her eyes but all the while was thinking ahead, seeing in her mind a Christmas-themed engagement party and a spring wedding.

They traveled the few minutes to Enterprise and met her father by the train stop, for the granary was right there. The history enthusiast had discovered one of the rocks he had heard about and was eager to tell them its size and shape and theories of its significance to early Indians. "Father, for heaven's sake, stop for a minute," she shushed him and got his attention.

"Dr. Kelley," JW began, "Your daughter has this day done me the honor of agreeing to be my wife. We ask your permission to proceed with these plans. I will treasure her, sir, forever." Minnie melted at his declaration.

Dr. Kelley's response was comical. He was truly surprised. After the clownlike look of wonder which covered his face came one of deep pleasure. "This match pleases me splendidly," was all he said before Minnie took over, "Thank you, Father. We'll go home now to deliver the news to Mother."

Minnie's family knew of the engagement for a week before JW thought to tell his family. When it occurred to him, he wired them the news. JW did not hear the giggles which happened after the telegram was read in the Hill Grove house, for George had a ball making fun. The family had expected this news because they all had seen the couple at Emma's party, had noticed their looks to each other, and Minnie's determined stand at his side. Tears of laughter rolled down George's cheeks as he said, "Our boy did not have a chance. This girl was bound and determined to get him and it looks like she did." He told a story, "Before Ohio was civilized, when the first settlers were in the area, there was a lot of dangerous game. Big cats, wild boars and grizzlies were seen on the edges of farms, and occasionally one snatched an animal or a small child. In order to rid themselves of these deadly threats the boys back then organized a huge, statewide hunting party. Each county ordered every able man to take a gun and join in a circle – a complete circle around the county line. With the whole area surrounded they would march toward the center and kill every varmint they stirred up. Those Kelley girls had JW surrounded like they were early settlers on a kill. It was only a matter of time before he fell." He so enjoyed the image of his son falling to a feminine predator that he laughed and laughed. "He had no more chance of escape than those ol' panthers." Plans were made for JW to bring Minnie to a Lambert dinner at Hill Grove.

By the time JW arrived in Hill Grove with Minnie, his father had settled down to an appropriate decorum. These last many years the family made the effort to go along with their beloved President Lincoln's suggestion for a November celebration of thanksgiving. Anna organized a big dinner in honor of both the thanksgiving and the engagement. She included Al and Libby and their families, Newton Glunt with his little son and even Harry rode the Ohio Central from Urbana to join in. JW had not thought to spread the news his way, but Anna did, and so Harry was on hand to celebrate JW and Minnie's betrothal. George toasted the couple, "I have not lost my son and now I learn I am gaining a daughter. Well, the more the merrier, Miss Minnie. Welcome to the family." There were smiles all around. Of course Anna wanted to know what timetable the young people anticipated for their plans. Minnie explained her family would host a Christmas Open House to announce the engagement, and then she hoped for a spring wedding. These words stopped the excited buzz of the conversation. *A spring wedding? Didn't Minnie know Emma's wedding was in March? Oh, Dear,* thought Anna. The moment passed without granting Minnie the courtesy of pointing out the complication, for Emma's date was set and the plans were in progress. It was not until the actual engagement party three weeks later the conflict came to light.

Minnie had not even a month to plan the Open House at which her engagement would become official. The intended bride made the decisions and arrangements in her parents' names for they were not able to help her, her mother for health reasons and her father because he had no expertise in entertaining. Her sisters, Dora, Cora and Lou, two of whom were already married and living nearby, helped with the arrangements and offered their homes to out-of-town attendees. It was a large gathering but then again, marrying one of the Lamberts of Hill Grove was a coup worth celebrating. The afternoon party was beautiful, from the intricately flavored food to the imported white daisies nestled in greens cut from nearby woods. John arrived the night before and was enchanted anew by the aura of beauty his fiancée radiated as their guests arrived. Dr. Kelley behaved with aplomb and glowed with pride on his daughter's behalf. It was ironic the seemingly absent-minded doctor could perform so well when the situation called for it. After awhile the doctor had had enough of small talk and implored JW to visit with him away from the crowd and sit amongst his displayed arrowheads in an old grain shed across the yard. JW went with his future father-in-law and together, on this important day, they examined stone specimens of an ancient civilization and surmised together what life had been like those many, many years ago. The doctor thought the young man came up with clever ideas which were, upon examination, quite plausible explanations for certain known facts. Through conversation they traveled the paths of old Indians and completely forgot the current circumstances they were in. After about an hour of this peaceful mental meandering, Minnie found the two men sitting in the darkened wooden interior and beckoned John to accompany her back to her guests.

On the surface, the two families and their select friends got along famously for Minnie's sisters were spirited, articulate and entertaining just like the Lamberts. Minnie enjoyed herself until the conflict over wedding dates came to light in a conversation with her future mother-in-law. Minnie was visibly upset. Anna tried to appease the disappointed girl by saying there could be two weddings, but Minnie would hear none of that. She didn't want to share her big event. Dora heard it first and found Cora and Lou, so together the Kelley sisters moved in to stifle Minnie's eminent tears and shore her up in order that the party not be spoiled for everyone. "Don't disappoint John," they told her for they knew their sister's yearnings for the man. She took their words to heart and acted her role as though she were Lillie Langtree, the actress. Anna knew Minnie was upset but defended the sanctity of Emma's day, even if Emma herself was less than enthusiastic about her March wedding. For John's future bride the conflict solidified a festering jealousy of the quiet and lovely Emma. Although Emma and Mr. Glunt arrived with a beautiful present, Minnie saw the gesture as smug for her vision was clouded by a green haze.

JW was relieved to return to Enterprise where he had little time to dwell on the peculiar moods of women. The uproar over wedding plans cramped his mind like a jammed typewriter. He knew Minnie had done most of the engagement party planning by herself, so it occurred to him her petulant behavior was because she was tired. He told himself it would all work out, and then he put his mind back on his business. He would be seeing her again soon enough over the Christmas holidays. He knew she would have liked an earlier meeting, but the travel was inconvenient for it was tied to train schedules and would eat attention needed for his business. But he thought nothing of dashing to Union for a few hours, usually on the late afternoon train to work on a project for his father redesigning the chassis they used for their horse-drawn carriages. Using bentwood and levers he was creating a smoother ride, keeping the wheels under greater control and assuring an effective braking system which would not throw all the travelers out onto the street. He had changed the configuration, making it lighter for resiliency. He intended to alter the vibration of the vehicle to avoid the resonance which rattled the trap in reaction to the road. He adjusted the old axles to be more sturdy and smooth running. It seemed every new idea he implemented hatched the need for looking at another part of the undercarriage. He worked on drawings of the designs in the evening in his room in his Enterprise home, intermittently with reading for pleasure and keeping the financial books for his own granary business. When he came up with an idea in Enterprise for the vehicle in Union, he was eager to put his hands to the task and would itch until he got down there to try it out.

Since he was a tyke, JW had absorbed himself in the mechanics of things. When his younger brother Christian came along, the tolerant young JW gained an audience, first in the outlaying farm buildings in Hill Grove and later at the factory site. The sight of the two brothers sitting together in front of some machine or tool had been a common thing during those early years. Christian Harry came up with an idea or two but mostly he listened and asked only an occasional question of his older brother. Now in the large, well-equipped factory workroom they hardly spoke, yet their hands communicated a lively conversation. Christian could follow what JW was doing and would point a finger or move a part as a way of suggesting a solution to the issue at hand. They even had a name for their overall endeavor. Their father honored them by spotlighting their work in his most recent promotions. They called themselves The Lambert Brothers Manufacturing Company. For the new undercarriages, the wood itself was integral to the design. They used bent wood but wanted to improve on their processes. They were working on soaking the wooden shafts and drying them in a brace, to bend and re-direct the flexibility inherent in the fibrous grain. This kind of mechanical experimentation to make it work better was JW's lifeblood. Back in Enterprise he opened a hardware store on Main Street, mostly so he could collect tools and use the back shed as workspace. As much as he invested himself in his business in Enterprise, at the end of the day he was thinking about such things as the number of coils per inch in ratio to the thickness of the wire. And on impulse he would jump on the train before it left with its bellowing belch of thick smoke and its load of grain fresh from his own rebuilt silos, so he could try out his idea in the Union workroom.

The businesses in Enterprise grew like saplings in Ohio soil. In the evenings in his new environs, he met with new friends, men who made him feel welcome at their own family's supper table, some local businessmen but mostly local farmers who shipped their produce from his granary. JW was respected for the service of his business, for his experiences as a farmer, and for his interest in mechanical things. The Swovelands were particularly gracious in extending a standing invitation every Thursday for a meal much like his mother served. Mrs. Swoveland felt concern the bachelor newcomer not be lonely, and at the same time she would give her friend Mrs. Schmidt a night off. Mr. Swoveland owned the drug store a short distance from the granary. The family helped their new friend celebrate his engagement to the unknown girl from Darke County much to the chagrin of a Swoveland sister whose doe eyes followed the good-looking businessman. After these suppers young Jim Swoveland accompanied JW on his walk home, eager for the chance for conversation. The younger boy understood the new neighbor had an interest in how machines worked. Young Jim had seen some trade magazines in his father's drug store and took it upon himself to deliver recent copies of *Scientific American* to JW at the grain elevator by the railroad tracks. JW was grateful for the gesture and allowed the boy to linger around the yard, for he was a cheerful lad and JW, away from his family for the first time, enjoyed his company. One magazine had an article about events in Europe related to the development of a gasoline-powered engine. The words rose from the page to meet JW's eager eyes. The article was about the type of engine he had seen when he was Jim Swoveland's age in the ashes of the tannery near Greenville. It told of the originator of that coal gas engine, Nicholas Otto. JW had precious little information except it had been built in France by a German designer. Before him now was an article about the outcome of a court case in France. Otto's company sued for royalties from a man named Carl Benz, who worked in Mannheim, Germany, for patent infringement on the four-stroke principle. Because an earlier inventor had mentioned this principal in a patent, the judge ruled it was not exclusive to Otto, so Benz need not pay royalties. Carl Benz, the article went on to say, was continuing to build four stroke engines whereas previously he had experimented with a two-stroke. Although the latter sold locally in Mannheim, he abandoned it because it was quick to overheat. The article further said a man named Gottlieb Daimler, an employee for Otto's company in the German city of Deutz, was continuing Otto's experimentation with a four-stroke internal combustion engine and had created a quiet machine. JW laughed out loud. That "quiet" probably meant the noise did not shake the rafters. At the same time he wondered how this was accomplished.

As John rode the train to Hill Grove for Christmas dinner with his mother and the family, he imagined himself traveling to Germany and France to see for himself what these men were putting together. It was a short train trip but he enjoyed every detail of his fantasy. He encountered no conflict in seeing himself among these great mechanical minds of Europe. In the same way he had spent hours with the boys in the machine shops in Greenville, or with his father's workers in Union City, or with the group which was defining itself in Enterprise, he saw himself sitting with Nicholas Otto, Gottlieb Daimler and Carl Benz, each picking the others' brains over such teasers as balance, durability, endurance, power, heat, sound and control.

8

Tinkering with New Ideas

The sun was too hot for dew and that saved the hemlines of the sisters and girl friends who came early to Minnie's father's house. They gathered to lay out the food they brought, to tie in place the nosegays they had dropped off the day before and to fawn over the bride, for this was her day. At twenty-four Minnie was relieved as well as excited this day had finally come but carefully showed only her excitement to her retinue who commented amongst themselves about the calmness, almost coolness, coming from the center of their attention. She had overseen the plans herself, the guest list, the menu, and the homemade decorations. With amazingly little bickering, her three sisters had participated with each step and thus encircled her as she orchestrated. One of Minnie's unspoken goals from within that circle was to shut the Lamberts out, for she found them overbearing. Her wedding was not to resemble the one which had occurred in the spring in which John's younger sister Emma married her Mr. Glunt. While Emma faded in her formal white dress, Minnie was striking in her stylish practical black taffeta. And there would be no influence of the evil alcohol at her wedding. Oh, it was not as bad as all that, she knew, but to draw stark contrasts reassured her she was not swamped by the Lambert luster which seemed to permeate all parts of her life. On this she and John agreed: their marriage would be independent of his large and powerful clan. They would be free to go their own way. It pleased her to set her own style, and on what other day was this better to happen than the day of her wedding?

Her compulsion to control began early, for the Kelley family had known hardship. The young girl had had to struggle at times to survive. Although her mother was a proud descendant of a Revolutionary War hero, known in the early generation for his bravery in the fight for independence, the pedigree faded for this family when the War Between the States lured the brother Minnie had not seen since she was two, the oldest son, from the struggling farm family. The absence of her son took a toll on Minnie's mother's health. Whether real or imagined, the woman suffered a series of afflictions and retreated from the care and concern of those who looked to her for their well-being. Minnie had pieced together in her own mind the reasons why her mythically esteemed older brother left home and why at the end of the War he headed right to California. When she was younger, she held to the childlike belief she was responsible for something terrible which drove him away and made him not love them. Later she turned to view her parents with suspicion for she imagined horrendous deeds must have been done to send him packing. Eventually Minnie learned it was more an accumulation of circumstances which repulsed him. Lonely and overburdened as a boy, he was saddled with helping a depressed mother and a distracted father whose attention for providing in those early days was sporadic. His mother was heavy with another child when the attack on Ft. Sumter signaled the outbreak of war. Thirteen-year-old George was infected by the battle cries, and soon after the baby was safely born he left to seek the far away glory of war. As the nation dissolved into civil war, the father also left for the Cause. At the age of thirty-nine, Thomas Kelley abandoned his needy wife and young children, the youngest a crawling baby, his land, and his farming profession to seek out the medic tents near the front lines in Virginia. His aim was to develop his interest in medicine and to test out his theories on healing. At least he came back, unlike his son, although he waited two years after the end of the fighting before he did. He took time to work in a hospital in Harrisburg but always held the intention to return to his family who now lived in the swampy back wood wilds of Darke County.

In the absence of her husband and older son, during those long war years and the two years after, the mother retreated into her depression. The young sisters scrounged to survive and to keep their mother alive. Lou was nine when her father left and thirteen when he returned; Cora was two years younger. They kept a vegetable garden, raised small fields of wheat and oats for bread and cereal, and brought the food home where five-year-old Orian looked after his baby sister Mary Francis and their stone-faced mother. The two youngest children gathered sticks for fuel, lugged water, pulled weeds and whatever other tasks their little legs and arms could manage. Orian's young mouth could not say "Mary Francis"; the syllables came out garbled and sounded like "Minnie" and so "Minnie" she became. During the cold winter months, more often than not with no fire, the fatherless family slept in the same bed for warmth, three girls, a little boy and their impassive mother. The dark cloud of this most personal of wars hung over their scrubby farm. While her sisters tended to other chores and before she could comfortably reach the kitchen counters or properly handle the cutting knife, young Minnie picked up the responsibility of cooking for the entire family under the sporadic instructions of her afflicted mother. It was an awesome burden. Her own legs were bowed from the rickets, for before she took up that knife, she had often gone hungry with the others. Eventually she and Orian kept chickens so they would have eggs. On special occasions they roasted a bird whose neck she wrung with her own little hands. When he was six, Orian learned to shoot from a neighbor named Phoebe Ann Moses who at eight helped support her struggling family by killing game she sold to the loggers' hotel near the Pennsy Railroad tracks. She had a sure shot and hit the birds in the head each time, not marring the meat of the body. By her instructions, the Kelley family added rabbit and squirrel to their menu. Phoebe Ann went on to become famous for her shooting and changed her name to Annie Oakley.

By 1870 the family was enjoying a few years of rebounding stability as the returned father sold his skills as a doctor and earned a reputation throughout northern Darke County up to Coldwater as a clever healer. He bought the house in Dallas where they now lived. In the earlier days they moved throughout the area, Wayne County, in Indiana near New Paris in Ohio and then to Washington Township in Darke County, squatting on high land cleared of trees abandoned before the Southern Rebellion by families headed farther west for kinder land in Minnesota and Iowa and for those who dreamed big, California. Nine months after their father's return, the youngest child and fourth sister arrived, Dora, an obvious disappointment to the father and mother who had pinned their hopes on a boy. For their own separate reasons, each had momentarily believed a little son would save them from the darkness of despair and discord. But God did not bless them with such, so the mother resumed her self-contained existence behind a shade drawn in her own mind, and the father wandered farther plying his trade as a physician and pursuing his endless eccentric interests in archeology, history, earth sciences and local Indian tribes: Miami, Iroquois, Shawnee and Wyondott. The entire country suffered during the economic recession in mid-decade, but Dr. Kelley regularly brought home animals and farm stuff if not money, so his family never went hungry. He had become a good provider.

Lou and Cora, both congenial by nature, did the best they could in their difficult circumstances. By the grace of God they believed what must be done is best done cheerfully, a motto captured in a needlepoint sampler hung on their wall. With a seven-year gap after Minnie, Dora born after the War was the youngest and was soon old enough to join in making life better. They all went to the county schoolhouse throughout the decade of the seventies and learned their letters. By the '80's Minnie spent time at teachers' college on the other side of Lima, and in turn Dora went too. The sisters made a study of style and manners. They were ambitious to appear cultured. They acquired a dog-eared copy of Catherine Beecher's *Treatise on Domestic Economy* and so studied fashion and homemaking. Minnie expanded her skills in the kitchen, and they all learned from each other. In spite of their mother's pedigree, they played up their father's French blood through their furnishings and food, for many of their neighbors enjoyed the same heritage. This served as well to distance themselves from being an Irish Kelly and they became active members of their Methodist church. Except for resurrecting their pride in their Revolutionary War hero ancestor Henry Horn, the four sisters joined in a conspiracy to hide the past. It was as though by ignoring their early hardship they willed it out of their lives and created the illusion of gracious prosperity. By the Centennial year, both Lou and Cora were married, each living with their husbands in nearby Dallas. Orian had moved to Toledo where he entered politics and was elected to a councilman's seat. Unlike the long-gone oldest brother George, the young fellow returned for visits riding the loud, dirty train which horrified his mother and sent her to rocking and mumbling to herself. Dora, the youngest, lived in the Dallas house with Minnie and their parents. Six years later, with Dora now sixteen, twenty-four-year-old Minnie was ready to take a husband and establish a home of her own. Unlike her sisters who married local men, Minnie had set her sights on a wider goal. When word of her father's relationship with John Lambert first reached the household, she knew what she must do and she did it. It was how this day came about.

Minnie was aware she had a perfectionist's streak, and was capable of curbing her own behavior in order to get what she ultimately wanted. Living through Emma's wedding was a case in point, for Minnie had anticipated it with loathing. Her sisters had warned her to make the day pleasant for John. It was HIS sister's wedding, given by HIS family, they said. And so, she honored his wish for the bride's happiness. As she made her way through that day, she made notes to herself of what not to do as she planned for her own wedding day. To others she was cordial and gracious. Before it was over, she surprised herself by having an enormously good time.

And now it was her day. Minnie lost her memory of the actual wedding. She could recall the sight through a bedroom window of the minister and first guests arriving, and that she was in the back bedroom to dress with her sisters. She remembered waiting there, for she would not appear in the parlor until the sounds of the borrowed organ played the strands of the bridal march. She can remember the sound of that music and knows she did walk through the hallway with her father, who whispered, "Je t'aime" as he let her go to take her place at John's side in front of the Officiant. This was the last of the celebration she can recall. She faithfully believes the minister recited the ceremony and both she and John repeated their vows, and she knows he kissed her right up there in front of everyone, the first time his lips had touched hers, and that the guests applauded. She just has no memory of it in her own mind. Her sisters and John's family have told her they had a very special time at the party; and they told her she seemed to enjoy herself as well. They all commented on how proud John was of his poised and smiling bride. Unfortunately, Minnie cannot recollect it herself.

But she recalls every detail of their evenings at the Red Rooster Inn. Taking their first night in Celina at the old Inn on Grand Lake where they had had tea on the day of their engagement was John's idea. Staying for four nights had been her suggestion, which he obliged with a wink and a sly smile. It was one of those moments which infuriated her. Yes, she offered the suggestion of prolonging their stay at the Lake. She was thinking of how relaxing it would be after the stress of the wedding and before taking their trip to the East Coast. He received it as risqué and his wink was bold. Her two impulses confused her: she wanted time to relax and enjoy the beginning of their wedding trip, but she did not want to admit or have him refer to the sexual excitement she felt. It was a force within her she both treasured and abhorred and a confusion he would play with throughout their marriage, for he was good-natured and kind while she was guarded and self-restricting. His affable generosity would win her over time and again.

When they finally arrived at the Inn, they were both tired after an eventful day. Although already in their mid-twenties, neither had had a prior love interest. Her older sisters had prepped her; John's father had taken him aside and given him advice. But all prior conversations had been labored and brief albeit well intentioned. The young lovers, not knowing where it would lead them, were ready to take the next step and expected to survive as countless other couples had done before them. Being farm folks they understood the basics. Minnie had prepared beyond her sisters' advice and had privately planned a display for her bridegroom, like a tableau, perhaps as a way of keeping this moment, so impossible to anticipate in fact, a bit under her control. Under the smart taffeta dress and her multicolored petticoats she wore ripples of white lace on her bodice, rows of which carried down each leg of her pantaloon.

John had reserved the newly decorated bridal suite at the Inn which included two second-story rooms, a spacious parlor and equally large bedroom, off of which was a balcony which looked out over the water. The rooms had oriental rugs, floral drapes, finely crafted large wooden furniture and a huge bouquet of fresh fragrant flowers on a round inlaid table standing in the middle of the parlor floor. The card in the lavish arrangement expressed love from his parents. Al and Eva had ordered the couple champagne which arrived in a silver bucket along side an expensive bowl of fresh fruit, grapes, pears, peaches and strawberries Libby and Dan had ordered over the wire. Minnie chose to ignore this flood of Lambert presence. "John, come here." The bride invited her new husband's help from the bedroom as her small hands worked the tiny buttons of her dress. "You see these small buttons? Do you think you could manage to unhook them without tearing the material?" Smiling firmly at his handsome face, she did not yet appreciate his dexterity with small parts. He approached her to begin his assignment, and she soon noticed how sensitive his fingers were, for he parted her sleeves in very little time. The sounds of the taffeta saved them from the silence in the room as they bravely experienced their physical proximity. Behind the dressing screen she freed herself of her outer layers and the practical whalebone stays she used as a corset over her slender yet generous body. She exited the screen to stand by the open door of the balcony where the lights around the shore gently flickered on the water. Her big moment had arrived. Decked in her rows of delicate lace she turned to show herself to him. He knew this was an intentional display and did his best not to rush to her in order to let the moment last. She could not know he never saw her dainty underwear for her female form bewitched him. "Lovely as the day in May," he quoted Longfellow to her. The warm July breeze across the water traveled in through the balcony door with a faint fragrance of honeysuckle touching her before he reached her, so his hands on her shoulders and back mixed with the sweet air for a sweep of sensual pleasure. The memory of his first kiss in that room stayed with her forever, for his wet lips on her mouth both shocked and thrilled her. After he did it several times she relaxed, and they both enjoyed connecting this way. They lay down on the bed under the soothing moonlight.

On the subsequent night they thought to look for stars. By shutting off the gas light jets in their rooms, they allowed the night sky to appear off their balcony. The day had been hot and the sky was clear, but the air moved in waves through the darkness. They were awed for the heavens were alive with tiny lights, some blinking while specks of light glimmered on the ripples of the lake. John recited the verse of his childhood, taught to the children by an uncle from Pennsylvania:

Star light, star bright,
First star I see tonight,
I wish I may, I wish I might,
Have this wish I wish tonight.

The two of them made wishes and devoutly kept their thought to themselves although the temptation to tell was great. John would have told but Minnie was insistent in not taunting fate. Their last night in Celina was moonless and the wind had left, allowing the stars in the night sky to reflect perfectly on the still surface of the expansive dark lake. It was late and all lights were out. Arm-in-arm on the balcony they looked out into a seemingly total dark world of stars and space. Their fancies took flight and their spirits did fly; the world seemed perfect and the future felt bright.

After their four nights on Grand Lake, they boarded the late morning Mackinaw train which came up from Cincinnati and rode far enough to switch outside Toledo onto the Northern Line to travel across Ohio into upstate New York. They planned to see the romantic Niagara Falls before pressing on to Boston. It was a short ride to Toledo where they caught the express to Cleveland. A thousand small towns flew by. Lake Erie kept them company bobbing in and out of view on the left. They covered the upper most corner of Pennsylvania into New York through Lackawanna and Buffalo. By the Canadian border, the young bride was so confident in her new role as intimate companion to her distinguished husband she slyly but unmistakably goosed him as they stood in the deserted depot steps. He laughed out loud. There they boarded the small old local train to the Falls which traveled along unremarkably until they rode across a spectacular suspension bridge. Powered by steam, their train had been converted before the War when it had been drawn by horses, the courses for whom were long since reclaimed by the encroaching wilderness except on the bridge where Minnie remarked on the relic, the parallel space on either side of the narrow track. John only grunted in response to her observations for he was engrossed in the expansive view as they passed over the deep gorge, and he knew she was chattering from height anxiety. He was also estimating distances and calculating the constructs of the wooden structure which held them, built by the same engineer who made the Brooklyn Bridge in another part of the state.

Their tour of the Falls was short; still, John had wanted to impress his new wife for he knew she was fastidious about details of her surroundings. The hotel where they stayed had been built in the boon years after the war. It displayed a luster of opulence which held back the vast foreign outreaches of Canada whose border was so near. There were large windows covered with wood slated screens which admitted the distant roar of the rushing river water as it spilled over the Falls. The room was moist like the air outside. There was a dynamic quality to the space, an expectation, like a strong force being held at bay. Perhaps the mood was enhanced by being so far away from home. Minnie had never traveled so far although technically she had been in two states, for she grew up sashaying back and forth across the Ohio/Indiana border. More likely that sense of eminent happenings was from the Falls themselves. John had tried to talk about hydraulic energy at dinner, but Minnie waved him off to critique the interior decorations of the large dining space. Although dulled by a cloud cover, the next day brought them sights for which no amount of reading or stereograph pictures could prepare them. Without the sun, they missed the sparkling rainbows of color in the bouncing moisture, but the penetrating spray in the air nonetheless bathed the young farm people as they viewed the horseshoe sweep of the Falls. The sound of the falling water precluded much talking, but Minnie's opinion about what she saw was expressed unmistakably in her eyes. Around them other couples loitered in each other's arms. Later in the summer the newly designated Niagara Falls Park would be dedicated by the State of New York.

In the morning, they traveled back across the Niagara Railroad Suspension Bridge to the train they would ride across New York State following the route of Clinton's Folly, the old canal. They passed Syracuse and Albany and traveled into Massachusetts and Boston where John had booked a suite at the Hotel Boylston. There they rode a new passenger elevator up to their room which passed walls covered in gold brocade Minnie noted, while the pulleys and wheels of the elevator captured John's attention. As friends from home had suggested, they ate their breakfasts at the Parker House to enjoy the bread and the rolls. So far away from Ohio, they strolled the Public Gardens and stepped onto one of the swan-shaped boats in its little pond. They noticed so many kinds of people with strange habits speaking a variety of languages. John asked questions about the excavation projects, for the Bostonians were lopping off hills and moving vast quantities of land to enlarge their busy city. When a steam-powered combination fire wagon went by on the street, John made notes of its estimated specifications to report to his father and Al. They heard about the Great Fire of a dozen years back which did an astounding seventy-five million dollars damage. It destroyed warehouses, churches and offices before the firefighters could drag the big pumpers out of the stables to the blaze. John saw a case for self-propelled vehicles, for the fire horses had been down with a disease and were convalescing out of the city. As a result, a lot of property was lost before the fire-fighting even began. Boston now had steam-driven streetcars John wanted to ride, but Minnie held back for fear of an explosion, and he would not leave her unaccompanied. Different companies shared the same tracks on the busy Boston streets. The resulting chaos at the corners was exacerbated by the drivers who yelled and cursed at each other as they vied to transverse their routes. On one stroll the newlyweds happened upon a massive squeeze and stopped to watch as the operator of a stalled streetcar struggled to realign the wheels of his vehicle to the iron rails on the ground, all the while other operators loudly harassed him and put on a show for their hot and impatient riders. As the Ohioans had observed in Celina, here also were red, white and blue buntings hanging from windows and doorways for Independence Day had just passed. Throughout their week they saw historic sites, heard opera and toured the Museum of Fine Arts. They ate leisurely meals overlooking the Boston Common where cows used to graze.

After their stay in the city, both John and Minnie looked forward to the relative calm of the seashore. With the help of the concierge in the hotel lobby, John hired a borauch and driver to take them to Cape Ann. As they approached Swampscott, the salt in the air made Minnie's eyes widen. She breathed deeply but avoided looking at John who kept an eye on the shoreline while jotting down notes. He wanted to remember the specifics of the relentless barrage of ideas which flowed through his mind – for example, ways to build up Enterprise to develop the community and draw more of the far-reaching farmers into the services of the granary, a vision begun on this trip. He would purchase engines and start milling his lumber and grinding grain by the railroad. He wanted to expand his hardware store. He thought of detailed ways to smooth out the ride for a heavier load for the carriages his father was building in Union City. He even made notes to pass on to Al about market contacts in each of their stops from Grand Lake to the Atlantic.

Minnie had been homesick as they ended their tour of the sights of Boston, but her excitement again took hold as she saw the soft sandy beaches running along the right side of the carriage, through the long sloping yards between houses. Large white seagulls swooped and called out their greetings. The far horizon stretched beyond the blue, breaking waves and Minnie could hardly believe her thought France was on the other side. White pillars rose three stories on the large Georgian porch of their hotel at Swampscott which had a lawn stretching to the beach. This was Grand Lake times ten! And the John Lamberts enjoyed it at least as much as their home state resort. Both had been eager to see the Atlantic with the smells, the constant noise and motion, the gritty, dirty feeling of the sand and the salty warm breeze. The vastness of the sea was matched by the vastness of the established East Coast wealth. There were huge private mansions to be glimpsed through the trees up and down the coastline which raised the hackles on Minnie's neck. John accused her of jealousy but she defended her condemnation of waste and lavish ostentatiousness. This was the age of the super rich, railroad barons and big money houses. Minnie was sure of their evil and confident in her judgments which John found too easy to poke fun at, for she was so high and mighty in her opinions. He did not take her too seriously and told her as they sat on the veranda of the hotel before their supper the fruity vodka drink in her hand had no alcohol. After a few sips she relaxed to the breeze in the air off the ocean and forgot about the unattainable amenities she had witnessed earlier in the day.

They walked on the beach, John in his long pants and leather shoes, Minnie in her bustles and little buttoned boots. They were miserable with the grit, but kept each other smiling until they accomplished the distance they had set for themselves. John perspired with the effort and Minnie gleamed. They agreed they preferred the hard, fertile black farmland they were more familiar with, but they conspired to keep to the story line of pleasurable adventure upon their return to their families. They sipped lemonade from a vendor at the seashore and purchased several items for their home in the row of artisan shops, an oak captain's chair from the eighteenth century, a large oil painting of the ocean and a nautical clock for the wall, all of which they paid extra to have packed up and shipped separately, so they would not have to lug them the rest of their trip. John wanted to buy gloves for his bride, embroidered and fashioned in France, but she insisted he not because they were expensive. He returned to the quaint little shop on his walk while she rested in the room by herself and tucked them in his valise to pull out as a surprise back home in Enterprise, perhaps for Christmas if he could wait so long.

Minnie had been homesick earlier and was now coming down with her second bout, so by the end of their stay at the seaside resort she was eager to board the Pullman train for the overnight ride home. She was homesick but not bored with her husband. For the past year she had loved the idea of becoming his wife; now she was in love with the man. The four nights in Celina launched an important union for them both. For him it was like four confining walls around his heart had fallen outward, and he now enjoyed the expanse of loving this woman. Unlike his wife, John remembered all details of the wedding celebration and filed them in a treasured locked box in his heart. He understood her preference he never speak of the things they did in private and he respected her wishes. Although they were first graders in the arts of physical love, they were pleased with themselves and guarded their secrets. Yes, he was content with the recent events of his life. He was a happily married man and his business was flourishing with opportunity abounding. While he sat on top of the world, his sister Emma was facing a different reality. She had her hands full with her new husband and his small son.

Along side his farm work, Isaac Newton Glunt was trying to start a husking and shredding business which kept him busy beyond the routine of a farmer. His farm was modest but his ambitions were strong. While he was out and about, Emma confronted her new living situation. The house, with fewer and smaller rooms, was older than the one she came from. She was used to working a kitchen which fed a large group of people. Initially the demands of tending this smaller domicile and feeding this smaller group of workers and family came as a relief. What she was not expecting were her husband's criticisms and lack of geniality. She told herself he was busy and still grieving, that with time he would enter into a familial habit. As for now, having inhaled his food at each meal, he left the table before she had a chance to sit down. He did not notice the care she took with her spices and presentation, but commented how this dish or that did not taste the way Allie, his dead wife, would have prepared it. Even though his house was smaller and the maid was compliant, Emma fell behind in her work. She was lethargic and sad and left her journal untouched. Mama noticed and asked if the stork were planning a visit, but Emma denied it. She could not bring herself to tell her mother about the massive difference between the two households. Her feelings had been hurt when the cleaning girl in her chatter had innocently told her Newtie had fired another worker when he married her. She had replaced a maid! Her days seemed so different now and so bleak. She missed her family, especially her best friend and sister. She missed her brother. He, with his new wife, was living all the way up in Van Wert County and hardly ever came home unless she counted Union City as home, for he still kept his work at the factory. In her sadness, she thought of Savina and how losing those kitchen-table talks with the Ohio pioneer left a hole in her life. Her grandmother had been a wise adviser and confidante. Having never felt so let down, she was stunned life could throw up such a cold stone wall. She told herself she was undergoing a big adjustment, marriage, and with time she would get used to it. Husband and new wife needed time to accept each other. They rarely spoke, except when he asked her in his businessman's clip about household affairs. Feeling like a schoolgirl, she tried to anticipate his needs so her answers would bring about his smiling approval, but that never came.

Anna knew by instinct Mollie would be helpful in raising Emma's spirits. The two girls had been as close as sisters could be. The watchful mother saw Mollie moping around the Lambert household missing Emma; so, she encouraged the eighteen-year-old to visit her newly wed sister at the nearby Glunt farm. Mollie began spending most afternoons with Emma, watching and playing with little Roly, Newtie's two-year-old son by his poor deceased wife. He was a happy little boy and the girls enjoyed his adventuresome ways. They played "buzzy bee" and "mousy creep" with him which made him giggle and bat at their hands. Their long skirts and corsets kept them from laying on the floor to play "Cat and Birdies" though they were tempted. Instead they chased and tickled him all over the house and yard until Newtie came home unexpectedly one afternoon. He caught them laughing over a game of Hide and Seek throughout the upstairs bedrooms and put a stop to the "roughneck play" in the house.

The girls put their heads together to think of a distraction for Emma's serious husband. Although he worked hard, the Glunt family financial situation limited the resources for adventure, especially in these strained economic times, so they devised a plan to go to the old family farm near Mechanicsburg. Emma and Mollie were young girls when the family moved from that farm, but they still had memories of the place and their times. The girls thought the visit would help Newtie forget the sadness of losing his wife and dear newborn child. His auxiliary business was much the same as what Lewis, and now Harry, too, had going from the Urbana farm. They owned the threshing machines which serviced the farmers of the area. After the harvest was in and the colder weather descended upon them, Newtie began to spend more time around the house. Emma made her suggestion and to her surprise he agreed to go. The trip did soften him a bit, enough so when she discovered after the new year she was pregnant, he was happy, and she took heart. She wanted to replace his losses, with herself as his wife and now a baby for the child who died. She thought about the pain the deaths caused him and without his asking, forgave him the unpleasantness he showed.

The train trip to Urbana was an adventure. Mollie held little Roly on her lap or walked with him up and down the center aisle of their railroad car while her sister and brother-in-law sat in silence in their closed compartment. The leaves were off the trees so they could look out from the train windows through the overgrowth near the tracks into the farmyards of the adjacent land. They saw fields of winter wheat and red clover, planted to replenish the soil. The day was warm for November and the train seats smelled sour, so they alighted from the confines of the car to stroll the platform of Springfield Station while passengers loaded up for the resumption of their journey. It was a short jaunt to the small town of London where Cousin Harry, as promised in his return message over the telegraph wire, was there to pick them up. His hair was still long and worn in a ponytail tied with a string down the center of his back as an on-going symbol of solidarity with, and remembrance of, his companions killed in battle. Harry was active in keeping the lessons of the Rebellion alive by helping the former First Lady Mrs. Garfield. He was assembling war equipment, collecting letters of the time, and writing out testimonies of stirring war exploits especially the 43rd Voluntary Ohio Battalion which was led by her husband, Major General James Garfield. Their efforts were now doubled for those who had fought were dying off. General Grant, the popular President and hero of Vicksburg and Appomattox, had died this past summer. In death he achieved what eluded his Presidency when war leaders of both sections cooperated to carry his coffin. Harry greeted his cousins with his gap-tooth grin and heaved their bags into the wagon. He had gained a little weight and seemed to have carved out some contentment.

The travelers planned to stay a week. In the evenings, Lewis and his intelligent wife, the former school teacher, read Shakespeare and Professor Longfellow's poems. They were delighted at the sisters' ability to recite many of the lines along with their recitation. Their children joined in as well as Cousin Harry and Given, the farm hand hired by George who now was more of a family member. They divided up parts and read *Much Ado About Nothing*. Newtie fell asleep in his chair, but Emma enjoyed the academic stimulation from her cousins. In the daytime Lewis and Harry showed Newtie their machines while Given tended to necessary chores. The old horse-driven thresher Harry had helped George with when he was a youth had been upgraded to a steam-driven model. They fired her up and let her run, the noise from which precluded all conversation but pleased all three of the men.

Anna's old friend Mrs. Longnecker had been dead for several years. Her husband had died before that, so Harvey, the son, now ran the family farm with his brother and sisters who lived together in the old family house. On their first full day, a crisp November offering, Mollie and Emma pulled a wagon carrying little Roly tucked under a rough wool blanket to visit their old neighbors. Emma had no idea ahead of time the fateful act they committed. They arrived to see, just like in the olden days, junk strewn over the yard, old tillers and rusting harvesters and a wagon with large, decaying wooden wheels covered in a tangle of bright yellow ironweeds. The Longnecker children, all grown up as were Mollie and Emma, welcomed their old friends. Mollie and Harvey Longnecker soon found an excuse to spend time alone together. On the walk home after that first visit, panic-stricken Mollie told her sister how he had tried to embrace her when they were out by the empty lilac bushes. Emma misunderstood at first, thinking the attempted kiss was the problem. But Mollie's distress was not over the attempt but over her own inability to kiss him back. To say he took her breath away was an understatement; she thought she was suffering a heart seizure and had nearly thrown up. She had had to sit down on the ground while her body shook roughly as she cried dry, raspy sounds. Harvey had been horrified and squatted next to her. He rubbed her back until she calmed down, then grinned at her apologies, for he was a tolerant, unassuming man who had seen a wide variety of behavior within his own family.

The next day, the girls with little Roly visited again and again Harvey invited Mollie into the yard. She repeated her efforts to tolerate his kiss. She liked the boy and was eager at eighteen to be a married woman. Because she had built a wall around herself, there were no boys back in Darke County who interested her or rather who did not thoroughly intimidate her. But Harvey was strangely familiar, like a member of the family almost. He was so boyish and eager for her kisses, apologizing and soothing her as he tried to get his lips on her. The second day she felt again like she was drowning for she could not catch her breath, and her chest was as tight as a fox trap. By the end of the week, Harvey had gotten a kiss and Mollie had shed enough tears to fill Lake

Superior. Getting close to him meant opening a part of her she tried to keep shut. Pictures flashed in her mind of a disgusting sore under a dirty beard, and she remembered the foul smell of someone's breath. She screamed in her sleep and the sound rang through the dark, unfamiliar house. Emma had heard the piercing cry and tiptoed with speed into where her sister lay, crawled in her bed and held her while she cried herself back to sleep. No one asked the cause of the outcry in the morning. The girls kept their closed counsel; both understood there was an inner devil afoot who needed to be fought and vanquished. They cast Harvey as a knight in shining armor, come to rescue Mollie from the turmoil of her memory. He could break through her fear and give her a normal life. Sunny and persistent, he was totally accepting of her waning hysterics and, at the week's end, thrilled to receive her kiss. Newtie made him promise to wire her father to ask for Mollie's hand in marriage. Harvey could not believe his good luck and strutted around saying God worked in mysterious ways for who could have anticipated this unexpected turn of events. Ironically, he called Mollie his saving angel, for his life was drab and it bored him.

Mrs. Longnecker had been Anna's first friend in Ohio, much to Savina's disapproval who had harbored resentment of all Longneckers for the attitudes and behaviors of a few. Anna had ignored her mother's criticisms and befriended the gentle wife of the irresponsible, good-natured man who died young as the result of his love of strong drink. Harvey's mother had given kind comfort to Anna when baby Savina died. Anna's answer to those who held grudges was we are all the children of God. George and Anna received the proposal of marriage with approval, and George wired back to young Harvey Longnecker they would be happy to receive his visit to hear his request to marry their daughter. His arrival was a point of commotion and excitement in the house, as Mollie was obviously flustered, eager to see him but subject to tearful bouts of self-doubt. Her three younger brothers both teased her and retreated in respectful concern. Anna, too, was puzzled to see her usually quiet daughter put on such a show and told her to pull herself together. Mollie calmed down after Harvey arrived at which time he made his request with aplomb. Harvey was proud to be accepted by the Lamberts whom his own mother had loved, and by Mollie, so pretty and shy. Together with Anna and George, Mollie and Harvey made their marriage plans. Mollie wanted to avoid a fuss and asked not for a formal wedding like her parents had given her sisters but for an informal ceremony in the near future. The engagement would be announced through the newspapers and through Anna's writing to far away family members.

Two weeks before her nineteenth birthday, on February 13, 1886 the young couple would say their vows in Greenville's St. Paul's Presbyterian Church directly after Sunday Services. Mollie wanted that setting for she took her love of Jesus very seriously and was fond of the minister Reverend Bumiller who had seen a sadness in the young girl and kindly assured her of Jesus' concern. Afterward they would return to the house for a quiet meal. As the marriage plans were simple, time was spent during Harvey's visit musing about the future in general. It made Mollie happy to see that Harvey was agog in the Lambert house; he was obviously impressed with the style the family had achieved. George, too, liked that attitude in his future son-in-law. Before mentioning it to Mollie, he offered young Harvey a job in his office. He was needing an additional man to help with correspondence. Mollie cried tears of relief at the news because she did not want to leave her family. Even though Urbana was not very far in distance, it was still farther than a hop, skip or jump. Whereas Anna believed young people needed privacy to adjust to marriage, she nonetheless offered Mollie's room to the couple, until they got their feet on the ground and could get out on their own. After this plan was agreed upon, George smiled a big, broad grin and said with authority, "By counting noses at my dinner table, after Emma married, I lost one. Now, I gain one. Lose one; gain one." It pleased him to say it.

Mollie's parents understood Harvey did not have much money to bring to the marriage; his assets were back in Urbana in the land he shared with his brother and sisters. When he returned to his Urbana home, he told them the extent of his good fortune which they accepted. With the price of wheat the lowest in forty years, it would be easier to lose Harvey than have an additional mouth to feed. Harvey's leaving meant they had to adjust. The next two oldest were girls. The younger dressed herself as a man and had worked the farm along side Harvey and their younger brother. She was the natural choice to take over as leader.

February came and Mollie married Harvey. The only out-of-town guests were a surprise. Levi Furst, Grandma Savina's son and Anna's half-brother, came up from Kentucky with his wife. After the Reverend Bumiller said his good-byes and the couple left for their wedding trip riding the railroad line to Chicago in over-sized velvet-covered swivel chairs bolted to the floor of the rumbling car, Newtie brought out a bottle of champagne and enough glasses on a tray so all the remaining relatives could drink a toast to "Emma's success." Emma nodded her head to her mother. She would be having a baby at the end of the summer. Anna cried. Her oldest daughter had become a mother at sixteen, hardly a time of celebration, and it was the only child to come along in fourteen years. Her second daughter lay in a grave for twenty-four years, gone but not forgotten. And now her third daughter, having married late, was to make her a grandmother again. Sure Al had little Maggie and Eva was finally expecting again but those were Eva's children. She expected her sons would go make lives of their own even if JW had picked the worst time to do so. But her daughters she expected to remain with her always. She could not explain her response to Emma's news except it made her deeply happy. Emma thought she had reason to be hopeful: her pregnancy seemed to settle her marriage, her dear sister seemed to have found happiness, and there was progress in her relationship with Minnie. JW's wife still held herself apart from the family but Emma had managed to engage her in a brief conversation outside the church. She wanted Minnie to like her for JW was the most important person in her life, at least until her baby was born.

Twenty-year-old Christian Harry sat in JW's Enterprise office in the corner of the wooden granary building by the railroad tracks while his older brother caught him up on his dealings in this small northern town. JW was explaining, "Even with the price of wheat where it is, my operation pays for itself with some to spare. I have money in the bank I want to invest in the town. People are good around here." JW received good shipping prices from family contacts in Springfield and he got good rail rates in Enterprise. His business was steady, convenient and the grain was high quality. Christian Harry knew from watching his oldest brother Al, who was involved with his father-in-law's concern in Greenville, that the elevator business could be lucrative. He understood JW was in a position to hire the sons of struggling farmers eager to work to supplement a dwindled income.

"You're better off than Al. The prices are the lowest in forty years, JW. Al is hurting just as his family is expanding."

JW ignored the talk of Al's finances. He knew his brother was building a larger home in Union City as well as expecting a baby. "I put money in a building over on Main Street. A couple of locals want a Town Hall, so we'll put it there. There's room enough for a jail. That slab behind the dump is better suited for raccoons."

"So, you're becoming a town father, huh? Building up the structures of civilization, eh?" Christian's tone was playful.

"I bought a Corliss and had it installed at the lumberyard. I'm milling my own wood now. A number of men around here want to build a music theater and I have a back up of lumber so I gave the okay to have it built above the town hall, a second story. Lewis was up here last week making suggestions." It had taken Lewis a long time to cross the several counties to Enterprise; with luckier train schedules the travel time could have been half of what it was.

"You are changing, big brother. Watch out for the ill effects of marriage! I see a John D. Rockefeller emerging and I had expected a Thomas Edison." Christian had a large smile which dropped years off his face. He had recently moved in to his grandmother's empty house across the yard on his father's Hill Grove property. The little house had seemed lonely, so still and empty since the lively old pioneer had died. Seventeen-year-old Frank moved in with his brother leaving only the two young boys still in the family house. JW looked at him with confusion, and then shook his head. His twenty-year-old brother was hinting at something. "Okay, I know what you want. After we eat I'll show you what I've been working on." With that kind of talk Christian Harry felt comfortable; he would be alarmed if JW abandoned his tinkering. He was glad to receive the invitation, for it made him feel special to be in JW's confidence, and in spite of his teasing, he was concerned about the placating effects of marriage. They walked the short distance to John and Minnie's home.

After an awkward meal with Minnie, for their landlady Mrs. Schmidt was pointedly banging cabinet doors in the other room, the two brown-haired men walked to a small, tarred wooden building which was behind John's hardware store on Crimean Street. One wall of the building had a wide hung door on a track from above. There, in the middle of a bright room crowded with tools, rolls of wire, measuring devises, rags, buckets of nails and a portable oil lantern for supplemental light, was what looked like a chassis with a lot of extra flourishes. With his hands on his hips, Christian stared at the configuration. "What are you doing?" He spoke softly and hung his words in the air, his eyes not leaving the formation of metal rods, springs, clamps, weights, wheels and plumb line. Unknown to his brother, JW had corresponded with a fellow up in Grand Rapids who had created a spiral coil which attached to two bars under the seat of a buggy and gave the ride a lot more stability; JW thought he might improve on his ideas. He walked to the far side of the skeleton of metal which seemed to float over the floor and pointed to a cross section of rods and springs toward the front of the model. "By putting this spring here I think I can eliminate the dumping that happens in most turns when there's no load in back." Christian Harry was immediately confused. His brother always assumed he understood principals he in fact had never heard of. He did not read the way JW did; he preferred adventure stories to science books and had just finished *Ben Hur*. But he did know the dumping problem, how passengers or cargo was often spilled, forced out of a vehicle as it awkwardly maneuvered a corner. But he made no pretense of knowing about balance and counter-balance and the effects of springs and their placement. His thinking and thus his expertise went to wheel design and the properties of the material used. He kept silent as JW continued, "I've tried different strengths of springs. Before I came up with this configuration, I tried placing this spring over there." He pointed from one place to another. This choice had meaning to JW, but the significance eluded Christian Harry. He remained silent except for an encouraging grunt. JW's words about the model were few, as he pointed and considered his own work in his brother's presence. This rather quiet conversation continued for an hour or more. Then Christian Harry hopped the late afternoon train back to Hill Grove.

That night, back on the second floor parlor of the widow's house, Minnie announced to her entrepreneurial husband she wanted a home of their own. She was taking a chance, she knew. She could hear the voices of her sisters in her mind's ear, telling her not to stress John financially, to let him make the offers and suggestions for their advancement. But she had waited long enough, almost four months. By observation she felt quite sure John's finances were in adequate shape. She knew he owned timberland up in northern Van Wert County which supplied his lumberyard where there was a brand new engine driving the large metal blades. If he can build the village an opera house, not to mention a town hall and a jail, he could build her a home. He does not even like opera, she harrumphed to herself. Besides, she told her conscience, it would be his home too, and she would make it a place he would be proud of. When Minnie presented her case, John was surprised to hear of his wife's discord with the landlady and the mystery of it prompted him to agree quickly to Minnie's demand. *A woman needs a home of her own,* he chided himself. Minnie continued her justification even though she had won his promise quickly. "We need a home to demonstrate your success, John," an assertion he did not feel but he had seen his father and brother act on the principal. So, after a brief search, a property was secured near the center of town on Banner Street, plans were drawn up quickly and construction began for a modest house with wide eaves and large rooms. The men of Van Wert County were well occupied the entire winter, constructing buildings for the town and the new home for the Lamberts at John's expense and thus fulfilling both John's visions and Minnie's for how to proceed with life in Enterprise.

As their first winter together turned into spring and the house received its finishing touches, including an indoor toilet in the basement, electric lighting throughout, centralized heating, a stained glass window from Cincinnati and furniture from both their family homes, Minnie discovered she was enciente. She was horrified at what she was called upon to endure for her condition. Her discomfort was debilitating for after throwing up every morning throughout the morning she was nauseous the rest of the day. Eating anything was difficult. John found and summoned a doctor from Cincinnati to examine his tiny wife. "Yes," the Boston-educated specialist said in response to the young couple's anxious questions, "she is small but should tolerate the delivery of a small infant easily." He shrugged at the sickness and called it normal. He roughed up John's shoulder and laughed, "Pray for a wee one, my man," John took offense and delighted in seeing the man gone from his house and his town, away from his vulnerable wife who was the one who alone faced the peril at hand. This doctor had no more compassion than an old rag. Both John and Minnie worried throughout the duration of the wait, John out of helpless concern and Minnie out of her indignation at having to endure the current discomfort as well as the dread of the labor. Equal to Minnie's ennui was her pleasure in being at the center of John's concern. As the time approached for the delivery, he did not leave Enterprise in order to be at her side when her labor began. As time marched through the pregnancy Minnie was visited by her three tiny sisters, the older of whom were mothers themselves. They psshawed her fear but exchanged dark, knowing looks among themselves and Minnie was not comforted.

Finally her time came. The labor went on for many hours and suddenly stopped. The contractions subsided yet still the baby was unborn. The Boston doctor was sent for. He traveled from Cincinnati on the Mackinaw Line, once he boarded a train, but had no train to board for four hours. He arrived muttering and irked, for he in turn had disliked these small town types who thought they could tell him how to practice medicine. The labor had resumed without him so when he entered the house, the midwife, the sisters and Minnie were hard at work in the large bedroom overlooking the front and side yards for their house was on a corner lot and the lawn was expansive. The lives of two Lamberts were in serious jeopardy. John and Christian Harry were smoking cigars in the parlor under the very bedroom where Minnie labored; every cry they heard through the floor boards brought another round of brandy. John sipped at his glass, sometimes taking in only fumes, while his brother drank deeply each time. As the hands of the clock worked their way past midnight, Christian Harry began making up word games, putting words together and cracking himself up. "Sassy chassis," he giggled and inspired, he enunciated, "classy chassis," and spit out a gaffaw just before he fell asleep. John kept the vigil all night by himself. He thumbed through a book of optical illusions and worked puzzles his father had bought in Chicago, but they were not enough to keep his mind off his wife. So, he read from *The Bible* intermittently with Darwin's *Origin of the Species*. John's parents had come up earlier in the day and gone home. Anna did not want to scare

Minnie by staying, to have her think they were there to comfort John in the worst of outcomes.

Just before dawn Minnie at last delivered her daughter, a sizable, healthy girl who shouted her presence with lustful cries. JW looked up from his book. He read the clock; it said six-thirteen. As the outside early light weakened the brilliance of the electric lamps in the room, the doctor and four women came down the stairs. When they proclaimed him a father, he allowed Lou to take him upstairs to greet his wife who cuddled the infant next to her spent body. The sweetness of his concern was not lost on his sister-in-law, who reported downstairs what details she could witness before she properly left the married couple to enjoy these moments in private. John was shocked at the sight of the new mother. Her tangled wet hair showed fresh comb paths near her forehead and her skin was white except for dark, swollen circles under her eyes. He had stepped quickly to their bed to touch her face; her smile was radiant through her waning distress. "Look what we have, John." She touched the soft blanket which surrounded their daughter sleeping innocently, unaware of the dangers which accompanied her arrival. Minnie would have preferred a boy, but was too exhausted to feel much reaction to anything so trivial as gender. John was delighted with his beautiful, perfect daughter. The new mother encouraged her exhausted husband to lift little Ethel Mae into his arms. He gingerly did; Minnie was too tired to instruct him which would have unnerved him, so in his best style he walked his little bundle over to the window. The new morning light coming through the bare branches of the horse chestnut showed him her perfect face and tiny fingers, each matched one to the other on remarkably large hands for a newborn and that face so tiny, round and sweet. The pulse of her little heart was pounding at her temple which alarmed him, but when he looked up to ask his wife if that were alright, he saw she had fallen asleep. Alone then with his daughter, he touched her gentle skin and studied her miniature features. Standing at over six feet, he was used to Minnie's smallness and often teased her for her tininess. Here was a truly tiny person and he was awed. Knocking at the door, Cora entered with that miserable Cincinnati show-off, but John smiled blissfully, for the doctor and the others had brought Minnie safely through her ordeal and together they had a new life to celebrate. The doctor felt Minnie's forehead and took hold of her wrist to count out her pulse. He made notes and spoke to the midwife, who politely agreed to all his instructions before he left. The young farm girl recently hired could take over now.

As that first week went by, Minnie began her recovery. Their baby slept soundly and ate like she had a hollow leg. Their families came for short visits. John sent a wire to Urbana to announce Mae's birth and to invite his favorite cousin the Civil War veteran to Enterprise to see for himself the most beautiful baby "this side of the Mississippi" for JW had in mind Harry's babies had been born on the other side. Harry arrived in two weeks with a bundle of family items from the Urbana farm attic thoughtfully selected by Lewis and his wife. Harry presented a little wagon he had designed and put together himself. The adults placed the child in the cavity and wheeled her around the parlor and on warm days, they bundled her up and took her outside. The prodigal relative stayed as planned for the Christmas holidays and then extended his visit at the Banner Street home throughout January, February and into March. He joined in the construction JW was underwriting by building beautiful stone walls around the granary yard. At the house, he lay a stone foundation for the combination barn and shed which would hold John's horses, carriages and tools for the yard. His craftsmanship created a rich ambiance. Many of the rocks were full of fossils, shells, bugs and pieces of wood left when the last glacier receded from the area thousands of years ago. The shale was easy to chip and could therefore be sized and placed face out to display the treasures of old.

Every day brought new delights to what the soft baby could do. Early on she could lift her head like an Irish body-builder. When she coordinated her hands, arms and wrists to roll herself over, John wired his parents. Her cooing was divine and she snored sweet little snorts when her sleep was the deepest. In spite of all that, John did go to work to keep the granary running and to manage his projects. He replaced the old steam-powered grist mill engine with a modern electric version, mostly because he wanted to study the large, stationary machine. At this time he began shipping lumber to the family plant at Union, for there was some financial trouble there and JW's price was right. His father set up a company in John's name to manufacture the handles which continued to sell after the rest of the corn planter became obsolete. Newly manufactured fire pumpers were backing up in the factory; his father and brother had tried too hard to sell an item they could not move. They were taking a bath in their own water equipment! The chassis continued to sell, most of them becoming fire trucks over in Anderson, Indiana at the Howe Fire Apparatus Company.

John and Harry sat on worn leather seats under a surried top behind a beautiful Kentucky mare as they drove around Enterprise to see all of John's projects. They ended at the Town Hall which had a jail out back and a music venue upstairs. On the ride, Harry was reminded of a walk around Springfield showing off construction projects to John's father in what seemed like another lifetime, for it was only days after George had arrived in Ohio over thirty years ago. The eight-year-old Harry had been proud to show his new-comer uncle the signs of success his father William had achieved in the fertile expanse of Ohio. Now the twenty-six-year-old JW took pride in showing his older cousin what he was doing in Enterprise. On this tour was the one lapse into seriousness Harry had when he spoke of his relationship with his father, "That was my father's big failure," he said out of the blue from the seat next to John. "He did not reach around my mother's problems to be a father to me. He never reached out as a man, and because I was a child, I didn't know how." Harry never once mentioned his own children. At several moments it seemed the three deceased loved-ones were crossing his mind. The twinkle in his eye became distant and a sadness passed over his smiling face. He had said something very kind after each of those moments, "Children are a blessing" and "Never underestimate the power of your love for your children." Harry's thinning, straight hair, now showing some fly-away curly gray, was tied in a knot at the back of his neck and proceeded down past his waist. As he stood on the street with JW after their tour of the new Town Hall, young Jim Swoveland approached him with a group of boys and asked about the length of his hair. The Civil War veteran launched into a forty-five minute explanation and gave the youngsters a history lesson out on the street.

John hired two boys to help the crippled veteran with the heavier tasks of his wall-building. Harry created designs with his placement of the stones and had the boys spread out each wheelbarrowful on the ground so he could see all of his choices for each addition to the wall. As they lingered over meals, Minnie had never seen John laugh so easily and she enjoyed Harry's company as well. He was full of stories of boats in St. Louis and Lewis' children in Urbana and even a few tales about the war, mostly railroad stories of explosions he and his buddies had set. When it was warmer, John tucked little Mae in his long winter coat to watch while Harry worked outside. In the second week of March shortly before his scheduled return to his home in Urbana, Harry did not appear for breakfast, as he unfailingly had each morning. As the minutes ticked by and still he did not arrive, John felt a knot tighten in his stomach. He excused himself from the table and left his wife and child to go upstairs to rap on the guest room door. When there was no response, JW opened the door. Harry was still in his bed, his cane carefully propped up against the nightstand, his covers unruffled. John saw immediately he was dead. He saw, too, the peaceful way he had gone out, for his face was at ease, his eyes still closed. His mouth had fallen open and his skin was as white as the sheets. He was outlived by his father and mother in Pennsylvania whom he had not seen in over twenty-two years. Congruent with that, neither of them nor his sister made the trip for the interment. Harry was buried in a simple plot near his Uncle Joe in Champaign County, the Lambert brother who died long ago of scarlet fever. Harry had been born on Lost Mountain and called Ohio his home. It was right the rich Ohio dirt receive him.

When the George Lamberts, all twenty-two of them, re-joined in Hill Grove after the small funeral near Mechanicsburg, they were tired and relatively silent throughout the meal. There was Lib and Dan and their daughter, Al, Eva and their two, of course JW, Minnie and the baby, also Emma, Newtie and their two little ones, Mollie and Harvey, Christian, Sam, Frank and Babe with Anna and George. Toward the end of the meal, George did manage to say, with his eyes on JW the new father, "Lose one; gain one." There were thin smiles all around. Mae most definitely responded to the wave of glances her way with a happy gurgle of bubbles which cascaded down her chin.

What a blessing Mae was, being the hand which brought Harry to Enterprise so the two special Lambert relatives could spend those weeks together. That time together comforted JW who knew he had lost a champion, both to himself and the country. Harry had been there at each point in his life when he needed a lift with a kind glance and words of inspiration. In spite of the terrible fear and pain Harry suffered in this life, he always found happiness where ever he settled because it came from inside him. He was affable and wise and he was devoted to John. Lewis told JW they were comforted Harry had been in Enterprise at the time of his death, sad as they were to lose him, for they knew of Harry's love for John William. After all of Harry's adventures and the years of worry the family had in not knowing his fate, there was a comfort in knowing the old Lambert farm was his final resting place.

9

Finding his Engine, Completing the Car

Looking back at the fall of 1887 John could see signs pointing toward disaster, but he did not see them as they happened. Even now he was blissfully detached from the sense of loss others were feeling. His elevator by the railroad tracks, which had held the combined grain of the farmers who traveled from far and wide, burned to the ground in a spectacular fire which briefly lit up the balmy October night sky. The hard-wooden frame had stood out as the inner orange glow consumed the thinner covering, which is how the charred black, skeleton-like edifice was left on this night so close to Halloween. Many citizens called the event evil because of the coincidence of happening so close to the holiday of ghosts and goblins. John thought it was a miracle he did not lose all his granary buildings that night or worse, that some one be hurt. His loss was the elevator and the value of the grain it held. He had been alone in his corner office calculating bills when he smelled smoke. Picking up the old kerosene lantern, he went to investigate. He walked only a short part of the expansive floor of the warehouse before he saw the glow from the silo on the other side of the far wall. He turned back clutching his light and ran to sound the alarm. Back in his office, he picked up the earpiece of his telephone on the wall and deftly cranked the mechanism. He heard Jessie, the operator's voice. His own voice responded automatically, "Jess, it's John Lambert. Seems my silo's on fire. Call the boys, will you? I'll get to the neighbors." Time took on a strange quality as he alerted those who lived close by. It seemed like no time elapsed before he got back to his building. He quickly ducked into the smoke-filled warehouse and ran to the other side to pull shut the thick oaken door which Al had suggested JW install for just this purpose. Emma was standing by the door at the yard as he rushed by. There was too much smoke to see what she wanted as he hurried to accomplish his task. As he ran out having secured the large, heavy barrier and as he saw help coming, he took a breath and came back to his senses. Emma was in Darke County caring for her children.

Men appeared within fifteen minutes of the original call for help with hoses and pumps and buckets to fight the flames which were growing with a huge momentum. John shouted to the first arriving volunteers to use the trajectory of the water from the hand pumper to push the flames out toward the tracks away from the two-story building, and after the boiler stoked up the automated pumper, to add its stream in the same direction. As more help arrived, waterlines were formed around the other side of the building to attack the burning silo from different points. This quickly brought the flames under control. Because John had been right there, the fire had been discovered early and much was saved. John ordered it rebuilt immediately, only larger.

The center of John's concerns was his work on the chassis, his businesses and his family, Mae and Minnie. At ten months, Mae was almost walking. She was always animated around her father. No girl had more clothes than this child who was pampered and loved by two parents. Their favorite occupation last summer was packing a picnic of fried chicken, sweet potato salad, coleslaw and jellied pastries, loading the surried barouche and driving out into the country for an intimate meal. John did not dwell on the fire, its cause or the profits which went up with the smoke. Fires were common enough and this one was minor in the great scheme of things. The losses put him in no financial jeopardy. He anticipated a bigger, busier commercial center in Enterprise which meant more folks moving to town. His building projects attracted workers, as well as other businesses, and these people needed homes to live in. He bought up property along Washington Street and around the corner on Elm. His first domestic purchase was motivated by one of his workers who approached him on behalf of his mother who wanted to sell her house but had no buyer; could Mr. Lambert suggest a buyer? John bought it himself, and two lots across the street, for his idea was to build more homes for the expanding community.

Minnie saw the elevator fire as an ominous sign and fretted over its origin and the damage which might have occurred. John took her worry as part of motherhood, like a lioness protecting her hearth and responded with good-natured reassurances. Eventually to her repetitious remarks he told her, "Mrs. Lambert, enough is enough. All is well." And then he told her of his property investments and suggested her sisters might want to use the properties for an extended visit over the winter. He proposed she tell her sisters Cora, Lou and Dora the homes would be for their use. Minnie melted with delight. She immediately took up the project of looking over the shoulders of the builders, making suggestions and planning accommodations to make the houses homey, like forbidding the destruction of any large tree. The small homes seemed to appear overnight. John's tactic was successful; Minnie was distracted. By Christmas, Minnie and her sisters had found old bed frames and kitchen tables for three little houses. Dr. and Mrs. Kelley with Dora could join the two Kelley girl families for a holiday celebration in what was now called Ohio City. John and Minnie's hometown had a new moniker and was no longer Enterprise; Dallas, too, was renamed Ansonia.

In January, John bought five more properties still thinking he was investing in Ohio City expansion. These were existing homes which were vacant for various reasons. Christian Harry and Frank, now twenty, brought up a wagon load of furniture for one of these houses, and John realized his plan to invest in property to accommodate the growing number of Ohio City residents was in fact a plan to accommodate members of his own extended family. Frank had been helping with legal matters, going over real estate transactions and making sure the deeds were in order, so it was reasonable he have a place to stay. Mollie and Harvey were offered a home by spring because Harvey was spending time in John's office helping out with his correspondence. Work was slow at the Lambert plant in Union. John himself offered another of the little homes to Emma, for he missed her and wanted to extend a welcome to her and her opinionated, out-spoken husband. Little Roly was four-years-old and Emma had produced two children of her own. In spite of a busy schedule, she managed on occasion to bundle up the three lively youngsters and travel the railroads to Ohio City. Newtie always stayed at home. During her visits, she and Minnie spent time sitting together at Minnie's kitchen table as well as out in the more formal parlor. Minnie was in confinement, not now entering the streets of Ohio City, for her second pregnancy was apparent, and it was unbecoming to allow strangers to view her condition.

Minnie was fascinated to hear Emma relate a story Mollie had told her. Mollie's sister-in-law from Urbana, the one who dressed like a man, had other unorthodox occupations as well as running the Longnecker farm. She liked to "commune with the dead" and worked a Ouija board in the parlor of the old family farmhouse. Sitting in a frayed dark velvet, hand-packed horse hair winged back chair, she would call upon the spirits to deliver their messages. She told her brother Harvey, who told his wife Mollie, who told her sister Emma, who directly related it to Minnie, that late last summer before the fire ever happened at the granary, she had had a vision of John experiencing financial setbacks, and she had seen flames in the sky surrounding his body. Chills ran up Minnie's spine. What a coincidence! Although the two women agreed the entire subject was silly, she and Emma concluded the image of being surrounded by fire was merely the picture of him with the blaze in the background. And as much as they tried to put to rest the eerie coincidence of what was predicted being so close to what actually happened, a nagging thought remained in Minnie's mind. She could not help herself but to request and Emma, in her effort to be helpful, readily agreed, to get Mollie to ask if any more terrible accidents were in store for John.

Minnie and Emma also talked about their children who occupied themselves with games of Parcheesi, spin-the-top and skittles. On this topic, Minnie held herself aloof. She envied Emma's brood, even though one was a stepchild. All of Emma's children were polite, inquisitive and helpful with little Mae, who seemed withdrawn and uncomfortable around her cousins. Emma did her best to encourage their cooperative play. Her ease with her children and her confidence in her guidance heightened Minnie's resentment as she was unsure of herself in this regard. Emma brought the children up to Ohio City quite a few times in the process of settling some of her things into the Washington Street home, only one block from the Lamberts. Cora and Lou were five blocks away. The older Kelleys, Minnie's mother and father, stayed in Ansonia with their young daughter Dora. Emma carefully observed her older brother to detect any symptoms that would indicate he had re-injured himself at the elevator fire and determined that he was healthy. The meal at Minnie's dining room table on the day Emma first came to visit was the first afternoon since Harry's death John had relaxed and lingered instead of rushing back to the office or the workroom. He took Beryl, Emma's youngest, up on his knee after he ate while the others nibbled at their peach cobbler and he sang "Doggie in the Window." The little girl loved it. Mae had her turn on his lap but the two older boys declined to John's exaggerated looks of disappointment. The children quickly learned to trust John's good-natured kidding and enjoyed games of cat-and-birdies on the hall-way floor. Minnie intervened to stop John from lying on the floor in his good clothes, but he usually wore work clothes. He spent more time at real work with the farmers and in his workroom with his machines and tools than he did meeting with businessmen and other community leaders.

John's workspace behind the Crimean Street hardware store was a busy place. Local folks liked to stop by when they discovered John knew about tools and farming. During the course of a conversation with the now ensconced businessman they could reap a solution to problems which had confounded them. He made suggestions for ways to fix tools so the local shop smith was busy re-building handles, sharpening new edges, adding a brace or an adjustable knob to bring new life to useful old friends. The JW Lambert Hardware business of Ohio City had started almost inadvertently. The owner began selling his own corn planter along side a few other products used and/or manufactured by his father's company in Union, boring tools, braces and the like. But John was not interested in running this business, so at his request, Al recommended Russell Smith, an old classmate of John who had traveled with Al selling Lambert products, to take over the daily running of the business. He had different interests than John and thus his contributions to John's endeavors in Ohio City relieved John of some of the more tedious tasks. John knew how to look at the bottom line and be sure all his bills were paid which set the overall tone. Russell introduced a large variety of machines and tools to be sold in the store. He thought up promotions which generated customers. John found the expanded retail warehouse to be a glorified tool shed. He roamed the space of the store hunting for ideas, studying the latest innovations or just musing on the work of other mechanically minded men. It was filled with everything from small hand tools, hammers and saws, to large field machines, tillers and harvesters. Russell had representatives from the other tool companies visit in Ohio City. These traveling businessmen spoke of John Lambert as a legend, for his invention of the corn-planter had for a brief time revolutionized farming. Many a friendly fellow would poke his head into the tarred wooden space across the alleyway out back to say Hello, be amazed to see John was so young, and steal a peek at what the inventor was currently up to. They caught a whiff of the lubricants John used, mixed with the onions constantly on his breath. John did not mind these calls of curiosity and often extended an invitation to enter. As a group he found them to be enthusiastic, optimistic men.

Along with the new friends, a regular visitor was Elwood Haynes. Elwood had gotten an East coast education at Worcester Polytechnic Institute, but did not lose his love of discussing the current innovations and their practical applicability. He had just finished another program at John Hopkins University and was back in Indiana to manage the Portland Natural Gas and Oil Company over where he grew up. The entire Midwest was springing up sources of natural gas and oil. He combed the countryside of Jay County, Indiana, inspecting, prospecting and protecting the gas fields and pipelines. His strongest interest was in chemistry and metals; he called it metallurgy. John saved up questions about soldering, stretching and strength to spark conversation with Elwood. Elwood believed it was possible to develop a metal which would not rust. Neither man could identify which of the two first spoke the words "self-propelled vehicle," John with his family history of carriage making and practical inventions or Elwood with his university book learning and need to constantly travel the backcountry for his work. The two harbored a fantasy of riding a carriage with no need of a horse. Besides business, this fantasy was based on a wide spectrum of wishes for thrilling entertainment, more personal convenience and faster fire fighting. Elwood brought John a newspaper article on Gottlieb Daimler's work in Europe. Daimler had been a mechanist in Nicolaus Otto's shop in Germany but was now out on his own with ideas which Otto quarreled with. Otto's stationary engines were innovative but cumbersome. Daimler was proposing a compact machine which would run on liquid, portable fuel. He seemed on track to developing a light engine with enough power to move a vehicle. His engines, using Otto's four-stroke principle, mostly had maritime uses. John was fascinated to get the update of Otto's and Daimler's work.

John and Elwood planned a trip to Chicago for the following year to visit the Industrial Exposition. It would be big and draw inventions from far and wide, more grand than the local shows this year in Cincinnati and Columbus. John wanted to avoid the Exhibition at the Columbus State Fair. It promised to be rife with political posturing. It was an election year and Ohio's Republican governor was a fiery speaker for veteran's affairs. When the Democratic President Cleveland suggested in a conciliatory gesture Northern families return Confederate battle flags to soldiers of the South, Governor Foraker went ballistic and pulled out a bloody shirt to illustrate his feelings. Too many Northern families suffer still because of Southern pride, he bellowed. Veterans, knowing they would enjoy a tremendous welcome and eager to raise their political voices, were planning the National Encampment of the Grand Army of the Republic. Ohio's numerous veterans would be joined by others from out-of-state. Tens of thousands of marching men would no doubt parade in front of large cheering crowds. John wanted to avoid all of that. He was in deep and private grief over Harry's death and could not speak of it to anyone, including Minnie, his family or any of his friends. He knew Harry would have been a big part of that day, maybe riding near General Sherman or Ex-President Hayes. The pain of the War had turned to memories of glory for many but for John, his grief was fresh. In his heart he blamed the War for Harry's early demise. Better to go to Chicago after the election where the emphasis was on progress, not politics and power. Elwood said they could expect to see an Otto engine in Chicago, for the exhibition was mentioned in *The New York Times*. When the time came, JW rode the train to Chicago, but the two men were not able to see much of vital interest.

John had a series of visitors in response to some letters he had sent out. He had kept notes on his contacts when he purchased his two stationary engines and managed to strike up a correspondence with some. Over the last few years he exchanged letters with carriage makers and carriage part makers from a few spots over the Mid West and managed to connect with a few kindred spirits also spending long hours in cubby hole workshops of their own. More lively was the face-to-face encounters with like-minded men. John enjoyed the conversations centered on mechanical puzzles and the work of producing and selling grain. He also enjoyed long hours to himself. John did not tell anyone, even Elwood, all that went on in his mind or all he managed to create in his workshop. John wondered about attaching one of Daimler's engines to a carriage frame. He spent hours calculating his estimates for the total weight of the Otto and Daimler engines being built in Germany. He had the prototype of the chassis for his father's Union carriage in his workroom, a model he had put a lot of time into improving over the last years. His father sold a lot more chassis than he ever did his fully assembled Union carriages for it featured clever adaptations and solid workmanship. Now John wanted to adapt it to hold a machine. In his shed he could take it apart and reconstruct it. He had plans drawn for adapting the chassis into a three-wheeled model. He played with possible positions for mounting a small engine like Daimler's. How would it effect the springs? The bounce from the wheels? The interplay with the road? What would the weight do to the dynamics of a turn? Should it be placed high or low? Forward or backward? Center or in dos-a-doe with the driver? What about two passengers? Surely any vehicle needed to accommodate at least two passengers and have enough space to carry the equipment for a picnic, clothes and blankets, dishes and glassware, baskets for food and beverages, and not tip or spill with any combination of cargo. How would power be transferred from the engine to the wheels? How would it accelerate? Brake? And how would each of those systems effect balance and maneuverability? It was a tantalizing mind game, better than all the Chicago puzzles his father could find.

The only exception to his silence about his mechanical experiments was with his father. The last time John was at his father's Union plant, he spent some one-on-one time with the older man. John told him about wanting to build a vehicle which would carry its own power and gave him a description of his experiments in Ohio City. He asked about taking parts from the factory to work on the chassis in the shed which his father easily offered. John had been casual in the telling of his purposes, but in fact his father now had a special confidence. George knew JW was up to something significant, but maintained the casual tone. As a way of pledging his own confidentiality, he suggested JW keep it under his hat, knowing his tight-lipped son would anyway. A self-propelled vehicle was a worthy idea; George had heard of such experiments in Germany and other places. He encouraged his son to play with his ideas and asked him to let him know if he had any success. The old entrepreneur was ready for the next Big Thing. John went back to Ohio City with the parts he had come for. He ordered construction to fill in the space between the hardware store and the small tarred shed out back in order to create space for storage and an office where he could see visitors and thus keep his work on the chassis locked up and private. He put a padlock on the big hanging door.

As busy as George was, John always found in his father an eager listener. John never used a superabundance of words with anyone. Neither did his father, although George could relax with a group of family or friends or even business associates and tell a funny story until all ached from belly laughing. John was largely silent in groups; he would join in the laughter but could not command a crowd the way his father could. Always George had encouraged JW's experimentation with mechanical things; he expected it the same way he expected his wife to do needlework or Emma to bake. George believed what his mother on Lost Mountain had taught him: *one practiced what one was good at, for to let a talent go to waste was a sin.* When George set up his manufacturing business years ago, he took his oldest son on as vice president. At the time John, as second-born son, took over the management of the large Darke County family farm which profited from grain, wool and hides for leather. John had grown up working in the fields of his father's first farm in Champaign County, so he knew the work and was respected by the hands. In Hill Grove he supervised the workers, handled the books, built a small granary right where the early railroad cut a corner of his father's land, and kept the tools and machinery running. It was the latter which took his main interest and his father knew it. At his father's encouragement and by delegating his other work, John spent long hours in the tool shed where he repaired and improved the equipment used on the farm. It was in this shed he designed a hand-held corn planter which looked largely like a hospital crutch and automatically dispensed exactly three seeds each time it was compressed into the dirt of the field. This was the Lambert Company's first successful product and until better methods came along, the Lambert corn planter sold hundreds of units and brought the family a nice profit. Wool prices dropped off sharply in the '70's. George sold off his sheep but the farm's other products had kept the agricultural production marginally profitable. The price of grain continued to fall through the '80's and George pulled out of the farming business all together. He kept land enough to grow only what the family needed. John and his farm workers now commuted to Union City to work in the factory manufacturing carriage parts, farm and work wagons and fire-fighting equipment. George's vision had been to make whole carriages, each completely assembled under one roof, which he did for a brief time. Now scores of manufacturers across the Midwest both made parts and assembled a finished product. John made suggestions for improving the over-all process of the production as he got to know every work post at the plant. He altered tools, changed prototypes and rearranged the process of assembly.

At sixty, George was trim and active. He and Anna played golf every weekend at the Greenville Country Club. Now that the last of their children were old enough to fend for themselves, they played bridge with a club including the Snells, the Houses, and the Denlingers. The card club would rotate locations and whoever hosted offered a lavish buffet. They traveled all over the common southern corners of both states, Ohio and Indiana, to participate in tournaments, and sponsored bridge classes in the church basement back home. They spent a lot of time with Al their oldest son and his wife Eva whose parents also lived nearby. Al's spacious new home was convenient to both sets of grandparents and served as the gathering spot. Al's older sister Libby and her husband, with their fifteen-year-old son, often joined the rest for Sunday dinner. Three of the men worked for Lambert, while Al also kept a hand in his father-in-law's elevator business. The Union Manufacturing Company was going to survive the recession; sales for parts were picking up. Last fall, George had had to cut back on the number of boys he employed, but he still fed their families through the winter and now he could hire most of them back. They had to shift around to new tasks, because the products were changing, but all seemed to adjust. George was an amiable boss who spoke to his workers by their first names, as they did to him. Never had one of the workers mentioned a labor organization even though unions were spreading all over the nation.

JW was too involved in Ohio City to feel excluded from the tight knit Lambert/Parent group around Hill Grove and Union. He spent most of his Sundays tinkering and his family time was devoted to Minnie, Mae and soon a new baby. He cared about his extended family, but it was hard to miss them because he spoke to so many of them so frequently. In May, George suffered a stroke on the golf course and the world seemed to stop. He was very sick. The family rallied to help, for someone needed to be by his bedside day and night, with the exception of JW. Minnie was seven months pregnant; because the first ordeal had been so dangerous he spent his time in Ohio City to be near her. He placated his concern for his father by wiring for information. His mother was good about responding, but it was Emma who sent the most informative descriptions of what was being faced, the entire process of learning to talk, eat and care for himself all over again. Alvan Ray was born in July.

John was pleased to be the father of a boy. Little Ray was a smaller baby than Mae had been and it was an easier birth for Minnie for which everyone was grateful. And it needed to be the last one; no more children. John was content with what he had and was sure these two were all he ever needed. Minnie struggled to be a good mother, but this little one was so demanding. She never totally regained her health after her first pregnancy and the pain ate away her patience. She loved Mae with her crown of soft, golden curls, enjoyed dressing her with ribbons and dresses, petticoats and little boots. The sweetest part of her life was showing the child off to John. Having a new baby changed everything. He took away from her pleasure with Mae and he himself was not very cute. His body was small like a plucked chicken and his facial features looked smashed together. John had no such feelings and insisted the baby be included along with Mae on Sunday family outings. Minnie knew her boy was a prize but to her he was also a demanding distraction. On her own initiative she hired three young girls, dressed them in starched linen uniforms and rotated their services for tending the baby. John thought he was seeing special treatment for a son, an esteemed male child; this new household organization looked right to him. Through it, Minnie found a modicum of relief.

While Minnie was expanding the home operation, John bought three more houses which he wanted to offer to his parents and two older siblings. In the past eighteen months he had bought six small homes which were all now occupied, at least part time, by Minnie's sisters and parents, two of John's sisters, plus one little home for his younger brothers. The Lambert/Kelleys in Ohio City were making a tradition of Saturday barbecue gatherings at the granary site, so how could he leave out Al and Libby and his parents? These were the only relatives he had not offered living quarters. Also on John's mind was the fact that, after his father's stroke, the others had helped out while John and Minnie remained in Ohio City to welcome their son. He had located the properties before discussing it with his wife, but gave her the respect of his apparent consultation. When she objected to his plans, he patiently heard her out, agreed with her logic and then peacefully told her they would proceed anyway. Yes, it was overly generous; yes, the three parties did not need housing; yes, none had ever worked in Ohio City; yes, they may never be used; and yes, they were houses but were to be called vacation cottages; but yes, John wanted to do this. Minnie's feelings were hurt, but she knew he was right. She recognized within herself her primary objection, which she never did voice to her husband. Those remaining three Lamberts were a powerful bunch and she was intimidated.

John asked his wife to oversee the outfitting of the properties. She contracted to install electric lighting and an inside flush toilet in the basements. She bought rugs, drapes and furniture, hired another two women, these older, to keep them dusted, polished and aired, and then had the yards planted with shrubs and flowers. She did an outstanding job in preparing these homes for she was inspired by her own feelings of competitiveness. Emma had pitched in. Minnie accepted John's sister's help begrudgingly; she preferred to operate alone. Luckily Emma assumed the role of assistant and so could be useful while not upsetting her high-strung sister-in-law. Most helpful of all was the economy. Property was dirt-cheap and help was easy to find, as farm folk needed money. After Ray's birth, Minnie's younger sister Dora came to help her sister until she recovered from what really was a chronic condition. She was a beautiful young woman and Emma could sense life back in Ansonia with the dark and reclusive Mrs. Kelley and the eccentric, traveling physician father was not the place for her and so encouraged her to stay in Ohio City. Whether she stayed or not was of no account to Minnie who simply folded her into her busy schedule. Before John noticed his young sister-in-law had moved in to his household, she had stayed six consecutive weeks.

As George recuperated, he took stock of his life. He was not one to look back and linger, but he could make an honest self-evaluation and was practical about the future. He and Al came to the realization a major economic step needed to be taken. In order to support the business during this time of changing production and sparse orders, George would sell the family home and all his private properties including the parcels specified for his three oldest children, while maintaining the plant and the Tennessee timberland. George and Anna would officially move in with Al and Eva whose two daughters were now seven and three. George could physically negotiate only the first floor of any home, so Eva tactfully created a downstairs sleeping quarters for her in-laws away from the rest of her family. She worried the children would disturb his rest and had latches installed on the sliding room doors, yet their visits proved the best therapy of all. She ordered a toilet installed on the first floor tucked under the stairs, to the shock of her neighbors, but it would prove to be invaluable.

Shortly after Christmas of 1888, the Van Wert Lamberts bundled up six-month-old Ray and two-year-old Mae who walked with the help of her nursemaid's skirt and hopped the train between snowfalls for Greenville and Union to visit the little fellow's grandparents. George had recovered enough to take the baby onto his lap. He laughed like a child himself at this newest male Lambert. John was not shocked to see the condition his father was in. He had been well briefed on what to expect and was optimistic about a full recovery. Behind the physical difficulties the brain was sharp; John saw the usual smart responses. He recognized his father's struggle as a shadow of what Savina's husband Levi had gone through who had been an old man already when the damage happened. George would appear to grow younger, for over the months he regained a lot of his assured step and the crisp twinkle returned to his speech. But, the unspoken question lingered on everyone's mind: would it happen again?

Anna thought about her mother Savina as she dismantled the contents of the large redbrick house she had lived in for over twenty years, for Savina had dismantled a home when her husband had had a stroke. It was an emotional job. Anna divided up objects which carried her trademark handiwork, chairs, pillows and wall hangings, of needlepoint and crewel. She got rid of wagonsful of junk or shipped them to Ohio City to help Minnie. She put aside a few treasured objects, the hand painted china from Italy, the punch bowl with the face of a President etched on each cup, for herself and should the young boys ever in the future get married and distributed the rest among her married children. The music box George gave her on a wedding anniversary was still in perfect working condition, just right to give to JW's persnickety wife Minnie. She brought the tall grandfather clock which had so dominated the farmhouse near Mechanicsburg into Eva's house, with the understanding it was on loan, for she did not have the heart to give it away. But Eva got the oak Captain's chair from Swampscott because Libby got the nautical clock and the large oil painting of the ocean. She gave Mollie the beautiful, gilded candlesticks which came from the Musselman home. Anna kept her collection of wool scraps which she used in the hours she spent sitting by her recovering husband. She cut small pieces on the bias and sewed them together to create a long snake-of-a-thing she would eventually roll and braid with other rolls and then shape and stitch into a rug. She intended the first rug to be a gift to her daughter-in-law Eva in appreciation of her kindness in letting them live in her parlor and eventually to make one for each of her children. It would take years; this was her way of declaring her intentions with living. When she was growing up as the unacknowledged child in a prosperous Philadelphia family, her sponsor, the lady of the house who was later revealed to be her grandmother, made a braided wool rug for Anna The project lasted for many of her young years and in hindsight can be seen as her grandmother's method of interacting with her forbidden granddaughter. It is a good memory in a sea of dark ones, for she had been lied to and denied, kept among servants although fed, sheltered and educated. The rug was something which said she was cared about. She had brought it with her to Ohio after marrying that boy from the mountains, the same one who was now by her side and making great strides in re-learning to feed himself. Ah, George! How scared she has been over the stroke. Now, he was recovering and she was regaining her trust in her vision of their living into old age together.

The time of George's critical convalescence was also the time Minnie most needed her husband's stewardship. She suffered pains in her hips and had two small children to maintain. Struggling to move throughout the day, she could not tend to all she would like to get done. Uncomplaining, she hired helpers and delegated tasks which freed up her concerned husband. After him, her top priority was her children, especially Mae whom she kept as the apple of her eye. Mae was a laughing, affectionate child but Ray was a brooder from the start. Already self-conscious about her favoritism, she half believed he looked at her through accusatory eyes, which deterred further her motherly attentions. Chubby, round-faced Mae, up on tip-toes, would peer through the yards of draped organdy covers into the cradle of her new little brother. With the electric lights lengthening their evenings, John occasionally joined this domestic setting in the nursery, and the strained threesome relaxed into a happy family gathering. Before long the baby was crawling. For self-propulsion Ray used only his elbows and let drag his limp legs and feet which sent his parents into spasms of laughter. His energy seemed endless. He quit taking his naps and wanted to stay up late at night.

In January John would turn thirty. For the last two years he had devoted considerable time to work alone in his private shed. He had been perfecting his chassis and the specifications for the needed engine. He had disassembled the big four-wheeled Lambert chassis long ago, the model that his father duplicated and sold by the score. John himself put an end to the work on his father's prototype at the point he started imagining a chassis which held the added weight of its own engine. A vehicle drawn by a horse disappeared from his thoughts, and he indulged in the exciting fantasy of a vehicle carrying its own power. To begin to build it, he took several basic components from the old chassis, cleared out the rest of the material from the workroom and reconstructed a new generation with guesses and ideas he had played with on paper. The current incarnation in his shed, this summer of 1890, was a three-wheeled undercarriage meant to hold the added weight of a large engine in the space he had created under the double seat for the driver and one rider between the two high back wheels. On paper he had devised a system for running gears, including a clutch and a steering device. He saw Carl Benz was using long leather straps to transfer power from his engine to the wheels, which John found illogical for they were cumbersome and heavy. He planned to use some good old American steel chains, which would be lighter than the Benz belts. He had come up with the design he wanted for the wheels, which he passed along to his brother-in-law Dan Cook. Pioneer Pole and Shaft would discreetly provide whatever design John requested. The power from the engine would engage the back wheels through a single large chain. He had recently taken a pencil to the drawing pad to sketch out his horseless carriage, complete with a surried fringe top and upholstered seats. John studied all he could find that was written about Carl Benz' car in Europe. His 1887 model shown in Paris was now in production in France. The little three-wheeler had sold but a few; reports were it could not take the hills. But it sold enough to indicate French interest in self-propulsion. A market was established.

Outside of his father, John did not discuss his project with anyone, especially Elwood Haynes. Since their fruitless day trip to Chicago in search of viewing engines, Elwood had seemed overly curious about John's project, pushy even, and on his last trip John had turned a cold shoulder to his old friend in order to avoid taking him to the shed which housed his work-in-progress. He had not heard from him since. Perhaps Mr. Haynes was up to something, as the two of them had talked in the past of their dreams of a self-propelled vehicle. John was unsure of his own project and too protective of his experiment to be able to discuss it with anyone new, except maybe his brother Christian Harry.

Christian Harry, now with Cousin Harry's passing commonly called just Harry, had little time to spend with John up in Ohio City sitting in front of the chassis throwing around ideas about balance and counterbalance. Harry's expertise in wheels gave him a marketable skill. Several winters ago he had opened a wagon and carriage repair shop in an old stable on the edge of Greenville. In these hard economic times, folks were eager to prolong the lives of their animal-driven vehicles and make do with what they had. Harry provided a reliable shop with a familiar name. The two youngest Lambert brothers, now sixteen and eighteen, helped out at their whim, for they were still thrill-seeking boys who enjoyed games much like they did as carefree youngsters in a prosperous household. The third youngest, Benjamin Franklin, a serious young man of twenty-two and the most visibly affected by their father's stroke, had taken to his books and studied the law while staying close to their Papa as he passed through his recovery. Eager to earn a lot of money from his shop, Harry hired the two youngest brothers to finish the mountain of tasks his business was generating but also hired more reliable help to be sure the work got done. It was the younger Lamberts' job to haul the worst cases in Harry's repair shop to Union so they could be worked on at the factory. This plan put the plant workers to the task until orders were up for Lambert-made products: buggy neck yokes and shafts, buckboards and wheel spokes and the original chassis.

As busy as Harry was, he found a summer afternoon to ride up to Ohio City to check on John. To Harry, John was constantly at risk of disappearing into the domain of The Marrieds. Harry thought his brother was changing; even John's ideas about the chassis were developing into something unique. Harry heard his older brother had refashioned the Lambert chassis by using more iron on the frame. Christian Harry objected, for being a wood man he resisted the new metals. John liked the strength of iron and steel for he saw it saved a cumbersome weight and bulk. Knowing their ideas were veering in different directions, he was relieved John received him with warmth, a generous meal and a walk over to the space behind the hardware store. They walked through the cavernous store and the offices sandwiched between the buildings. At the door to the old shed, John turned the key and the padlock swung open so he and his brother could get into the darkened workroom. The smell of oil and metal met their faces. John cranked the knob on a large hanging glass bulb, for he had had the place wired for electricity, and light flooded the room. The thickly built triangular chassis was up on three thin wheels, the rear ones much larger than the small centered one out front. John studied his brother as he was the first other human to view his secret project. Christian Harry was taken aback for it looked so different but he moderated his reaction. "This is the heaviest buggy seat I've seen," he said referring to the entire chassis, so-called for it is the seat to the body of the carriage.

"It's not for a buggy." JW said simply, as though that explained everything. One of John's overall goals was lightness, so Harry's words made him cautious. There was a long silence as Christian Harry took the time to take in the view. This contraption was so different from anything he had ever seen. Their father had made two- and four-wheeled chassis for years; he and JW had worked on them together. This shape confounded him. He saw chains and masses of wire representing gears that he did not understand. He waited for what he considered an obvious occasion for an explanation, but John just looked at his small iron sculpture as though it could speak for itself. Finally Harry asked, "Then what is it for, JW?"

"Not a carriage as we know them, but for a horseless carriage. I want to fit an engine right here." He stepped up to the side and hung his hand over the rear center part, fingers outstretched and pointing down. Now Harry knew the whole of what he was up to; his brother was designing a horseless carriage.

"An engine?" Harry asked. John nodded and keeping his left hand hung in the air, he bounced the corner nearest him, still keeping his suspended hand level. Harry understood from the gesture more of an explanation than John's words gave. Their old style of communication was still there, having survived new businesses, marriage to Minnie and fatherhood twice over. Harry tried to make conversation to draw out a verbal explanation of what he was looking at, "I see you have been studying Anchor Circle?"

"The wheels, you mean?"

"Yes, these big, tall wheels." Harry pointed to the rear of the chassis.

"I actually got those off of the old Ordinary bicycles Sam and Babe used to have. Mama bought them the new safety bikes and these were discarded. The front wheel is off a barrow. Eventually I'll have Dan build custom ones. Meanwhile, the left is Sam's and the other is Babe's." John gave a slight smile.

"You like 'em for the fancy way they can take a turn?" Harry liked displaying his knowledge to JW. The high wheels were a current fad in wagon and carriage design.

"They're amazing. Funny how you can improve something so much with only a simple idea."

"Have you seen the pneumatic tires? I've seen a few at my shop."

"The bubbles?" JW grinned and nodded his head. The air-filled rubber tires struck him as funny. "Anything to make a smoother ride. I'm keeping this thing simple," he nodded to his work. It was a theme Harry had heard from JW all his life. The tall, brown-haired Harry looked more closely at the chassis on wheels. He stepped up to the side and touched it. He bent to one knee to get eye-level and took a closer inspection. The workmanship was flawless. The soldering, the sizing, the angles and attachments lined up perfectly. Harry lamented the thin iron buckboard replacing wood but kept it to himself. John let go of his stance over the metal and stood back. He could see Harry was taking this seriously. He bent his left leg and put his boot back against the wall. He pulled out a cigar, clipped the end and lit it with a long match. Harry looked up at the sound of the flame. John pulled a second cigar out of his pocket and offered it to his brother.

"Sure, I'll take that." He stepped over, accepted it and John gestured toward the door.

"Okie-dokey, then, let's go into this office." They re-locked the padlock on the door to the old shed before they settled into the newly painted room between the two old buildings. The desk was an old door thrown over a couple of crates and invoices were stacked on it. This was the space Russell used to meet with salesmen to go over orders for the hardware business. The brothers picked out seats from the five mismatched chairs collected from among Minnie's remnants and sank into comfortable conversation.

"You're making a steamer then?" Harry assumed a logical conclusion. There were several steamer-type self-propelled buggies around, including one in Greenville made years ago by a card-playing friend of their father, actually a distant relative by marriage, whom the boys had met when they still lived on the farm near Urbana, named Alfonse House. He had put a large, heavy steam engine on a carriage originally built to be pulled by a horse. The result was too rough a ride for usable streets so he ran it outside of town as a novelty. It served as a lightening rod for curiosity and criticism. The awkward machine was actually quite dangerous with its boiler and copper tub of water heating up to 212°. Reasons for sticking with the horse had a lot of neighbors nodding to each other, but others were clearly interested in the self-propelled idea. John did not answer, but instead put a well-worn copy of *The American Machinist* in Harry's hands, opened to a page about an engine designed by Nicolaus Otto. John let him look at the words then said, "Remember that engine I saw in the burned down tannery north of Greenville?"

"I remember your telling me about that."

"I'm betting I can locate someone on this side of the Atlantic to put together a machine like that, small enough to fit on that chassis in there," he said as he tossed his head toward the wall behind him. "Fueled by gasoline."

Harry looked confused. "An internal combustion engine?"

"That's what I'm thinking. I'm asking around now. I want a mechanic who knows about this." JW pointed to the open pages on Harry's lap. The younger brother nodded in understanding and glanced down to finish looking at the article and the photograph of the small, light petrol engine with its large metal driving wheels. It was about thirty inches high and 110 pounds. Otto seemed to have definite ideas about generating power and some success in putting his engines to work.

"Small enough to ride around under the seats on that carriage?"

Sucking on the cigar, John grunted in the affirmative.

"That small and still big enough to move the vehicle?" Harry's questioning showed he understood John's intentions.

"Benz has done it already in Europe," John told him as he blew smoke over his brother's head. Harry pushed his meaty lower lip out and nodded as though convinced.

"You think they would sell?" the newly successful businessman asked his older brother.

"That's what I want to ask you. I know a lot of people are tired of taking care of horses or waiting for a train."

"True, horses leave a messy legacy, too. And they have this annoying habit of expecting to be fed every day," Harry joked. John smiled at his brother's supportive comments. Then Harry dropped the joking, "You envision a machine that could travel city-to-city?"

"Long distances, yes."

"That would be an attractive quality to a lot of buyers, especially salesmen."

"I thought of them, and doctors too. But I don't see selling vehicles like this on a broad scale," John said. "We're talking about a high-priced item, a strong, quality machine. It would be a matter of money buying convenience."

"Al would know about this better than I do. He has traveled to more places. The fellows I talk to are mostly farmers. But, I'll bet there is a market for what you have in mind. Most people, particularly the farmers, won't give up their horses. That doesn't mean there aren't a lot of other folks out there who might be interested."

The inventor agreed, "No, not the farmers. Men with extra cash. A Sunday afternoon in the country would be a pleasure with no horse."

"True. It will sell, JW. There will be some who call this kind of thing the work of the devil." Harry's merry smile returned.

John remained serious, "I may be married to one." Harry shot him a quick look. JW continued, "Oh, I'm not complaining. I like a woman with an opinion and Minnie has definite opinions. But before we get back to the house, I suggest we chew spearmint leaves. The smoking, you know." Harry nodded conspiratorially, as mystified by the institution of marriage as by what John meant by his comments. The afternoon was surreal to Harry, for the machine in the shed was strictly the result of John's imagination.

After Harry left John was in a better mood than he had been in in weeks. His mind was flying. The inventor could see himself riding the mechanical carriage down a long country road, wind in his face, trees whipping by. He could envision competitive races to promote his idea, just like his father had done for the corn planter, which would demonstrate what the machine could do with speed, endurance and power. He could see ribbons of roads to drive fast on. He could see self-propelled vehicles in the fields, helping to do the farmer's work. He saw motor wagons quickly arriving at the very lip of any fire with equipment ready to pump. He wanted to find other men interested in the construction, men who respected the integrity of the work and who were not interested in flying off with someone else's ideas to make money for themselves. John knew enough of the world to guard his project. Still, he would refine and test his ideas with other men. Seeing Christian Harry was reassuring. He did not laugh at John's idea or scoff at the chassis' changes. Telling Harry made the possibility seem more probable. Maybe he really could build a vehicle propelled by its own gasoline engine which would sell like the corn-planter. The similarity would not be in the number of units, for his new idea was much more complicated, but like the corn planter in that it would put his father's factory back into high production and make every one a lot of money.

John stayed up late the day of Harry's visit to pen letters. He had been compiling a list of names. He had been sharpening his wits on a circle of curious idealists interested in new adaptations for self-propelled transportation; perhaps one of them could help him unearth an engine. He poured over his copies of correspondence from when he bought the engines which ran the lumber mill and the granary. To that he added names from clippings of newspaper articles and advertisements. He wrote to companies that manufactured steam engines and electric motors. He was searching for statistics and specifications as well as an outfit or individual who could help design an Otto-type petrol engine. The best pen pal he cultivated came from Lansing, Michigan. John had originally written to Ransom Old's father, for the father manufactured stationary steam engines as well as casings. The Olds family had started in Ohio and re-located to Lansing to open a machine ship while the father attended Lansing Business University. Since 1880, the Olds Company was moderately successful in building and selling simple, small steam engines. When the father realized the Ohio man was more interested in information and correspondence than he was in purchasing machines, Mr. Olds passed the name of John Lambert to his son, also a curious, observing man who liked to tinker with the New Ideas about building better transportation, selling more American goods and using the natural resources God provides. The two had exchanged letters over the past months. In his, the Michigan inventor spoke right to the heart of John's own intentions by confiding to this distant stranger he wanted to build a successful self-propelled vehicle, a horseless carriage. Both men understood "successful" meant salable and that meant Ran was a potential rival in the future marketplace but the bond of mutual discovery for both men was too strong to let financial competition spoil their fun. John confided the same thing. Ran's idea was to use steam power; John's interest was in the Otto-Daimler model of using gasoline.

Like Phonsey House, Ran had already built and run an experimental self-propelled vehicle. He placed one of his father's steam engines on a three-wheeled carriage. Ran wrote to John at length of his experiment, of hauling the cumbersome thing out to the edge of town, heating up the machine and riding for several harrowing moments bouncing over the rutted, muddy road before toppling off in one direction, as the vehicle stalled in another. John used Ran's words to visualize the sight and laughed until tears ran down his cheeks as Ran intended him to do. The stalled vehicle was again dragged by a team of complying horses (who in fact ruled the roads) back to the workshop where Ran could continue to adjust and re-design. John did not know where to begin to tell Ran his critical thoughts. Their projects were similar yet very different. John kept to himself his vast understanding of the chassis and his belief a self-propelled vehicle could not be made by converting a horse-drawn carriage. It needed to be built for the purpose of carrying the weight. The three-wheel model was attractive to both inventors for it seemed to involve fewer problems with maneuverability than a four-wheeled design. John knew the simpler three-wheeler would be lighter as well. The pen pals based their thinking on the established practice of a two-wheeled buggy being pulled from the center by the propulsion of the horse, which provided a smoother ride and easier handling than a four-wheeled vehicle. Pictures from Europe of experiments there showed mostly three-wheeled projects. The French Benz was a three-wheeler.

September brought an unexpected boost. John had read, and at the same time Ran Olds wrote he had seen the news, about a new law in Wisconsin enacted in response to a successful steam-powered car built by one of its citizens. The law offered a monetary reward to inventors of self-propelled vehicles and set standards in order for their cars to qualify – how far it must go, how much it can pull and other specifications. This institutional endorsement legitimized their new idea and gave the two men, one from Ohio and the other from Michigan, huge encouragement to develop an alternative to the horse. The Badger State legislature also sponsored a race, a write-up of which had been mailed to Ran from a friend in Green Bay and Ran passed it on to John. The race, largely a showcase for the idea of a horseless vehicle, had two giant entrants, both steam-powered: a seven-ton vehicle and the other nearly five tons with only one forward speed. John's neck almost ached at the thought of the jerk which would put the machine in motion and he chuckled to himself, "Stop or Go!" Only one vehicle finished. The winner raced for two hundred miles and achieved a six-mile per hour average; that's over thirty-three hours of travel!

All of this fascinated John. He had visualized situations similar to what was actually happening in Wisconsin. It gave him tremendous heart for his project and filled him with determination to get the job done. He pulled out his wallet and unfolded the paper holding the thin white-laced clover he had carried since the first day he visited Ohio City. He had found the little four-leaf beauty by the front step of the widow's house. He dared not touch it, for it was so dry it may crumble. JW knew the story of the framed four-leaf clover from Lost Mountain, symbolizing God's presence. God had been generous to him all along and there was no reason to believe the source was not infinite. In the same way he had found arrowheads and fossils while he was out in the fields, and the same way the black land yielded up lush and large harvests, that's how he expected his ideas would bear fruit. If he tried, he would be rewarded. It would come in the same show of God's generosity symbolized by the four-leaf clovers which now routinely jump out at him. He found them in the weeds circling the granary yard, in the grassy neighborhoods while visiting family and along the way walking to and from work, a couple times a week throughout the green seasons. He had dozens of them pressed between the pages of books he put back on Minnie's shelves. Faith in his idea was secure in John's being, a part of his expectations. If not this idea of a horseless carriage, then something else would catch hold in the marketplace. All it would take is effort and good timing.

He made a big push to come up with sources for what he would need to complete the vehicle: the gears, an engine and a body. A body of leather seats and an awning roof were not such a deviation from current standards so that pieces could be easily ordered to suit John's needs. He was confident of that and it could be done last. His current concerns centered on the source of propulsion. John needed an engine. He entered autumn still without a suitable lead in his search for an American shop capable of putting together what he had in his mind. He grew frustrated. For the first time in his life as the easy-going introspective second son and third child of ten in a hard working, healthy home, he experienced jolts of annoyance. The thought of how long it was taking was a physical sensation that would grab and rattle him. His development of the chassis, the idea for the center location for the engine, the type of wheels, the running gear design and the device to disengage the gears, was done. The gestation period for his final idea seemed endless. He was so eager to have the picture off the sketching pad and into material existence he could taste it in his mouth. He walked home the long way at night to exhaust the flame of frustration so he could sleep. Too often in bed that surge went up his spine, and he lay awake ruminating over details and combing lists in his mind of stones to overturn to look for that engine. He woke from his sleep in the very early morning most days of the week with the picture in his mind of the engine IN the space under the seat. And for a moment it would seem real. The contrast of his dream to reality pulled him out of bed. As usual he kept his eye on the newspaper reports of new patents. Among the list in mid-December was the name of a man from Cleveland who was applying for patent protection for parts on a stationary gasoline engine. His name was John R. Hicks. John knew he had found his source. He wired Mr. Hicks that afternoon and briefly outlined his situation which included his willingness to fund an effort to complete an engine specifically for his project, and his intentions to be in Cleveland at the end of the week. When a return wire offered a meeting time, John made his plans to travel across northern Ohio to Cleveland on the same trains he and Minnie had taken on their honeymoon.

Before leaving, John intended to let his wife in on his secret project. He got an opportunity that evening after the nursemaid had quieted the children and left for her own home, about a half hour walk. In spite of the cold weather, Dora was down the street spending the evening with Emma. They were stringing cranberries and popcorn as garlands for the houses. The John Lamberts shared a fire in their front open parlor, each sitting in a balloon-backed chair covered in toile de Jouy material with scenes of the French countryside. Minnie held a thin silver needle in one hand with a colorful wool thread trailing. Each time John glanced at her, a different color strand billowed behind her quick little fingers. He held a copy of *McClure's Magazine* on his knees and slid his finger down the page as he glanced through the text. Minnie was chatting about the number of times Emma had been to their door in the past week. "Really, John. Does not the woman ever go to her own home? It is like she lives in Ohio City." John was preoccupied as usual. Thoughts of the chassis, and now the engine and whole car, never leave his mind.

"She means well, Minsy. She wants to be helpful and she knows you have a lot to do." Minnie was silent seeing again how strong and unshakable was his loyalty for this sister. His eye saw the glint of her needle as he continued, "Besides, she has a rough go with that husband, I gather." Even up in Van Wert word got to John about Emma's husband and his involvement in the secret neighborhood meetings where talk was bombastic and members re-enforced each others' fears regarding outsiders, Negroes and

Jews. "I heard through the grapevine our Newtie is in trouble with the law. He was involved in a plan to disrupt a poetry reading, of all things, because the poet was Paul Dunbar, the Negro fellow from Dayton. They're calling him a "white cap". I hear there's a subpoena out on him. He's on hiatus, gone for awhile." Minnie raised her eyebrows without missing a stitch. She was shocked and oddly gratified. *So, Emma's husband Newtie was a member of the KKK.* Minnie allowed herself to understand it was better for Emma, even necessary for the children from John's point of view, to be away from Darke County. "Don't be hard on her." It was not the first time he had instructed his wife to be kind to Emma, but Minnie was on a mission to make a point to John about his sister.

Minnie missed her older sisters, Lou and Cora, who were busy with their own families in their old hometown Ansonia, as Dallas is called after the Postmaster picked the name from a clock. She felt a bit left out of their world, while Dora, at twenty, lived for all intents and purposes with her and John. She was strained caring for Dora, for she was adventurous. The young girl had cut her hair into bangs against Minnie's wishes; but worse, Minnie had caught her spirited sister riding a bicycle, one of the new ones, with her legs straddling the machine to turn the pedals with her feet. Minnie was nearly prostrate from indignation at such behavior especially because it had been done in front of neighbors. And Emma defended the girl! She was tired of their whisperings and smiles. But complaining about Dora's behavior, or Cora and Lou's silence, would not do any good. So she addressed the irritation at hand. John interrupted her thoughts; "Why don't you send Dora to Quiet Nook, that cultural camp near Anderson over in Indiana, Mrs. Lambert? Let her go to a few plays, attend a few lectures, breathe in the culture. Give yourself some elbow room."

He disarmed her without hearing the depth of her feelings. And quick as a flash she added, "Perhaps Mr. Glunt's errant wife would go along to chaperone her."

"A sound idea," her husband smiled at her. She could not tell if that is what he had intended in the first place. "You and I will go to Chicago, attend a few plays ourselves after the holidays. Maybe you'll see someone you want to book. How about a poetry reading?" He could be a devil and Minnie knew he was teasing. Paul Dunbar may be a gifted poet, but she would never run the risk of a race riot by inviting him to Ohio City. Minnie ran the rental of John Lambert Hall, which was the first floor of the granary, and also the rentals for the small theater, which was the second floor of Town Hall. Lewis, John's thespian cousin from Urbana, fed her names of entertainers for he and his wife encountered theatrical people. They also knew lecturers and showmen. Minnie was repulsed by deformity and so shunned the traveling shows of nature's mistakes, the snake boy whose arms and legs were too long or the one hundred-sixty-year-old Indian who never spoke and might have been carved from wood except for the slight detection of breathing or the Siamese twins, two pathetic girls who shared the same legs and who knows what else up under their broad skirts. No, she did not do business with circuses. Minnie allowed farm organizations and political groups, theater and intellectual entertainment. Among her bookings was a childhood acquaintance from those horrid years during and right after the War of the Rebellion. Minnie had had her old neighbor to the Banner Street house, where their husbands joined them for a formal dinner by candlelight. Conversation was sweet and fantastic. Hers is a traveling show with her husband known as Buffalo Bill; she had given herself a new name too: Annie Oakley. Minnie had tried to get the man in the white suit Mark Twain to come entertain the people of Van Wert County with his sayings and story-telling, but his latest book *The Adventures of Huckleberry Finn* was a mad seller, and he is now too big a draw for her space. To Minnie's horror, her mother-in-law offered to give the Van Wert Lamberts the old Steinway from the Hill Grove home. John diverted her to donate it to the little town theater instead. So, the facility now had a piano. Minnie was on thin-enough ice sponsoring dramas, scripts for which she gave to members of a certain committee from her church ahead of time to filter for moral lapses. She drew the line herself at musical entertainment, for she could not bring herself to offer the devil so convenient a tool as the rhythm and beat of a concert. She found plenty of venues to fill her schedules, and folks came from far and wide to attend the performances. Of course, with a full-time coordinator working in an office in the Town Hall, Mrs. Lambert merely over-saw the operations and attended only selected engagements herself. She considered this activity to be civic duty, to bring wider ideas to the poor farmers. She also earned a moderate profit for her husband. She smiled bravely to her husband's generous offer of the Chicago trip. Many of the county's elite went on Chicago excursions. She would go but she preferred to stay home. If only her sisters could afford such a trip, they could come along and make it bearable.

"And speaking of traveling," John said, "I'm going to Cleveland on business Wednesday night."

"Overnight, then?" Minnie put her needlepoint down in her lap. "What possibly could your business need in Cleveland?" She did not like it when John traveled. He dashed about on quick trips all the time but rarely was gone overnight. She worried he would not return, that a freak accident would claim him if he went out of her realm. She worried about his safety rather than admit her dislike of sleeping alone.

"Yes, overnight. I'm going to see a man about an engine. I'm hoping he'll build me a portable engine."

"You want to carry around an engine? John, that would be dangerous," Minnie blurted out.

John bit his cheek rather than show his mirth at her mistake. "No, Minsy, nothing like that. What you call my hobby is rapidly becoming a Thing, Mrs. Lambert," he said mysteriously, raising an eyebrow.

She had resumed her handwork, so had to stop to look at him. "A Thing, dear?"

"I've built a wagon that will take its own motor, a mechanical road vehicle. If I can get it to run, we may put it to market."

He breezed over details and only said the gist of it. She heard he intended to launch another new project and looked at him with affection and concerned wonder. *For a man who can't fold a napkin, he sure gets out in the game.* He took a good look at his wife and thought to himself, *Boy, is she beautiful!* They beamed sedately at each other, each proud of the other. "Tonight is a good night for strudel," he announced with a casual gaze and a sheepish smile. It was their private language for her intimate shows in their bedroom. He never tired of seeing a glimpse of her lace, or the more satisfying experience of her displays in the boudoir, designed for his pleasure. Others may have missed her beauty, for she wore a strained look most of the day. When she relaxed for these moments, for she loved showing off for him, her beauty shown through. She believed her transformation in the bedroom was divine inspiration, sanctified by Holy Matrimony, and never admitted to herself her own sexual lust. John went along for the ride. As she heard his request, the concerned wonder on her face blinked to pure amazement. Her body turned hot in an instant and a deep red crawled up her neck and cheeks. She was steaming inside her corset and under the yards of cloth in her long, fitted skirt. He reveled at the visual effects of his words as he saw the little pearls of moisture appear on her coloring brow. He knew she would not dare to call him on his playful trap, for she did not like to speak aloud of such things and acted in the parlor as though there were eyes and ears in the walls. "Later," he concluded, letting her off the hook and twinkling with glee. She smiled as though to herself, still not recovered from his reckless talk. Wordlessly, she picked up the needlepoint and he continued in a more serious tone, "I'm not the only man working on this idea, but I think my ideas are worth playing out."

"A wagon that has a motor?" The words finally registered; *he was talking nonsense.*

"Yes, self-propelled."

"Propelled?"

"By the motor," he encouraged her to visualize a carriage with no horse, a vehicle moved by its own energy source.

"I never know what you will think of next, John. You're telling me you want to build a horseless carriage?" There had been stories in the newspaper of various attempts, mostly comical, using turpentine, gunpowder, giant springs, and rubber bands, even wind sails.

"Yes, but I'm keeping the whole thing under my hat," he said pointedly.

"Don't worry; I won't tell anyone," she could honestly say. *A horseless carriage! Horses would never share the road with a motorized monster!* Every engine she had ever seen was large, loud and smelly. And scary. Her emotions turned on a dime again, "John! You're not dallying with fuel are you? This man in Cleveland will handle that, right? Oh, Darling, you know I don't ask much, but please, don't surround yourself with fuel. You know how absent-minded you can be ...."

"Calm yourself, Mrs. Lambert. No, I don't know I'm absent-minded at all. You have nothing to worry about."

Knowing she had gone too far, she stopped. Then in a low tone she ventured out into her objections again, "Fire seems to find you, John. Emma was just telling me the story of your poor little cousins and that horrible fire on Lost Mountain. No wonder your Aunt and Uncle left Ohio. I don't want to be a widow, John." Minnie had her own logic and would not be cowed. She was remembering another conversation with his sister in which Emma told her about the fire in Hill Grove and her husband's blatant disregard for his own safely by running into the burning shed and pulling out the barrel of fuel. That may have been heroic and saved a larger fire and greater loss, but nonetheless, it left him quite ill for many months. Maybe those acts started a chain of events which led him to her, for her father treated his illness, but the facts of his behavior remain. Minnie's insides had turned to water as fear ran through her. *He'll blow himself up!* She bit her tongue, kept her hands busy and her eyes on her work.

"That was on Lost Mountain, Love, long ago." John respected her even when he was the object of her illogical determination. She held her fearful look. "Now, now. I promise I will be careful." He soothed her rather than argue and, as always, it worked. Minnie allowed him to offer his reassuring words for she felt confident her own words had met their mark. Her show upstairs that night was especially pretty with equally successful results.

In two days John was on the shore of Lake Erie. He remembered the time he and Al visited Cleveland with their father. He was young then and had grown up taking care of the big, old steamer engine George had bought, new fangled at the time. Now, at thirty, he was back to arrange for a special engine for himself. That first engine changed his father's life dramatically; maybe this one would change his. Cleveland, with its easy access to supplies of natural gas and with its rail connections to the East, as well as Cincinnati and Chicago, had become a large, urban center. It was home of JD Rockefeller's giant Standard Oil Company. The city's tall buildings and busy shipyards were bigger and the hazy air was smellier than when he had visited as a lad. Now, the area's rich reserves of coal and iron ore have made it one of the largest iron and steel cities in the country. Its steel replaces iron for rails and beams for building. Trains can run faster and buildings are bigger. John had traveled most of the night but was clear-eyed this cold crisp morning. He had stepped off the train and onto an electric street car to ride to the viaduct neighborhood on the shore of Lake Erie. Inside the ornately decorated building, John rode in an elevator to the towering heights of the eighth floor to meet John Hicks. Mr. Hicks was impeccably dressed and held his head in a way that would put off most strangers. John offered his hand in greeting and explained his interest at this time was not in a stationary engine but in a portable one. This seemed to signify something for the pale, thin man and without an expression breaking his face, Mr. Hicks summoned a clerk. The young fellow entered their conference and to Mr. Hicks' dictation, penned a license arrangement granting John the right to manufacture gasoline engines embodying the Hicks' improvements for use only on land vehicles other than railway or tramway cars. He knew the American shipping industry was ready to use the internal combustion engine, as the Europeans were doing, but he could not imagine a salable private self-propelled vehicle. Mr. Hicks had sought patent protection because he wanted to adapt the European gasoline engine to American interurban and local mass transportation. He envisioned using the gasoline engine to drive public transportation to replace the current electric system, the interest for which was increasing among politicians and community leaders alike. Gasoline was abundant and it was dirt-cheap. Newspaper and magazine editors also endorsed the idea of developing mass transportation and called it a better priority than the development of iffy individual motorized carriages.

Grateful for the generous terms of the license, John shook hands with Mr. Hicks, even though he suspected Mr. Hicks thought him merely a dreamer and that a horseless carriage was a far-fetched thing. Everyone knew it took a large vehicle to carry even the smallest of possible engines. In a display of charity for the man with his head in the clouds and because he seemed to enjoy hearing himself talk, Mr. Hicks told John about a gasoline engine on a boat which was now in New York harbor. John knew of the vessel; it ran with a Daimler engine. To know it was on an American shore was exciting. John kept a cool exterior but his adrenalin told him he had to go to New York.

John's trip would have to wait until after the large Christmas gathering Minnie and Emma were planning in Van Wert for all the Lamberts and Kelleys of Darke County. The granary hall was spacious enough for a two-story-high evergreen tree surrounded by tables and chairs for all the extended family, a list topping thirty and possibly hitting fifty. Santa, actually Christian Harry dressed in a red and white velvet suit carefully hidden behind fake white whiskers, would arrive in a sleigh pulled by John's mare who for an unknown reason permits a wire-contraption to be strapped to her head to simulate a reindeer's antlers. The women planned to pull back the large sliding door to allow Santa to drive the sleigh right into the Hall, to surprise and delight the children. After the party, John promised himself, he would slip off to the railway station and get on the overnight Pullman for New York City. But first things first: Mr. Hicks gave him the name of the German immigrant who had been his engineer on the European engine and who had a shop not far from where they sat looking out from their perch in the sky to other buildings several blocks away. Beyond was Lake Erie, the direction he walked into the moving air on this frosty December day to reach Mr. George Wacholtz' shop in the Lowell Machine Works building.

Because Mr. Hicks had telephoned Mr. Wacholtz, John was taken right in to his workspace. The square-framed man had an accent as thick as his mustache and his demeanor was serious, even sad. He was not chatty and the two men got right to business. The engineer initially asked for so much money John thought he had misunderstood the English numbers spoken with a clipped, guttural timber. When he understood, he thought the sum was a ploy to turn him away. Still, John persisted and with further talk ascertained Mr. Wacholtz was indeed interested in his project. John was not used to big city costs. In the end, Mr. Wacholtz came down in his price and agreed to do the work for two hundred dollars. He would start immediately, for all that was needed was at hand. John wrote out his specifications for the valves, plugs, pistons, rods and of course the dimensions of the frame. He wanted the agreement to include the ignition device which Mr. Wacholtz insisted he could do. John was happy to see the engineer was using Babbitt bearings, for he was familiar with the brand and considered it the best. With the help of Mr. Hicks' recommendation and through Mr. Wacholtz' willingness to try, the Ohio businessman decided to gamble with his money and give this fellow a chance to develop what he had in mind. John was convinced Otto's principle of the four-stroke process was the way to go, so finding an engineer who understood and agreed with it felt like a fifth stroke of luck. He was willing to take a chance to get his engine and this arrangement seemed reasonable. Being eager, John went ahead, for he had no alternative at hand.

The two drew up a final contract wherein Mr. Wacholtz would design and build a three-cylinder internal combustion four-stroke gasoline engine to John's specifications. The materials were standard and therefore accessible. Every sentence the man said seemed to signify an end to the conversation, but John noticed if he stayed put, the educated mechanic would verbalize another gem of information. As John lingered after handing him the $200 bank note and settling their agreement with a handshake, Mr. Wacholtz asked if John needed upholstery. When John nodded, more to see what the man would offer than out of real need, Mr. Wacholtz offered the name of another immigrant with a shop in the same building, Mr. Perry Santoro. John made it his next stop. Mr. Santoro was a small man with a big smile that activated lines all over his face. The warmth generated from his eyes made his messy shop glow with welcome. He offered the small-town businessman a seat on one of the many deep-cushioned chairs, each in a different stage of re-dress, a gesture neither of the prior gentlemen had bothered to offer. Mr. Santoro seemed ready to entertain John all day. He spoke glowingly about Mr. Wacholtz and talked about his own experience with tanning in such detail John purposely re-directed the conversation to the business at hand. He gladly gave Mr. Santoro his order.

It was not all serendipitous accomplishment for John on the waterfront. He had done his homework. Pursing his goal of over-all lightness for every part of the engine, he had discovered an idea for a fabric crankcase. Through his research at home he knew of a manufacturer in Cleveland who had developed a process to treat burlap by which it could be formed into a crankshaft cover. John dropped by this location to learn his man would not return to the facility until the next morning. John left a note requesting to see him early; then, confident Minnie knew this was a possibility, made arrangements to stay in Cleveland overnight. The next day he watched as the gentleman demonstrated the oil-proof quality of his treated burlap. After making an agreement with the man, John headed toward the train station but made two stops before traveling home. He dropped in on a longtime Lambert business associate to order the final rendition of the running gears. His was a unique design which let the driver steer the vehicle with a pedal at his foot. The leaf springs for the gears would be made of bent wood from his father's factory, for it was the best bent wood John could find. It was soaked in formula developed by Christian Harry and would be ordered as soon as JW got back to the western side of the state. John knew it was time to put his face to the wind and lay down the money for all he needed. Now that the conceived vehicle was springing to life, John made a second stop and ordered the rest of the body, including the frame for the top which Mr. Santoro would cover with material matching the seat. Once back in Ohio City, he would order the wheels from his brother-in-law at Pioneer Pole and Shaft. Snow began to fall as he traveled the rail line home across northern Ohio. He watched big, fat flakes out the window, along with the continuous looping of the telegraph wire. Snow joined rain and sleet as he rode south away from the Lake toward home.

The family Christmas celebration in John Lambert Hall was the next day. John hardly had time to rest before the festivities began. He quickly came to his senses about dashing off to New York. As curious as he was to put his eyes on a Daimler engine, he decided to let it go for now and tried to relax with his family. The Ansonia Kelley sisters had rehearsed their children to lead the singing of carols, *Silent Night*; *Hark, The Herald Angels Sing*; *Oh, Christmas Tree*. John sang with the rest as he held a squirming two-and-one-half-year-old Ray on his lap, when all of a sudden Santa Claus clattered into the big room on his sleigh, along with a wave of cold air from the large opened door. Having just turned four, Mae was dressed for the party like a little lady wearing hat and gloves and holding a black pocketbook embroidered by her grandmother in pink and gold. She clapped with delight at Santa's entrance, while the ever-in-motion Ray, who was noticeably small for his age, stopped spellbound and did not break his trance even when Santa bent to him with an outstretched hand holding a gift wrapped in lace ribbon and gold-printed paper. As John helped his young son open the present, he could not distract the concentrated gaze of wonder from his little pinched face for the boisterous and animated Santa, expertly played by Christian Harry. John laughed that afternoon until his own belly ached, and by evening the smile muscles on his face were sore too. He spent little time with the adults, for he enjoyed the children more. He was distracted by his project and held it in his mind constantly. Yet, he did not want to discuss what he was doing, not even with his father–in-law who would have been enthusiastic but had no sense of the market place, or with any other Ansonia in-laws, or with his own father or brothers. They were too eager for a new product and would not contain themselves. He might as well call that Chicago reporter Davis himself. He thought about how he had heard Minnie say, *Premature chatter is bad luck.* No, it was not the time for presentations but the time was coming. It was a relief to play with the youngsters. He exclaimed over each treasured new belonging and re-enforced their awe at Santa's mysterious way of knowing exactly what each child had wanted. He tickled and laughed his way through the event. Emma had outdone herself in the kitchen where she baked holiday breads, pies and even a strudel, a piece of which John ceremoniously centered on a beautiful plate of imported Italian china and presented to his busy wife, who blushed like a bride as she received it into her graceful, capable hands. John's eyes twinkled with a secret as their eyes met for only a second and she said, so poised, "Why thank you, John. How thoughtful!" The rest of the food was equally delicious, roasted meats of lamb, beef and turkey, mashed potatoes, candied yams, peas, beans and creamed pearl onions, which were John's favorite.

The day after Christmas, just like the day before, John received a wire from Mr. Wacholtz stating he would need more money to proceed. As before, John wired money. He and Minnie made their trip to Chicago. They stayed in the Auditorium Building near the shore of Lake Michigan, a Louis Sullivan structure of massive masonry and a marvel to them both. Together they walked through the entrance under a ten-story tower. The hotel was only a part of its use and among the tenants was the Engineers' Club where John poked around while his wife shopped in Marshall Field's Wholesale Store down the street, which was really more like a village for it covered an entire city block and was seven stories high. Along with various packages, Mrs. Lambert picked up several bolts of fabric for the dressmaker's yearly January stay during which new clothes and household supplies were replenished and refurbished.

When they returned to Ohio City, there was another wire from Cleveland and John again wired money to Mr. Wacholtz. By New Year's Day, the price had climbed to a whopping $3,300.00 and John put his foot down. He wired Wacholtz to ship the unsuccessful engine to Van Wert. He would take it into his own hands. The German engineer packed it up and sent it immediately. He included an apologetic note with his drafted drawings, all of which John poured over. The young inventor had all the pieces delivered to his shed. He stoically deflected all inquiries as to the contents of the large wooden crates which were pulled from the railroad car by a team of his granary workers and brought by mule and wagon to Main Street. They were unloaded and carried through the eighty-foot implement showroom where Russell and the boy stood wide-eyed, and deposited in the familiar workspace which could be locked and so maintained under his own direction. This mysterious process was a repeat of earlier in the week when other boxes had similarly arrived. The contents of those crates had been eagerly unpacked by John alone, examined in privacy and then added to the growing vehicle. The newly arrived running gears were fit into place onto the chassis, along with the braking system and most of the drive train. The wheels, the seats and the buckboard were among the contents so John assembled or readied them for their place on the entire machine. He used roller chain to connect the clutches to the wheels and was confident they would outperform Benz's heavy belts. John was curious to test how seamlessly his beveled gear transfer would work between idle and top speed. That had been his own idea. He had thought, why make notches when an incline makes for smoother action. There were numerous innovations woven into the whole, each one on the inquisitive man's mental list to mark the outcome.

John set the motor up on three, thick elm planks, then found if he suspended it between two, he had better access to the whole. He needed to view it, as well as get his hands around on it. With the rest of the vehicle taking shape in most of the room, the space for work on the engine was short. Still, it all fit. John's concern and concentration were on the question at hand, to do what Wacholtz could not do, to get the thing to run. He examined the flywheel and crankshaft, the connecting rods and pistons, and the three combustion chambers. He studied the water jacket around the cylinders connected to the three-gallon tank for the cooling system. What he needed to do was devise a method to ignite the four-stroke process. He had little experience with what he had before him, just what he had read and the repair work he had done on the big stationary engines of his own and his father. Nonetheless, he saw this was the problem. It was the time to go to New York. His mission was to find out how Mr. Daimler solved the problem of this step in the engine's work.

With a worried look and fake smile, Minnie waved him goodbye with the two children, one at her skirt and the other squirming in her arms. She wondered where all this would take them and despised the fear which lurked around her as he rode off. John was on a wild man's adventure, traveling on loud trains, rarely at home, heading for a far-away coast. The train could hardly move fast enough for the excited farm-boy-turned-entrepreneur. Each stop was agony; the hours of waiting to change trains in Toledo and Cleveland and Pittsburgh felt like an eternity and John could not sit still. He walked the length of the train, passing through cars and stepping over the deafening metal riggings between them. Their noise and the sight of the large steel gears were cathartic. On the long ride across Pennsylvania, he settled down to reflect on the latest developments. He envisioned his vehicle and allowed himself to further his fantasy by envisioning its production and sales to gentlemen across the country.

If Cleveland looked big and dirty, New York City was a jungle which made it look small. Buildings were packed close and streets were narrow; human trash mingled with the dirt of the animals in the road. Streetcars and buggies, carts and wagons, some pulled by men, some horses, mules or oxen, clogged the streets. John made his way to the harbor and after asking around, located the Harbor Captain, a jovial Irishman named Matthew Murphy. Only his name gave away his heritage, for the thick hair on his head was curly bushy black as well as the single long eyebrow sitting across his splotchy red face. "Captain Murphy, thank you for your time." John pumped his hand. The Captain welcomed the well-dressed Ohioan onto his tugboat and proudly swept his hand in an arc. "And welcome you are to my living room," he grinned, his accent only slight and meaning the entire Hudson River Bay. He emitted a slight smell of alcohol but his gray green eyes were sharp as he directed his craft to the larger boat which was the object of his guest's interest. "But you'll get no invitation onto that vessel, Mr. Lambert. They have waited long to refuel and plan to set off with the tide this afternoon." The luck of its still being at bay amazed John, and feeling a quiet assurance, he still insisted on trying. As the Captain maneuvered the tug through the congested harbor, John fixed his gaze on an inspirational sight, Lady Liberty holding high the torch of freedom. He felt proud as Punch to live in this land of exemplary democracy where anything was possible and pleased to show off that opportunity with new arrivals he had encountered from Germany, Italy and now Ireland. He knew somewhere in him his experiment might prove to be worthy of national attention. A man of means in Minnesota, Boston and Florida, everywhere alike, would have the same reasons for driving his own self-propelled vehicle. The Captain continued, "No, Mr. Lambert, I don't mean to correct you, but I arrived in New York from Newfoundland...Canada." John could hear his wife's often spoken explanation of her own name, "No, Kelley with a second e. It's a French name, not Irish." Every story was of interest to the curious man from Ohio.

John's easy manner won him an unlikely invitation onto the boat carrying the Daimler gasoline engine, and he was granted a brief visual inspection. But he was refused answers to his questions with the crew who claimed no knowledge and no access to the engineers who did know. John had to rely on his own eyes and his own elementary knowledge of what he saw. And he saw a great many levers and various mechanical movements connected with the mixing and igniting device. He high-tailed it back to Ohio, taking the time on the train to draw out what he had witnessed. His trip gave him the concept to draw air over the gasoline to make a vapor. At home he could not answer Minnie's questions about sights in New York, for his only memories were connected to that engine.

While John was away, Minnie was beside herself. She gave her nursemaids, who were a pair of sisters, extra pay and they stayed on into the evening to put the children to bed but also so she would not have to be alone. Here was a night she would have welcomed the lively Dora's presence but her younger sister was in Ansonia, their old hometown, attending parties in Darke County and keeping the senior Kelleys company for the holidays. It was not often Minnie used the telephone as John was so comfortable in doing. Looking for consolation, she cranked the box on the wall and had the operator ring up Emma's newly installed telephone. She only requested a visit, for words spoken over the wire had a way of finding their way around town. When Emma stopped by the next day with her three children in tow, and while Minnie watched her own precious Mae and precocious Ray begin games with their cousins, the inventor's wife made a special, private request: would Emma find out for her what that Longnecker woman across the state has to say about what John was up to, for Minnie truly did not understand, and most urgently, would he be safe. Emma soon talked to Mollie who spoke with the woman intended, her sister-in-law, during a New Year's visit to Champaign County and word came back John was up to something important! The eccentric woman sent the message he may suffer injury in the coming year but he would be basically sound. That was hardly re-assurance enough to drive away all of Minnie's demons with the granary fire fresh in her mind but she did hear the "important" part and she liked that just fine. She knew her husband was special. She resolved to keep an eagle eye out for any violation of her safety rules, the list of which expanded daily: stay clean, keep busy, be polite, eat sparingly, do not play with fire. She worried he did the latter, although he called his activities "work." He insisted he encountered the use of fire in the course of his "work" but she did not understand how his tinkering on the side with fuel and fire had anything to do with his running the granary, the lumberyard, and their properties. He was an enigma to her, and a good husband. She would do her best to steer him on a safe path, to protect him.

Once back in Ohio City, John slept deeply. He lay in bed beside his wife and dreamed of streaming through the land on a machine with controls at his hands and feet. Birds were amazed. Horses backed away. There was freedom in being able to move the way the eyes see. There was sky and no trees. Bugs and wind hit his face. Fast. Into the unknown. He awoke unrested, spoke very little and went to work by himself on his project. In his workshop behind the hardware store, over the course of thirty-two straight hours, he developed a carburetor which he called a "Vaporizer." He built a device which pulled air past a heat source which warmed it enough to draw the proper proportion of gasoline into vapor to travel into the cylinders. Then he tried it on the engine. He would fire the charge with a make and break ignition. The set-up seemed promising. The sun was low in the clear sky by the time he had put his ideas into their proper places on the engine, thereby making it ready to be tested as it sat on the two planks on the floor of his shed. When he played with the crank, it seemed to want to hold. Tempted as he was to turn it full force and try to fire the works, he resisted. He knew should it work the noise would penetrate the walls, and he was not ready to answer any questions, even from the congenial Russell. He had promised Minnie he would be home for dinner. As planned, he would wait until night to give his experiment a run when the veil of darkness would give him the privacy he wanted.

The front parlor was filled with light, warmth and toys, the latter a special exception due to Christmas. After Epiphany, all Christmas things would be put away and Minnie would lead the family into a new season. She came out to the hall at the sound of the door opening to smile at her husband. She was relieved he was home and she would not have to send food to the hardware store again. She did not linger to get his kiss on her cheek for she was busy in the kitchen; she turned to the back of the house before he could hang up his hat and coat. Mae got up from her game on the floor and ran to him. He liked when his daughter could be spontaneous with her affection, when the baby shown through the young lady she practiced to be. Completely ignoring his loss of a night's sleep, for he was jacked up on adrenalin, John was before long on his back on the floor and his two children were squealing in delight, as first one and then the other leapt in to touch their Daddy as the big "cat" on the floor feigned a ferocious demeanor, growled and swung his mitts at the youngsters. Minnie knew when one of the "birdies" was caught, for she heard the crescendo of yells and shrieks while the little one received "tickle torture", the price of getting caught.

When dinner was ready, the family sat together and said grace:
Father, bless this food we take,
And bless us all for Jesus' sake. Amen.

It was easier for John and the children to sit still after the exhaustion of laughter dispelled their exuberance. John looked around at his family. He believed he was on the verge of something big enough to possibly affect all their lives. He had faith in the future. He hoped a self-propelled car would be the ticket to that future, but he was willing to let a Bigger Hand have its influence. He had felt that Hand in the last two weeks removing obstacles and placing pieces of the puzzle in his path. Some called it fate; he thought of that larger force as God. Feeling profoundly grateful for that Hand and for his talent for seeing mechanical solutions, for having the ideas to try different things and to be able to string those ideas together to devise a marvelous new thing, he honored his family by adding to the short grace, "Jesus, we thank you for each other." The food was delicious, leg of lamb roasted with rosemary and garlic and eaten with mint jelly, creamy mashed potatoes with dark pan gravy and another favorite, braised onions over steamed carrots. A charm seemed to glisten in the air. He knew the engine may not run tonight, but he had faith. Tonight would be his first official try.

It was already pitch dark when John went back to the hardware store, let himself in the front door, walked across the dark storefront and into his private backroom. The echo of his boots scraping across the floor followed him through the offices and died as he stood to turn the knob for the light hanging over the chassis. There was his dream, almost fully dressed with its buckboard and assembly of chains and gears, wheels and brake. The space waiting in the center would be filled, and then crowned with the black leather seat. Tonight the vehicle was background to the little engine in the corner of his workspace. John lit the heater and lingered to let the room warm. He poured the large jar of gasoline he had bought at Swoveland Pharmacy where Mr. Swoveland had had the good sense not to ask why, into the feeder tank. Any spillage disappeared into the hard-packed dirt floor. Putting on his apron, he casually checked over the moving parts of the engine and used his handkerchief to dab at spots of fuel on the engine's surface. He silently reasoned with himself if it did not work with simple persuasion tonight, he would walk home and return with the light in the morning.

Finally, the room felt warm enough and the time right. He stood before the machine and bent to apply the crank. Holding loose to the handle, he let it rock in its place to feel the work of the engine before he cocked his shoulder in preparation. When he felt the sway of the piston's movement join with his own rhythm, he gave the crank a turn. Nothing happened. To try again, he let the handle find its place in his hand, carefully tucked in his thumb and syncopating the machine with the muscle in his back, he threw in another full turn. This time the engine coughed. It was a beautiful burp of a noise which cut through the air and up John's spine bringing goose bumps out on his skin. He put the crank back to its spot, made his connection and swung it around again hard, evoking a cough, cough, cough. John's mood was soaring, like drinking brandy too fast. He placed the crank again, felt it make movement, paused to exhale, drew a quick breath and turned the crank one and a half turns. He was rewarded with a full piece orchestra striking up in unison. The engine runs! John set the throttle and looked over the loud machine from every angle to see the phenomenon. Through the eyes in the back of his head, he noticed the room vibrate to the rattle of the noise. This rattle contained a strained rhythm which grew more lopsided with a worried intensity and before long, the sound which filled the room cut silent. John saw immediately the outer end of the crankshaft was broken. He sat and listened to his memory of the engine running before him. The sound had been fantastic. The engine had run for perhaps a minute, but it had run. Now his life was changed.

Eventually, he locked the shed door with care by twisting the long, metal key and listening for the clip to clasp. Then he hesitated, as though looking through the solid door to what was behind it. He was weaving something out of nothing. His pleasure in the possibilities thrilled him. Inside was what he had to show for two years' work. No, three years; he had started, really, before Papa's stroke. Although still a bit shaky on his feet, George spent most of his time with Al, John's older brother. There was nothing new in that. They both had been caught up on these latest rapid developments and as John had predicted, they were like the children had been as they waited for Santa's presents. At their insistence, he had promised he would wire any dramatic developments. John knew the wire would prompt their immediate presence to see the gasoline engine run, so he played with wording for a message for when it was time to signal his milestone. John smiled in the dark street as he turned and walked away from the store. He began to whistle, not a song, just toots with a lot of stops and pauses. Down the block he grinned broadly for he realized he was whistling the rhythms of the motor. Walking helped him think, so in spite of the cold, he took a round about way home. By the schoolyard, he looked up at a favorite place to gaze, the dark cap of the sky, and looked for the constellation of Orion's Belt to locate his favorite sparkle Sirius. He made a wish, "I get to ride in my horseless carriage."

At home he fell into a deep, dreamless sleep and in the morning he set to work on repairing the engine. His choices were to rebuild the broken crankshaft or to adjust the engine to take a shorter crankshaft. With no local man to call who could help rebuild, he knew his only choice was to sacrifice a cylinder, an action he was more curious about than dreading. It would certainly make the engine lighter, a concept he had long esteemed, and it might even make the entire work of the engine more efficient. However, that evening when he tried to restart the engine, the crankshaft broke again and he faced the same dilemma. Now with only two cylinders instead of the original three, he was not so confident of the outcome. Yet, without responsible alternatives, he had no choice but to make the same adjustment. To his delight, the engine with one remaining cylinder willingly perked and ran. Having found the right combinations, he ran his gasoline engine on and on and the shed filled with dense blue and white smoke. John found the smell delicious, like the Coco-Cola he drank with his brother on the back porch, for Minnie would not allow an effervescent drink in the house. He shut down the engine and locked up the shed before heading to the telegraph office.

As JW was arranging for his message to be sent, fifty miles away his mother Anna was washing dishes with her two young granddaughters aged nine and five and telling them stories of childhood in Philadelphia. She left out all reference to bloodlines. Now that she was living in someone else's home again, she was reminded of her early days. "We used to have our milk delivered every morning, just like you do. We'd hang a pail on a hook outside the back door, and the dairy farmer would come by with his milk wagon before the sun was up and leave good, fresh milk. On the farm if we needed some milk, we would just walk across the yard to the cow barn and get some right from the source." The girls, each holding a damp towel and wiping alternate dishes, rolled their eyes at each other. Their grandmother continued, "We bought vegetables from the vegetable peddler, just like here. But girls," she hesitated and, implying importance to her words, looked them in the eyes, "the quality of the produce is better in Ohio." She nodded in agreement with herself, an unconscious gesture mimicking her black foster mother. "Yes, we eat better here." The girls hardly remembered the Hill Grove farm she was referring to, yet Anna had been a farmer's wife most of her life.

As the females washed dishes, Anna's oldest son and her husband were deep in conversation in the front parlor, the only available sitting room as the other had been turned over to the older Lamberts as a bedroom. Happily ignored, Anna's daughter-in-law Eva was quietly doing handwork between where the men sat and the fireplace. She knew the masculine conversations by heart, yet the Lambert men approached their subjects with fresh attention every night: the stock market, the price of wheat, the rail strikes, the upcoming elections. Eva wondered if they had any idea of how repetitive they sounded. She had heard them speculate about marketing potentials for what Al's younger brother JW was up to in Van Wert. Especially her father-in-law expressed faith in his experiments. He said they had "good bets on the table with John William." She did not understand because she did not know the story of the corn planter. But the men were aware of promise in the air and had a mutual sense of anticipation, so when the telephone rang on the wall in the entryway, they looked at each other with knowing hope. Al got up to answer the ring.

"Yes, Clara. OK. Thanks for ringing us, Clara. I think I'll come down tonight to get it. Yep. Thanks. Our best to your Jake." He hung up and grabbed his hat. George had pulled himself up and Al offered his arm to his father. Their unusual behavior caught Eva's attention, "You boys look like a fire brigade responding to a bell. Whatever are you up to?"

Al explained briefly to his wife, "There's a wire for us at the station. Clara doesn't have Jake to run errands tonight. He had a club meeting or something. And instead of waiting until tomorrow, we are going to go down to pick it up. It's likely we will head up to Van Wert from there."

Eva had turned her face back to her stitching. "Well, watch out for Indians." She smiled, for it was a phrase she loved to say because her father used to say it to tease her as a little girl.

Outside the two men were making swift decisions. They were sure the wire was the one they were waiting for from JW. They would walk the mile to the Western Union station to pick up the message. They would leave the carriage and the horse in the barn because if the news were really good, they would be on time to step on the train to Van Wert. In the excitement George's pain disappeared, and he kept up with Al's steady pace down the long dirt highway to town.

The operator handed the night letter to George, for it came addressed to him. He opened it and looked at the words. "RUNNING LIKE BUTTER STOP" was all it said. When Al read it, he let out a yell. Maintaining decorum, George moved him outside while apologizing to Clara. There Al danced in a circle around an imaginary Mexican hat as George would have done had he been able. George cut in, "Let's get on the eleven-o-six."

"We're on," Al confirmed. They chased each other back inside the telegraph station and Clara clicked the message over the wire to JW they were coming. She got an immediate wire in response telling them "ALL SYSTEMS ON HOLD TIL TOMORROW STOP". Al and George had Clara tap out: "COMING ANYWAY STOP". And they did.

JW knew the train schedule and met them at the granary stop at nearly midnight. After tipping the engineer, he helped Al get their father off the train and into the waiting carriage. John was nervous because he knew the perils of showing off. It is likely the engine would not start out of pure orneriness. The only folks out on this cold January night, they moved down Crimean Street to Main and stopped on the darkened street in front of the long façade of the hardware store. Because of the cold, after unlocking the door to the store and rearranging implements to create space, John pulled his horse and the carriage passed the hitching post outside into the shelter of the hardware display room inside where she waited until further notice. In the back shed, John instructed the other two Lambert businessmen to sit on crates to the side near the heater. He went over to turn the crank of the engine. Except for the sound of their boots on the shadowy showroom floor and one or two words from John in the crowded workroom, there was silence. After awhile John started the engine. The contrast of the silence to the pounding onslaught of noise sent the two factory partners jumping from their seats, but the prevailing song of the engine drowned their cheer. With a broad rather private smile on the inventor's face, John adjusted the throttle to keep the machine at a low rumble so the men could talk. George was somewhat skeptical so small an engine could drive the vehicle which was taking shape in the rest of the room. Having found a fulcrum in the showroom which he brought into the shed, he picked up the third elm plank and used the two to test the engine's strength. He tucked one end of the plank on the flywheel and then as the engine ran, he began to bear down, increasing his weight to pressure the engine while John gradually opened the throttle to produce more power. George was tough in his test and the engine battled back with confidence, meeting his demands with aplomb.

"That's amazing!" George exclaimed as John turned off the noisy powerhouse. Al was less than congratulatory for he was holding back his praise for the show of the completed self-propelled project, but he complimented his brother on the success of this step. The two out-of-towners examined the vehicle behind them, much of which was new to them. Al and George pointed and discussed all aspects of JW's work as though he were not in the room. John went from following their dialogue to letting his eyes wander over to the engine. Next he would mount it in the vehicle and put it to the final test. If he had been a betting man, he would have confidently gambled his house, his properties and his businesses on its success. Still, John wanted privacy for the first real run. Al and George were inclined to talk business and John allowed business matters to foreclose the mechanical thrills in the shed. The three men extinguished the heater and took the carriage back to the Banner Street house but not before John's faithful, patient mare expressed her feelings about the noise she had heard. JW had to talk softly into her ear for several minutes before she would perform her job.

It was way past midnight but Minnie made her Lambert men comfortable before going back to her own bed by slicing some bread and offering them bacon and pea soup. Discussing possibilities and trying to make plans, the men stayed up until almost dawn. At the end, all plans were stalled to give JW time to go back into the shed to finish construction. The two Darke County men managed to sleep a few hours before they rode the mid-morning train to Union, with a promise to return in a week. It was assumed the vehicle would be together and running by then. JW apparently needed a break, for he slept fourteen hours that day and did not get back into the work shed before the end of the week. There were checks to sign, letters to dictate, foremen with questions, all for his other enterprises. As well, he attended a poetry reading with Minnie at the Town Hall Theater, which he owned. Familiar faces greeted the well-dressed couple as they took their seats in the small wooden hall. The program was put on by the county grammar school; local children took turns reciting passages written by the now departed Henry Wadsworth Longfellow. Their efforts were sometimes painful as a word or phrase needed prompting, but most performed without stumbling over the melodic lines. The words of the poet and the faces of the children took John back in time to his own growing up. He let his mind wander to an idealized picture of cold evenings around a warm, bright fire with Mama and Papa, Al, Libby, Emma, Mollie and Christian Harry. Aunt Margaret from Lost Mountain had been there too. They had entertained each other by taking turns standing at the hearth to recite favorite lines from Professor Longfellow's works. The short program ended with a Lambert favorite *A Psalm of Life*, recited in unison by the two dozen students:

In the world's broad field of battle,
In the bivouac of Life,
Be not like dumb, driven cattle.
Be a hero in the strife!

John, with Minnie at his elbow, left the building feeling on top of the world.

In preparation for seeing his father and Al, the young inventor returned to the shed and took the last steps to assemble the car. He called Russell to help move the engine to the chassis where he bolted it tight. After swearing his reliable helper to secrecy, John allowed him to stay while he fired it up, the first time in daylight hours. As it had been doing across the room, the tight little engine with its single cylinder put on a good show for John's old friend and business associate. John was happy to see that its journey to its place on the chassis had done no harm. Russell had always been formal with John. He did not reveal his true opinion of what he saw which, if he had, might have insulted his old school chum who after all was his boss. He put on an enthusiastic face and shortly afterwards excused himself back to his customers, relieved to leave the fuel-soaked air. He thought John was neglecting his businesses, out on a limb and wasting his time. The true machines were in his shop on proper display for the men of the county to learn about, buy and use.

With all parts installed and the engine in place, John attached his new seats which had come with an encouraging note from Mr. Santoro successfully communicated in the man's second language. John knew the thick leather upholstery with the wooden spindle arms had been assembled with the same effort and pride as the letter, and it looked handsome in its place on the vehicle over the engine. The two tall, sturdy rear oak wheels had arrived along with their smaller front counterpart from the Pioneer Pole and Shaft Company as had the other ordered pieces. All were fastened in place. The small town entrepreneur did not attach the matching square black fabric top, but left it leaning against the back wall of the shed with its fringe dangling any-which-way. Before Russell let the clerk in the hardware store go for the evening, John had the boy rearrange the plows, tillers and harvesters on the showroom floor by pulling some to the center and some to the corners and edges, thus creating a clear path ringing the giant room. When the boy left to join his family for the evening, John and Russell pulled the machine out of the shed through the old hanging door, passed the offices and into the expansive interior of the store. Russell said good night and John lingered alone only a few moments. There was his car, ready to drive. He hesitated and considered gratifying his excitement by riding in it right then and there, but he knew better. He would fire it later in the evening in the comfort of solitude.

Directly after dinner with his family, John returned to his project. It was hard to believe a month ago he had not even located his engine. With a crescent moon in the sky, John thought how this was a time of firsts, first month of the new decade, first running of the gasoline engine, first showing it to his father, first showing an outsider and now, the biggest first of all: his first attempt to drive the vehicle. In a way he was blasé, for all his pieces were to his satisfaction and his mind was faithful to his science. By his calculations, tonight he expected his self-propelled experiment would perform accurately. The evening was young, so he would wait until folks were off the streets and settled in their homes. On his walk over he nearly stepped in fresh horse droppings. Soon the pile would be frozen, having sunk by its warmth into the ice of the street, same as other remains accumulated through the winter which dotted the way and made March seem so dirty.

Once inside, John lit the heater although the big room still had warmth from the day. There was no wind to blow January air through the cracks of the building into the cavernous show-room. As he walked the oval clearing to double check his path, he heard all was quiet in the neighborhood. Now was the time. The car was positioned with its wheels angled toward the length of the room. Standing at the side by the engine, John turned the small crank that appeared from the shaft and moved the engine in its place. It responded at once and the room came alive with sound and smoke. John's mind kept working but his body was as light as a feather from excitement. With the engine running, he jumped up on the seat to set the car in motion. He used a lever to accelerate the engine and put the beveled differential to work. As the wheels made their first revolutions, the start up was surprisingly smooth. He was off! After the first rotation he could not stop. Round and round he went. With no one else present and no one accounting for his time, he drank deep of the pleasure of riding. Ah, the thrill of the ride! The feel of the rumbling engine under his seat! He commandeered his control of direction by the two pedals at his feet. Round and round he went. He ran the thing until the fuel tank was empty and he was in fact too tired to crank it up again. Then he left a note on the front door of the shop for Russell. It said he would meet him here at the store's opening to roll the vehicle back to the shed. Until then, he was not to open the store to the public.

Despite his precautions to keep his experiment a secret, word was flying around Van Wert county about what John Lambert was doing behind locked doors. Some accurately guessed what the popular businessman was up to, at least in general terms. If he had taken the time to investigate to hear some of the rumors, he would have been entertained indeed. *He had built a machine which could fly to Europe; he had built a machine which could travel back in time; he had nearly blown himself up and was scarred beyond recognition.* Criticism blew hard too: *If God had intended us to get around by mechanical means, He would not have given us horses.* Defending their animals, some were calling John a man who worships a mechanical God. Whisperings stopped when Minnie was present, but Emma heard it all from the girl who helped with her laundry. JW had not explained his project to her, but she had heard hints. She told the laundress, "Don't be silly, Cally; you use a telephone and wouldn't say that about Mr. Bell. You use electric light and don't think poorly of Mr. Edison." But the ignorant girl could not see John's contribution might have any comparison with the larger than life reputations of these inventors nor could she imagine something so historical being invented in her own hometown. John paid no attention to rumors; he was too busy making his dreams into reality. His car ran! He had driven his self-propelled vehicle, no horse, no reins, no bridle or bit, but a machine which ran to his direction. Surprisingly, included in the triumph of his successful ride John found a portion of the evening's activity unsatisfying and could not shake the sensation of being like a tiger pacing in his circus cage. John and a disapproving Minnie had taken their children to Van Wert to see certain parts of the Ringling Brothers' Circus. They watched the animals deemed educational by John's Methodist wife, including the tiger who paced constantly in his small cage. John understood how the big cat must feel. He wanted to run the car in the open to test his machine's ability and to fulfill his dream of covering the ground like a free-running beast while feeling the wind in his face.

The same weekend JW would be showing his father and brother his fully-assembled self-propelled car, Dr. Kelley accompanied his youngest daughter Dora from her Christmas visit in Darke County back to the home of his son-in-law John Lambert. Although none of the involved individuals had ever uttered a word to the effect, all accepted Dora's place was in Ohio City with her sister Minnie and not in the square little bedroom of her parents' home in Ansonia. From the same afternoon train, Christian Harry and Dan Cook alighted with Emma and her children all of whom had traveled together from Greenville. Minnie of course knew this. In her expectancy, she had opened Emma's home and left a large crock of beef stew for their dinner and built fires ready to be lit in her home and in the rarely used Kelley cottage. John's wife routinely proved herself of hearty pioneer stock as she took the reins of the carriage and traveled the village streets to do her errands, with or without an assistant and in spite of constant pain. Later in the evening, having found their own way to Minnie's well-lived-in home on Banner Street, George and Al joined Minnie still sitting at the cleared dinner table with Dora, Dr. Kelley, Dan, Christian Harry and John. Emma had taken the hint and happily stayed in her own home with her three children eating their hearty meal before early bedtimes. Newtie as always stayed in Greenville. John had earlier explained to Minnie the four Lambert men with Dan Cook would arrive on business. She took his words at face value and did not imagine the history her husband would be making that night, for the moment had come for John to unveil his assembled project. When the moment was at hand her father was included in the posse which walked to the hardware store that night. The doctor assumed he was going to be bored by talk of Lambert business matters. What he found himself witness to was anything but routine: John had built a working horseless carriage!

On the walk over, Jim Swoveland the druggist's son happened to be returning from an outbound delivery. Expecting to be alone on the road, he was letting his nag set a slow pace home in the crisp, quiet night when he came upon the unusual gang of six men in long dark coats. *Were they specters?* His heart beat in his throat until he realized John was among the unfamiliar group, unrecognizable in the shadows of the street lamps. John called to him, "You, Jim, it's John Lambert." Nineteen-year-old Jim let out a "Geez" and before long, John invited him to join the prospectors. And that is how it was seven of them in a line entered the hardware store and six took places along the edge of the deep room. Inside the eighty-foot showroom was a clearly discernible pathway which had been deliberately created for the purposes of the evening.

The vehicle put on a performance which made John proud. The happy engine started up with the second turn of the crank and John was off and riding, the power under his seat, the tall wheels turning true. He made it around the long warehouse floor once and as he passed his father and the others including young Jim Swoveland, he waved in simple happiness. As he headed around again, guided by the controls at his feet, the other men could not contain themselves. Al's arms were spinning like a windmill and George headed down the room limping to meet the on-coming, self-propelled vehicle. Dr. Kelley followed George half way down the makeshift runway out of curious wonder as JW came around the far end of the room. They stood back as the lacey vehicle and its beaming driver passed them, slowed to a stop by young Jim and motioned for him to come aboard. Jim, the drug store clerk who as a youngster had picked John out as a friend, now climbed into this first gasoline-powered horseless carriage for a ride to become John's first passenger. John drove him around twice before slowing the machine for Jim to jump down and motioned for another spectator to take his place, George the father was first. After each had had his turn, Al, Harry, Dan and Dr. Kelley, John rode the machine out of the showroom, passed the offices filling them with blue and white smoke and stopped it in the shed just big enough to house it where it could be locked away for the rest of the night. John hopped down and pumped the hand of both brothers Al and Harry while his brother-in-law Dan put his hand in too. "Congratulations, JW. What a sight to witness! Congratulations." Young Jim dashed home, late to his parents' expectations but carrying a tale which would quell any argument over schedules. John's older brother was seeing dollar signs and in his enthusiasm, was talking fast, "We can assemble them at the plant. Papa and I will take care of that and the marketing. I have ideas for promotion." JW was not listening to the content of what was said because he could only feel the exaltation of having shared this experience with others. On the way out of the building, George put his arm on John's shoulder in a congratulatory gesture and said, "This is the first of its kind, JW. We'll start a new trend. People will want these all over, all over." He was happy and John could see that. George continued his comments along the same line as they reached the street. All the way home the out-of-town men talked at once while John half-listened. Even with the moment so new, JW had an idea itching at him which might improve the front wheel of the car. He tried to shelve it in his mind in order to take in the excitement of the evening. Under his heavy coat, he was shaking with suppressed laughter and pleasure.

10

Fun with Speed

The promotional letter for the clever new car had long been written in John's head, so when Al assumed he was leading the sales effort, John put his foot down. It was a big step for a little brother but a lot of time had passed since the tiny toddler ran the streams of Champaign County following the adventurous older Al who relished his leadership then and still, but as was appropriate in the current circumstances, now acquiesced to the inventor. John's letter with John's signature was sent to over five hundred individuals and businesses, a list of contacts collected from his time in Ohio City and of keeping his eye on the possibility of this day, stationary engine workers and executives, likewise for carriages, wagons and bicycles, interested implement salesmen, actors and show people, country doctors, even farmers and folk who had dropped by through the years including Ransom Olds and Elwood Haynes. The brothers brainstormed for a list of personal friends, all their relatives and names in the news. They alerted Dan Davis their contact at the *Chicago Tribune* who wrote a short item which was picked up by the national wire. Al had a large clientele from his dealings in Union with Papa, hardware and wood men, fire fighters and fire equipment producers, politicians and some leaders of industry, so the letter was circulated nationwide. The brothers made calculations together and placed the price of a completed car, including leather seats and surried top, at $550.00. John described his vehicle in his January letter as having a single cylinder, four-cycle gasoline fueled engine with a make and break ignition. It had chain drive with two forward speeds, up to fifteen miles per hour. Astonishingly, total weight was only 560 pounds.

Al and George turned their attention to setting up the means of production within the Lambert factory facility in Union City. They agreed with Libby's husband Dan Cook of the Pioneer Pole and Shaft Company the easiest conversion was in Dan's wing of the Lambert buildings. Dan was organizing a satellite plant in Indiana with plans he would now enlarge and could thus afford to give up significant space in Darke County. Meanwhile, in Ohio City, John continued his business of upgrading and improving his project. He ordered another engine from Mr. Wacholtz to work on in the back shed. He now kept the vehicle at the granary, where it could be run inside John Lambert Hall. Thus Russell was left to resume some kind of normalcy for the farm retail business, as much as possible with all the curious neighbors dropping in to ask their questions about John's new machine. With the story out, Russell was telling all he had seen and heard to the villagers. Likewise down the street at the drug store, Mr. Swoveland was weaving tales of his own involving sales of gasoline and bragging about what he had first taken as fibbing from his son. Jim emerged as a celebrity for he was a first-hand witness to the marvel John Lambert had made. Neighbors were telling neighbors and as spring approached, Ohio City experienced an upswing of visitors. They came in hopes of catching a glimpse of John Lambert but more importantly his machine. The girls at the sandwich shop noticed an increase in business by Valentine's Day, and by April Fool's Day, they were more than doubling their usual total of tips.

At first John did not take his phenomenon onto the streets of the village. His biggest frustration was in the condition of the roads. Even with all the development in the last few years, there were precious few stretches of road smooth enough to allow him any kind of free ride. Deep ruts lined all streets and the tree stumps which dotted most thruways were a true impediment to all travel. With each infrequent snowfall and thaw this winter, the ruts became deeper and much harder to negotiate. The small town captain of industry waited until nightfall to satisfy his lust for a ride in the open air. He discreetly made arrangements with long-time customers of the granary, farmers with large fields just outside of town. A couple times a week he would break through a consenting farmer's fence so he could open the throttle on the evenly plowed land settled and frozen for the winter. Under a full moon, John thrilled himself in the cold silvery air, his cheeks ablaze with excitement and wind burn, his chest heaving with warmth and exertion while keeping his balance on the spindle seat as the spirited car shot around the open fields. He took a few tumbles when the car would upset, but he was never knocked out nor did he break any bones. Small cuts and bruises from wrestling with the vehicle did not bother him. He went out alone at first, and then began inviting others, Harry, young Jim and his friends, even Dr. Kelley. Instinct told him not to ask Russell.

Maybe the vigor of his ancestors from Prussia, which after all was settled by the Vikings, propelled him to push the power of his machine too far. Maybe it was some foolish pride in himself for his accomplishment that blinded him from taking more caution. Whatever the set-up, a serious accident occurred. John's in-laws had arrived one weekend in January for a visit. John took his curious father-in-law out after the evening meal for a ride on a friendly farmer's field. In their glee, they ran through an unexpected wire fence which broke after impact near Dr. Kelley and raked across John, cutting his hands, ripping his clothes and opening his upper lip. Blood spilled over his mouth, throat and clothes. The car had mishapped while traveling at approximately five miles per hour and peppered on while John momentarily struggled for control; he quickly cut the engine with bloody fingers. Dr. Kelley took a long look at John and handed over his clean handkerchief while instructing the injured driver to press it to his face. "Sit still and hold this here." He adjusted John's hand. "Hard, now. Give your lip a tight squeeze." He saw it was a deep and ugly cut. Scanning the edges of the field, the sixty-year-old doctor located what he wanted and sprinted to a large elm. Quickly, he stooped to scrap the bark at the base of its trunk before sprinting back across the frozen ground. He held a spongy moss dripping with icy pellets of dirt. Leaning across the high seat toward John, Dr. Kelley breathed into the cleaner green side of the moss and knocked it against his shoe before putting his hot breath again on the moss and moving it from his mouth to John's bloody upper lip. John's body was in shock, so the pain had not begun. The moss coagulated the heavy flow of blood. The immediate crisis was over before John realized how much danger he was in. The two of them rigged up a bandage by tearing out the lining of John's coat and wrapping his face but leaving his eyes free so he could see to drive. Although light-headed, John had no intention of abandoning his car or walking back into town. The valiant Dr. Kelley was happy to turn the crank, sit on the seat and be driven home, for he knew his patient would live. But what a sight Minnie received when she went into the kitchen after hearing the back door! Her husband and father had chosen that entrance in an attempt to avoid her. They tried to wipe off the worst of the blood before she saw the spectacle, for John knew full well of her fears. He had loosened the bandage and collar as her father heat water and was wringing out rags. The room was not big so she could quickly see the red blood coloring the neck of her husband's clothes, and at the same time she let out a shriek, not for fear of the blood but for the reason it must be there. John turned to face her with his bloody hand raised in appeasement to her outburst, which only widened her eyes more. The injured inventor turned back to the sink in silence. Her father was the first to speak. He did not look at his daughter but to his patient and said with a calm manner, "It's just a little cut with a lot of blood, nothing to be upset about. It might have ruined your husband's good looks but he never had any anyway." John's good looks were well recognized throughout the family. John could not react, for his face was now at the doctor's trained hands but Minnie smiled. Her shoulders fell from their position up by her ears and she came to John's side. Her father continued, "It wasn't a fall so there was no bump, no concussion."

"I knew something was going to happen."

"Nothing much happened, Minsy. I'm all right. Your dad will have me patched up in no time," John managed to mumble.

Somewhat appeased, Minnie went to the front hall to fetch her father's black bag. Upon her return Dr. Kelley rummaged through it and came out with a needle and thread. Without hesitating, John reached for a hidden bottle over the shelves by the sink and poured a tall glass of bourbon, which he quickly drank. Minnie raised an eyebrow at the forbidden drink, but turned her back to heat another burner on the stove. She insisted a beef consomme would hit the spot for John and her father on this cold night, which it eventually did, although John had some trouble swallowing under his swollen upper lip. His father-in-law put in over fourteen little stitches using animal tissue for thread which would disintegrate as the cut healed for a job other men would have used seven or eight large loops and thus he saved much of those good looks. The doctor did not call his children's attention to the several additional stitches on the underside of the lip inside John's mouth. The skin around his eyes was already turning deep purple. Her father put a few stitches on John's left thumb and right knuckles, as well, before walking to the cottage he shared with his wife which had been a gift from his son-in-law, the Big Shot around this town now banged up like a barroom brawler.

Minnie put John to bed and held his hand as he fought sleep. He wanted to tell her what had happened but he could not keep his eyes open. His exhaustion was softened by laudanum from the doctor. She sat for a long while and shivered in the dark as she dramatically thought her father saved her dear husband's life. She knew about the vehicle of his dreams now running in reality. *His toy*, she called it. And she had heard him tell stories of his experimental rides. She had been used to that even though she did not like it. As much as her concern centered on her injured husband, she saw a new vision of her father. All of a sudden there was meaning in his healing profession. The image of a silly country boy gave way to a dignified scientist and skilled surgeon. She rubbed John's hand and cried uncharacteristic tears as she thought how precious he was to her and how much she loved them both. In the morning, John told Minnie about the ride in the fields but left out the daredevil nature. She listened while he related the heroic response of her father in the events of the night before. The worried wife shared her new respect for the country doctor who had used his old fashioned medical knowledge based on his love of the Indians to stop her husband's extensive bleeding. She made her own confession about contacting a medium because she was so confused and worried about what he had been doing over Christmas. She declared the Longnecker woman had predicted this injury and she, Minnie, was relieved it was over. She told him the part about his being up to something Important and his laughter at that made his face hurt. Remembering the strange but gentle uniqueness of his old Longnecker companion, he lightly made her promise not to talk to the medium again for he said she had planted ideas in her head. Minnie never actually promised but took his direction as an expression of intended protection, caring and love.

While John's face turned stunning colors of purple, yellow and green and the cut healed along with the other nicks and bruises, he returned to the shed to make adjustments to the vehicle. He came out with a design for an improved, more sophisticated steering system. The blacksmith made him what he needed for the improvement. It was easier to give the front wheel more maneuverability than to change the middle rut down every public road, the line in which the noble beasts of transportation put their steady hooves. The two wider parallel grooves in every road were not so deep, for wheels vary, as do axle length and the width of vehicles. Smoothing the road is a constant civic concern for public ease and happened only rarely, usually in the spring. Turning his tiny front wheel to change the direction of the carriage to the left or right had been nearly impossible. The runabout had no leg to lift! John wanted more bounce and bigger play in the front. He built a new stirrup-type steering mechanism and used good American steel for a strong tiller stick. Thus he was able not only to steer with his feet, but also with his hands.

The pain in his face kept him quiet for maybe a week. Still itchy to ride, he contacted his younger brother Harry to come to Ohio City and go out with him, which he did on the weekends in late January including John's thirty-first birthday. John had completed and installed his new steering system, so the car handled more smoothly. Against Minnie's unspoken objections, the two brothers, old buddies, took to the fields. With Harry as a companion out in the open space, there was yelling and hollering, all under the extreme noise of the engine. In spite of experience and new scars, John gladly pushed the limit on turns. The car performed ably. Afterwards, if the night were not bitter cold, they would smoke a congratulatory cigar before pouring in the last jar of gasoline and cranking the engine one more time.

While the winter kept the ground hard and the skies held back the snow, the vehicle could be driven down thoroughfares to the outskirts of town and the easier terrain of the open fields. In the relative privacy of moonlight, John enjoyed his invention. In clear daylight hours, he occasionally ventured out from John Lambert Hall sitting high on the black leather seat behind the tiller stick. He drove in the neighborhood along a straight path as the ruts in the road dictated, taking corners sometimes with help, but never backing up for John had made no mechanical provision for reverse. Throughout February neighbors grew accustomed to the sound of the engine and knew it heralded a crowd. Many hoped to be offered a ride and even more just hoped for a glimpse. They followed the car like dust trails after a comet. Dogs barked from the safety of their porches to defend their territory from the belching mechanical invader. Neighbors came to their doorways, some just to look, others to wave greetings and still others to shake their fists. Horses veered, startled and rebellious, unaccustomed to sharing their road with the strange, smelly contraption making so much noise on their street. What a sight to see the young businessman and town leader, grinning in his perch with his satisfied countenance, waving to faces familiar, curious or merely friendly.

During the time John's injuries cleared up, letters of inquiry began arriving in response to the mailing done by the brothers. One was from Elwood who wanted to visit. John put him off long enough for his facial colors to fade and to grow a mustache to cover the rude red scar. He could not shave his sore lip. The mustache filled out, Elwood stepped off the train from Greentown his new home, and John forgot what had ever made him feel uncomfortable with the Indiana businessman, educator and tinkerer. Elwood was gracious in his praise of John's invention. Only when he claimed to be planning production of a self-propelled vehicle as well, did John doubt his sincerity. John suspected Elwood was staking out territory more than he had concrete plans. But it did not break the host's pleasure in re-connecting with his old friend, a friendship which went deep for John. First of all, it had been Elwood who solved the case of his two sisters' unhappy episode in Hill Grove and, more generally, because the two men had so much in common, most prominently an infatuation with riding in a self-propelled vehicle. John let Elwood turn the crank to start the engine and get behind the tiller to drive the machine himself. The former farm boy openly shared the riding but kept details of the chassis, body and engine vague except for the glimpses Elwood could grab. The Hoosier never asked to make a close inspection and John never offered. It was a courtesy to John, the inventor, and John appreciated the respect. On the same token, John basked in sharing his glee with Elwood. They talked about a litany of uses for the riding machine starting with the work of an oil field worker as Elwood had been. His visit lasted long enough to catch up on many subjects and share the news of the day. They talked about the discovery of natural gasoline in Alexandria just north of Anderson in Indiana. Elwood said people all over Madison County were madly drilling because they all figure there is bound to be more and sure enough, some have made strikes. Imagine owning a modest dirt farm, making a strike and spending the rest of your life in luxury without ever working! They marveled at what other men considered a fine dream, but the dream did not touch either of the engaged, accomplished men.

On the first Saturday after his birthday at the end of January, the newly mustached John took the car up to Main Street and pulled to a stop in front of his hardware store. He answered questions about his mechanical contraption from those gathered and drew attention to his hardware business. Whatever men of the area, from in-town and throughout the county, who happened to be there on this cold winter day, stepped forward to get a closer look at the heavy drive wheel, the nifty little glass Vaporizer, the chains and gears and such, whatever they could see and discern, for it was unlike anything anyone had seen before. They commented on the tiller steering and were awed when John pulled up the seat he had been sitting on to reveal the receiving tank which held the fuel for the engine. The success of his outing in front of the store inspired John to promise rides the following Saturday inside John Lambert Hall. Early the next weekend, folks in their warm winter clothes gathered in the yard outside of the granary in anticipation of being offered a ride. Word of the novel opportunity spread so that lines grew longer than the shadow of the silo. Mothers forbid their daughters, but their sons could not be dissuaded from partaking in the thrilling new activity, to ride in a car. Inside there were no tree stumps, patches of ice or deep ruts which make driving outside problematic. The loop inside the first floor of the large wooden building provided an easily acceptable duration for a whirl. The granary workers who helped with the event kept the hanging doors open so more people could see and so the smoke would not grow too thick in the room. The patient inventor started and stopped his vehicle all morning before heading over to Main Street, where he would again call attention to his hardware business. Minnie thought it was showing off and refused to come down to the sight, but allowed five-year-old Mae, not little Ray, to go with her father and a nursemaid, Emma and her three children, to look but not to ride in the car. Mae was a clever, alert young girl and quickly caught on only boys were going for rides. She was fascinated by the noise and carnival atmosphere with her father at the center of everyone's attention. She watched her two boy cousins take their turns going around in a loop. Her good-hearted father accommodated each citizen, young or old, willing to climb up beside him and partake in the brand new activity. Like Americans everywhere, many people of Ohio City were enchanted with new inventions of all kinds which propelled American progress, from steel-girder construction to the zipper.

On subsequent Saturdays John brought the car to his hardware store on Main Street. He was lucky there was no snowfall on any of his "show-off" Saturdays. Unknown to most citizens, John had arranged for sawdust to be packed into the ruts of the main block, to give his car a chance. With a crowd of perhaps eight children and twice as many adults who happened to be there to watch, he maneuvered the vehicle around tree stumps. It being Main, there were only three prominent round examples left on the village street; being too difficult to dig, they were left to rot out. Other modes of transportation, horses and wagons, mules and carriages, to name a few, gave way to the fifteen-minute show of the amazing self-propelled vehicle. The obstacle course on Main Street was a showcase for the car's capabilities, and folks cheered as he veered around the stumps and again completed the block-long course while the strong little engine snorted and popped. People came out of the stores and stood along the curb to see the dynamic entertainment. John allowed the vehicle to slow to take the U-turn smoothly at the ends of the block. On the last turn by the railroad tracks he kept the throttle low as he came up the street and put on the brake in front of his store across from where a familiar figure was coming out of Leasenhoff's bakery. John knew her as a prominent member of the church committee which advises his wife on the content of the Town Hall programs. Dressed with a dangling fur around the collar of her chestnut brown coat, the middle-aged woman did not look happy as she quickly took in the scene on the street. She caught John's eye high on his seat and held it. Innocently, he thought she meant to greet him. He stepped down to the street while the car rumbled beside him, just short of the now growing crowd in front of her. "Good morning, Mrs. Smalley," he said. Although uncommitted to her congregation, for he had been raised in a household of practical Protestants, John had been to services at St. Stephen's Methodist Church with his wife, had prior introductions with the woman, and so, using his Lambert manners, he extended the gracious hello.

At the same time just yards away from Carmean Street, Minnie turned onto Main, driving the carriage pulled by their patient mare who was undaunted by the noisy vehicle with which she had long been forced to share her road. The inventor's wife was accompanied by her current prize assistant, a girl from the Moogle farm. She arrived just in time to witness Mrs. Smalley tongue lash her husband, "Where do you have to go, anyway, in that thing? It's noisy and the roads weren't built for it. Stick with a horse, Mr. Lambert, as God intended all of us to do." Not until it was too late did she see Minnie, who had heard all.

Minnie put the reins of the carriage into the hands of the startled but capable farm girl, and in spite of the pain in her lower back, a constant companion from childbearing and malnutrition in early childhood, she forthrightly climbed down from the carriage. She walked with purpose to her husband's side whereupon, barely hesitating but with a glance to Mrs. Smalley, she put her hands on her hips. Without a word she climbed up to the high seat of the three-wheeler, the first time anyone had seen a woman in that position and said to her husband in a pitch for all to hear, "May I have a ride, Mr. Lambert?"

As though without a care in the world, John said in his timbrel voice, "Of course, Mrs. Lambert." Chuckling to himself at how outside criticism converted his loyal wife to his project, he tipped his hat to Mrs. Smalley and then properly tended to his wife's request. The dumbfounded crowd moved away from the shaking machine while he stepped up to the seat beside his wife. As he pulled the vehicle away, the rising noise of the engine ended all conversations in their wake. The woman in brown stood still as she watched them go, her jaw having dropped to her chest, her hand, white-knuckled, clutched her bag of donuts and dinner rolls close to her chest.

Mr. Leasenhoff had seen the event from his establishment. He came out to sooth Mrs. Smalley and help her into her own horse-drawn carriage, the reins of which were held by her ten-year-old son who had been looking at John Lambert's unusual vehicle. He was so absorbed in what he saw he missed his mother's conversation and current predicament but the boy expertly maneuvered the two of them down the block as John and Minnie reappeared from around the other way. John stopped the car and jumped down to help Minnie alight and then handed her back on to the waiting Lambert carriage. John then asked Mr. Leasenhoff if he wanted to climb aboard the humming and popping horseless carriage. The round, friendly man in white aprons climbed up the beautifully crafted machine. "Ya," he said, "It's a beaut, Mista Lahmbet. She's light but she's strong, eh?" There was flour on his cheek and he smiled to John to show he approved and held on with both hands as though for dear life. He loved the ride and he figured he did his business no harm in being able to tell of the thrilling vantage of the rider's seat and of being up close to the gleam in John Lambert's eyes as he drove the dancing vehicle on its unique and graceful bentwood springs. All parts were on springs which gave the ride an airy feel. With Mrs. Smalley gone from the block, people clapped and whistled for John's car.

True to John and Minnie's prenuptial intentions, the Lamberts of Ohio City had indeed established a life in which they were the central authority of a full and busy existence. As close as they were to their relatives in the southern county, they did not hear all the family news. The last time Emma saw her husband was in their Darke County home a few days after Christmas. Although he never traveled to Van Wert County, Newton appeared with the family at gatherings around Greenville. On the night in question, their three children had been asleep in their beds. The house was cold, for it did not have the new heating but still relied on the fireplace. Emma had let the flames settle to build it back up before she got in bed for the night. As she had done for each of her children, the oldest being hers as much as the two of her own body, she ran the warmer through the sheets of her bed. Shortly after she settled down in her white flannel nightgown with the broad lace collar made by her Aunt Margaret, she dozed. In no time the front door opened with a wave of cold air, and she heard her husband stomp his boots on the foyer rug. She had not expected him and did not want to speak to him, so decided to feign sleep. After a few moments his form filled the bedroom door, the smell of whiskey found her nose and he took the two steps to their bedside. Without a word he grabbed the comforter, the blankets and the sheet, and yanked them to the foot of the bed. There was no feigning now as, exposed, she wordlessly and instinctively pulled herself up the pillows on the backboard. At the same time, he swung his arm around and swatted the colored vase on the bed stand to the floor with a loud splintering crash, but he did not touch her. Putting his face right into hers, he slurred steam, "You're not worthy to fill her shoes. You'll never be half of what she was." Then he turned and stormed out of the room and the house.

He blames himself for Allie's death, Emma's thought came to her like a headline, part truth, part denial of his cruelty. He came back with jewelry the following morning as she was packing all her and her children's things. This time was the last and she would escape to live permanently in the sanctuary of the small, comfortable house in Ohio City. With their marriage strained long before this, he knelt at her feet to present the pearl ring which did take her breath away. Emma understood this was as close as he could come to apologizing and again, without his asking, she forgave his ill behavior. No words passed between them about last evening's unpleasantness and he left the house as abruptly as he came. By afternoon she and the children were on the train with Harry and Dan going back to Van Wert. She told herself she could not trust him again. *A tragedy*, she thought. *He could have a good life, if only he could forgive himself for something that was not even his fault.* On the train, she looked at the ring still on her finger and slipped it and her gold wedding band into her pocket. She would put them away. As long as he blamed her, he would be a threat. She arrived at the house her older brother had bought, and later in the week enjoyed his reassuring presence when she brought her children to join him and his family and Dr. and Mrs. Kelley for a late holiday meal. Her sadness blanketed the event but with the excitement over the success of the new project no one asked or said a word. She did not know about the indictment or Newtie's need to be scarce. She did not know he was a White Cap, so could not understand Minnie and John's assumption she had not seen him or comprehend they saw their silence as a courtesy to her.

Emma had other reasons for looking forward to a fuller life in Ohio City; her sister Mollie lived there with her husband Harvey Longnecker, John's chief bookkeeper and faithful assistant. The couple had moved from Hill Grove into one of John's houses in 1888 and Harvey was soon overseeing all three of John's businesses. After being argumentative with a bristly Minnie, Mollie had become reclusive. Once Emma moved up to Van Wert County after Christmas, she learned the rest of the story. She discovered Mollie had the daily habit of sipping and napping while going through a bottle of sherry. She was overly quiet, her clothes were not pressed, her skin had no luster and the house was a mess. It broke Emma's heart which she kept to herself for it was her nature to shoulder emotions. She never voiced the changes in her own marriage and no one asked about her lack of a ring. She took it upon herself to break her sister's self-imposed reluctance toward life. Emma thought about what her grandmother Savina would do and planned what she would say so when she cleverly confronted Mollie with her worries over her health, Mollie was receptive. The childless woman confessed her inability to be physically intimate with her patient husband, "I'm a failure as a wife. I can't face Harvey and he's a good man." The ghost of a foul-mouthed stranger seemed to be in the room and there was little the compassionate Emma could say. She held Mollie's hand while she cried, then poured sherry for them both. It had been ten years since the assault in the hen house. Mollie turned twenty-four at the end of February.

Emma's children often spent an entire day with Minnie's children and nursemaids. The third floor of John and Minnie's home was one large playroom complete with scaled down furniture and lots of toys. The yard was a playground used on sunny days, the crown jewel of which was a long swing hanging from a tall branch of the huge horse chestnut tree. With the children thus occupied, throughout the winter months the two sad sisters spent their afternoons together. Soon Mollie's naps disappeared and luster reappeared in her cheeks. The girls dove into housekeeping, polishing silver together, scrubbing floors and letting the cold outside air sweep through their small rooms. These were tasks they had done together as girls. Laughing hysterically, they beat out the old carpets and drapes Minnie had found to place in their homes. They traveled the thirty minutes by train to Van Wert and on to Lima to shop and bought ready-made clothes and objects to use in their houses. With Harvey's making out so well at John's lucrative businesses, Mollie paid for most of their items.

John had barrels of fun driving his vehicle over the frozen ground of Van Wert County but by March the temperatures had softened the roads, so going abroad in the mud was difficult. After the thaw John took the vehicle out on to the streets of Ohio

City only once, which was enough to experience their impassibility. The warmer, wet weather was good for growers but rough on roads. While farmers could reclaim their fields for planting, it was useless to try to run the wheels through the deep muck. It was like wading through molasses. It defeated the spring of the chassis and jeopardized his thin wood wheels. A few weeks into April the temperatures had climbed enough to coax daffodils and tulips out of the ground and the roads began to dry out. During this Lenten season of austerity and sacrifice, the fervent Minnie insisted John give up his "show-off Saturdays". John conveniently accommodated his devout wife and waited until after Easter to resume venturing out. He wanted to please the visiting tourists, advertise his businesses and he indeed relished showing off the object of his enthusiasm. On a sunny April 25, after Easter, he drove the sensation the short distance from its granary garage to Main Street and was standing by his machine in front of the Lambert Hardware establishment about noon surrounded by a sizable crowd of friendly inquisitors when Russell came out of the store, squinted in the sunlight and announced, "JW, there's a fire at the lumberyard. They ask you come right away. The information came through the telephone."

John gave his resting machine a turn of the crank, hopped back up behind the stick and scooted down the street. He disappeared in a cloud of smoke, dust and barking dogs. Jumping down in the granary yard and asking questions at the same time, he ran to where Harvey was waiting for him in a horse-drawn wagon. In a flash they sped north of town. The smell of fire was in the air and the sky over the treetops ahead was laden with dark smoke. They arrived to see no pumper truck, for the town had lost their only one. A bucket brigade of mill workers were dousing a burning pile of ready timber stacked higher than a man's head. Another team was working the manual pump to shoot water into a hot and smoking heap. The large mill building, the obvious origin of the fire, was a dark cindered memory. Active flames continued their feast on the remains of the wooden structure and what was left of the blades and machinery including the large Corliss steam engine which had provided the power. The workers had let the mill building go and were struggling to save the timber in the yard. Still, sparks had spread behind the building so that entire stacks of freshly milled wood on the far side had gone up in smoke. The owner and his assistant John and Harvey sat in dumb silence on the wagon seats while the horse twitched and complained to be shown such a sight. They saw what could be done was being done. The mill hands had saved some of the inventory and the office shed, a valiant effort. Both businessmen knew what this loss meant, John to his overall hopes of shifting his focus to Union City, and Harvey, the figures for lost labor, lost product and disappointed customers. "Looks like it came from the engine room," John said aloud.

"Yep, it does." There was nothing else to say.

John spent the rest of the afternoon dealing with the crisis. He spoke to his men, made some phone calls and set up a few meetings to salvage customers and get advice. Then he headed to Union City. Unknown to him, down in Dayton, a friend of his father got word of the Lambert loss. Tyler Kuhns guessed at the implications for the family's pending production decisions for the horseless carriage John had built. Believing John's contraption would be a hit, he did not want John to lose his chance at popularizing his new invention. Ty, too, was infatuated with driving machines. Mr. Kuhns had first met John's father years ago in a church basement at a bridge game, and then with his wife, got to know George and Anna at subsequent tournaments. He was the owner of a large mill and lumberyard south of Dayton which supplied material for hundreds of homes built in the fertile area where five rivers come together, the Miami, the Great and Little Miami, the Stillwater and Mad Rivers. Without being asked or even expecting payment, he had a freight car loaded up with the most regularly used sizes of his milled wood and shipped it by rail to Ohio City. When the train with its goods arrived at John's granary, the mill workers were rounded up and the inventory was brought north of town on the short feeder railroad line. Harvey was on hand Monday afternoon to witness the astounding unbidden gift. In the months to come he connected the dots and in his opinion the gesture kept John Lambert in business. The fire could not have come at a worse time for every spring saw a surge of construction and was therefore their peak season. It would be six months like every year until the top autumn numbers of the granary came in.

John knew the fire spelled disaster and was giving the situation his full attention. As the wood made its way north, he traveled south to huddle with his father and brother in the Union factory executive office. He had wired his brother Al about the fire and announced the need to meet. FIRE TOOK LUMBERYARD STOP REASSESSMENT IMPLIED STOP WILL ARRIVE MON AM STOP. On the train he had time to do some thinking. *How*, John wondered, *could they consider production of an iffy new product with the financial disaster now upon him?* He had lost his lumberyard and the loss included not being able to supply the Lambert factory's need for raw wood products. Once in Union City, JW found Al in no mood to discuss any new plans or contingency measures. He had no attention other than expecting Eva to give birth any day. He was so sure it would be a boy. After two daughters the oldest brother declared himself overdue for a son and he was convinced he would get what he wanted. His marriage felt the weight; Eva resented the pressure to perform the trick of producing a son. The entire household was being held hostage to the ensuing labor. Anna and George, still living under Al and Eva's roof, wanted their oldest son to have a son. Libby's boy or Emma's two did not bear the Lambert name and so did not hold up in this primitive of standards. No one mentioned little Alvin Ray Lambert who lived out-of-town in Ohio City. Due to their guilty wish, for what if it were a girl?, Mama and Papa strived to say nothing. The silence was deafening to Eva, who also wanted a boy but felt lost in others' anticipation. She spent much of her time with her sisters and in her parent's large, richly decorated home. Al could muster little concern for the loss from JW's lumberyard fire even though there were consequences to him. He did not think through the implications and talked only of his expanding family. He wanted a big celebration after the birth and was weaving his plan for all who would listen. Papa was 100% along for Al's ride. With little advice and no answers, JW headed back to Ohio City disappointed, but he did receive a warm invitation to bring Minnie and his children to Union as soon as the boy was born. JW had gone through these periods before in the relationship between his father and older brother in which no one outside could intrude. He shifted his attention away from reacting to the familial situation in Union and focused on his priorities. He had the recent fire very much on his mind when he stepped off the train at the granary. Oddly, folks were smiling like Cheshire cats in the commercial yard, in contrast to the gloom and dark clouds he felt under. No one told the secret but each encouraged him to make his way to the lumberyard. *They must really feel sorry for me,* he explained to himself.

When he arrived, he could not believe his eyes: beautiful blond, fragrant wood, piled in stacks everywhere, ready for sale. Where could it have come from? His foreman told him the story. Like a guardian angel out of nowhere a gift had arrived and saved the day. John got on the horn and immediately ordered new mill equipment and put a team of his men to the task of erecting a replacement building. But first he ordered an inventory of the gifted shipment and had every piece and every size listed. He told Harvey to get a cost estimate of every last item and have it shown to him. He knew they were back on track and could fill the most troublesome orders.

Minnie heard the tale of the latest fire and did not like it but could not complain. With John's not being at the site when it started, she could not hold his fuel or his absent-mindedness accountable. She simply patted his hand with empathy and reassured him intelligently, "We'll get along, John. Whatever we have to do. I'm happy with all this or nothing. I know how to make do with less. But we should see to it the village gets one of those Howe fire trucks your family has ties to." It was an excellent suggestion.

Like a spring lamb, the boy Eva sought came into the world and gratified the male-hungry wolves. Baby lust was at an all time high in the rural red-brick Darke County home as all older family members followed in awe each opening and closing of his fists, each daily development in facial response, body functions and overall cuteness. In honor of the birth, Eva planned a large baptismal party over several days for friends and neighbors, all her relatives and her husband's entire family. Eva's two sisters had large families so the numbers of guests were staggering. She was never fond of JW's wife Minnie; the two had never shared more than a cordial how-do in the presence of others. While Minnie was invited of course, her parents and two sisters in nearby Ansonia were not included on the extensive guest list nor was Dora who lived under Minnie's own roof. Minnie was furious over this, but said nothing even to John. She fortified herself by making a trip to Chicago to shop and so dressed her family in an extensive and expensive wardrobe. She made arrangements to rent an entire furnished home in Greenville to maintain an independent headquarters for the three-day affair. John considered it a logical decision based on convenience for they planned a two-week stay to socialize with out-of-state visitors. It was the longest time he had spent in the Union City area since he moved away eight years ago.

The Urbana Lamberts made their way to the Lambert springtime soiree which inspired the Pennsylvania Lamberts to do the same. News spread to Iowa and Minnesota that George's brothers and sister, with all members of their three families, were making the trip from Philadelphia to Ohio to join Margaret and George and their families. With that the two far-flung sisters, who had wanted to visit since George's stroke, rallied at the chance to effect a complete family reunion. It was the first time they would all be together since the siblings went their separate ways maybe fifty years ago when they set out from Lost Mountain. During that time long distance travel has changed from ox and cart to powerful and comfortable locomotives. Aunts and uncles, cousins and spouses, children and grandchildren made their plans to travel to Ohio. Seven of the eight original Lambert family gathered; the eighth died long ago of scarlet fever. Incoming Lamberts took over the Greenville Hotel. The three days of celebration hosted by Al and Eva were spent mostly on their lawns surrounding their home, close to the newborn's nursery. The late May weather was cooperative with warm sunshine and damp coolness in the shade. The fragrance of lilacs filled the air; John and Minnie strolled the awakening gardens and orchards while the children joined the others for competitive games, tether ball, croquet and baseball. Al was proud as a peacock and held Homer Parent Lambert in his long, lacey white gown for hours on end. The father was always careful to keep the little bonneted face out of the sun. Minnie had brought a beautifully wrapped baptismal gift which she graciously presented to Eva, but she purposely never approached the new child. Such antics never crossed JW's mind. The weekend climaxed at St. Paul's Presbyterian Church for the formal Baptismal service and a catered roast beef dinner for all back home during which Eva, Homer and Al sat at a special table situated under an archway of roses, a symbol of their marriage.

John's clever gasoline buggy was the hit of the weekend, at least in Minnie's green eyes. She preferred to extol his invention than to collude in deifying Eva's funny-looking baby. It was the final conversion to supporting her husband's love of a self-propelled vehicle. John had worked hours in Ohio City to be certain the new car would be in shape to give rides through the weekend and had arranged for designated stretches of roadway by his brother's Union City house to be leveled with saw dust and rollers. Gasoline was plentiful and cheap, so that was no problem. The original engine still ran happy; even the jostling ride on a flat-bed train did not disrupt its mechanisms. It ran smoothly for showing the zippy gas-powered runabout to all far-reaching members of the Lambert and Parent families who were from Iowa, Minnesota, Boston, New York and Philadelphia. John knew these people would go back to their local communities and tell what they had seen. He gave rides up and down the road in front of Al's home far from the crowds of guests. As long as he would keep it running, children and plenty of adults waited or rode and enjoyed the loud, smelly, bouncy marvel.

In the crowd was Warren G. Harding with his fiancé Florence DeWolfe, an older divorcee with five children who talked about their plans for a July wedding as Minnie had had. The tiny Mrs. Lambert, who disapproved of divorce, gave the stout woman some strong advice; the cool older woman looked right over her head and humored Mrs. Lambert adeptly. Mr. Harding was editor of the *Marion Star* and interested in politics at Florence's urging. But the Hardings were not the only political celebrities in attendance. Most exciting was the presence of William McKinley, whom all hoped would be Governor soon, for Republicans wanted him to unseat the Democrat James Campbell now in office.

Before embarking on their long return voyages, the Lambert visitors planned to spend time with each other. On one of the days, William offered to pay for a photographer; George hired one from Greenville. The professional set up a portable room with wicker seats on Al's lawn for maximum natural light. George organized picture sittings in any number of combinations of formal groups, for they all wanted posed keepsakes. No one ever thought to include the gas-fueled buggy.

On the last occasion they all were together, George stepped ahead of his two older brothers into the role of Master of Ceremony and was in his element. He started by toasting Grandma of Lost Mountain for being the "benefactor of our youth" and led waves of laughter making affectionate jokes about everything including his relief at being free of "those noisy Parents" which gratified Minnie. He remembered loved-ones not with them, Cousin Harry, their parents Mike and Betsy, and Joseph, the one missing brother who had known the names and paths of the stars. George told the gathered group, some as a reminder, others for the first time, of their special ancestor Aunt Star, who although weak had found much to contribute. William, obviously prosperous, stood to salute his equally successful younger brother. His wife Lizzie wore gloves to cover the scars on her hands from a fire long ago. Of all the toasts and remembering, not a word was said about the War or past fires, but the reunion nurtured each individual for the bonds of affection and concern were strong. George called for silence and gained everyone's attention to give the floor to Given, uninvited by Eva but welcomed by all Lamberts. Projecting his voice, the humble farmer announced to all present Margaret was to be his bride. A cheer went up for he was like a member of the family already. He had run the Urbana farm with Lewis since the 'seventies, when George moved his young family to Hill Grove, and had worked side-by-side with Cousin Harry both before and after the War. Margaret, the youngest of the old Lost Mountain crowd, had lost her husband in a mill accident and had been living on the Urbana farm since Cousin Harry came walking back into their lives. It was too late for children but not for happiness. George echoed, "We all are sorry to have lost Harry in the last few years. But we welcome Given into the official Lambert clan." He paused and said with a smile as big as the ocean, "Lose one; gain one." Those who knew family history especially appreciated the sentiment.

During his time in the Greenville area, John saw his brother Harry was over-burdened by their younger brothers, Sam and Babe, now nineteen and sixteen. The two boys had made Harry's living quarters in Greenville their own, and while the responsible Harry worked long hours at his successful vehicle repair business, the young ones loafed about on his furniture or joined their friends in a circle chatting in front of the drug store. Occasionally Babe went to school. He said he slept on his books to learn what was inside after he heard of a man named Edgar Casey who could do that. John thought they should strike out on their own and so approached Harry about putting his foot down. John remembered when he was their age; he had the responsibility of running the farm while Al and their father got the factory started. These two could make better use of their time and relieve Harry of shouldering their load. Together the older brothers had a sit down talk with the younger ones. John especially encouraged them to find fortune on their own.

When John and Minnie got back to Ohio City, he resumed his usual activities, but she had to recover from the overload of information she had been bombarded with during the two weeks away. The time spent in Greenville was an eye-opener for Minnie. Still angry over her family's not being included at the Greenville Lambert party, she needed to settle the score. She hit upon an idea, a perfect retaliation for what she felt was Eva's deliberate behavior. She would host a gala for her annual Fourth of July event. She had her plan up and running before consulting John. Her party would out-shine what her sister-in-law had achieved. She talked to her two older sisters Cora and Lou from Ansonia about inviting their own extended in-law families because numbers were important. Of course Dora was with her. Always a good delegator, she recruited Emma and Mollie to help. Emma showed her resentful sister Mollie how to go along with what the forceful Minnie wanted, to save irritation and make better memories. Emma would bake pastries, breads and a decorated cake depicting General Washington. Mollie would make red, white and blue pompoms for each table and decorations to strew about. The Ansonia sisters planned activities to entertain the children; for example, first to tie turkey feathers onto dried corncobs and then to compete by throwing the missiles into a basket or through hoops for prizes. There would be no music but an orator was hired to read the *Declaration of Independence* and the *Constitution* including the *Bill of Rights*. At dusk they would all ride to the edge of town for a public firework display, not so grand as in Greenville but as fervently viewed. John expected his extended family to gather for their annual Fourth of July celebration at JL Hall. He figured something about his marriage would be included as it had in past years. Their sixth anniversary was the next day. When Minnie told her husband she wanted to make the party bigger this year, he nodded with sweet temperament and agreed after the meal was finished, if it were running, he would offer rides in the old car with Harry as first alternate driver.

The roads were firming up, so John could reliably venture out of John Lambert Hall with his loud machine under him. He headed for the center of town to bring his attraction to the front of his hardware business. On the way, Jim Swoveland flagged him down and when John slowed, young Jim jumped up to the seat. John took his rider up and down the blocks of the village. Jim easily hopped down when needed, to pull the tiny front wheel out of a rut to make a right angle turn. They steered clear of any street slathered in mud. Deep in conversation about the various merits of construction with wood or with steel, John pointed to a passing building to illustrate an architectural point. He was guiding the car toward Main as the usual small groups of four to five towns-folk gathered on either side to watch their approach. Just then the tiller got away from the driver's gloved hand and the front wheel veered sharply to the left. It had hit a root and the breezy buggy skid into a hitching rack on the side of the road. JW and Jim sat stunned on the perch of their seats. A number of men knocked against each other just to rush to set their hands on the rumbling machine. They worked together by John's direction to pull the car backward and back on to the street. The engine never missed a beat as John and Jim then continued on their way up the block to the Hardware store. It was the first public mishap and much talked about ever since. John got tired of hearing about it because it occurred due to a skip in his concentration on driving. He took to responding to the ribbing the boys gave him with serious talk about the power and potential of the machine. Before long, in many minds the mishap became evidence of the success of John Lambert. It was a clever trick on his part to make the mistake an object lesson on the power of his product but his reputation for fairness led the way.

On one of those Saturdays in June, John brought the car to his Banner Street driveway beside his house. He was scraping dried mud from the vehicle's large oak wheels by the fossil-filled wall when five-year-old Mae appeared from around the side of the house with her nursemaid and brother Ray who sat in a hand-painted wagon that had been a gift from Cousin Harry. His sister held the handle and pulled her load up near her father. With her round sweet face and blond curls, she melted her father's heart each time he looked at her. "Well, here comes the Sugar in my coffee and my favorite little Sunbeam," which was his current nickname for the boy. In all this time except at Al's party and then only at a distance, little Ray had not had the privilege of a look at the thundering, potent machine, let alone a ride. Minnie kept the three-year-old tight under her protective wing when it came to activities involving motors and fuel.

"Has Ray ever gone for a ride, Papa?" Mae knew boys rode the high seat of the loud, smelly contraption which was the object of so much of her father's attention.

He smiled at his children, "No, sweetheart, he's a bit young for so high a seat."

"Roly and Albert got a ride." She referred to Emma's two boys.

"You want to see your brother in the car?" The accommodating father offered to lift the boy up into the still car. Once up there, the little boy stood perfectly quiet in front of the seat with two fingers in his mouth and held in view everything his father did. As Mae watched from the ground, her Papa pointed to the tiller stick and the buttons on the leather upholstered seat. He showed them the underside of the seat cushion to reveal the metal receiving tank. John put a passive Ray back into the wagon and offered Mae a trip up to the spindle seat. She accepted by raising both little arms to her father. Her mother would have been horrified to see either child in so precarious a position, yet she herself had sat there while the machine ran! Mae climbed up to the seat and put her hand to the tiller stick. Pretending to drive, she made motor noises and then clapped her hands and smiled big. Her father was thoroughly enjoying himself. "So you like it up here, eh, young lady?"

"Oh, yes, Papa, I do." Her face had a gentle, trusting expression.

"Well, maybe someday I'll make a big motorized carriage just for you, sweetheart. Now hop on down, like a good girl. That's right." He helped her back to ground level and watched as they continued on their tour of the yard. The young nursemaid responsibly presided over each movement.

Before the end of June, John put two of his residential properties up for sale. They sold easily and he used the money to pay the notes for the new equipment at the lumberyard. The inventive second-born brother reasoned that by the Fourth of July the older company leader Al could leave his baby boy in the nursery, come back to earth and focus on business. He wired his suggestion to meet on the morning of Minnie's party in his corner office of the wooden granary. They had decisions to make. Inquiry letters needed to be answered. On the appointed day, over coffee and cherry cobbler, Frank, Al and George met with JW. They quickly set a deadline for collecting car orders. They wanted to give the idea a chance to hatch, but not wait forever. At the end of August they would make the decision to produce John's prototype or not.

Eva, Al and their children, all John's family and all Kelley's came up from Darke County as well as the Urbana Lamberts from Champaign County to attend Minnie's day-long patriotic extravaganza. Minnie's closest brother Orian came from Toledo with his family. He was the brother who had learned to shoot a rifle from Annie Oakley, but the fabled oldest brother still living in California never even heard of Minnie's Fourth of July event. To pay tribute to her own anniversary, Minnie and John sat on a raised platform under a banner made of red, white and blue carnations and listened to the reading of the orator. John cocked his ear to the reader between winking and waving to little nieces and nephews.

An invitation to the day's events had been extended to Tyler Kuhns, the leading lumberman in southern Ohio. He made the trip to Ohio City with his family by train. The older man spent a lot of time standing near the horseless carriage, talking with John about market factors and sales possibilities. To his surprise, John presented him with a check which covered half the cost of his generous gesture after the fire. The young businessman promised to deliver the balance in good time. The gentleman pocketed the note and punched John's shoulder, then continued offering his opinions on the business outlook. The optimistic Mr. Kuhns insisted new roads were coming. "Within five years America will be ready and there will be a market. Keep at it. You'll get there." These welcome words fondly reminded JW of his now departed Cousin Harry. Prior to the food and entertainment, John's motorized attraction was shut off and put away but not before both his children got to ride in the invention, first Ray and then Mae. They were held in the tight and reliable grasp of their Uncle Harry while John slowly rolled the vehicle in a loop by the silo. Harry had brought copies of a newspaper he had come across in Greenville called the *West Side News*. It was published by two grandsons of old Mr. Koerner whom they used to visit. Al and JW remembered the grandsons Orville and Wilbur running around the Koerner farm.

Too many weeks had passed without an order to purchase a car, and John's logic caught up with what he knew in his heart. The vehicle would not sell. He realized the roads were not ready for his intricate machine. The roads in Ohio City and Van Wert County were typical of the condition of the highways all over. Lack of adequate roads was reason enough to make buyers shy. John read the journals, *American Mechanist*, *Scientific American*, *Harper's* and the newspapers from Greenville, Dayton and Chicago along with the *New York Times* and occasionally found reports of developments overseas, or rather lack of developments. England passed a law requiring the driver of a horseless carriage to proceed down the road behind a flagman sixty feet ahead to warn citizens and beasts of the oncoming danger. This was meant to forestall plans to run such machines and it worked. The man who bought up the patent rights in England had no intentions of going into production and simply filed them away. Only in France, where they had the best roads to accommodate the self-run vehicles, were sales making headway; still the numbers were small. Karl Benz was selling only a limited few of his three-wheeled machines. The European news was writing on the wall for the American market. "It is too early in the game," John shrugged. The outside news was hardly a damper on the affable inventor. No matter what the public thought, he was infatuated and he had no intention of giving up his project perfecting the vehicle with its engine. John was patient and believed, like the Daytonian businessman had voiced, the time would eventually come when gasoline buggies could be successfully put on the market.

The early Lambert euphoria brought by the cascade of immediate interest in the assembled project faded to the general observation no orders were ensuing. Week after week passed with no definite deal. By August, of all the inquiries, there was not one single order for the car and the decision was made out of their hands. Al called the expected meeting and introduced the idea of turning their attention to producing a stationary version of John's engine and putting that to market. He believed farmers would turn from their old steam engines and try the more compact and efficient gasoline power as sea captains and boat enthusiasts have done. The motor boat business, like bicycling, was booming. Their manufacturers were riding the crest of a craze. Gasoline propulsion did not require a supply of coal or dangerous fires to boil water. The most important feature of the new-style engine was the portability of its fuel. It was not tied to location as with natural gas. John had read Otto's machines were being marketed successfully in France. Many of the inquiry letters asked about the tiny gasoline engine strong enough to drive the carriage. Al listed bakers, tanners, publishers, farmers, small businessmen who run ovens, fans, presses, tillers, threshers, cutters, cultivators, reapers, mowers and water pumps, workers who lift and haul loads and run construction machinery. With that he smiled at JW. The nifty gasoline engine JW had brought to life could be mounted on a frame and sold as a stationary, lightweight and powerful energy source. "Yes," John smiled in return when he said, "I can do that."

Al told John they wanted to print up some pamphlets and proceed with a sales campaign for the engine right away and John gave his OK. George said, "Make hay while the sun shines." They were getting in early on the small gasoline engine market, which was a big advantage. John let his engine take precedence over the vehicle in order to apply himself to what would be successful on the market for he was not shy about earning money. He liked the gasoline engine's power, noise and smell as well as the clever and intricate systems which combined to make a magnificent whole. Between enjoying rides in his car, he would hence work on improvements to the new prototype engine he already had up on a sawhorse frame in the tarpaper shed behind the hardware business. He let fall for now the ideas he had for the rest of his project, the complete self-propelled carriage. The brothers signed a deal and gave birth to the Buckeye Manufacturing Company. John was President, Al was Vice President and their younger brother Frank, the lawyer, was Treasurer. He drew up the papers of incorporation. Harry was asked to be included but declined for he had all he could handle at his thriving repair shop in Greenville. With no formal designation George, now sixty-five, served as counselor, consultant and arbiter.

Once the decision was made, JW spent most of his days in Union City. Only on weekends was there a chance to fire up the internal combustion engine on the three-wheeled carriage and take it out for a spin. The hot sun of late summer dried the dirt roads to a hardness which invited John to attempt the common thruways throughout the county. He took off on a dry September Saturday in his motor buggy to a stretch of road he knew between two farmers' fields which for some geological reason rolled up and down like the waves of a stormy ocean for a half mile stretch; perhaps it is the remnants of an under-ice stream from the moraine which moved in and out of the region eons ago. The land dipped and climbed five to six feet several times in that short distance, but the peppy car made it a fun course. With no nearby place to turn around, for effecting a back-up was nearly impossible solo, the fun was frustrating because it was so short. Trapped by sweet-smelling corn plants higher than his head, again and again John made the twenty-minute ride to his U-turn to return to the stretch to run over up and down in his amazing animated car.

When the cold weather came again, John planned to dismantle the original engine from the chassis in order to test ideas he had been collecting for improving some parts, the undercarriage, the engine, the running gears and steering. Before that happened, taking a cue from his father and Uncle William, it occurred to him to photograph his unique vehicle. He called a Van Wert professional Walter Lewis and commissioned him for $1.25 to make the picture. John spent hours brushing and buffing the top with its fringe, the leather seats which rose to a high shine and the metal foot space and buckboard. John wanted an uncluttered location which did not appear to be outdoors for he wanted the lines of the car to stand out. Minnie's young farm girl assistant insisted her father would be happy to supply the setting for the event and with arrangements made, the two men set out with the cameras in John's unique sensation to drive the three-quarter miles northeast of town to the Oliver Moogle farm. But this first attempt yielded no photographs for the negatives were ruined. On his second try, taken in the granary hall, Mr. Lewis created a suitable souvenir of John Lambert's unique and operational motorized buggy.

Using a story told from their childhood of George's sending men into a competitor's store allegedly to buy an item but actually to collect information and report back to George, and unknown to JW, Al concocted a plan to check out the Sintz Engine Company in Springfield, the largest manufacturer of stationary gasoline engines in Ohio. Theirs were mostly for marine use; a few ran printing presses. Al contacted Lewis in nearby Urbana who took the undercover idea to his thespian heart and pulled off a caper which yielded a lot of information. Most of what he reported served to verify Al's already assessment, Sintz's newest offering, a two-cylinder model, was not in direct competition with the proposed Lambert product. Lewis provided size estimates of the two facilities Sintz and Foos in Springfield from which the Union City boys speculated about production numbers. This espionage project provided some good hints which helped in their set up decisions.

As a lawyer, the fourth Lambert brother Benjamin Franklin (there were six boys all together) offered important skills to the business venture. He sought John out to give advice he emphasized with a written version. He wanted to help John apply for patents on his improvements on the gasoline engine, first and foremost his Vaporizer called a carburetor. John did not need convincing; he had heard his father speak to the importance of legal coverage for his inventions. New ideas were precious commodities. He remembered Papa saying, *"As men searched for gold in California, men search for mechanical inventions in Ohio."* To expedite things, one of John's Banner Street neighbors, who was a lawyer named Alex Davis, worked with him one evening to draw the application figures. His wife signed the form as a witness along with her sister who was visiting from Toledo. At another time, Frank wrote longhand as John explained his carburetor with its novel combination and arrangements of parts to commingle air and gasoline vapor. The young advocate added the pictures to the written description and sent the entire application to Washington.

During one of the meetings with his inventive brother, Frank offered a story at the end of which he said he would pose a question. John listened to the story. Frank had been with Al and their father at Eva's table in Union for a Sunday dinner which included Mama and the girls. At the meal, Frank told Al and George about the research he had been doing on patents which could possibly affect their plans. The biggest concern he found was William Steinway's purchase of the rights here in the States to the patent of Daimler's principles as applied to the stationary gasoline engine for marine purposes. Frank told Al and their father he advised securing a waiver from Steinway to avoid even the possibility of a lawsuit over patent infringements. The courtroom is where many life-or-death battles were being fought among American businesses.

"Steinway, as in piano?" Mama entered the conversation.

"That very Steinway, Steinway in New York. They manufacture stationary marine engines under the name National in Hartford," young Frank confirmed.

Anna spoke right up, "I can handle that," to everyone's amazement. "Don't you boys worry. I will write to Mr. Steinway. I think I know how to get him on your side. I can get him to agree to your waivers. Get them written up, Frank." No one laughed, although no one understood how she could make those assertions except George. He remembered a magical evening when it seemed the room they were in filled with angels, to hear the sounds coming out of the most beautifully crafted wooden box he had ever seen. When Anna composed her letter she told the old New York businessman the story of a young Philadelphia serving girl who, long before the war, fell in love with a farm boy from the mountains. While courting they went to a concert featuring a new instrument and gained a spiritual experience which enriched their long lives. She described their purchase of a Steinway piano as soon as her husband was successful at farming. He had, she wrote, gone on to greater success as a manufacturer in Ohio with their sons, one of whom has now built a single cylinder stationary gasoline engine intended for farm and industrial use. She spelled out her full request he grant the enclosed waiver and then placed her name at the bottom of the page.

Having told the story, Frank asked JW this question, "Should I mail the envelope containing her letter?" JW said, "Sure." And sure enough, the papers were promptly returned with the necessary authorized signatures. Also enclosed was a kind note informing her to assure her son that his work would not be cited for patent infringements on his account. Further, he wished him good luck in the business venture. Anna was now on board as a participating contributor to John's project.

Al began receiving orders for their little gasoline engine at a wildfire pace. The fraternal partners' plans for converting the factory space was underway, pieces were ordered and John was ready to present his prototype of a stationary internal combustion engine. He himself would teach the men who would do the actual work of assembling each engine, some of whom had worked with John on the farm when he was a teenager, while others knew him from his days at the Union factory. He organized the workstations and supply closets. Moving forward with production, they would stall widespread distribution until the patent was granted.

John had only rare opportunities to pay attention to his old fun-filled automotive project but he did get his vehicle disassembled. He wanted to start work on ideas he had to improve the running gears. He left most pieces in storage at the granary, parts he would experiment on later or on which he had no plans to alter, Mr. Santoro's surried top and leather seats, the buckboard and the three wood wheels, big pieces of the chassis with the original engine. The rest he brought over to the shed behind his hardware business. But his work was stalled for the priority was to shepherd the production of his little powerhouse motor and that took most of his time.

As he passed Celina and Grand Lake over and over in his now daily commute between Ohio City and Union, he noticed the leaves outside the train window had turned bright yellow and orange and were falling off the trees. He was spending a great deal of time on the train and it was beginning to annoy him although it was a short jump across Mercer County between Van Wert and Darke. He began to imagine packing up his family and relocating near Union. Then he would be on hand to give this new business venture the commitment it needed. On a November evening with a cold nip in the air, he brought the subject up to his wife who surprised him with her response, "This town is too small for us, John. I want the children to attend schools with more resources. Mae likes first grade, but I'm not sure the teacher knows more than she does." The parents decided then and there to move to Greenville. John did not suspect Minnie's views were fueled by her current discomfort at her church, which was so much the center of her tie to the Van Wert community. She was experiencing a rough patch and thoroughly disliked not being in control. A group of ladies had been scandalized to hear the story Mrs. Smalley told. On a Sunday morning, they had decided amongst themselves Minnie Lambert was entirely too permissive in regards to the horseless carriage of which they did not approve. They wondered how far her behavior would go, for they believed the rider's seat was certainly no place for a woman. Minnie did not know the specifics of the charges against her, but she did not like being asked to pick up the report for her Town Hall play list whereas it had always been delivered in the past. She had ordered the clerk at Town Hall to do the errand. It was not the only affront she encountered during her time at her religious commitments; she could tell she was the subject of gossip. She inadvertently hit the nail on the head in her letter of good-bye published in the St. Stephen's newsletter. In it, ever dramatic, she asked "her dear brothers and sisters in Christ to respect every man's right to experiment and build, which men are doing all over this country. I invite you to join in my gratitude for their hard work and for their inventions. These industrious men should make each of us more proud to be an American because their innovations fortify the nation and lead the progress of civilization."

Shortly into December, while the John Lamberts researched their living place possibilities in the Greenville area and debated the proper time to transfer their daughter to a better school, disaster again struck in Ohio City. For the second time in four years John's granary burned, this time to the ground. Perhaps the distraction of the Buckeye Manufacturing Company led to a lapse on his part; no one was around to make an early detection. He did not want to contemplate the obvious loss, so he left that to Harvey. It did not immediately occur to him he had lost pieces of his beloved car, the cute fringed top and the deep, well-crafted leather seat, to name but two. The event seemed to eliminate any hesitancy John or Minnie felt about leaving Ohio City. The next day Minnie arranged for the lease of the same Greenville home which they had stayed in before. She signed the rental agreement but it would need the signature of her husband to make it legal. Meanwhile, he ordered the granary completely rebuilt for the purpose of selling it. His men complied and were quick; the plans for construction from four years ago were still on file. By December the granary was on the market, along with John's Banner Street home and all but two of the smaller residential properties, another two of which had been sold in November. John had mailed the balance due to Ty Kuhns at that time. As they prepared to leave Ohio City, John promised Minnie their next home would have a horse chestnut tree in the yard, but his pledge was for his own sentimentality.

Mollie and Harvey did not want to leave the Van Wert area. Not a social couple, they were happy to spend their evenings reading to each other and working word games. It was agreed Harvey would stay in Ohio City to tie up loose ends for John and commute, when needed, to Union. Emma used the excuse of keeping Mollie company to stay in her brother's old town. John wanted to reinforce her security so he and Minnie signed the real estate deed over to her; thus they made her the sole owner of the home she lived in. With no desire to be back in the Greenville area, she encouraged her children to work at their memorization and shout out their mathematic tables with confidence at the Van Wert County School. She then insisted their consistent attendance was a priority.

The large home inside Greenville the JW Lamberts had stayed in last spring was available immediately, which suited Minnie. She was as busy as a pie peddler but, with help, she packed up her furniture and household items and secured them in a barn belonging to one of her sisters in Ansonia, only eight miles from Greenville and brought her family's personal belongings to the Victorian-style home and began spending nights there. Minnie was immediately miserable in Greenville. Her father's sudden death soon after her arrival did not help. The monochromatic dreariness of the November funeral day became engrained in her mind as "Greenville," an image of sadness even springtime could not diminish. She decided muddy Main Street was impossible to cross on foot and so she never tried it. Her sisters gave her ideas for where to shop which left her feeling dwarfed by their established presence. Minnie was sensitive to their feeling sorry for her in what they called John's diminished circumstances. She made up her mind to find her own church community to join and avoid the parish north of town attended by Cora and Lou. She let her sisters believe she was involved with her husband's family and let Eva believe she was busy with her sisters and then wallowed in her solitude with self-pity. She was grieving for her father, but blamed everyone and everything around her, except John, and so isolated herself.

Before the Christmas holiday, the John Lambert family traveled by train to the Kuhns' home in Oakwood, a lovely community south of Dayton. The chauffeur met the traveling party at Dayton's Union Depot and brought them to the rolling green hills of a neighborhood spotted with grand homes and wooded parks. He directed the carriage into a large circular driveway. Inside the mansion was an aviary. Their holiday meal was served under a cavalcade of glimmering light from a large crystal chandelier. John and Minnie were proud of Little Mae who dazzled and entertained the adults for she was a beautiful child who liked people.

John never second-guessed Minnie's plans to make a post-Christmas visit to Urbana. Margaret, now Given's wife, was delighted to receive her and watch the children, with their nursemaid, while Minnie did an errand. She drove herself directly to the Longnecker farm and sat in the Longnecker parlor in its clean, out-dated state. The psychic woman wore britches and a man's shirt and sat in the large, winged-back chair in the center of the room with her legs encircling a round table which held a burning candle and a bowl of water. She never looked at Minnie and Minnie only stayed fifteen minutes but what Minnie heard brought her a sense of purpose and lifted the anxiety which kept her from sleeping. Minnie would soon be moving west and so problems in Greenville were not of great consequence. John would be successful both on his own later and now with his brothers. The strange, gentle woman said she saw him smiling, covered in mud, sitting in a four-wheeled horseless vehicle "with lanterns for eyes".

John knew without a psychic he had found success with his brothers. They were in production and storing the nearly complete engines. They were holding off shipment until they heard from the patent office to get the all important number so they could stamp it on plates to be secured to every machine. Al was already talking about a need for more factory space if orders continued to expand at their current rate. As a final break with Ohio City, John made a deal with Russell to make him owner of the hardware business. He would take over all functions in name and fact and make payments to John until an agreed upon sum was reached. The inventor businessman paid the current young clerk extra to box up his projects in the tar paper shed and he gave a few moments' thought to the loss in the fire of the parts to his beautiful car. It was painful, but most of the parts which were lost were more standard, and thus the easier parts to replace. The original re-built engine was now being replicated a hundred times over. His life was so changed, and changing still, that the unique vehicle and it's fun seemed from a past life. Then John arranged to put the lumberyard on the market by advertising in Columbus, Toledo, Indianapolis, Dayton and Cincinnati. He found a buyer he felt good about, a young German man with an Ohio wife ready to start a family. He spoke to his workers who agreed to give the new owner a chance. Word of the patent being granted arrived in May and orders for engines went out immediately. Although some were prepaid, now significant cash started to come in and there was much celebration in Union. For the rest of the year, production and sales went well and Al upped his talk of expansion for 1893. The Lambert men knew their brother-in-law Dan Cook was doing well in Anderson, Indiana, so they reasoned they should look west. John remembered what Elwood and others had said about the gas boom there and on an early spring day he volunteered to go scope the place out. He hopped on the train for the short ride to Anderson's Pennsylvania Station. On his first exploration of the area, he learned there was plenty of commercial property available to buy and build on with natural gas fields all over the state.

John read the writing on the wall. Along with Al's talk of relocating the factory was Minnie's complaints about Greenville and her obvious interest in moving again. He and Minnie traveled together on the next train trip to Anderson to look over what both wanted to be their new home town. While there, John set up meetings with town officials. On his next visit, he made his plea to them bold as brass about cutting a deal for the Buckeye Manufacturing Company which, he explained, would bring business to the area, hire local workers and put the name Anderson on the commerce map. He was pleased with his performance before the city fathers and credited his cunning to aping his older brother the salesman. The politicians had listened politely to the Ohio businessman's proposal but the conclusion was foregone. Other companies were already receiving their natural gas for free. The fuel came right out of the ground and boosted the local economy. While JW was busy in Anderson, Al collected offers from Union City with the idea of expanding in their current vicinity. This entailed two sets of government for the small rural town straddled the state line. He was not offered nearly what John procured. The brothers made the decision for Anderson and John located a two-block parcel of land for the future site of the Buckeye Manufacturing Company on Sycamore Street between Third and Fifth. It had all the variables he demanded; first and foremost was easy access to The Big Four Railroad. Then he tied up the deal with a trip to the bank. In the spring of 1893, he opened an office adjacent to where they would soon break land and from there hired a crew. He sent out orders for construction of the spacious production site Al and Papa had designed. Itchy to be at his own tinkering, he had arranged for the boxes filled with the items from the tar paper shed in Ohio City to be sent to this new office which had a large rear room that opened out onto an alley. He was now commuting regularly to Anderson from Greenville on the Belle-fontaine line.

On one of his days in Anderson, he dropped in at the Howe Fire Apparatus Company and approached Bud Howe to introduce himself. Mr. Howe knew who John was, but went along with the humble self-introduction and welcomed the newcomer to Anderson. He primarily did business with the Lamberts through Dan Cook and of course knew Al and George. Over the years, he had heard of John but never met him. JW wanted to purchase a fire fighting truck to send to Ohio City. Mr. Howe showed him around his facility in person so John could select what he wanted. Mr. Howe had the papers written up and even had John sign them. The truck was sent and arrived anonymously as John had requested to the thrilled but not fooled people of Ohio City. Mr. Howe never intended to charge John for the order because he wanted to show courtesy to the inventor. The Indiana businessman knew the value John's innovative features on the Lambert chassis added to his product. The details of craftsman-ship in the design John was responsible for gave his trucks superb balance for tearing around corners when speed is of the essence. Proud of his superior product he knew saved lives and grateful for John's engineering expertise, Mr. Howe had been hon-ored to meet the inventive genius of the Lambert family.

With construction starting for the new, larger facility, John and Minnie volunteered to pack up their children and move to Anderson. Minnie could not leave Greenville quick enough. She collected the family things out of storage and moved to her own larger domain. What a relief to claim a town her own again! The John Lamberts found a modest three-bedroom house close enough for the inventor to walk to the construction site and comfortable enough for his wife to be happy. Next year they would build a home more to their liking. As she held the hands of her two children to walk up the path to the new Lambert front door, little Ray pulled away from her grasp to pick something up. Minnie, with the gentle Mae still holding tight, watched as the five-year-old presented his mother with the treasure he had found on the ground, a tiny, dark green, four-leaf clover. He had seen his father do this trick many times. In fact, John found four-leaf clovers all over town, so many he gave away most and pocketed only a few which he stuffed in loose papers, his daily diary, whatever was handy. He could not help it. Each place he went, in a green patch in front or nearby or along the way, he would look down and his eye would catch an irregularity of shape. Nine times out of ten, he bent down to pick a four-leaf clover, rarely a fooler. He recently gave a particularly large one to Minnie who then listened to a rare and brief telling of a story from her husband's childhood. "The day our dog Rex died, I found fourteen four-leaf clovers." It was little Ray's find Minnie carefully pressed and then displayed along with dried violets and rosemary sprigs in a beautiful oval frame made out of one piece of burled cherry wood with a glass bubble face.

The new Anderson residents John and Minnie sat in their new parlor. Minnie asked her husband, "Do you miss your little buggy, darling? Do you regret not selling them?"

"No, Minsy. I figure, lose one, gain one." He looked sideways at her. "I may not be selling my car, but the engine is selling like hotcakes." She reached over and squeezed his hand, relieved his motorized car project was now in the past. He did not mention he was making plans to design a new prototype.

The first guests the new residents invited to their Indiana home to help them celebrate another anniversary was an old

Hoosier friend Elwood Haynes. He, with his wife Bertha, traveled on the Cincinnati-Chicago Line from Kokomo where they had settled the year before. They were all delighted to find themselves facing a future of closer proximity and greater opportunity for friendship. The men had much in common before the bond of inventive inclination; both were one of ten children raised in Midwestern homes with prominent fathers, one a judge, the other, a manufacturer. Of the two men, one was awed by the education of the other; and the other was a touch jealous of the other's mechanical ability. They discussed an item both had seen in the newspapers. A pair of brothers from Springfield, Massachusetts, the report said, claim to have a gas-propelled, converted horse carriage. Elwood had gone to college in nearby Worcester in the Bay State but had never run into these fellows. He told John he was still working on his plans to put together a gas-propelled vehicle. He had recently made the acquaintance of two brothers in Kokomo, Elmer and Edgar Apperson who ran the Riverside Repair Shop, and he believed they had the mechanical aptitude to build to his specifications. JW knew Elwood had a way of playing things up but he listened with an open mind. *As far as either report goes,* he thought, *well, boys like to spout grand intentions on both sides of the Alleghenies.* He knew the long careful process he had walked through to come up with his design. Even then, he ran into numerous practical problems. John wondered how far along Elwood really was. When Elwood talked about using a Sintz upright marine engine, JW saw the content of Elwood's plan. Like the Duryeas in Massachusetts, Elwood was going to place an existing engine in a carriage designed for a horse. John's project was different; his lost car including all of its parts had been made expressly for the purpose it served. John smiled to himself but he did not gloat.

Thinking of his promotional campaign, Elwood asked John whether he would mind if he, Elwood, called his proposed vehicle "America's First Car". John went along and said he would not contradict his friend, and in truth, he really did not object. He was intrigued and enchanted by the dinnertime conversation which was softened and deepened by the presence of both wives. If Elwood and these Duryeas were so keen to go into production with a vehicle propelled by a gasoline engine, they must believe the public interest is, or soon will be, there. John's mind went to the room behind his new office and he pondered his intention to draw and build a new prototype self-propelled car. He had enough pieces of his old vehicle for a good head start on a new project. Back at the candlelit dinner table, Elwood's request impressed him as picking a fight with the Massachusetts brothers. Elwood wanted to get his mark on the public before they did, for the item in the paper had said the Duryea brothers were planning a go of producing their version of a horseless-carriage.

It took a hop, skip and a jump to get from Anderson to Kokomo; it took another hop, skip and a jump to get from Kokomo to Chicago. That is what John and Elwood planned to do with their families in the cooler weather of fall to visit the Windly City's Columbian Exposition. The six hundred twenty-three acres of shows and festivities on land and water included a replica of a Viking ship John wanted to see and was crowned by George Ferris's giant revolving wheel, a sound answer to the steel wonder Eiffel Tower of a few years' back, which was sure to delight the children. There would be wagon builders, bicycle makers and engines. John and Elwood looked forward to seeing the fourteen-passenger tramcar to be run on a circular track by a Daimler motor.

There was more to look forward to; Ran Olds and his wife were planning a visit in August.

As the first wave of Lamberts stepped over the state line, a second wave was close behind. Harvey was now commuting between Union City and Anderson while still living in Van Wert County. Mollie and Emma made plans to leave Ohio City and move together to Anderson before the start of the academic year. Emma's children would join Mae who was entering first grade at the Columbia School. At this time Harvey signed over the Longnecker farm to his two sisters at JW's suggestion, "Let the Urbana farm go; leave it to your sisters. They may need it." JW also advised his brother-in-law to buy a home in Anderson and backed him up at the bank. It was a skittish time for bankers and Mr. McCullean of Anderson First National was grateful to have the Lambert accounts. Harvey and Mollie were happy to have Emma and her children brighten their home. She paid her own share of the cost thanks to JW's discreet generosity. No one mentioned Newtie who, no longer under indictment, was farming and working at his threshing business in Darke County.

Other Lamberts saw the course of events and considered their own move to Anderson. Most pressing were George and Anna. George had chronic pain from his early years of farming but was basically recovered from his stroke. Anna wanted her own home, so George talked it over with Al. They agreed, much to Eva's relief, that plans should be made for the older Lamberts to move to Anderson, the new home of the Buckeye Manufacturing Company. "A small, in-town bungalow would be perfect," Anna proclaimed. John, confirming it could be done, stepped forward to oversee their arrival in Anderson. In addition, after conferring with his mother, he bought a grave site by the Anderson River and arranged for Baby Savina's remains to be brought there to the Maplewood Cemetery. Lillies of the valley, transplanted from the Urbana farm, flourished on the long sloping bank of the Anderson River.

As the days slipped by before he left Ohio, George lay awake beside his wife of thirty-eight years; the pain across his shoulders kept him from a long night's rest. It would break through his sleep-state like a crying baby and was just as demanding. Periodically through the night, he would have to get up and walk through the dark first floor of his son's home, rolling his shoulders in a gentle motion, trying not to bump into furniture in his groggy state. It only took a few minutes to loosen the pain. More times than not, when he crawled back into bed he got back to sleep. A new chapter was beginning in their lives and that old sense of adventure stirred his body like a flame. George thought of other challenging adventures he had faced over his life: leaving Lost Mountain for Philadelphia, marrying Anna and moving to Ohio, first Champaign then Darke Counties. Now they were off to Indiana. Oh, the leather he sold! The bags of wheat he shipped out! The decision to try manufacturing, the thrill and terror, but always an exciting sense of adventure. With these thoughts, he fell back asleep. Dreaming that sense of adventure, he saw himself in a large factory room, with sunlight streaming in through the copious windows onto row after row of chassis, four-wheeled chassis, each newly assembled. He knew in his dream these were part of a large manufacturing effort to produce complete self-propelled Lambert vehicles. George awoke amazed. He knew in his heart he had seen what would eventually happen. JW would soon get his horseless carriage on the market and be a big success in the future.

Epilogue

1950

The old man sitting on the stone wall had one leg extended to the gravel driveway. With his elbow balanced on his other knee, he was lining up and attaching thin metal strips to a fanlike device. He was completely absorbed in his task and never noticed the middle-aged woman who pulled up in the black Ford sedan. She called in greeting to him as she went in the large wooden-framed house.

"Father!" She reappeared at the side door and jolted him out of his reverie. "Didn't you hear me?"

"Sa," he resisted returning from his otherworldly realm. His nonsense syllable was his stepping-stone back to the present. He lay the weaving down on his knee, his fingers still intertwined with the material which was beginning to look like an Indian headdress. He lifted his clouded eyes and tried to focus out over the driveway. "Yes, Mae. See here, now, you have my fullest attention." She was standing beside him by this time and placed her arm on his shoulder. Ever since her mother died, she had taken care of her father. She bent to give him a ceremonial kiss he accepted by tilting his cheek. "Yes, darling daughter. Now what is it?"

"Did you remember Bill is coming from Dayton with Evelyn and the children?" Bill, the one and only son of Mae's only brother Ray, made infrequent trips to the Indiana branch of the family. Today he was expected to arrive with his Missouri wife and John's two great-granddaughters. There were three great-grandsons and a great-granddaughter already but none to carry on the family name. Now Evelyn had produced a second girl, luckily one cute enough to almost make up for not being a boy.

"Why, yes, of course. They're bringing their new girl. Of course, I remember."

"I think you should clean up. Come into the house now and you'll have plenty of time. What is this you've been working on?"

"I wanted to send Bill home with one of my brooms. I'm calling it a broom so those boys from the hoe company won't come down and complicate my life again."

"It's a rake, Father, whether you call it a rake or a broom." She sighed. "Never mind." Her father had received a patent on the lawn rake which he had designed here in the old wooden horse shed. After selling the patent rights to the manufacturing giant American Hoe and Shovel Company out of Toledo and with no thought to the contrary, John had continued to make them one by one here in the yard for all of his neighbors and friends. One of his homemade items must have been passed to someone's hands from American Hoe who took offense their exclusive design was circulating free of their label. A snappy young lawyer had tracked down the domestic "manufacturing source" right here at the house. Her eighty-eight-year-old father had been sued and a judge ordered him to cease and desist from his production of rakes the rights of manufacture of which now belonged to The American Hoe and Shovel Company.

"Let them sue me and take me to court. I'd like to see a judge tell them once and for all to be content with the money they're making. My rakes don't rob them of much of their market. Ridiculous!" He finished the last adjustments to the spread on his lap by snapping it into place at the end of a long wooden handle. Mae nodded in tolerance and gave him a hand as he stood up next to the wall. Together they walked across the gravel that had staged such colorful and powerful luxury machines in his heyday as a pioneer of the automotive industry. The daughter understood he gets lost in his work and his body gets stiff from the abandonment. Mae's two children and their families were vacationing at Wawa Lake and so would not be joining them for Sunday dinner. Patty, Bill's sister, lives in Massachusetts with her Connecticut husband and their two baby boys. But John's elderly sister and close neighbor Emma was expected to arrive with two strudels she still baked herself.

Evelyn and Bill were driving their four-door Chevrolet across Route 40 which only one hundred years before had been the dirt-packed National Road bringing settlers across Pennsylvania to Ohio and Indiana. When all were together, Mae presented an elegant dinner in the wood-paneled dining room as her mother had done through the car years for guests including Ran Olds, Jonathan Maxwell, Will Durant, Henry Leland, the Dodge brothers and just once, Henry Ford and his wife were guests. After dinner, the current gathering reassembled in the parlor where Grandfather John lit a cigar, Bill sipped a brandy and the three women enjoyed coffee out of imported cups. Before little Ann fell asleep on the hearth rug Aunt Mae had pulled out a set of toy wooden blocks for her, and her great-grandfather showed her a music box with a pop-up ballerina which he let her hold in her slender little hands.

"Grandfather, do you want to hold the baby?" Bill held a bundle of blankets over the lap of the kind-hearted inventor. A tiny fist was waving above the folds. John docked his cigar in the ash tray on a table at his side and held up his hands. His grandson took time before removing his own hold on his second daughter to be sure she was securely held on the retired businessman's knee. Round-faced Carol Jean studied her great-grandfather and held on to his sensitive finger. She was cooing and fully engaged in conversation with the older man who seemed to understand the range of ideas the child was conveying. He chuckled and his old face beamed with pleasure. Bill watched and his heart filled with emotion. As the child and her ancient relative wrapped up their intense interaction, Bill reminded his grandfather of their games of checkers when he was a boy.

"Well, did I beat you, young man? Or could you get the best of me?"

"Why, Grandfather, I'm not sure I remember," Bill smiled.

Emma reached out and gathered up the baby, freeing the men. With a word to the mother, the elderly woman took the young child to the kitchen, propped her up in the highchair and talked to the little thing while she washed the dishes. She was leaning on a stool as she worked. "Maybe you'll inherit the itch to write." She loved books and had once dabbled in writing herself. "Keep your great-grandfather in mind for a subject. He's a genius." She paused with her hands in the water and smiled at the observing infant, "Well, he's been a wonderful brother to me and a wonderful husband and father. But he also built the first gasoline automobile in America. I know, I was there. But he won't tell you. Maybe you'll tell, you cute little button."

Back in the parlor the men had embarked on a conversational trail of bringing up pleasant memories with Mae joining in and Evelyn relegated to listener. Many of the earliest stories centered on the old Lambert Automobile Manufacturing Company. Grandfather wanted to tell stories of driving the cars in various unlikely locations and brag for Mae she was the first female in America ever to drive a gasoline powered automobile. Bill wanted to hear about the business-end of the company, but John was more interested in remembering old relationships and the special moments which carried the feelings of adventure and affection.

The young William Lamberts stayed longer than they intended. Evelyn finally put her foot down when Ann awoke as the large Ansonia clock over the mantel struck four. Carol Jean was asleep near Emma who had just finished drying the silver. Before rejoining the crowd, John's sister slipped a worn leather sachet tied with stiff string into the soft blankets beside the little girl. Standing, the rest were having their good-bye talk. Evelyn guided her husband through the large entrance hallway toward the door. Bill, on some level, suspected he would not see his sweet, old grandfather again. With extra care, he bade him good-bye and saluted as he pulled his car out of the driveway onto the shady, neighborhood street. His wife was sitting beside him; the baby in the bassinet was on the backseat; little Ann was blowing kisses from the rear window and the newly made rake, er, broom, was stowed in the trunk of the vehicle. Mae wrapped her hand around the crook of her father's elbow and stood waving a handkerchief. The intelligent face of her father smiled and mouthed "bye" to the car he could not see, which so smoothly and quietly drove out of sight.